GYPSY
HEARTS

For Clark
AND Bharati,
MENTORS IN literature,
AND GENEROUS FRIENDS
iN liFE.

Also by Robert M. Eversz
Shooting Elvis

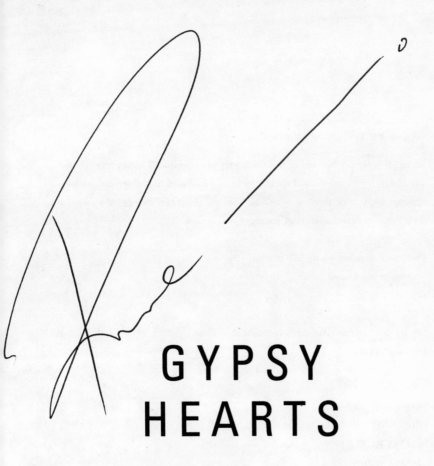

GYPSY
HEARTS

ROBERT M. EVERSZ

Grove Press
New York

Published simultaneously in Canada
Printed in the United States of America
FIRST EDITION

Library of Congress Cataloging-in-Publication Data
Eversz, Robert.
Gypsy hearts / Robert M. Eversz—1st ed.
p.   cm.
ISBN 0-8021-1609-4
I. Title.
PS3555.V39G97   1997
813'.54—dc21   96-40085

DESIGN BY LAURA HAMMOND HOUGH

Grove Press
841 Broadway
New York, NY 10003

10 9 8 7 6 5 4 3 2 1

To Prague as it was then.

Homicide is not a sin. It is sometimes a necessary violence on resistant

and ossified forms of existence which have ceased to be amusing. In the

interests of an important and fascinating experiment it can even become

meritorious.

Bruno Schulz
The Street of Crocodiles

WARNING!

This book is a lie, a confidence trick, a wicked jab in the eye of truth. Read at your own risk. Those with high blood pressure, heart problems, weak nerves, and particularly those under psychiatric care, LEAVE THIS BOOK NOW. Management will not be held responsible for the consequences!

GYPSY
HEARTS

1

The story begins with a strapping youth walking across a bridge in Budapest. A rain-slashed night not fit for man but perfect for young beasts. The youth walks as though wave-tossed. His eyes are hard, his lips cruel, his forehead void of the evidentiary marks of thought. He shouts a command—*Stride, feet, stride!*—but the pitching river of concrete and steel tangles him to his knees. His mouth stretches wide to roar a defiant belch. He belches, therefore he is! He belches again, beer-drunk.

A second figure stalks the youth from behind. The brim-shade of a fedora cloaks his face to a cleft or scar down the center of his chin. His right arm is plunged elbow deep into his overcoat pocket. A gun? A knife? A book of poems he tries to keep dry in the driving rain?

The youth gasps and belches, laughs and belches, farts and belches. The last belch, dangerously moist, leads him to contemplate the Danube as an impromptu vomitory. He measures distance and arc and wind direction. Trajectory is a simple problem but the wind confounds him. It gusts and swirls without rhythm, and each sudden updraft is sharp reminder of the consequences of miscalculation.

No witnesses move hunched against the wind. No rain-specked lights glide toward the bridge. The hat-hid man lopes forward. The pocket of his overcoat hides his right hand. His knuckles strain against pocket cloth. Bent against the rail ahead, the evening's quarry. Cable slaps against steel plate. Teeth grind. Pocket seams stretch to snapping.

A swell of music please, a march and shriek of strings like Bernard Herrmann composed for Hitchcock, ominous and razor-edge hysterical.

The youth half turns and cocks an arrogant eyebrow. No one would dare to. Not to him. And not this runt of a hat-hid man.

A sliver of gray in the rain.

A startled shout.

Blurred flailing, all hands and feet.

By Newton's law, a limp sack of punctured mortality plummets neither faster nor slower than raindrops dripping off the bridge railing. It descends as though borne by rain, wind gurgling through gaped mouth. A splatter of flesh against water, and red gushes into the dark Danube.

If this were a movie script, that is how I should pitch it. My former trade. Worked in The Biz, as the movie business is called in Southern California, pretending none other exists. Writer-producer credit on a number of projects. First-name basis with major Hollywood players. Condo by the beach. Porsche in the drive. Poolside sex with starlets, buttocks tickled by the shadows of palm fronds. All by the tender age of twenty-five. But this isn't a movie script. It's a confession.

The story begins on a train, clattering into the Central European darkness. The Orient Express. Paris to Budapest. Opulent carriage of mystery and romance. Outside the gilt-framed windows, moonlight bounces like silver coins on a taut shroud of February snow. Inside, the elite recline on red velvet and eat their fill of roast mastodon, poached spotted-owl hearts, and marinated tit-lark tongues.

False start!

Anyone traveling the Orient Express since 1939 would recognize that scene as fabrication relying on old Agatha Christie novels more than truth. I must begin with the truth.

This story does begin on a train. It is night, and February.

But the Orient Express is like any other Central European train: fouled with cigarette smoke, beer piss, and rank sweat from the newly liberated socialist masses. My fool of a travel agent had booked second-class passage, and I sat trapped in a cramped cabin with two Poles, who chain-smoked and quarreled in a language that sounded to my ears like grinding glass. I tried to read, barricaded behind a copy of the *Herald Tribune,* but a shattered concentration clawed the words to syllables and serifs. When the Poles' quarrel abruptly ended with the appearance of a bottle of vodka, I grabbed my bag and escaped to the dining car.

I had no intention of eating what passed for food on that train, but the occupants seemed recently scrubbed, if not particularly compelling, and I did not desire a quick return to my boon Polish comrades. At the insistence of a waiter, I was coaxed into joining the table of a portly man who sported a neatly trimmed beard, like the actor Philippe Noiret, to whom he bore a more than slight resemblance. To be forced companions was an annoyance to both of us, and he seemed relieved that I was content to drink mediocre Hungarian wine and stare out the scarred window, ignoring his attack on some goulash-looking thing the waiter had brought to him shortly after I'd arrived. When finished, he clattered the spoon to his empty plate with a musical sigh of such pitch and duration that I inquired, "Indigestion?"

"*Non, simplement incapacité.*" He wiped his mustache with sharp short strokes of the napkin and observed, with the discreetly contemptuous tone the French reserve for those of my nationality, "*Vous êtes américain.*"

"*Bien sûr, et tu es français,*" I responded, switching to the informal form of address. Let him guess whether I was insolent or merely ignorant of French grammar.

The man replied with the classic Gallic shrug, and I thought that would be the end of it, cross swords once and withdraw, but when I returned my gaze to the window, he continued, this time in English, "What do you think of your wine?"

"*Ce n'est pas français, ni californie,*" I answered.

"*Exactement!*" he cried, as though my strictly factual observation, intended to sever the conversation, was of great insight. Signaling the waiter for a fresh glass, he filled it with a Bordeaux he said had been pulled just that morning from his wine cellar. I sniffed the bouquet, rolled a drop around my palate, and pronounced it *exquis,* which, though an exaggeration of the wine's modest merits, pleased him. He introduced himself as Monsieur Marcel, from Fontainebleau, a château town on the outskirts of Paris. There was no way out but to respond with a few of my own particulars, preferably false. And who am I? The hero of this fool's tale.

Richard Milhous Miller, christened after the thirty-seventh president of the United States and fondly nicknamed Nix by that scion of a used-car dealership empire, my father.

I told Marcel I was a film producer and screenwriter from Hollywood and directed the conversation toward discovering a subject of mutual interest. We found it soon enough: women. Despite his happy little family back in Fontainebleau and a fifty-year history of indulgent dining habits, Marcel was, if you'll forgive the vulgarism, a pussy hound.

I normally shun casual traveling acquaintanceships as the lowest form of human interaction, but Marcel's erotic obsessions aroused my interest. He claimed he traveled to Budapest once a month, on business, his visits contiguous to a weekend, when he would invariably seduce one of the local women. His methods were simple and direct. He learned where available women congregated, usually one drinking establishment or another, and, settling in at the bar, ordered cognac in a commanding French baritone. If a woman met his glance twice, he approached with a complimentary remark, such as admiring her hair if it was long and lustrous and an obvious point of pride. He insisted on buying her a drink, most commonly French champagne, and never lost an opportunity to commend the woman on her taste, believing compliments from a Frenchman were the sartorial equivalent of the Burning Bush. From such moments, a shared bed was *fait accompli*.

Discounting the unfailing charm of a French accent, Marcel was not the image of Adonis. When I suggested doubts, he pulled from his breast pocket a wallet-sized photo album and splayed the evidence of his conquests before me. The women were photographed in restaurants, bars, and the occasional bedroom. Nothing artistic. Flashbulb exposures of bleached faces advancing inexorably on drunkenness. A few could have turned heads in daylight. Several were out-right slatternly. Most were ordinary, with the curse of the ordinary: a nose too big, a chin too weak, eyes set crooked in an otherwise attractive enough face. The film caught each in an expression of confused desperation, like refugees afraid of missing the train, who don't know if they will be allowed to board, or to what destination the train will take them if boarded, but needing at all costs to escape the station.

Marcel's commentary accompanied the photographs: Katalin, a twenty-seven-year-old shopkeeper with water-melon breasts; Ilona, a waitress who liked Marcel because she liked French champagne; Margit, an art student who nearly caused a scandal when she later came to see him in Fontainebleau. I wondered whether the snapshots were part of the excitement or trophies of the score. Did his hands tremble when he pulled out his camera, pretending the idea of taking a snapshot was spontaneous? I stopped him at a photograph of a thin young girl with immense brown eyes. The flash had caught her full red lips parting around the filter tip of a cigarette. The girl couldn't have been over twenty. Contemplating the tension between her innocent eyes and the carnality of those lips, I asked Marcel how he managed to seduce her.

"*Curiosité,*" he said. She had never slept with a French-man before. The French have a reputation for romance. Most of the women he seduced were curious. Some hoped he might take them away to a new life in the West, but Marcel never enjoyed the favors of the same woman two weeks in a row. He was married and had no need for a relation-ship. "When I first bed a girl, I give her a red rose and tell her our romance is young and beautiful as this rose, but when the petals of this red rose fall away, so must I."

The gullibility of women never ceases to astonish me, but that so many could fall for such romantic swill was a revelation. This was my first inkling that the former Iron Curtain countries might be a sexual playground for a Westerner of some style, and the local inhabitants seduced as effortlessly as easing a virgin leg into a pair of jeans. Thus it was I arrived in Budapest with a sense of purpose. But Budapest has little to do with my story, until much later, when other events came into play. I did meet a Monsieur Marcel on the Orient Express, but Marcel is not the story.

The story begins when the train arrives in Prague, where I have plans to live for six months or so, until the cooling of certain legal difficulties, which have recently embroiled me, allows my return to Southern California.

No, the story begins later still.

The story begins the night I accidentally vomited on the shoe of a woman who, much later in our relationship, would try to kill me.

2

I met Katerina at an outdoor café in the shadow of Prague Castle's St. Vitus Cathedral, identifying her nationality and the nature of her visit by the Polish language guidebook she read above her espresso. She wasn't the type to attract me at first, not that I'm so disciplined as to narrow my choices to one type over another. Later, I learned to appreciate her eyes for their intelligence and trace of mischievousness. Even her stylish flair with clothes—riding pants, black boots, and olive-green coat—was not enough to make her attractive at first glance. She seemed unnaturally pale even by Slavic standards, her skin broken at the chin by a small constellation of blemishes. Her hair curled so vigorously that, when the wind blew, matted tendrils writhed like a hat of snakes from which the rest of her unremarkable face seemed to shrink in terror. But tourists crowded into every chair at the café except the one opposite hers, so it was natural to ask if I could join her. She agreed. We politely ignored each other during the subsequent half hour, Katerina reading her guidebook and myself penning observations in a notebook, until she tried to pay the check and discovered her wallet missing.

I helped her to reconstruct events: she firmly remembered using the wallet to buy tram tickets earlier that afternoon and concluded it had been stolen sometime between purchasing the tickets and coming to the café.Pickpocketing is a common problem throughout the major cities of Europe, and no less so in Prague. I did what any decent person would have done: took care of her bill and offered to lend her whatever money she needed to survive the next few days.

It helped that we got along well. I promised to take her to the police station, but we soon lost track of time touring the castle and the winding streets of Malá Strana below, reasoning together that her vacation shouldn't be a complete loss. I had lived through the last of Prague's winter and the first of her vaunted spring by then and knew the city well enough to amuse the first-time visitor. When later that afternoon we arrived at her hotel, she allowed me to pay her bill, scrupulously writing down my name and address so she could later repay me. The cab then took us to the wrong station for the evening train to Warsaw, and by the time we arrived at the correct one, her train had already left. As the next train wasn't scheduled until the following morning, I offered her the couch in my apartment. Several hours later, as a result of two bottles of wine and a shortage of blankets, we shared the same bed and let the gravity of our sexes take its course. In the end, she hadn't shortened her vacation at all, and as the train pulled away protested that she didn't mind so much losing her wallet because she'd found me.

After dropping Katerina at the station, I wandered the medieval labyrinth of Staré Město, Prague's old town, exploring those hidden streets where the renovator's brush had yet to reach and the walls retained a patina of Communist neglect. Prague resembled a Potemkin village then, with the major tourist zones a facade for the crumbling ruins a side street away. After years of living in newer-bigger-brighter Los Angeles, any evidence of decay held me in morbid fascination.

A few hours before midnight, I walked to Lávka, a popular dance club with picture-postcard views of river, bridge, and castle on a hill. Lávka was the meeting place that year for the lawyers, economists, advertising executives, government advisers, returning exiles, small entrepreneurs, and big business interests that comprised the advance army of Western civilization. Various male acquaintances and I often met to drink on the back patio and pick up tourists, who flocked there upon spotting it from Charles Bridge, the fourteenth-century span of stone that arches the Vltava River. Two years after the Velvet Revolution, tourists flooded into the country along the Elbe River to the north, over the mountainous spine of the German border to the east, and through the pine hills of Moravia to the south: Scandinavians, Germans, French, Italians, and Austrians retracing with the instinct of migratory birds the invasion paths of their ancestral tribesmen. They massed at the borders and descended upon Prague each weekend, rape and pillage reenacted as shopping, drinking, and whoring. Most went home a few days later, hungover and laden with Soviet army hats, epaulets, watches, and other memorabilia of the victory over the Evil Empire.

Some stayed, particularly the Americans, entranced by Prague's shabby beauty and carpetbagger economy. Those least qualified for business employment in the West immediately became business experts in the East. English teachers were in such great demand that a passport was deemed ample qualification, and any native speaker untutored in the mysteries of grammar could find work teaching others what he did not know. Most Americans stayed a year, perhaps two, if particularly desperate to avoid responsibility. A few had intentions to settle in Prague on a more permanent basis, but this sort was rarely encountered and was notorious for learning to speak the local language, befriending the inhabitants, and exhibiting other disturbing characteristics of going native.

Andrew was the only Lávka regular I considered a friend, perhaps my only friend in Prague. He sat on the back patio, accompanied by his guitar case and a beer, deep into a characteristic crisis of spirit. Though I considered Andrew my best friend at the time, we had known each other for just under two months; we didn't know each other at all. But his moods were no secret. He was proud of his moodiness, having made the common error of mistaking it for emotional depth. After he failed to respond to an amusing erotic anecdote about Katerina, whom he had met the night before, I gently chided him about his silence.

"I had a bad shopping day," he confessed.

I cocked an eyebrow, a conjunctive in the lexicon of facial gestures, meaning *And?*

"Don't you ever get upset that you can't buy anything in this fucking town? Like, all I wanted was a simple tube of toothpaste, it didn't have to be Colgate or Crest, something from Germany would have done, but I didn't know the word; then I picked the word out of the dictionary but I couldn't pronounce it. The clerk looked at me like I was a complete idiot, so I showed her the word, and she shook her head and moved to the next person like I stopped existing. I repeated this, like, in four different stores, took me the entire afternoon, until finally someone gave me a tube of something, and I don't even know if it's toothpaste. God only knows what's in it, certainly not fluoride or tartar control."

"Sure, but on any night of the week you can find over twenty types of Czech beer. You have to consider what's most important in life."

"I hate beer!"

Heresy! Shouting such a sentiment in Prague was the Czech equivalent of condemning apple pie in Washington.

"I'm tired of drinking too much and waking up the next morning with a hangover and some woman I can't remember meeting the night before. It's an empty, stupid lifestyle."

Andrew's behavior was little different from that of most young Americans in Prague. He smoked and drank to excess. He lived for the favors of sequential lovers. For the first time in his young life, he lived more than one hundred miles distant from his family. Familial conscience had faded to a crackling voice on the telephone. He had no friends from home. No family priest. No school. No government. No one was watching. Nothing was forbidden. God doesn't punish what God doesn't see. My God, who had never been the most omniscient deity to begin with, bailed out over the Atlantic or was, perhaps, discreetly pushed.

"I'm thinking of leaving Prague," Andrew confessed.

"Don't be such a whiner," I counseled. "If you go back to the States, you'll be crying within a month because not only will you be stuck in some stupid job, you won't be able to afford to drink and no one will want to sleep with you."

Andrew with great concentration bit a loose flap from the cuticle of his thumb. "I wasn't thinking of going back to the States, at least not right away."

"You can't afford Paris," I said.

"A refugee camp just opened in the countryside. For Yugoslavs, mostly Bosnians. I thought I'd go there for the summer, teach English to the kids."

My grin spread unconstrained. Though I felt the occasional wild impulse to do good, I never considered acting on it. The nobler sentiments of altruism and charity seemed irrelevant to the demands of the modern world.

"What's happening in Yugoslavia is terrible," Andrew insisted. "We should do something about it. Maybe teaching English isn't enough, but it's better than turning a blind eye."

"Hey, look everybody!" I shouted. "It's Mother Teresa with a penis!"

My jibe seemed appropriate and clever, and I couldn't stop myself from laughing out loud. It was then that Andrew hit me a childish blow, the flat of his hand across my jaw. I stared at him in disbelief. He said, "You're such an asshole."

"Certainly you don't—I mean, Andrew, please," I stuttered.

He pulled violently away from the table, grabbed his guitar case, and fled. I expected someone to rally to my defense, to approach with a commiserating word or hand. Neither came. I'd been told before that contrary to my initial charm I'm not a very likable person. I flagged a passing waiter and ordered six shots of Johnnie Walker. I'm good at first impressions. I practiced introductions for months in the first sallow bloom of my youth. Stood in front of a mirror and grinned, testing blends of sincerity, intelligence, and emotional warmth, with a dash of devil-may-care for spice. The icebreaker first, the clever little tale that always gets the smile. *Indeed, Nix is an unusual name, and there's an interesting story behind.* . . . Say just enough to impress, hinting modestly at important matters not at liberty to be discussed. Feign understanding and interest. Sparkle. Move on, before the conversation bores to distraction and the undisciplined truth slips out. I've since learned tricks to keep the deception going. Some people have known me for years and have yet to discover anything genuine about my character. But I weaken at times, from greed for human companionship. I can be fooled by the ruse of friendship. My attempts at intimacy have always met a bitter and lachrymal end. Apparently, the more skins peeled from the atrophied onion of my heart, the more pungent the odor.

The waiter returned with my drinks. I lined the glasses straight, knocked the first shot back, and noted the time on my watch. Nothing to be ashamed of, my feeling wounded. Even a monster has feelings. King Kong fell for Fay Wray. The Hunchback of Notre Dame burned for Esmeralda. And who was more human than Frankenstein, struggling to fill with blood and broken bones the emptiness in his newly wrought soul? Rarely is the monster appreciated. Five minutes later, I tossed down the second shot. Perhaps Andrew hadn't meant it, not really. It wouldn't have depressed me, had I not loved him. Loved wasn't the right word. Love was an empty sentiment. The brotherly bond of an older brother? Avuncular affection? Unrecognized homoerotic longing? I considered distant synonyms for love and failed to find one adequate to the situation. I glanced at my watch and emptied the third shot. I was more capable of murder than love. The murderer is a creation of genetics and chance, and as blameless as any predatory creature acting according to its character. May as well blame Lucifer for being a devil. A brilliant thought, really, the monster as victim. *You have been chosen, willing or not, to . . .* After the fourth shot, my thoughts wouldn't hold still or, rather, I lacked the intellectual time-space coordination to grasp them. The whisky hit after the fifth shot, unscrewing my head at the neck. I can't remember drinking the sixth.

Sometime later I tried to chase down my head, which had risen from my shoulders and drifted above the dance floor. I lurched into the crowd and blindly groped the space where I thought my cranium should be. A woman bared her teeth in laughter, thinking my frantic search a new dance craze from the West. I shouted something I can't recall. An unfortunate elbow sharply reminded me of unsettled matters in my stomach, which insisted on prompt exposure. I glanced wildly about for the bathroom. It lay at the bottom of a steep stairway. Not enough time or physical coordination. I pushed my way toward the railing. The crowd didn't willingly yield passage. I was jostled, sung to, pushed, and danced around. A raised cobblestone or inadvertent foot tripped me up, and I sprawled onto my hands and knees near a table at the edge of the crowd. The choice of time and place was no longer mine. A dog on all fours vomits where the urge takes it, on the master's white carpet or not.

"You disgusting man!" a woman shouted at me, her English accented by a barbaric tongue. I looked up to a face as cruel and sensual as the illegitimate spawn of Brigitte Bardot and Genghis Khan. I felt a violent thumping in my chest and wondered why my heart should knock about so fiercely, then noticed the thumps coincided with the vomit-splattered tip of her shoe slamming into my rib cage.

"Get away from me, you disgusting man!" The woman commanded, her blows like those of the horsewoman falling onto the indifferent ribs of a beast. She raised her heel and gave me the thrust of it. I rolled onto my back. She towered above, gloriously enraged. I laughed. She understood! Most women would have shrieked at a man spilling his guts at their feet, but not her. She instinctively understood I was disgusting, loathsome, vile. I was a beast, to be beaten and kicked into submission. An odd idea speared my brain and fixed it like a lump of meat awaiting the spit. If she could come to love me, intuitively knowing my true character, then perhaps I might be redeemed. The next evening, I would present her with my charming self, the dashing, considerate, and intelligent man many women found irresistible. She would know immediately I was a fake. But what type of fake? Might not the mystery intrigue her? I could charm her intuition to sweet sleep, and, like so many others, she might believe I was the gentleman I pretended to be. Later, when conscious knowledge of my true monstrousness met her initial instincts, love and loathing might find balance in understanding.

I crawled home stained and soiled but exhilarated by unreasoning hope. To vomit on a woman one night and win her heart the next was absurd. At most, I could expect a strained acceptance of my apology. But I felt certain I could succeed. I would bring her a dozen red roses—no, three dozen. I would scribe some witty bon mot on a napkin, order a bottle of champagne delivered to her table, and patiently wait for her reply. When she first discovered the generous gentleman to be the vomiting fool from the night before, she would certainly ask my name, accept my offer to sit and share a drink or two. Such a display of style and grace would soften her heart. She would have no choice but to fall in love.

3

I staggered to my feet just after dawn, head pounding in syncopation with violent knocking at the door. Memories from the previous night floated in the wreckage of my hangover. Andrew. Six shots of Scotch. Rude kicks to my rib cage. The vomit-flecked pumps of an enraged goddess. Curses tumbled past my teeth. How could I have been so stupid? I swung the door open to a pair of State Policemen, one dangling an arrest warrant and the other drawing a bead on my forehead with the barrel of his Walther P-38.

"Up against the wall, American *schweinhund*!" One commanded, shoving me into the hallway.

"You can't do this! I'm an American citizen!" I protested.

A fist slammed into my kidney.

"You're not in America anymore," he sneered.

"Capitalist exploiter of the heroic masses," the other taunted.

I felt the brutal tip of the P-38 press against the temporal bone behind my right ear and rued the day I accepted a package from that shadowy figure from the CIA who appealed to my sense of patriotism and duty to country. . . .

An inspired fiction, of course, springing into my imagination the moment I put my eye to the peephole and spied two policemen in the hall outside my door. I have a talent for sudden paranoid fantasy, enriched by the vast repertoire of scenes from my years studying movies and television. The two policemen who appeared that morning were far more terrified of me than I of them. One presented an official-looking form while the other hid behind his back, as though I might, if offended, resume the Cold War and so return the country to Soviet hegemony.

"I don't read or speak Czech. If you have a problem, talk to the American Embassy," I suggested, and closed the door.

Two minutes later, the policemen mustered the courage to knock again. In the meantime, I had artfully lathered my face with shaving cream to demonstrate complete indifference to their visit. I snapped open the door.

"Please, I have an appointment. I told you to contact the American Embassy if you have any problems. I have many friends in the American Embassy. I'm sure my friends in the American Embassy can handle this." I was certain that, like trained dogs, they understood only a few key words, two being "American" and "Embassy."

One's hand braced against the door when I attempted to swing it shut. "You come," he commanded.

I gave my most scathing look to the back of his hand, which failed to convince him to remove it from my door.

"Am I to understand that I'm under arrest?" I asked.

He rattled the form in front of me and repeated, "You come."

The man seemed determined to carry out his job. I considered conflict escalation as the more entertaining alternative to conflict resolution. I could push him backward, slam and lock the door. They wouldn't break down the door to get me. Later, I could claim it was a misunderstanding.

"Very well. I need five minutes," I said, holding up five digits, then pointing to the shaving cream on my face.

One's hand dropped away from the door. I repeated the words "five minutes" several times, flashing my fingers in the space between the closing door and the jamb. One stepped reluctantly back. When the lock clicked into place, I sprang the dead bolt. Done. It would take a bomb to get through that door. I ran water in the sink and proceeded to shave, admiring the steadiness of my hand on the razor. After rinsing, I wandered into the living room, a towel pressed against my chin to staunch the flow from a few small cuts, and estimated the drop out the back window. I lived two floors up in a courtyard apartment. The courtyard was littered with broken beer bottles, rusted piping, molding carpet, shredded cardboard, and the desiccating corpses of various small mammals. The average communist and the white-trash American have at least this much in common: Both are too cheap to discard anything of possible value and too lazy to dispose of the completely worthless. Assuming the jump didn't break my ankle, I could walk unscathed out the front door of the apartment building.

I selected from the closet charcoal-gray slacks, a white shirt custom tailored to my specifications, Canali silk tie, and Armani checked sport coat. It was important to dress well when conducting any official business in what was then

Czechoslovakia. The Czechs had lived so long in a class-less society, while secretly longing for its opposite, that any presentation of wealth and style intimidated them witless. If the State Police wanted to ask me a few questions, I would accommodate them with answers of my own choosing. It made little sense to run from a powerless adversary. Perhaps I could even learn something to work into a future screenplay.

It was a dismal spring day, gray and wet. With a few thumps on the dashboard, the driver convinced the wipers to streak across the windshield. I had expected to be taken to the police station in a Tatra, the ominously black trademark car of the Czech secret police, but my two policemen drove a proletarian Škoda. In Czech, *škoda* is both proper and common noun. As a common noun, *škoda* means "pity." Escorted up the steps to police headquarters, I pitied how low the minions of Czech law and order had fallen. I was led through a bewildering set of corridors, sat on a bench, and made to wait.

A half hour later, the door to my left opened. My guards ushered me into a small office, where two men casually ignored my entrance, one to study a file folder on his desk and the other occupied by the rain falling beyond the window. The man behind the desk wore a cheap brown suit. On a salary equivalent to two hundred dollars a month, the suit was a sign of honesty. Its ugliness was a matter of personal choice. He gestured toward the chair, a sound like the dry grind of a garbage disposal in his throat.

"I don't speak Czech," I said, sitting. "If you wish to interview me, it will have to be in English."

"Passport, please," he said.

I handed over my passport and watched him study its pages. I sniffed a reek of cigarettes and poor personal hygiene. The random angled spray of hair indicated his barber was a talentless disciple of Picasso and Braque. His face was all lopsided smudges of gray and pink, held into bare coherence by dark and rheumy spots on opposite sides of the lump that served as his nose. Likely broken a few times and never set right. I judged him a man who would consider timidity a weakness.

"Now that you know who I am, I would like to know who you are," I said.

The man glanced up from his study of my passport, startled by my voice. His pouched eyes were apologetic. He either hadn't heard or didn't understand.

"Who are you? Your name," I said, as slowly and clearly as possible.

He searched the clutter on his desk and uncovered a nameplate hidden between a stained coffee cup, a dead spider plant, and a stack of file folders. The other man had not moved since my entrance. He dressed like an American —tennis shoes, off-brand blue jeans, lumpy sweatshirt, windbreaker. I wondered if he watched the sky, raindrops roll down the window, or my reflection in the glass. The man behind the desk set my passport aside and opened the top folder on his stack.

"Problems, Mr. Miller. We have problems with you." He sighed.

I read the name on the plate—Petr Zima—and assumed the jam of consonants before the name was a title of some sort.

"I'm deeply distressed to hear that, Mr. Zima. I also have a problem. With the Gestapo tactic of sending two policemen to abduct me from my apartment on a Sunday morning."

"I read in your passport you are here three months now. It would not hurt to learn some Czech."

I laughed at the absurdity of his suggestion. Learn Czech! Learn a language with seven incomprehensible grammatical cases in a country of sixteen million impoverished creatures! I said, "This is a very small country in an English-speaking world. I don't think it's reasonable to ask the world to speak your language. You should all speak English."

"*Learn English or die,* as the expression goes in my country," the man at the window carefully pronounced, his eyes fixed on the glass.

"It isn't a question of life or death, but of being irrelevant."

"Irrelevance is the same as death to a small country."

"Do you have some official capacity here, or are you employed to stare out the window and utter profundities?" I asked.

"He is my colleague, from Mad'arsko," Zima answered.

"Where the hell is that?"

"Hungary, in English. I'm from Budapest," the man declared, and turned at last to face me. His was the darkness of the Hun who once raged down from the Mongolian plains to plunder Europe. His eyes had no light in them at all, as if the pupil of each had swallowed the iris whole. He introduced himself as István Bortnyk. He said he was a cop, using the American idiom, and attended the interrogation to observe Czech legal procedure. An obvious lie. I wondered what a detective from Budapest could want with me.

"I am very sorry to disturb you on beautiful and sunny Sunday, Mr. Miller," Zima pronounced with careful irony. "But I hear complaints, and it is my job, whether I like it or not, to look into complaints. To ask questions, take notes, and apologize if complaints are not correct. This is why I ask you to come." He shuffled through the file folders on his desk and opened what I presumed to be mine. He read, nodding his head at one passage, shaking his head at another, until a final wince testified to a telling blow against my character. Still, his voice managed to register surprise when he announced, "I have reports here from several young women. All say they go to café or club, meet you, and same night their wallet is stolen. It's too much for coincidence, I think."

"Several young women," I repeated, with all the arch dryness I could muster from the frantic chase of my heart. "Name one."

"Please, we are not stupid," Zima said.

"Neither am I. If a specific person has made a specific charge against me, I want to hear it."

Zima lifted a form to rheumy eyes and, after careful study, produced the name Victoria Goddard.

Ah, Victoria. The first word she screamed after realizing her money had disappeared was *police*. I tried to convince her that the local law was not as friendly or competent as her neighborhood bobby, but she insisted on making the complaint. I had no choice but to let her go, alone of course, and hope her lack of Czech and the laziness of the local law would spell the end of it. Apparently, it hadn't. Never underestimate the indignant outrage of an Englishwoman.

"I am aware Miss Goddard had her purse picked, but I don't see what it has to do with me."

"You were there when it happened."

"So were a couple hundred others. She lost her pocketbook at Lávka on a crowded Saturday night. You certainly don't expect me to believe that Victoria accused me of taking it, do you?"

Zima allowed the question to hang in the air, then dropped his eyes back to the file folder. A persistent clicking chipped away at my concentration. I traced the sound to a ballpoint pen in Bortnyk's hand, the tip extending or retracting with each rhythmic plunge of his thumb. Zima cautiously turned aside the top form in the file folder and, without moving his eyes from the next document, fumbled at a familiar spot on his desk, shook a cigarette from a pack of Czech Spartas, and lit it. The clicking of the ballpoint was as annoying as a dripping faucet. Did he really think such low-level psychological harassment would unnerve me? Zima must have hoped his long pauses inspired terror of the unknown, but all I felt was a suffocating heat. The office was unbearably hot. I cursed the decision to wear a sport coat. In a matter of minutes, I had sweated through my clean white shirt. Neither Zima nor Bortnyk seemed to be troubled by the heat. What evidence did they have? Several more rabbits could spring out of that hat. Anna, Hanna, Helga . . . several others whose names I couldn't recall. The trouble was not knowing. If I knew what they planned, I could defend myself. I could prepare answers. I fought a desperate urge to loosen my tie and wipe my brow. I must show no weakness. What if they had evidence? I was certain the sweat was popping out my forehead. There could not be any evidence. I had been careful, and no searches were made. I didn't have to say anything. I wished I could stop sweating. One look at the sweat on me and I'd be condemned. But neither paid the least attention. Zima read, preoccupied with his papers. Bortnyk stared out the window, clicking his pen. They knew nothing.

I cleared my throat and said, "I asked a question. Did Victoria Goddard accuse me of any impropriety?"

Zima didn't bother to look up from his papers.

"Why do you think you're here?" Bortnyk asked. The question was artfully ambiguous. Did he call for supposition on my part, or was the reason for my presence so obvious only an idiot couldn't see it?

"I don't have any idea—" I began.

"Margit Szabo," Zima announced, interrupting me.

"—why I'm here," I finished.

I waited for Zima to continue, because though I'd deliberately completed my sentence, displaying my calm and lack of guilt, the name was not meaningless. It had been called out to make me jump. But Zima had no intention of rushing his investigation. He stubbed out his cigarette, lit another, and returned to his documents. I had met Margit during the first cold month of spring. At the time, I was certain she hadn't suspected anything. How could she? I was a perfect gentleman. Margit was barely twenty, as fresh and sweet and lightly browned as unpasteurized cream. She was so grateful after I rescued her from an embarrassing financial situation that we frolicked nonstop for three days. In fact, it was difficult getting rid of her. She had secret yearnings to be a movie actress. My experiences in Hollywood suitably impressed her, and I think she was overwhelmed by my generosity. I was the rich and famous American of her fantasies. She was crying when I put her on the train to Budapest.

"So, you know Margit," I said, twisting around in my chair to face Bortnyk.

It was the only possible explanation for the absurd scene the two were playing, though Bortnyk did not respond to my question with so much as a glance.

"Are you a friend or family?" I asked, and noted with satisfaction a determined nonreaction in the tensing of muscles along the ridge of his jaw. "I've heard that in some countries a foreigner dating a local woman risks being abducted at gunpoint and threatened with death. Is this the Hungarian variation on that theme? When a foreigner compromises a relative's virtue, you resort to legal harassment?"

His dark face went darker still.

Zima looked up from his documents. His eye met Bortnyk's. Bortnyk dipped his head, terse and murderous.

"Margit Szabo," Zima repeated. The name was a broken shell, drained of its ability to inspire fear. "I want you to say me how you meet this young woman."

I crossed one leg over the other and examined the handsome cut of my Italian loafer. I was a bit of a cad, if the truth be known, not above taking amorous advantage of a young beauty who wanted it. No crime. Many would admire me. That would be the limit of my confession. I risked a quick sweep of my brow. "I met the young lady in question at the café in Obecní Dům, where we shared a table by chance." I turned to address Bortnyk. "Obecní Dům is one of the world's finest Art Nouveau buildings. I don't suppose you've been there?"

Bortnyk nodded, reluctant to be engaged.

"Inside, in the café? Then you know how crowded it can be when tourists are in town. There wasn't a free table that afternoon, so I was forced to share one with Miss Szabo. Not that I found her disagreeable. I had hoped for a little privacy, to work on a screenplay for a film I plan to have produced here."

"You walk into café and see Miss Szabo. You sit at her table," Zima said, not interested in my screenplay.

"Is it a crime to share a table in a crowded café? I thought it was local custom."

"You misunderstand!" Zima exclaimed, though he knew I understood perfectly well. "We do not formally accuse you of crime. Please continue."

"There isn't much to it. As I said, I sat at her table and jotted a few notes down. Miss Szabo and I began to talk. When it came time to leave, she looked in her purse, and—"

"Who spoke first?" Zima interrupted.

"I don't see how that matters."

"An unimportant point, but please answer."

I made a show of rifling through the rusted cabinets of memory.

"I did. My pen ran out of ink. I asked her for a pen. I keep a full supply of pens just on the verge of going dry, you understand, so that I might use them as a pretext for starting conversations with pretty young girls."

"Where did Miss Szabo get pen?"

"I have no idea."

"You did not see her take it from purse?"

"If I did, I certainly don't remember now. This happened two months ago. A silly little tragedy with a happy ending."

"Where did Miss Szabo keep purse?"

"I don't recall."

"She put it on chair between you, for safekeeping?"

"Miss Szabo's *purse* was the last thing on my mind."

A sharp exhalation of breath from Bortnyk blew across the room.

Zima asked, "Did you leave table at any time, say, for example, to go to toilets?"

"I may have. I really don't remember. It's quite possible I did. Coffee is a powerful diuretic."

Neither of them had the faintest idea what I meant.

"It makes you pee," I explained.

That they understood. Zima even smiled.

His line of questioning carefully traced the logic of the crime. Choose the victim, establish contact, gain her trust, snatch the wallet, and slip off to the bathroom to dispose of all but the valuables. The moment comes to pay the bill, and poor Miss Szabo can't find her wallet. She's confused, flustered, alone in a strange country. The handsome young man at her table gallantly offers to pay. Miss Szabo gratefully accepts, too upset to ask herself why her eye didn't catch, when she opened her purse to loan the pen, the glaring breach of a missing wallet. If she did not notice the wallet was missing then, it was picked after the handsome young man joined her.

"This is embarrassing to both of us," I said to Zima. "You have a colleague, maybe a friend as well, upset because a young American seduced his relative. He invents a ridiculous charge and convinces you it's the truth. But if you look at the logic of it, that I stole Miss Szabo's wallet so I could get rich on her zlotys or florins or whatever the hell the Hungarian currency is, the accusation makes no sense. These are not convertible currencies, and Miss Szabo herself told me the sum she lost was insignificant by Western standards."

Bortnyk slipped behind my chair and whispered, "You are a smooth operator, Mr. Miller." His position forced me either to twist uncomfortably or allow him to shoot accusations into the back of my head. I looked at Zima, who gazed out the window. Bortnyk's voice breathed in my ear. "I asked myself many times if you were crazy. You did not need the money. Only a crazy man would take such stupid risks. But now I know you are not crazy. You are a very clever man."

"Do you know how much money I spent bailing Miss Szabo out of her jam?" I complained to Zima. "First, I paid all her expenses: meals, drinks, entrance fees. She needed money to buy a little something for her mother, and I gave it to her. I even bought her train ticket back to Budapest!"

"You used the money from her purse, didn't you?" Bortnyk whispered.

"Absurd!"

"You stole her money and then used that same money to wine and dine and win her gratitude."

"Are you her father?"

"I think you like to steal from young women so you can rescue and then seduce them."

"You're her uncle. That's it. Her uncle."

"These women think you generous, romantic. But you laugh at them. They are fools! You steal their money and they sleep with you! It is ingenious, this scheme of yours. A great joke!"

But it's just a game! I wanted to cry out. A harmless erotic amusement, a charade of financial bondage. No one gets hurt. I give full value. A romantic tour of Prague, bed and breakfast included. What woman on holiday doesn't yearn for a romance with a sympathetic and sexy man? I enliven dull vacations, provide fodder for postcards, am something to tell the friends back home and reflect upon in old age. I have a drawer full of letters thanking me for my generosity. One or two mailed bank drafts as repayment, which I returned, complaining that to be repaid cheapens the deed. I haven't pocketed a haler or kopek from anyone. If any change remains after our time together, I discreetly slip it into a pocket, to be found later, with fond thoughts of my kindness. I defy anyone to show me the harm done.

"You are a sick and repulsive man. A thief. A petty purse snatcher."

Calumny!

"I think you've said enough," I began, quite calmly, despite the rage bubbling from my chest. A petty purse snatcher! Me! "I refuse to discuss this without the presence of consul from the American Embassy. I am in Prague to write a multi-million-dollar screenplay for Paramount Pictures, a production which I hope will be of benefit to both our countries. To be hauled into a police station on a Sunday morning and slandered by a cop from Budapest is an outrage! Obecní Dům is a notorious hangout for Gypsies. Every day, one long table is packed with these creatures—black marketeers, money changers, thieves—and yet, based on the jealousies of this cop, you allow me to be accused of the crime of Miss Szabo's missing wallet. You have no evidence, and the logic of the accusation sounds ridiculous. I did it as a joke? I have been very patient with you, but now I must protest! I am an American citizen! I can speak with Ambassador Shirley Temple Black tomorrow! Are you looking to create a diplomatic incident?"

I must admit to shouting toward the end of my speech, overwhelmed by the injustice of the accusation. A petty thief indeed! Zima's eyes lifted apologetically to Bortnyk. Wary sarcasm returned to his voice. This was intended to be a friendly interview, he said, and he was sorry if I had taken offense, when no offense was meant. I was free to go.

"You're not filing charges, then?" I asked.

"Not at this time."

"Can I expect more police harassment in the future?"

"Please, Mr. Miller, it's time for you to go."

I stood to leave, but couldn't help a last attempt to satisfy my curiosity regarding Bortnyk.

"You're her uncle, aren't you?"

"I'm her fiancé, you fool."

"A little old for her, aren't you?" I said, without thinking.

He was on me before I had a chance to react, landing a right hook just above my ear. I threw my arms over my head and staggered back against the wall. His fists slammed into my ribs. I imagined one breaking off to pierce my heart.

Zima slowly rose from his desk, decided his friend had revenge enough, and pulled him off. I straightened up and
noticed a tear in my custom-tailored dress shirt. Savage
bastard!

"You're a witness," I said to Zima. "I will be in touch with
Ambassador Black in the morning. Charges will be filed."

4

The week I arrived in Central Europe I noticed with preternatural awareness that something foreign had lodged a few inches deep in my cerebrum just above the right eye. The tumor seemed no larger than a speck at the time, a few hungry cells at most. The symptoms were not much different from those reported by migraine sufferers: light sensitivity, striations of color rolling down the back of my eyelids, and a dim awareness that some alien living thing, lodged behind the skull, gorged on brain tissue. It was no use consulting a doctor, certainly not in Czechoslovakia, where medical science had barely advanced past the hammer-as-anesthetic stage. If I flew home, the family neurologist would predictably conclude that nothing in the CAT scan was indicative of a tumor. How could a doctor locate something not yet visible? Meddling friends and family would ridicule me privately as a hypochondriac. I estimated a year or two before the tumor gathered enough mass to be noticeable. After my night at Lávka and morning at the police station, I was not surprised to feel my brain swelling up in rebellion. With any luck, aspirin and the quiet dark would shrink the pain to a bearable throb.

When I approached the front door to my apartment building, a voice called my name in a piercing shriek that dispelled hope of suffering peacefully. Andrew darted across the street, shouting my name as though he found a long-lost brother.

"Must you be so loud?" I whispered, pressing the spot on my forehead behind which the tumor must lie.

Andrew laughed with the peculiar idiocy possessed by the innocent, a good-natured sing-along kind of laugh. "Hung over, are you?"

He followed me through the door. A letter from the States poked from the mailbox. I plucked it out and climbed the stairs, Andrew babbling behind. He apologized for hitting me, didn't know what came over him. He had been a little drunk, not that alcohol was an excuse, though in all honesty it had to be considered a contributing factor. His ridiculous complaints about being unable to find toothpaste—which he realized made him sound like the spoiled young American he suspected we all were—and then the desperate act of slapping me so upset him that he wandered all night through the streets of Prague. As he watched the sun streak through clouds over the city at dawn, his spirit had suddenly cleared, and the course of his future action gleamed straight as the rays of sunlight striking his eye.

It was too much for me to bear. His insistent sincerity nibbled at my patience, until I could no longer restrain myself and cried out, "Murderer! Get me the aspirin."

Andrew hurried into the bathroom. I tore open the letter. Vexing news, written in my Cousin Dickie's childish scrawl. He planned to visit Prague upon graduating from that surfers' college he attended in Santa Barbara. I crumpled the paper and tossed it aside, upset that I needed to plan my vacation around his visit, to ensure I wasn't in town when he arrived. Prague suddenly didn't seem far enough away. Andrew rushed up with the bottle, fumbling at the childproof cap. I lined up the arrows and popped the top. Four pills spilled into the palm of my hand. I chewed them to pulp and washed it down with mineral water.

Andrew opened a window and lit a cigarette, blowing his smoke out of the room. "I've lived with myself for a number of years. I have a certain self-image. What I won't do. What I'm not. What I want to be and sometimes think I am, until an incident like this happens. Then I realize I'm perhaps the opposite. My true self is not the same as my ideal self. Am I making any sense?"

"You're apologizing for trying to kill me," I guessed.

"Don't exaggerate."

I approached the mirror and examined my mouth for cuts and bruises. "You knocked loose half my teeth."

Andrew's face appeared over my shoulder in the mirror. He dismissed my injuries with a smirk, and said, "I've decided to leave Prague for the summer."

"To teach English at the refugee camp?"

"Don't you sometimes feel—particularly here in Prague, where so many people have nothing—don't you feel like you have too much privilege? Like maybe it's wrong? That a little bit of hardship and suffering is good for the character, good for the soul?"

The laughter howled out of me.

"You think I'm being naive?"

"I think you're being a saint."

Andrew flicked his cigarette into the courtyard and closed the window. "You know, Nix, I don't want to offend you or anything, but it's difficult to be your friend."

"What do you mean?"

"For one, it's impossible to tell when you're joking."

"But dear Andrew, I'm never joking."

He stared at me, uncertain if I joked still further or told the truth. I grinned ever wider until he realized that perhaps the opposite was true; I never told the straight truth. Shocked by that momentary glimpse into my character, or so I imagined, he backed toward the door and looked at me strangely, fingers trembling on the doorknob, awaiting, I feared, the moment he could politely flee.

"Have you ever been to a Catholic mass?" he asked.

The question startled me. "What does that have to do with anything?"

"There's a Gregorian choir at St. Jacobs. Want to come along?"

I suspect Andrew thought he might see me, if not saved in the arms of the Church, then within spitting distance of its feet. We walked the crumbling baroque neighborhood briskly. A reenactment of Aztec sacrifice rites could not have interested me more. Andrew claimed his interest was aesthetic to my anthropological and was all for slinking into the back row, but I wouldn't allow it. I dragged him as near to the altar as the crowd would allow. The priestly minions filed in soon after we settled and performed a series of incomprehensible gestures involving cloth, candles, and biblical texts. The service was conducted in Czech and Latin. I understood little. The rituals soon passed from the quaint to the tedious. I glanced about the church. The interior swarmed with saints, prophets, apostles, and angels swooping and trumpeting like so many acrobats in a holy circus. My gaze drifted to the cherub-infested ceiling and down a ghastly figure of St. Agnes, carved as a wooden giantess to stare with saintly severity upon the worshipers and crush them if they transgressed.

Like a host forgotten at his own party, a small figure of Christ stood alone at the end of the pew, attracting my eye simultaneous to the first chanted note from the choir. The sacred heart burned eternal in his chest. His crucified palms spread open to embrace the faithful. I looked directly into the wooden eyes and remembered a youthful time when I believed his myth. His arms seemed wide enough even for my sins. A memory of innocence struck me: a boy too young to have doubt or carnal knowledge crying at the dramatized death of a movie Christ. The memory weakened me. I wished a return to that effortless purity of being. My brain emptied. The choir's voice filled my chest like a balloon. I surged into the vaulted spaces, soaring with the chant, the charade of personality sloughed off in the desire for spiritual union with the God of the cave.

A young Slavic blonde in the next pew, attracted to the spiritual glow in my countenance, glanced over and met my gaze. She smiled with sensual frankness, then blushed and turned away. An absurd fantasy shot up at me like an arrow, of stealing down the steps leading to the crypt and jumping her bones amid the stone coffins of her Bohemian ancestors. The shriveled remnants of conscience pumped and gasped and choked out a dribble of shame. I plummeted to earth with the dust of heaven on the seat of my pants and hoots of angels in my ears. I felt a sudden kinship with Lucifer, the rebel angel tossed out of heaven. A God-chosen chump to play the loyal opposition. Condemned to eternal villainy for the greater good of God. Terrifier of innocents, straw demon for the righteous, bogeyman to keep the faithful shivering in their sinless beds. Like Lucifer, I would have preferred to sit at the right hand of God, rather than catch that same hand across my chops.

The shame passed to disbelief. That I could believe in a clutter of dead statues brought on a chuckle, and the longer I considered how I had been fooled by an attack of sanctilepsy the louder I laughed, until my roaring echoed through the vault to contend with the priest's litany. Stares swiveled to fix me with vehement disapproval. Andrew's elbow dug into my ribs, always the most ticklish spot in my anatomy. I howled with laughter. Soon, a brown-robed monk with a bowl cut hustled to the pew and competed with Andrew to be the one to pitch me out onto the street.

This was not a fantasy. This actually happened. Do I disappoint you? Did you expect a different sort of villain, a brutal man of action who, though you might not agree with his motives, nonetheless is admirable in his directness? Or perhaps a faux villain, someone who initially appears to be evil, but—as his motives and character come into focus, an unhappy childhood here, a good deed sprinkled amid the bad there—you realize is not such a bad fellow after all? These are not me. I am not a hero with a tragic flaw. That I should be so heroic, to be brought low by a single flaw! I began low and shall end no higher.

Perhaps my judgment was not sound—I now consider many of my attitudes and decisions at that time loosely hinged at best—but I thought my best chance for salvation lay in my towering goddess of the vomit-flecked pumps. When I arrived at Lávka that night, my nerves were strung taut between the dread and hope of meeting her. The back patio held a scattering of tourists in the fading light. I chose a table with a view of the castle and waited for a girl selling roses by the bloom to pass through the club. One or two often did, plying an extortionist's trade among the couples. I needed to buy at least a dozen. If I bought a dozen and my goddess did not appear, I could place the roses in the lap of another woman and smiling mysteriously leave without a word. If such a woman were single, I might reap some benefit the next time we met.

"Out looking for new victims?" a voice whispered in my ear.

I twisted to match the voice with Bortnyk's face. He had a beer in hand, and not likely his first. That he knew my habits irked me. Quite possibly he had been at Lávka the previous night as well, watching my argument with Andrew and subsequent disgrace. Paranoia. He had not then known my habits or what I looked like. He pulled a chair from beneath the table and reversed it before sitting, propping his elbows on the chair back as he drank. Unexpectedly, he smiled.

"Not happy to see me?"

"I'm overwhelmed with joy. Police harassment is near the top of my list of entertainments."

"I'm not a policeman tonight," he corrected. "I'm off duty and out of my jurisdiction. Tonight, I'm just a man."

The glint in his voice did not bode well for my personal safety. Never before had I been looked at with a frankness so warmly expressive of death. In his tar-black eyes gray flecks of light lay submerged like bones. I began plotting escape routes. If I got up and walked out, he would catch me in some dark alley and turn me into a police statistic. I'd need to be clever. Defuse his anger first. Argue that I was as much a victim in this as anybody. Confuse him with a little pretended humanity.

"Look, I'm sorry about all this."

"Fuck you and fuck your apology."

"She took off her ring. I didn't know she was engaged."

"I don't care what you knew."

I smiled. Shook my head. Threw my hands into the air.

"I'm at a loss here, Detective. What do you want me to do?"

"Die," he answered.

"Eventually, I will. But not soon enough to please you, I hope."

I told the truth when I said I had no idea Margit was engaged. The injustice of my situation galled me. Not that I was above sampling another man's fiancée. I resented being guilty of a crime I had no previous knowledge of committing.

"How did you find out?" I asked.

"Margit told me."

"I thought women tried to keep their affairs secret."

"It's the last knife they throw as they walk out the door."

"She left you?"

Bortnyk drained his beer and signaled a passing waitress for another. It was certain that the longer this went on, the more he would drink, and the more he drank, the more likely he would start swinging at any imagined provocation.

"Do you know what a stinger is?" he asked.

"A cocktail?"

He lurched forward and clamped my wrist to the table. "I'll give you a hint. It locks onto the heat of the target's engines."

"A missile, then."

"The target rolls, the missile follows. The target accelerates, dives, the missile follows. No matter what the target does, the missile follows until it makes contact with the source of the heat. Then it explodes."

"Impressive."

"I operate the same way," he said.

I shouldn't have laughed. I didn't want to antagonize him any further. Like that afternoon at mass, I couldn't stop. I gripped the edge of the table, helplessly waiting for the fit to blow over. Bortnyk watched, anger lines flexing the length of his jaw. When the tears stopped flowing and I could breathe once again without tittering, he said, in a voice he might use to order at a restaurant, "I want to break your bones. Arms and legs and face."

"I'm not worth it."

"You're a thief."

I backed my chair away from the table and stood. "I'm not a great guy. I'll admit that. But I didn't steal the wallet from your fiancée's purse."

"You stole my fiancée," he said.

"Please. I didn't steal your fiancée. I merely borrowed her."

I turned and walked quickly from the table. The sparse crowd did not offer enough cover for immediate escape. I clipped rapidly down the steps leading to the bathrooms. There were two exits from the bottom of the stairwell: one back the way I came and the other surfacing near the entrance. I wondered how well Bortnyk knew the club. If he was any good as a detective, he would have a clear blueprint in his head. I resisted the temptation to sprint up the steps to the front. Bortnyk would know the club had only one exit.

A toothless, grinning attendant took a two-crown admission fee at the bathroom door. My lungs rattled and wheezed in the fetid air, a sign since childhood that my nerves were close to snapping. I unzipped and stepped up to the urinal. The old bastard collected two crowns from every full bladder in the club, and the urinal still smelled like a urinal. Not like in America, where the toilets smell like perfumed oases. What if Bortnyk followed me into the bathroom? My back was to the door. He could sneak behind and smash my face into the porcelain. The thought pinched my bladder. I zipped up and approached the mirror. Three months in Central Europe had bleached the last traces of Southern California from my skin. The indispensable benefit of a suntan is that it masks the paling effects of fear. Ten deep breaths to calm the nerves and clear the brain. Then it was up the steps again to the back patio.

Bortnyk had disappeared, our table claimed by a group of tourists. I backed into a corner, shielded by a pack of young men sniffing for women near the bar. I waited. Bortnyk raced up the steps from the bathroom and sliced through the crowd toward the table. I slipped inside, strode briskly past the front bar and out the club. Well into Staré Město, the old town of Prague, I finally paused at a dark corner, unzipped, and listened for pursuing footsteps above the liquid splatter on cobblestones.

Instead, I heard the clatter of a woman's heels, amplified by the arched promenade across the street, where a squat Gypsy called to a young man waiting for traffic to clear. Startled, he darted between cars, a smirk clenched in his teeth. The Gypsy returned to her archway predictably bored. I recognized the attempted transaction and the street. The better-looking hookers worked for hard currency in hotel bars or wandered Václavské náměstí, a broad avenue popular with tourists. Customers didn't need hard currency on Perlova Street. The hookers priced themselves for local clientele, workers and clerks who couldn't pay the hundred-plus deutsche marks charged by the hookers walking Václavské náměstí. Perlova was not the street to find the busty young blonde of healthy vulgar fantasy. Any hooker who could command more than a fleeting glance under a streetlamp would not work here. Perlova was the street of the fat, the lame, the diseased, the freaks. I had heard rumors that the mayor of Prague was a frequent visitor. Perhaps I might lodge a complaint about Zima and Bortnyk. I pushed out of the shadows and, peering into the dark under the arched promenade, spotted a face so startling I stopped in the middle of the street, convinced my eyes had contrived an apparition. What astonished me about the face was its location, no higher than waist level, though the woman did not appear to be sitting or kneeling. The same height a child's face might be. But what would a child be doing on Perlova at night? A horrifying thought. Was she that dollop of freshness to slack the jaded's thirst? And if so, how much?

Child, woman, or other, a streetwise awareness twisted the creature's head when I stopped and stared. A gleam of white flashed in the darkness, hip-high. The sight astonished. It was smiling at me! The creature called out in a stained voice and breached the dark so I might see it better. White plastic go-go boots, pink hose, red coat parted to reveal sagging voluptuousness beneath a black miniskirt and tight white pullover. A contiguous slash of hair the size of a mustache hovered above its eyes. Its lips were obscenely red and full. The lips of a carnal goddess. A stunningly incongruous genetic gesture. I was driven to ecstasy. Another monster! My soul mate! A midget Gypsy whore!

I approached, trembling. Another smile, quick as a knife flash. She spoke to me in German, batting her eyes in grotesque coquetry. I told her I was an American. I appreciated monstrousness and was willing to pay for it. She understood no more than two words of my monologue: "American" and "pay."

"Fifty dollars," she said.

I pulled a hundred-dollar bill from my sport coat and watched the greed in her eyes. She wouldn't examine the bill too closely. Not that I worried. I'd passed such bills before to black-market money changers, always with a camera around my neck and a map of Prague jutting visibly out of my pocket. About half the time the bastards tried to cheat me with worthless notes, discontinued bills from the communist era or Polish zlotys, but not even the shrewdest questioned the legitimacy of my hundred-dollar bills. "Mad money," I called it. I avoided banks as a precaution. An expert with a loupe and strong light might notice the hundred was a color Xerox seamlessly printed onto a bleached dollar bill. I'd bought a hundred of these bills from a friend, at ten cents on the dollar. It pleased me to fool the black-market money changers.

The creature tugged on my arm when I showed her the bill, whispering the other word in her English vocabulary: "Room." A room was too private for what I had in mind, contemplating the obvious anatomical advantage of waist-high lips. I dangled the hundred above her head and countered the pull of her arm with a step in the opposite direction. She resisted, protesting with the same word, "Room." I tugged my arm free and stepped onto the street. The bill fluttered in a cool breeze. She wheedled, cajoled, begged. I didn't understand a word. When I turned and crossed to the opposite curb, her uncertainty was compromised by greed. I was almost touched, the way she clutched my arm.

I led her to a dark wedge where two buildings unevenly joined, and with a simple gesture demonstrated the service I wanted performed. A line of trash cans screened her from the street but left me visible from the waist up. She took the hundred and went to work. It wasn't the most artful handling I'd ever experienced. She insisted, with rude pulls here and there, on hurrying the act to its contracted conclusion. I didn't oblige. A hundred dollars, even in counterfeit, entitled me to some drawing out of pleasure, and if she wasn't interested in providing it, I could.

The physical sensation she provided was of minimal interest. My sexuality always has been primarily cerebral. It was the idea of the event that excited me. That I was capable of such a perverse idea and had the lack of decency to act upon it lent new perspective to my personal degradation. The novelty of experience justified almost any act to me then. I was engaged in a game of dare with my conscience. What rules could I break, what unspeakable acts could I commit without incurring the wrath of conscience? I sought liberation. If I was capable of paying a midget Gypsy whore to fellate me in the shadows of a public street, few acts could constrain me to decency. I could satiate any whim or desire, without fear of conscience's reprisal. I could be the freest man on earth.

Deep into my reverie, I noticed a billboard had been newly riveted to the side of the nearest peeling baroque town house. I blinked at an iconic hamburger and golden obelisk of fries as though confronted by hallucination. The first sign of a free market economy had arrived to the street of whores: Prague was soon to have a McDonald's franchise. I began to laugh. The midget whore pulled away, startled by the sound. The confused twisting of her absurd eyebrow, that solid slash of hair across her brow, seemed funnier than the McDonald's billboard, or maybe it was the unexpected juxtaposition of the two. I laughed harder. The whore backed away, terrified.

"Don't stop, really, it's okay, this is what I like," I said, laughing.

"*Ďáble!*" she shouted, angry and afraid.

She turned and ran, short legs churning furiously, to the safety of her arched promenade. A man built like a sprung suitcase stepped out of the shadows and shouted at me. Her pimp. He'd grown so stout the buttons on his shirt stretched to popping. I laughed at him too. He advanced into the middle of the street, shaking his fist. I fell back into the shadows and laughed at everything.

5

On the street corner outside my apartment building, a beggar with hands joined like flippers to his shoulders routinely exhibited his appendages for coin. Prague was a city of the deformed and disfigured. The route to Charles Bridge featured a half-dozen beggars who waved stumps or signs proclaiming disability. Plastic surgeons were in short supply, and the routine orthopedic care taken for granted in the West did not yet exist. Those struck blind stayed blind. Those not deformed were infected with one virus or another caught in the packed warrens of the metro, where an ill-timed breath doomed. I sat hunched at the far wall between cars and sang to myself a litany of the infected, of the flu-ridden, cold-caught, polio-victimized, valgus-deformed, arthritis-afflicted, cataract-blind, pockmarked, clubfooted, and hare-lipped, of that crippled gob of flesh, post-communist humanity. I sprang free when the compartment doors slid open, glad of my Southern California fit body, pleased that my deformities were as invisible as wormish meat inside the immaculate shell of an almond.

As I rode the escalator toward the surface, a face as assured in beauty as a Botticelli angel appeared above. At first, I thought her an apparition and stared in a pose suitable for adoration, but as our escalators converged her features sharpened to a familiar and cruel sensuality. My goddess from Lávka! I all but waved my arms in panic as I watched the swift and stepped steel river opposite mine rush her away. At the top I leapt the barricade and plunged back into the metro. An arriving train whipped the air. I ran to one platform and then its opposite. Crowds gushed toward the escalators. The raven back of her head surfaced briefly as she ducked into a metro car. The warning chime sounded. I pounced at the nearest door and wedged into the mass of passengers. She stood at the opposite aisle, hand gripping the rail and head resting gently in the crook of her arm. I did not directly watch her; instead I sought her reflection in the window encased by the sliding doors and even then dared no more than furtive glances, fearful of catching eyes in the glass.

Two stops later, a swarm of tourists looking for the guidebook graves of dead Jews swept her from the train. I followed a few yards behind, plotting methods of casual introduction there in the metro and again on the street, as I followed her wanderings through the medieval labyrinth of Staré Město. By no great coincidence she stopped at Obecní Dům, which contained a café and Art Nouveau interior incompletely obscured by a peeling veneer of Stalinist bric-abrac. The café filled rapidly with tourists most afternoons, though the occasional Czech could still be seen nursing a cup of coffee, and, as I mentioned to Inspector Zima, the Gypsies routinely commandeered a corner. She settled into a table near the fountain at the back of the café, marble nymphs frolicking over her shoulder like members of a divine retinue.

I slipped into the bathroom for a quick inspection. No gnashed particles wedged between teeth, hair stylishly awry, back of the sport-coat collar turned down, polo shirt casually unbuttoned, and blue jeans cinched around an admirably slim waist: an informally elegant look calculated to appeal to the widest possible range of women, from the slumming countess to the backpacking sorority princess. I sneaked another glance inside the café. Luck joined seamlessly to plan. The last available table had just been taken. I approached with seeming annoyance at the crowded ambiance and asked, in Czech, if the chair at her table was free. In the bathroom mirror, I'd practiced a look of shocked recognition dissolving to embarrassment and boyish apology. I almost launched into the routine unprompted, but when she stared as though never having seen my face before, the apology stuck to the back of my throat. I must have looked idiotic, gaping down at her like an actor dying under the weight of a missing cue.

"I asked if this chair was free. The restaurant is quite crowded, and I'd like to sit down," I blurted and tapped my fingers on the chair to further communicate my intent. Her eyes traveled the cut of my jacket and the well-kept, rugged planes of my face. I began to tremble, waiting for recognition to barb her lips. "It's a custom in this country. If a chair is free and there are no tables." A sudden horror struck me, that I had confused my goddess at Lávka with this a stranger, that this was not Her. "You do speak English, don't you?"

"I'm expecting someone, but please sit down," she said.

Expecting who? A boyfriend? I hadn't considered the possibility of her having a boyfriend. A woman of her beauty and poise does not remain long without consort, unless some intolerable obstacle daunts her suitors. I could wheedle the information from her without revealing my intentions, but what if she said yes? Disaster. I planned on winning this woman. We were to have a whirlwind courtship and exchange vows in the heart of Old Town, on Staroměstské náměstí. Love would change me. I'd become not just likable but lovable. New friends would flock to us. I'd enter a café and a half-dozen people would drop by my table to chat, seek advice, or warm themselves in the glow of charisma. The thin soap-shell of this fantasy shimmered as it neared the bursting pinprick of a boyfriend.

So I asked nothing and played the idiot, gawking at her, with a half-dozen possible remarks, rejoinders, replies, questions, observations, and apologies vying to be the first propelled past my lips and jamming instead against my teeth. I sat down. It seemed impossibly lucky that she did not remember me from that night at Lávka. Judging by a barely half-amused smile, she was wary of my trying to pick her up yet found the prospect somehow ironic. Was she merely demonstrating good manners in not recognizing me? I couldn't decide which was more objectionable: She knew perfectly well and withheld formal recognition to torment me with the uncertainty, or my face was so unremarkable she promptly had forgotten it. Another explanation suited me better: The discrepancy between the monster sick at her feet and the dashing figure I cut at the café table was so great it never occurred to her the two were the negative original and positive print of the same image.

She resumed studying the menu. I was about to offer my inept assistance in translating food items when I remembered the menu had a perfectly capable English section. An irrational fear seized me; I was to be eternally trapped in an adolescent nightmare of sweaty palms and conversational fumblings. The best strategy was to retreat into indifference. I pulled a notebook from my coat pocket and flipped it open. This technique has worked for me several times in the past. The woman watches as I scribble intensely across the page, lit by the pale fire of genius. I don't pay her the least bit of attention. Her curiosity mounts as I fill the pages.

"What are you writing about?" the woman asks, finally overcome.

"You," I reply.

I wouldn't resort to such a cheap trick with a goddess. I had better ruses. But first she'd have to ask. I scribbled on page after page a list of movie stars I'd seen in L.A. restaurants and, based on observed detail, could claim I'd met. She read the menu, ordered coffee, admired the ornate carved interior, and paid no attention to the frenetic chase of pen across page. The natural melancholy of her face was guarded by a sharp glance and cutting smile, which I encountered when I connived an accidental meeting of our eyes. My fear stilled to irritation that I could be so easily disregarded. I decided to employ a gambit reserved for the hardest cases. I threw my notebook down on the table. The resounding thump jumped her eyes to mine.

"I'm stuck," I said, clearly frustrated, yet appropriately deferential to her privacy. "Do you mind if I ask you a question?"

Her smile was oddly predatory, as though she was accustomed to advances from bold young men and awaited the moment she might cut me down.

I said, "Imagine you're a young businesswoman recruited by a Czech armaments company."

"Why?" she snapped.

"It's a dramatic problem I'm trying to solve."

"You're a writer," she said, her accent mysterious to my ear but the tone of contempt clear.

"A writer-producer," I corrected.

"And what does a writer-producer do?"

"He makes more money than a writer."

The corner of her lip turned gently toward her eyes. I'd pleased her. She said, "I'm not a typical person. I can't give a typical answer."

"The woman in my story isn't typical."

"I'm a businesswoman then."

"You're dating two men in Prague: one an American, and the other Ukrainian. You discover the American is an active CIA operative. The Ukrainian is an ex-KGB agent. What do you do?"

"I confide in the better lover and betray the other."

The swift decisiveness of her reply startled a laugh out of me.

"I warned you I was not typical."

"You didn't warn me you were murderous."

"I like strong men."

Did she intend an invitation in that remark? I whispered, "The studio is talking about Tom Cruise as the CIA agent."

"They must pay you very much, if you write for Tom Cruise."

I shrugged modestly.

Without warning, she stood, set her purse on the table, and said, "Watch this for me while I make a call."

Had I a camera, I would have framed the shot like Hitchcock. The brass clasp of the purse looms huge and sharply focused in the foreground, while the much smaller figure of its owner recedes into a blurred background. When the owner exits the frame, only the purse remains, immensely irresistible. The shot would symbolize the terrible temptation to the protagonist. Was this a test? She was supposed to be different. She was not one of my harmless erotic pursuits. I imagined there was a God in heaven testing my resolve. Or perhaps she knew my weakness, just as she recognized the beast in me that night at Lávka. I would not yield to the temptation. Still, there was the irrefutable fact of her purse on the table and my history of unreliable honesty. I glanced casually about. No one watched.

The purse accidentally fell to the floor, jarring free the snap. I bent below the table. No one could begrudge me a peek, to make sure nothing had broken. Her book was regrettably the only visible content. The choice of reading material disappointed me. *The Firm*. Even I read Grisham. I couldn't shut the purse again with just that to judge her. I nudged the paperback aside. A train ticket and passport, clipped together for safekeeping. I fished them out for a quick look. She was Danish. Monika Andersen. Born in 1968. A good-luck omen, the year of Nixon. Not a bad likeness on the inside cover. The train ticket was Prague to Budapest, open departure date, first class. A receipt slipped from the back passport page and fluttered to the carpet. I became sharply conscious of the passage of time. I dropped the passport back into the purse, snapped the lip shut, and returned the purse safely to the tabletop. The receipt lay blank side up on the carpet. I flipped it over. It was from

Gerbeaud. I knew Gerbeaud. A café in Budapest with delightful pastries. I stuffed the receipt into my pocket, loath to leave it as evidence.

I jotted a few words into my notebook, pretending disinterest when Monika returned to the table with a tall brute at her side. She introduced him as Sven. Her paramour? Sven scowled down at me. Was it possible he had witnessed the business with the purse? He did not seem pleased to meet me—the natural reaction of any man introduced to a potential rival. I studied him as he lit a cigarette. Thick lips, broad nose, wide cheekbones, an arch of blond hair slicked back. And big. A couple of inches taller than my near six feet, and built like a prizefighter. The sensitive type of brute women adore.

"You in the movies?" he asked, studying me as I studied him.

"In the business," I corrected.

"Done anything I've seen?"

"I don't know what you've seen."

He kept his eyes fixed on mine when he turned to Monika and asked, "What was it you said he was? A writer?"

"Writer-producer," she corrected, quick to my defense.

"If you're such a successful writer-producer, what are you doing in Prague?"

He came straight at me, jabbing away. To be considered a threat pleased me, but the best I could do in the situation was adroitly parry everything he threw and walk away unscathed. Later, I could engineer another meeting with Monika and ask what she saw in such a lout.

"I have a development deal with Paramount Pictures. The studio likes the story and the story takes place in Prague, so they pay me to come here and write it." By a miracle of timing, a waiter strolled by, pretending to work. I asked for the bill and said, "I'd tell you more, but I'm late for an appointment."

Monika's hand dropped casually onto my wrist. "I'm sorry, but my brother sometimes is a little protective."

Brother! Only a sudden contraction of will kept me from laughing in loud joy. A protective brother! How charming! Will he walk a dozen paces behind us as we court, like the relatives of old Europe? I wanted to stay and impress them both with my conviviality as well as my accomplishments, but the waiter, in a rare display of efficiency, insisted on presenting me the bill promptly after I'd requested it. I had little choice but to leave or prove my fictitious appointment a lie. But first, I needed a theatrical set piece to demonstrate the power of fate.

"I don't blame your brother for being suspicious. Prague is overpopulated with scribblers, unpublished and unproduced, all pretending to be the next Hemingway. It's worse than Hollywood, where every other wait-person is trying to peck out the great American screenplay. To tell the truth, Monika, I'm ashamed to admit I write anything at all."

"How did you know my name?" Monika asked, sharp-eyed.

I looked confused. It's one of my better looks. One eyebrow drops low while my eyes pace their sockets, searching an escape from befuddlement.

"I'm sorry, but I don't," I confessed.

"But you just said it!"

I appealed to Sven, palms floating in bewilderment.

"You called her Monika," he confirmed.

"But that's the name of the character in my story!" I cried, triumphant.

"I don't believe you," she protested, but a smile broke through the disbelieving smirk on her lips, like that of a child presented with a magic trick.

I flipped open my notebook and presented the most recent entry, documenting Monika's remark about the CIA and KGB agents, the character name clearly identified. And the crowning proof, a character note for the female lead, named Monika, written on a page dated the month previous and left blank for just such an occasion. She took the notebook and thumbed through it, arriving at the cover page, which listed my name, number, and local address.

"What kind of name is Nix?" she asked.

"Just a nickname," I answered.

"Are you a thief?"

Her question startled me. Again, she knew. But how?

"English slang," she explained. "If someone nicks something, they steal it."

I responded with a watery laugh and the idiotic remark, "But you aren't English?"

"No." She handed back my notebook. "Monika isn't an English or American name. You should change the name of your character to something more American, like Debbie or Sue."

I considered telling her my character was half Danish but, like an actor aware of the fine line between brilliance and hamhandedness, decided not to push too strongly the limits of disbelief. "She's half Czech," I replied.

"I'm also half Czech," she answered somberly.

For several seconds, we were suitably speechless with amazement. Was is it coincidence or fate? As a native Californian, I have a cultural weakness for the most tenuous evidence of the supernatural and almost completely forgot I'd invented my half of the sudden mystic congruence of our lives. I backed away from the table, eager now to leave, as the old adage goes, with the audience wanting more.

"Perhaps I'll see you again—at Lávka," I offered and immediately regretted the choice of venues.

"Perhaps." She smiled.

I left the café cursing my idiocy. Luck rules most games of chance, and romance is no different. I'd pulled off a few brilliant strokes and made a few blunders. Mostly, I'd been lucky she hadn't seemed to recognize me. To suggest Lávka was egregious stupidity. One good look at me, in situ, might stir that earlier memory I was anxious to suppress. If her interest survived the shock, an appearance by that cuckold Bortnyk would chase me from the scene.

CUT TO:

EXTERIOR—LÁVKA BACK PATIO—NIGHT
ON CASTLE—lit up like a jewel box this beautiful summer night.
PULL BACK—to Monika staring at the castle, waiting for Nix to return.
A MENACING FIGURE parts the crowd and taps her shoulder.
She turns—

DETECTIVE BORTNYK
(flashing badge)
Budapest Police Department.

MONIKA
Yes?

DETECTIVE BORTNYK
I'm sorry to disturb you, miss, but we have reason to
believe the man you were just speaking to is a petty
thief and seducer. Could you please check the valuables in your purse?

THE END

No matter how charming I'd been, a well-informed accusation from Bortnyk would poison her embryonic tenderness and abort the relationship. I crossed the square outside the café and waited near the stall of a street-side bookseller. I wasn't foolish enough to trust to luck. I waited no more than fifteen minutes. Sven and Monika walked out of the café arm in arm. Such touching sibling affection! I followed them past the old railway station into a neighborhood of crumbling plaster and coal dust. Tucked in a corner was Sven and Monika's hotel, the Merkur, a stripped-down, no-star accommodation, it's original turn-of-the-century coat of plaster and paint peeled indecently to its ankles.

A cab lounged at the curb. I instructed the driver to take me to police headquarters and tapped insistently at the meter until he sullenly turned it on. That Monika was poor pleased me. Not that I'd fallen for the cliché of the princess in rags made virtuous by her poverty. Rich young women, though encouragingly hedonistic, are less impressed by wealth and achievement in others. It's expected and gives no real advantage. A poor woman is more likely to have unfulfilled ambitions. The fantasy of escape long inhabits her dreams. A suitor with elegant habits and real-world accomplishments is part of the fantasy. Not the wisest basis on which to start a permanent relationship, but effective enough in the short term.

The addled old man at the front desk claimed Inspector Zima was out of the building, then in the building but at a meeting, then out of the building again: all in the most incomprehensible cacophony of German, English, and Czech. After fifteen minutes of wringing misinformation from him, I still had no idea where Zima was or how to find him. Losing patience, I whipped out my passport and lectured about the rights of an American citizen.

"Mr. Miller!" Inspector Zima called from behind my back.

He stood at the end of the adjacent hallway, file folder in hand and smoke-yellow teeth flashing behind a grin of deceptive goodwill. I rushed up, ready to let roar with the indignities of the previous evening's encounter with Bortnyk.

"But why did nobody tell me you were here?" he protested before I could begin.

"But I—!"

"Stop!" he commanded, and tugged portentously at his ear, a clandestine gesture intended to convey the information that people might be listening. He strode vigorously through the maze of corridors and ushered me into his office, where he asked, shutting the door, "How is your very good friend, Ambassador Black?"

I resisted the temptation to paranoia. He had not called Ambassador Black and asked about me. Ambassador Black had not said she'd never heard of me.

"I'm not here to discuss my relationship to Ambassador Black. I'm here to discuss the behavior of your colleague."

Zima tossed the folder onto his desk and lit a cigarette. He watched me for a moment over the smoke and said, "The mafia, Mr. Miller." He could have said almost anything and made as much sense to me at that moment. *The potatoes, Mr. Miller!*

"Did you know we have more than five mafias in Prague? Serbians, Russians, Ukrainians, Chinese, Romanians, and Italians have mafia now. Weapons, drugs, money laundering. Only local country not to have mafia here is Czechoslovakia, if you don't count taxi drivers."

To be polite, I smiled at his jest. "Last night, your friend Bortnyk—"

Zima held up the palm of his hand and opened the folder on his desk. "New crime is to follow merchants. *To neni Amerika*. This isn't America. We have no checks here. Good joke in English. No checks in Czechoslovakia. Businessman puts money into briefcase, hundreds of thousands of crowns, and drives to place where money must go. Somebody follows and bang! Takes his money. That is my problem."

Zima closed the folder.

"You do not interest me. *Vůbec ne*. Not at all."

"Are you going to do nothing?" I exclaimed, vexed.

"We will arrest thief, I hope."

"Not about your stupid merchants. About Bortnyk!"

"But Mr. Bortnyk is not my responsibility. If you want to make complaint, you must contact Budapest police."

"I'll contact the local English language press is who I'll contact," I threatened. Prague boasted two weekly newspapers, both with a jaundiced eye for scandal. "I will not be harassed by a mad Hungarian!"

"I think you're safe for some days. His train left this morning."

"Thank you for the information." I bolted from the chair, annoyed at the game of fetch he'd forced me to play.

"Stop!" Zima called.

I turned at the door. Zima looked down at the sheaf of papers on his desk, face wreathed in smoke from the cigarette pinched between his fingers. He carefully turned the top paper over and said, "I hope you become more like other Americans. Enjoy a little harmless fun. Drink too much beer, smoke cigarettes, play guitar on Charles Bridge, find young American girls to sleep with you. Then go home. If you continue to rob tourists, I will arrest you, even if it displeases your good friend Ambassador Black."

6

The next morning the title page of a new screenplay flew from my imagination with astonishing ease. Satisfied I'd made a good start, I rose from my desk and put a pot of water to boil. The movie would tap the knowledge of Central and Eastern Europe I'd acquired since moving to Prague. A great love story, peppered here and there with elements of a thriller. The lead character would be an innocent American, someone here to teach English to the natives, a naive but boyishly hip young man who possesses some special talent that triggers at a key point in the action, saving the day. Maybe an English teacher isn't the right occupation. Better yet, a young American business-man. Not a carpetbagger capitalist, but someone with ideals. Like somebody from Greenpeace. Why not Greenpeace exactly? The lead character, we'll call him Tom, is a Greenpeace executive who becomes accidentally embroiled in the smuggling of radioactive materials from the Ukraine. A perfect irony! But how does Tom get fooled into acting as a smuggler? A woman, of course. A heartbreaking Slavic beauty fresh off the steppes, untouched by the carnality of Hollywood. We'll call her Julie. Later we discover she was smuggling uranium to pay for an operation in the West to save the life of her crippled younger brother. A message movie with foreign locations, tragic love, stirring action, and a cast of thousands. A perfect vehicle for Tom Cruise. Julia Roberts for the Slavic beauty. Tom and Julia in the same picture! A sure hit!

I sat down to write, the cup of coffee warm in my hands, and . . .

Nothing. My fervent swarm of ideas diminished to a few stray buzzings or, worse, became inexplicably cliché-ridden between the moment of inspiration and inscription. I stared out the window, thinking about the seven-figure sale I was certain to make once the script was finished, if only I could get it successfully started. The greatest writers suffer from writers' block. Some say the greatest novels were never written at all!

Shadows shifted over the piles of refuse in the courtyard as the sun tipped above the rooftops. A cat in heat rubbed her back on a patch of sunstruck ground and howled. I closed my eyes and thought about the hundred ways the film might begin. A short time later, I fell asleep.

I couldn't remember what I had been dreaming when the phone woke me: something simultaneously bright and dark, like underexposed film projected onto a blank screen. I can never remember my dreams. I glanced at the clock. Nearly four. I answered the phone to a woman's voice calling, "Good afternoon!"

The telephone line hummed and popped as I struggled for a response. Margit? Helga? Karin?

"I called to say I hope you haven't forgotten me."

"Of course I haven't! How are you?"

"You really don't know who this is, do you?"

The woman's laugh, sharp and clear as glass, jolted me to sudden perspicuity. "Monika! How did you get my number?"

"If you don't want women to call you, don't print your phone number on the front cover of your notebook."

"Yes, well, I don't normally," I began, hoping for a clever rejoinder, but wit remained frustratingly out of reach. I cleared my throat to hide the incompletion and waited for her to launch into the reason for her call, fearing she might have lost something at the café and wanted to ask whether or not I'd seen it. Paranoia. I hadn't tried that one with her. When the conversation stalled for several seconds, it occurred to me that she was as interested in me as I was in her. I said, "I missed you at Lávka last night. Will you be there tonight?"

"Not tonight."

"Where, then? When can I see you?"

"You could try the hotel café at eight. Do you know where I'm staying?"

The Merkur, of course. I said, "No idea."

"The Hotel Paříž. Just around the corner from where we met."

After we hung up, I decided to be charmed by her little lie. It was the kind of lie I might tell, had I been poor. She was ashamed of having to stay in the shabby Merkur. The Hotel Paříž was one of the city's finest hotels, a brass and oak museum piece in the Art Nouveau style. It fit her image like a glass slipper.

The rest of the afternoon did not pass quickly. At five I began to dress, unable to restrain myself any longer, but no matter how many times I changed my mind about which shirt to wear with which jacket and pair of pants, I had completed dressing by half past the hour. For two hours I tried to read, but my eyes wouldn't stick to the page. Minutes after the last remembered sentence I would catch myself staring out the window lost in an absurd romantic fantasy of saving fair Monika from a gang of uranium smugglers. I tossed the book aside, annoyed that love aroused from my imagination such incipient adolescence, and hastily walked to the Hotel Paříž, arriving a half hour early.

When the waiter came to take my order, I asked for mineral water. Couldn't allow myself to get drunk. A fine surprise that would be, if the moment Monika walked into the café I opened my mouth and once again vomited on her feet. I regretted arriving early. She might not come at all. If she does, the anxiety of waiting will have destroyed my nerves. The waiter approached, balancing a platter of drinks colored a comforting amber and one clear bland fluid which he deposited at my table. She had recognized me as the vomiting fool. She despised me. She had called to execute her revenge. She laughed, knowing I eagerly awaited a woman who never planned to show up. Only alcohol could dim the lightning strikes of paranoia flashing across my brain. I clutched the mineral water between my two hands, gritted my teeth, and when the waiter next walked past ordered a Scotch, which I drained in one long draught.

Monika arrived punctually fifteen minutes late and, no doubt surmising that my early arrival signaled the greater of our impatiences, greeted me with a radiant smile. Her waist was cinched to a delicate thinness by a gold and blue sash with a zigzag weave, and below her ballooning Turkish pants I glimpsed an ankle so exquisitely formed I nearly swooned onto the table. I tried to think of something to say. Something sharp, incisive, astonishingly perceptive, and revealing a profound understanding of human civilization. My mind blanked. Say something coherent, then. Anything. A grunt or groan will suffice. I tried smiling. I had waited all afternoon to talk to her, and now that she was before my eyes waiting for me to speak I could think of nothing save the crushing movement of time. Much better to stroll grandly in, twenty minutes late, some adventure fresh as air on my lips.

"Nice day today," I said.

Idiot. Her head barely lifted from the drinks menu.

"I wouldn't know. I spent it with lawyers."

"Legal trouble?"

"Are you afraid I might be—what did you say I was yesterday? Murderous?"

"Of course not, I just was trying to, to, to. . . ." I was just trying to make conversation, trying not to appear stupid, and failing at both.

Monika looked up from the menu. The right corner of her mouth hooked toward her brow. I'd never seen a smile so cruel. She asked, "Are you nervous?"

"Nervous? No. It's been a day. A tough day, I mean. Nice too. Nice but tough. You know. Here and there. But the lawyers?"

"My family owned property in Prague before 1948."

"The Commies then?"

"Nationalized it. With everything else in the country. Banks, factories, apartment buildings. You couldn't even keep a house."

"I heard about some new law, something about giving it back?"

"The restitution law. First you have to prove it belonged to your family, so we talk to lawyers all day. My brother and I."

"Where, by the way, is your brother?"

"At Lávka."

I laughed out loud at her cleverness. No wonder she didn't want to meet there, under the watchful eye of big brother. I had to get my nerves under control, had to remain conscious that Monika quite likely wanted me as much as I desired her. I ordered a bottle of Taittinger from a hovering waiter. Didn't want to seem cheap. Was it really possible that Monika didn't remember me? That I had seen her quite by accident in the metro and she had later called to arrange this private evening away from her brother? I asked, "I don't suppose you've eaten?"

"I'm famished," Monika confessed. Eager as I to meet, she hadn't eaten a morsel all afternoon. I suggested we dine in the adjoining room, by Czech standards a nice little three-star affair. We ordered appetizers, talked our way through a menu heavy on old Czech favorites like broiled boar livers and poached asshole of antelope, and once we had made our selections I asked, "What did your family own, that you hope to get back?"

"A palace."

"What kind of palace?"

"Seventeenth century, with the usual Socialist improvements."

"I've never met a princess before."

"I'm not a princess."

"A countess, then, or a duchess."

"I'm not. I'm a bastard."

"You could be a Gypsy for all I care."

"A Gypsy? Explain what you mean."

I heard both shock and outrage in her voice but couldn't determine why the notion should so upset her. Gypsies were everywhere in Prague; even the casual observer perceived the hostility they engendered in the Czechs, who mostly considered them members of a criminal underclass rather than an oppressed minority. I said, "It was just an example. I didn't mean—"

"Didn't mean to insult me, or didn't mean to be racist?"

I brought a forkful of cold goose heart to my lips, but could not convince my mouth to open, and returned the morsel to its plate. I said, "What I meant was, it doesn't mean anything to me. I'm American. You know, classless society."

"Can't someone be both princess and Gypsy?"

"I didn't mean to insult anybody."

"I'm not accusing you. I'm asking."

"Gypsies are nomads. Fiddles and no fixed addresses. Nontraditional ideas regarding private property."

"You mean thieves."

"In other words."

"Why don't you just say so? Why hide your racist attitudes behind complicated language?"

I didn't remember how the argument had begun. Should I attempt to explain, change the subject, or snatch the knife from the appetizer dish and rake it across my wrists? With an angry toss of her head, Monika disciplined a raven lock of hair that had tumbled to her eyes. She seemed obsessed with this Gypsy thing. Why couldn't one be Gypsy and princess both? Her skin was too light, her eyes too green. But a single ancestor one or two hundred years ago would leave scant genetic evidence. Call it deduction, a lucky guess, or proof that Monika and I knew each other in ways that defied conventional logic. I said, "You're part Gypsy, aren't you?"

Monika set her champagne glass aside, carefully folded her arms together on the table, and stared at me for several long seconds. The full meaning of the look evaded me. More than one of the seven basic emotions were always at play in her eyes, and the combinations encrypted more often than revealed. My perception astonished her, that was clear enough, but her eyes when I had the strength to meet them also expressed fear and anger. Unsettled, I moved to refill her champagne glass. She said, "This is the second time you knew something about me you couldn't know. My great-grandmother was half Gypsy."

"And a princess?"

That I guessed foolishly persuaded a smile to cross her lips. When I returned the champagne bottle to its nest of ice, the fear was gone but not the anger. The anger never completely disappeared from gesture or glance. She said, "An orphan. Her mother was a young peasant girl from Kostalec, a village not far from Prague. Married at fifteen to a farmer."

"A Gypsy farmer? Doesn't sound typical."

"The farmer was Czech. So was the peasant girl."

"Then how?"

"The farmer worked the girl and beat her when he drank. She had food and a roof, but I don't think her life was much more than that. One day she heard music coming from the woods, someone playing a violin. She crept close and hid in the bushes to listen. The Gypsy playing the violin was young and handsome, and I'm told even now the Gypsies remember how beautifully he played."

"She fell in love?" I guessed.

"It's a story the old women in the village still tell, handed down from their grandmothers. Every week the Gypsy would play in the woods, and every week the peasant girl would come to listen. Sometime later, a baby girl was born. The farmer suspected his wife was unfaithful because the baby's hair was black, but he couldn't be sure because her skin was white. When the Gypsy began to play in the woods again, the farmer followed his wife and killed them both with an ax."

"Jesus, what a story. You could make a film with that story. High-octane music behind, something by the Gipsy Kings."

"I could get rich, selling my great-grandmother's murder to Hollywood?"

The sarcasm startled me. "It's a habit of mine," I admitted. "I always think in terms of film. Blessing or curse, I don't know. It's the way I make things real."

Monika reached her hand toward my face, and her fingertips lightly traced the line of my jaw from ear to lips, a gesture I found both intimate and intimidating. She said, "You're so American."

"How so?"

"Movies are always in the present tense. Movies are now. Movies don't live in the past. Just like Americans."

After dinner, we strolled through the neighborhood, pausing to admire the ornate Art Nouveau cornices and crenelations of each building we passed. I feared she might ask about my family legacy, and if I chose to tell the truth I would have to confess my descent from a long and ill-distinguished line of used-car dealers. To forestall a lie, I asked how she could expect to inherit a palace, descended as she was from a Gypsy and peasant girl.

"Because the story doesn't end there. Each generation passes its history to the next. The story never ends. My great-grandmother inherited her father's black hair and love of music and her mother's fine Slavic features. She was beautiful, one of the great beauties of Central Europe, but the villagers hated her. The cause of murder and scandal. Half Gypsy. When she was fifteen, her grandparents gave her a one-way ticket to Prague. Her only contact was a distant cousin, a dishwasher in the Hotel Paříž."

"You mean where we had dinner tonight?"

"At the turn of the century it was the best hotel in Prague. The cousin thought his fortune was made when he saw how beautiful the Gypsy girl was. He promised fancy clothes and jewelry if she agreed to have sex with the rich guests of the hotel. She refused, so he threw her to the streets. That night, she wandered Prague until she came to a garden. She wanted to curl under the bushes to sleep, but the night was warm and the moon full, so she began to sing. The song was full of sadness and a little fear, because the river was just across the garden, she could hear it rushing against the banks, and she thought when the song ended she should throw herself into it and drown."

Monika and I walked along a wall fifteen feet high, buckled and crumbling the length of it. Electric light and a parked car were the sole twentieth-century relics in a gray and brown cityscape of cobblestones and peeling baroque town houses. At the end of an alleyway the river Vltava rushed black as the night sky, sprinkled with city lights. Monika stopped at a gated arch. I peered through the bars and from the garden of fruit trees and rose bushes recognized our location as second only to the castle in the rank of famous noble residences.

"This?" I said, laughing in surprise.

"It's funny to you?"

"Valdštejn gardens. I never expected."

She put her finger to my lips and said, "The story is serious. No laughing."

"No laughing, " I promised.

Monika pointed to the dim outline of a building across the garden. "Count Valdštejn was working late that night, past midnight, when he heard the Gypsy girl sing. He hurried to the window, and the vision in moonlight below was so enchanting and her song so moving he summoned his chief steward and told him to bring her to the palace. In his study, the count discovered the Gypsy girl was as beautiful by candlelight as in moonlight. The count being a count and the young girl a young girl, it surprised no one in the palace when a few months later she became pregnant."

Monika pulled me away from the gate. We walked the riverfront and across Charles Bridge, pacing ourselves to the rhythms of Monika's story. "The count wanted to set her up as his mistress in a small house in the country, but the chief steward was afraid of scandal. Society allowed the count to sleep with any Gypsy girl he desired, but not to accept one as formal mistress. The count was unhappy but agreed. She was sent back to her grandparents with a small sum of money.

"The news of her arrival and, later, the birth of a baby girl, spread through the village, and from the village to the surrounding farms, and from there to other villages and other farms. One Sunday, the grandparents left the girl alone to attend mass. No one really knows what happened that morning. When the grandparents returned, they found every stick of furniture broken. In the center of the hut lay an old farmer, a butcher knife stuck in his chest. The baby slept unhurt in her crib, but never again until the moment of her death some years later would so much as a cry escape her lips."

"Old farmer?" I asked, confused.

"Her mother's husband and murderer. They had never punished him for the crime. You could kill unfaithful wives back then."

"What happened to the Gypsy girl, I mean she killed the guy, I guess you'd call him her stepfather?"

"A young boy from one of the farms saw her last. He heard her singing and hid behind a tree to watch. She was sitting on the banks of the Vltava, sewing stones into her badly torn dress. When the boy returned with his parents, the Gypsy girl was gone. The villagers say they can still sometimes hear her singing at that same spot. One of them took me there, but I didn't hear anything. Just wind and water."

We had strolled to Národní Boulevard by the time Monika finished her story, and as we neared a crude banner stretched across the walk, she pulled me aside to listen to a throb of music coming from stairs at the end of a corridor. The spray-paint lettering on the banner read UBIQUITY. I knew the place as one of the more notorious new nightclubs, a haven for illicit drug use and casual sex run by a couple of North Americans. The moment I explained the nature of the club, Monika wanted to go in, and though I protested that we were overdressed—indeed, anything other than ripped jeans and black leather would be overdressed—I felt relieved that the course of the evening did not lead straight to a shared bed. I was only too eager to strip a relationship down to base desires when the woman was a participant in a game I played for my amusement. Monika allowed me no detachment. She inspired fear as much as love, and, stripped naked, my emotions might prove more powerful than my ability to perform.

The noise in the club was intolerably loud. The first few faces that bobbled past us in the smoke and dim light bore such idiotic grins I concluded free samples of ecstasy were being dispensed. The din crushed Monika's shout before I caught the words. I assumed she wanted a drink and stepped toward the bar. She grabbed my hand and pulled me in the opposite direction, to the writhing mass at the center of the dance floor. The frantic flail of arm and leg reminded me of ground zero one millisecond after detonation. I shuffled my feet, bobbed my head, and every now and then shrugged my shoulders in rhythm to the beat. Monika had a Mata Hari talent for seductively deceptive movement, seeming to move this way while flowing that, distracting me with a bright gesture of hands to conceal that she had suddenly disappeared behind.

When the tempo slowed to a less frantic beat, she caught my hand and pulled me tight against her body. Her womb felt hot as a kiln. Despite my best efforts to maintain carnal discipline I swelled the space between us. I shifted my waist to an oblique angle, embarrassed by my body's betrayal of etiquette. Monika laughed and squirmed her hips into mine. "I feel you" sounded in my ear like a child's accusing whisper. Her breath stirred the hair at the base of my skull. I let my hand slip from its safe perch above the small of her back to the cleft of flesh below and with firm pressure guided her onto my thigh. I've always received high technical marks, though sex rarely touches me. My body moves with the vigor of a conductor's baton coaxing music from an orchestra; no matter how thrilling the music, the baton itself remains stiff and insensate. But that night and in that public place, her lips splitting simultaneously across my neck and thigh,

Monika splintered my certainties like a dark wave snaps a stick of timber. Though I strained to conceal my wild trembling, Monika must have guessed my condition. I surrendered control and gushed. A hand roughly grabbed my shoulder. I turned to the strobe-lit face of Monika's brother.

"Sven! Come dance with us!" Monika cried, so innocently even I believed her.

Sven brushed me aside. I was too discomposed to know what to do or think. He shouted something incomprehensible, face strobing incandescent and black. I recognized the language as Danish by guess more than ear. It could have been Hungarian for all the sense it made to me. Dazed, I smiled and shrugged my shoulders. The response seemed to make him angrier. He stepped closer and shouted again. For a moment, I thought he might hit me. Monika slid between us and, taking my arm, led me a few steps distant.

"I'm sorry, but I have to go now," she said.

"Is something wrong?"

"Nothing at all," she answered, though I knew she was lying.

"Your brother, what was he saying?"

"He's been drinking too much, that's all. I have to make sure he gets home."

She extended her hand. I looked at it a moment before I realized that despite what had happened between us on the dance floor, I was expected to politely shake it good night.

7

Prague was a cornucopia of amazing sex stories at the time, of outlandish couplings comprising every imaginable position, location, number, and nationality of participants. Both sexes recounted their adventures with competitive passion. Though I'd frequently entertained friends, acquaintances, and strangers with amusing anecdotes about one erotic escapade or another, I didn't know how to begin talking about Monika or the disturbing emotions she evoked. A mild but persistent nausea unsettled my stomach. Concentration evaporated at the briefest memory of word or gesture. Moments after sitting down to a task, I would catch myself staring out the window in Monika-induced reverie. I so rarely had feelings that I didn't know how to discuss them, but more than ever

before felt driven to talk. As evening approached, the anticipation of seeing her for dinner that night so agitated my
nerves that I could no longer tolerate the cramped silence
of my apartment.

Jo's was the most dependable bar in which to find English-
speaking company at any given hour. The beer was cheap
and everybody liked its owner, an affably randy Canadian
notorious for having vowed on his thirtieth birthday never
to sleep with another teenager. Cheap beer drew the expatriates, and prominent mention of the expatriates in
guidebooks drew slumming tourists. The bar was typically
crowded and loud, but the few faces I recognized that
evening I didn't like, and none of the strangers seemed
interesting enough to warrant more than brusque dialogue.
I was uncertain how to act when meeting Monika again, not
knowing if I should acknowledge the previous night's sexual
encounter on the dance floor or pretend with good manners that nothing had happened. I was on the verge of confessing my dilemma to a backpacker from Seattle when I
spotted Andrew and his guitar poking through the crowd
at the entrance. I naturally assumed he looked for me and
raised an arm to signal my presence. The arc of Andrew's
gaze passed without deflection. I shouted his name. He
ducked out the door before I finished the second syllable.

By the time I breached the crowd and gained the street,
Andrew's figure was already distant, striding toward Charles
Bridge. When I caught him by the elbow, he claimed he
hadn't seen me at the bar and hadn't heard me shout his
name. I stared at him with the theatrical disbelief of an
arched eyebrow. He glanced at his feet and fiddled with
a latch on his guitar case, while staring at an invisible mark
over my left shoulder.

"Come back to Jo's. We'll have a drink," I said.

"Can't. I have a lesson."

Like half of the twenty-something Americans in Prague, Andrew taught English at a local high school which paid him according to his qualifications, which is to say miserably, as Andrew not only hadn't taught English before, he hadn't taken so much as a grammar course since his own high school years.

"You're not angry with me about my laughing fit in church, are you?"

"I don't have time to talk about it," he said, and hurried off. I twitched as I watched him weave through the crowds, burned by sparks of paranoia. Andrew was lying. Had he been in a genuine hurry, he wouldn't have stopped at Jo's Bar. When he saw me at Jo's, he fled, and fled again after I caught him on the bridge. He didn't have a lesson. He found my company so repugnant that he fled in revulsion.

I'd never followed anyone before, but as I'd seen over a hundred films with character A trailing character B, it wasn't a difficult skill to master. It never would have occurred to Andrew that I followed. There was little risk in his turning suddenly to recognize me in the crowd. He strode so briskly it was a strain to maintain both silence and the proper distance when we entered the snaking streets of the Gothic quarter. At Staroměstksé náměstí I slowed, knowing that against the backdrop of cake-colored baroque and gray Gothic structures I could easily keep him in view. At the far end of the square, beneath the bronze figure of Jan Hus, a woman stood and waved. Even at that distance I recognized her as uncommonly pretty, if a bit wholesome for my tastes, with wheat-colored hair hanging to the small of her back. Andrew greeted her with a kiss that lingered too long for a teacher-student relationship. He had lied about the lesson. When they turned together and walked hand in hand from the square, I saw expectation had fooled my eye. The woman walked with awkward determination, lurching to the right and straightening again with each step. I narrowed the distance between us when the layout of the streets allowed. As they neared their destination, a bar and café called Hogo Fogo, I dashed to the corner and peered. At that distance, no more than twenty feet, I could make no mistake. The woman's right leg was noticeably thinner and ended in a shoe several sizes larger than her left, compensating for the deformity of a clubfoot.

My fears about the loss of Andrew's friendship evaporated. His character was naturally noble, at least in comparison to mine, and I contemplated the possibility that he was drawn to the weak, crippled, and monstrous from an instinct to heal or reform. Those of noble character have dark secrets of their own. I had heard stories of men who could scarcely contain their excitement around women with one or more amputated limbs. Perhaps weakness and deformity in others hardened certain of his tissues while softening his heart.

The possible solutions to the riddle of Andrew and the clubfoot so beguiled my thoughts that when I saw Monika waiting for me at Restaurant Parnas I nearly failed to purse my lips when she deftly parried my hand to kiss me on the mouth. The swift intimacy of the gesture surprised me as a statement of romantic fact, like the greeting of one lover to another. If it was not technically correct to call us lovers at that moment, we seemed lovers in some future moment I hoped was fast approaching. As we drank champagne and waited for the appetizers to arrive, the slender elegance of her hand, lightly bronzed by candlelight, so dazzled that I reached to touch it, but Monika chose that very moment to withdraw the hand to her lap, and I, fumbling to give some new purpose to my sudden reach, nearly dashed the champagne bottle. At first, I thought little about the incident except my clumsiness, not suspecting that Monika used gestures as an agent of control and would not be subject to the gestures of others. I trickled a few drops of champagne into her glass, which, like mine, had not been in any immediate need of refreshing, and thinking back about her story of the night before, remarked, with hidden petulance, "It's a long shot, isn't it, your laying claim to Count Valdštejn? I'd think other people would have stronger claims than an illegitimate great-granddaughter."

"I'm not just his great-granddaughter," she said, and coughed violently into her napkin. From her crimson flush and wild eyes I feared something had stuck in her throat. She hid her face until the fit quieted and her breath returned, but when the napkin dropped away she wouldn't approach my glance. "You see, the count's blood runs twice in my veins," she said.

"What kind of riddle is that?"

Monika took several cautious sips of water, seeming to debate her response with each. "I'm sorry, but it's a little shocking," she said.

"I don't mean to pry—" Though of course I did.

"The count is both my great-grandfather and grandfather."

"You mean he, ah, he . . ." I stuttered, with fitting hand gestures.

"Yes."

"But how?"

"When his lover—my great-grandmother—drowned herself, their baby was taken to the palace."

"The count adopted her?"

"He gave her to a scullery maid, put her to work in the kitchen as soon as she could walk. She never said a word growing up, never cried once since that day the old farmer was murdered. At fifteen, she was as beautiful as her mother. One day, the count lifted her skirts from behind. The girl fought, but as she couldn't cry out or protest—"

"He knew who she was?"

"You think incest stops people? I think it turns them on."

Monika lightly traced the outline of my fingers, a gesture so arousing I crossed my legs beneath the table to constrict the sudden swelling of blood and allow concentration.

"He used her a month or two, no more than three," she said. When the girl's condition was discovered, the chief steward quietly married her off to the gardener's assistant, a shy and muscular young man frequently scolded for having his feet on the earth but his head in the sky. It was to everyone's great surprise that the girl and the gardener's assistant fell deeply in love soon after their arranged marriage. The gardener's assistant, who had never felt confident enough about his intellect to talk about any subject in public more controversial than the weather, discovered his tongue in the girl's silence. Her inability to contradict him with anything more than a glance, which most often adored, encouraged him to express his views and discover that, despite his long silence, he held strong political convictions. One of these convictions was a sense of injustice at the aristocracy's wealth, which led him by degrees to socialism. The groundskeeper overheard the gardener's assistant talking one day about Marx and accused him of communist agitation. The two began a fierce argument that came to blows. When the chief steward investigated the incident, he attributed the assistant's new political views to jealousy over the parentage of his wife's child.

A baby girl was born to the couple during the summer of 1938. The gardener's assistant was promoted to gardener, and his political temper cooled in the new heights of his career. Two months later, the Munich pact was signed, ceding the Czech Sudentenland to Germany. In spring of 1939, the Nazis marched into Prague. Jews, Gypsies, and Socialists were declared enemies of the regime and sent to concentration camps at Theresienstadt and Buchenwald. The count was interrogated and given the choice of collaboration or death. The count chose collaboration. When the groundskeeper reported that a Socialist agitator and his Gypsy wife served at the palace, the count did not attempt to dissuade the Gestapo from their fascist duty.

The gardener's assistant died two days later in interrogation. The chief steward managed to hide the baby with a family in the country, but the mute girl was sent to Theresienstadt. A rare survivor who met her there said that a few days after the girl's arrival, an SS officer drew his pistol and shot her through the heart. A few months later, the count was taken to Gestapo headquarters, where he fell out of a third-story window.

"Fell?" I repeated.

"It's an old Czech riddle. If a body is discovered below an open window and no one saw the fall, did it jump, slip, or get pushed?"

"We should write a screenplay," I said.

"About?"

"Your family. A feature film, maybe a miniseries. Julia Roberts for the Gypsy girl," I suggested, amazed myself at how perfectly suited she was for the role.

"And Tom Cruise?" she asked, laughing.

"The gardener's assistant. Of course we can't make him an outright Communist, but maybe a young entrepreneur type with a social conscience, someone who tries to rise above his station—maybe he wants to open his own greenhouse raising vegetables or flowers or something—but is cruelly slapped down by the count, who is still in love with the Gypsy girl. We have to play with the ending a bit too. I like throwing the count out the window, but we can't pay Tom and Julia three million apiece just to have them die in the end."

"But that's what happened."

"We'll give it a slightly different twist. Tom disguises himself as a German officer and finds Julia in the concentration camp. The SS guy wants to shoot Julia on the spot, but Tom, he suggests they let her think about it overnight and hang her in the morning. Imagine the suspense! Tom Cruise—maybe we can make him part Jewish too—disguised as a German officer in a concentration camp, with Julia scheduled to hang in the morning! Then they escape! Over the border, to Switzerland!"

"And the baby, what happens to her in this Hollywood ending?"

"That's the tragic part. *They have to leave her behind,*" I said, the corner of my eyebrow tipping heavenward with great significance. Grand romance, stirring fight scenes, nail-biting suspense, and, when the tail credits roll, not a dry eye in the house. Then, for the sequel, Tom returns to Prague as a resistance fighter, on a mission to find and rescue Julia's baby!

Monika said, "Sounds very Hollywood."

"You never go see Hollywood films?"

Monika shrugged, meaning she did, but didn't like to admit it.

I said, "That's my point. Everybody goes. I respect the European attitude of art for art's sake. But the problem is, art is business and business is money. If you want to make films you have to make money. Europeans make films based on intellect, meaning they're mostly enjoyed by intellectuals, because after all, if we're going to be candid about this, not many people are interested in or capable of intellect. Hollywood makes films based on emotions, so they make films for everybody, because everybody has emotions. One system is elitist and the other panders to the lowest common denominator. The question then is whether to make films for the public or for twelve intellectuals in an art house in Paris. Me, I'll take the public and a fat paycheck." Listening to myself speak, I realized I might sound too commercial. No artistic soul. The truth was, I did feel capable of that special personal project, though I had never bothered to articulate it. It wasn't my fault the market for such projects didn't exist. It was the system. I said, "I'd love to write one of those small, personal films one day. Nothing I'd like more than to forget bankability, pay-or-play, and merchandising deals and make a film that comes from my heart, that would define the world as I see it, something really me, you know?"

Monika hid her laughter in a crumpled napkin.

"What?" I said. "What's so funny?"

Her face flushed red behind white linen. "I think you'll make a hundred million dollars one day," she said.

I took it as a compliment.

Admiring the views of Prague from Charles Bridge later that night, I waited patiently until the angle of Monika's gaze dropped from the castle, and then I kissed her. I had anticipated a kiss more romantic than passionate, but Monika had other intentions. She turned her hips and screwed into me.

Her mouth found my neck, my throat, my mouth again. I let my hands cascade down her sides and eddy under the hem of her miniskirt. When I gently slipped the elastic bands and brushed her sex, she leaned back against the stone ledge and I thought of our two bodies igniting in free fall from the bridge, the rush of air blowing our burning clothes above our heads as we drop, entwined, burning like fireworks to a cindered terminus.

"Someone's coming," she said, and with a deft twist left me pressing my groin against a patch of stone and wondering if a pun was intended. Two pairs of Doc Martens clomped past and stopped at the next statue. Giddy voices. American slang. Shaggy hair and slackly vacant faces. Hippie-spawn. Like many young Americans in Prague, they fancied themselves musicians. They sat cross-legged, an upended hat for tips placed in front. Their guitars strummed out a paean to rebellious youth while two voices began a hopeless search for harmony.

Monika approached the musicians, took a coin from her purse, and dropped it in the hat. Her small act of generosity annoyed me. A couple of young girls drifted past, sat in front of the empty hat, and began to sing along. Soon a small crowd would gather, the smell of pot would waft through the air, wine would pass from hand to hand, and the voices of brother and sisterhood would rise in chorus. What inanity. I took Monika by the arm and invited her to my apartment. She broke away and ran to the middle of the bridge, where she leapt onto the ledge and caught the sleeve of one of the bridge's nineteen stone saints. Profiled against the night sky she looked so like a goddess among saints I solemnly kissed her slippered feet, then not so solemnly licked her ankles and calves.

"Come home with me!" I cried.

"I can't go home with you."

"Why not?"

"You won't understand," she said.

There are few challenges more compelling than one to understanding. "Sex isn't that important," I lied.

"Sex is important. But with Sven here, I can't."

I must have groaned when she mentioned her brother.

"I knew you wouldn't understand."

"I understand you're a grown woman who should do as she pleases."

"When everyone around you dies and just one person is your entire family, you do not just do as you please, grown up or not."

"I'm afraid you lost me there."

"I told you about my family."

I blinked once, twice. The Gypsy girl, the count, the gardener's assistant. I had taken Monika's story as fairy tale, had forgotten that to her it was real as history. I said, "The baby who escaped the Nazis, that was your mother? But how did you get to be Danish?"

"How did you know I was Danish?" Monika seemed not just surprised but alarmed.

"You told me."

"I have an excellent memory for this. I did not tell you."

Her passport. I was an idiot to forget a minor detail like that. I so believed myself an honest man with her, I mistakenly assumed I was one.

"You just seem Danish. Your accent."

Monika's stare did not forgive. Was it possible she suspected? I ransacked memory for a clue and said, "You and your brother were speaking Danish last night, in the club."

Monika climbed down from the ledge and leaned against

the hem of a saint's robe, deciding whether or not to believe me. I didn't question why my knowledge of her nationality should be so important. She said, "My mother escaped to Denmark in 1968."

Nineteen sixty-eight. The year of Nixon, Prague Spring, and the invasion of Czechoslovakia by the Warsaw Pact nations.

"She was running from the Russians?"

"Not at first. She knew a Danish man there, Sven's father. When the Russians invaded Czechoslovakia, Mother stayed. Maybe she knew, even then, that she was not going to have good luck. She died, with Sven's father, in a boating accident when I was five."

"My God," I said.

"It's bad luck in my family to fall in love. Sven is all I have."

"But he's your half-brother after all, not your husband."

"You saw how possessive he is. If he thought I loved you, I don't know what he'd do."

"Is that a warning?"

"If you want. I meant it to be a confession. Confessions never have just one meaning."

"What if I confessed I'm already in love with you?" I said, and even though I felt astonished such words could come from my lips and not be an outright lie, I wasn't certain the words were mine; it seemed I cited lines in front of a camera. When she kissed me in response I was struck with the feeling that *Cut!* would be called at any moment, the true feeling between us would dissolve when the director announced it a take, and we would march back to our separate trailers to prepare for the next scene.

"Tell your brother you need time alone," I begged. "Travel by train to a little town I know, Český Krumlov. I'll book a room there. Will you do it? Will you come?"

8

E arly the next afternoon I went to the American Express office on Václavské náměstí, where the first of every month I drew $750 from my account in Los Angeles. That same day a like sum was deposited into my account from a trust fund left by my grandfather. The size of my inheritance was much larger than such a paltry stipend indicates, but owing to the watchfulness of my father, who served as executor of the will, I was not allowed to touch the capital or enjoy the full benefit of interest payments until I reached thirty years of age. Father did not trust the salubrious effect of money on my character. He wished to keep me out of the gutter, but close enough to smell it, in the vain hope of encouraging a work ethic. His strategy was thwarted by Prague's post-Communist economy, where

$750 was a princely sum. My rent, which was double that of anyone else I knew, totaled $300. I lived quite well on the balance in a town where a buck could buy a movie ticket, a pack of good American cigarettes, or a liter of the best beer in Europe. When I needed mad money, I traded a few of my photocopied hundred-dollar bills. It gratified me to obey the letter of Father's rules while violating their spirit.

I began to pack for Český Krumlov late that night. According to plan, I was to leave the next morning. Monika would take an afternoon train to avoid her brother nosing out the true purpose of her trip. We were to be gone three days. First thing, I counted out a dozen lubricated supersensitive condoms from my drawer and tossed them into a suitcase. Call me an optimist. Then casual clothing, a book for skimming on the train, and, lastly, a Hasselblad camera I'd bought, following my French buddy Marcel's example. Just past eleven a persistent finger on the buzzer forced my eye to the peephole, where on the other side of the fish-eye lens stood Monika in a fetching black minidress. The prospect of early consummation trilled through my groin.

"Put on your coat," she ordered when I swung open the door.

"Are we going somewhere?"

"To a nightclub."

"But isn't it late?"

"You don't want to be with me?"

"Of course I do, but why don't we just stay here?"

I tried to catch her in a casual embrace and maneuver both of us onto the bed, but she adroitly slipped into the entry hall.

"If you don't want to go with me, that's okay," she said, clearly meaning that if I didn't go with her, I might not see her the next day in Český Krumlov. I grabbed my coat and met her outside. A taxi waited by the curb. I reconciled myself to the probability that I would not sleep more than a couple of hours that night. The taxi careened through streets designed for peasant carts and the occasional horseman, streets no longer than one hundred yards laid out at oblique angles, like sticks bunched together and dropped. When the taxi sped around a corner, I took advantage of centrifugal force and leaned into her. She pushed me away but fell into my arms on the next curve. As we kissed, her hand slid up my thigh. I said, "I want to know every inch of your skin, every ripple of thought through your mind. I want to know your past, your present, your future."

When we kissed again, lights flashed behind my closed eyes: her face an image pulled down, registered, and shot through with light twenty-four times a second. Although my sexual experiences were many and varied, everything I knew about love came from Hollywood, as I had been able to love only vicariously, through the performance of actors on screen. Celluloid moved me in a way that flesh and blood could not. That night in the taxi I sat in the dark of my eyelids and watched a movie of myself kissing Monika. I became not only the audience but the actor performing the scene, and the man on whom the actor based his performance—I even felt in some vague way I directed the scene. Though I'd watched myself perform before, I'd never felt the performance connect to the man, and this merging of theatrical and human identities fulfilled me in a way that I had never before experienced, not even in the sanctity of a cinema.

There was something naturally theatrical about Monika, and when I contemplate why she alone has been able to awaken human feeling in me, I'm always drawn to the similarity between her and certain Nordic actresses, particularly

Garbo and Bergman, who could convey with a gesture, glance, or single spoken word the existence of a rich and tragic past. I envied Monika the Old World charm of having a past. I had a Los Angeles past: bulldozed, paved over, rezoned, and rebuilt to gleaming modern standards, a past pounded to dust by skyscrapers and ribboned in freeway. Every now and then when something troubled me and I didn't quite know why, I hired an analyst to pull from my tarry depths an old bone. We cleaned it off and admired it together and guessed its meaning: a cancellate fragment from an uncaring father, or the compact splinter of a distant mother? The truth of the archaeology didn't matter. Invent a history to give it reason. But of the immediate past, the remembered past, the uninvented past, I had none. The future continually reinvented me.

When I opened my eyes again, the road had widened and the taxi hurtled at great speed through what seemed to be a canyon of stacked concrete blocks. A light rain drew slashes across the passenger window. Squares of light gleamed in monotonous pattern beyond the glass. Squinting through the rain, I caught the blurred suggestion of laundry hanging from a balcony.

"*Panelaks,*" Monika said. "Socialist housing for the masses."

The driver executed a dizzying combination of turns on streets identical, one to the next, and pulled in front of a concrete apartment building claimed to be our destination. I stepped into a landscape of tramped mud, asphalt, bits of toilet paper, broken glass, and the smell of spilled beer. Rows of identical apartment blocks crumbled into the mud. Modern ruins. I asked Monika what could possibly interest her in such a dismal environment. She led me to the nearest ruin and through a set of glass doors to a sepia-skinned man—

I took him to be Indian or Pakistani at first glance—who demanded a hundred Czech crowns from me before allowing us to pass. The floor trembled with a retrogressive disco beat.

"You've discovered an underground music club," I guessed.

"This is the culture house for Romanies," she said.

My step faltered.

Concerned by my sudden sweat and paling skin, Monika asked, "Are you all right?"

No. She did not say that. In my imagination she said that. She noticed nothing. I needed an excuse to stop, turn around, go back. She pulled me down a hallway lit with a single sputtering incandescent. At the end of the hall spilled a rough stream of brown skin and black hair. My glance darted from one half-obscured face to the next, searching for a familiar hook of nose or twisting brow, any prominent feature to aid recognition of the Gypsies with whom I exchanged my counterfeit bills. How was it possible that Monika, who seemed to know everything, did not notice that I was turning to stone? She led me into an auditorium muddied by cigarette smoke. A hundred men and perhaps fifty women sat at cheap cafeteria-style tables or danced at the opposite end. The moment I entered the room the men began to whisper mouth to ear and the women to stare coldly in my direction. Monika claimed two chairs at the back wall, asked what I wanted to drink, and when I stuttered out my answer merged into the crowd at the bar.

As the only non-Gypsy in the room, I was watched by everyone; those few not looking directly at me watched in the expressions of those who were. I resisted the urge to glance wildly about, looking for the face that would recognize me, shout an accusation in a language I had no hope of understanding, and in that crowded room begin my dismemberment. I took slow deep breaths of secondhand smoke. No one could possibly recognize me. I took precautions when changing bills. Baseball cap, jeans, tennis shoes, map in hand, and camera strapped around my neck: a perfect caricature of the American tourist. Dressed that night in Armani herringbone sport coat and black slacks, I bore no resemblance to that other creature. It occurred to me I was staring too long at my hands, clenched together on the table. I casually glanced around. Naturally everyone noticed and immediately looked away, so that it appeared no one watched. A good front was all. I must pretend confidence. A smile cracked my lips apart. I was cleverer than any man there and need not be afraid of anyone. The man next to me huddled over a mug of beer. His teeth looked like a line of infantry decimated by machine-gun fire. He glanced my way. I held on to my smile. He measured me in sections, like a butcher might a cut of meat, and sank his ruined teeth into the head of his beer. I shouldn't smile, I decided. Monika set my drink on the table, a double Scotch on the rocks, and said she wanted to dance.

"Here?"

"If you don't want to, I can dance by myself."

Monika alone on the dance floor would be dangerous provocation. The DJ played a song by Queen, the most popular group in Prague that year, though most of the natives were happily ignorant of the slang meaning of the group's name. Where were the fiddles, the slashing dancers in peasant skirts or shiny chinos, the raging fire, the bottles of wine; in short, where were the Gipsy Kings? The young men affected the Western look of jeans and button-down shirts, the young women miniskirts, dark hose, and floral print blouses, and together they danced the same amorphous disco found all over the world. Their sartorial style varied little from one individual to the next, as if a group decision had been made to adopt that particular veneer of Western culture, with variations unacceptable. I shuffled my feet and bobbed my head and tried to keep close to Monika, who could not sway her hips in any way not charged with sexual invitation. The men watched her like hungry prisoners. The women looked like they wanted to poison her. I was mostly ignored.

"You've been here before?" I shouted above the music.

"Several times."

We returned to the table, where I bolted my Scotch.

Monika said, "The men here are different from the Czechs. They're violent, and violence interests me."

"Why?"

"Because death interests me."

I normally considered death obsessions evidence of an arrested adolescence. My normal perceptions never applied to Monika. Just as her every gesture held profound meaning, her brooding over death seemed instead proof of a tragic nature.

"I don't think I'll live to be thirty," she said.

"Nonsense. You'll live to seventy."

"But I don't want to live to seventy. I don't want to be old. I don't want plans. I don't want a job, family, pension. The past is death. The future is death. That leaves only the moment." Monika took my face in her hands and kissed me. I could taste the melancholy on her lips and traced along the dolphin surfaces of her tongue a delight in personal tragedy. Monika seemed as much in love with her history as bound to it. I closed my eyes and drank as much of her as I could hold.

"Burroughs said kissing someone is like sucking on a thirty-foot tube, at the end of which is a sack of shit."

The comment snapped our lips apart. Sven smiled down at us as though his comment had been a joke, but I sensed nothing well-meaning in his display of teeth. He set two glasses of amber fluid onto the table and sat across from me.

"You drink Scotch?"

I looked at the glass, not knowing if I should accept.

"Monika knows I hate this club. That's how I knew you'd be here tonight. Monika has these people in her blood, from her mother. Me, I'm one-hundred percent Danish. You ever read Burroughs?"

"You mean the guy who wrote *Naked Lunch*? Saw the movie."

"What about Bukowski?"

"Sure. Mickey Rourke in *Barfly*. I didn't think you were the type to read."

"Sven writes. Poetry," Monika explained.

I couldn't have been more surprised had I learned an ape could dance a polonaise. It appeared Sven was a brute with a sensitive soul. I asked, "Publish anything?"

"That's what I like about you. Straight to the point. Am I successful? Do I make money. Not as much as screenwriters, I can tell you that much. All the poetry in Europe combined doesn't pay as well as one Hollywood screenplay. Come on, drink up. I'll make a toast."

I picked up the glass, expecting a cruel joke or insult.

"To my sister."

Innocent enough. I drank. The Scotch tasted rough and bitter. Some swill of a bar brand, distilled anywhere but

Scotland. Sven drained his to the clear bottom of his glass and asked, "Have you fucked her yet?"

Monika said, "Don't do this to me, Sven."

"He should know. That's his right. He should know the risk he's taking."

I downed the last of the Scotch, fought the urge to bolt from the table, smiled at Sven as though sincerity could win him over. I said, "The way Monika and I feel about each other, it isn't just sex."

"You're not going away together."

"We're leaving tomorrow," Monika confessed.

"You know what happens to the men who go away with you."

"Nothing happens. Nothing at all."

Sven stuck a cigarette between his lips and struck a match. The light seared into my cerebrum. I rubbed my eyes, fighting a precipitous and inappropriate fatigue. Sven smiled at me, pleased about something he didn't care to share with the table.

"She told you about her family, I'm sure. That romantic story of everyone dying young and tragic. It's all true. Everybody around Monika comes to a bad end, except me."

"You shouldn't listen to him," she warned. "He gets like this whenever someone is interested in me. He just wants to scare you."

"Did she tell you about the terrible luck of her boyfriends? They always seem to meet with accidents. They fall off things. Get hit by cars or trains or buses. Cops find them in alleyways, robbed and beaten, sometimes stabbed."

"Every time I meet someone, you come out with these crazy stories."

"He needs to know the truth. It's only fair he should know the risk he's taking."

"You're being a bore."

"I'm sure she told you she has death in her past and death in her future. It's my feeling she overplays that part. Too melodramatic, even for Hollywood."

"You're not supposed to say that."

"You started to care for this one a little more than the last ones."

Monika rose from the table and nearly pulled Sven off his chair. "I need to talk to you, alone. Now."

Lethargy seeped like anesthesia into the nerves lacing my brain. My vision began to blur. I said, "Monika." She turned to me and when I looked at her it was like looking at glass.

"I'll be back in five minutes," she said.

Monika's black minidress vanished in the crowd. I thought about getting up to follow, but I couldn't convince my legs to support the weight. It seemed that I was suddenly and horribly drunk. I cradled my head in my hands to keep it from dissolving. In the distance, I saw myself sitting alone at a table surrounded by Gypsies, and the figure that was me kept getting smaller, as did the Gypsies, until I could no longer distinguish myself from the others. We were all diminishing together, a dot surrounded by darkness that promptly extinguished to darkness itself.

9

Sometime later, the brutality of individual consciousness returned. Nerve cells synapsed up and down my spine, reporting the particulars of weather conditions and suspected damage to body parts. A careful analysis of conflicting sensory data concluded that my face lay flattened against a pebbly surface and the rest of my body twisted behind in the unnatural angles of a bomb-blast victim. I blinked the grit from my eyes to a diffuse gray light. A few minutes before dawn. Cold. A sour smell of puddle at my lips connected to a memory of vomiting. I rolled onto my back. The movement unloosed a miasma of nausea and pain. A tumor had gorged itself on the vital tissues of my cerebrum and begun to seep poisonous cells into my stomach and small intestines. I crouched on hands and knees and retched a spidery gruel. When breath returned I stood on trembling legs and attempted to hang memory to the hook on which I had awakened. I had spent the night amid a cluster of garbage cans. My Armani coat was gone, and with it my wallet. Could I have left my coat in the Gypsy club, too drunk to safeguard my possessions? I felt pockets. My keys were missing. A circle and band of bare skin chilled my wrist where a watch had been. I had been stripped like a corpse of my shoes. I dimly recalled the previous night's altercation with Sven and the horror of being too drunk to remain conscious.

I walked cautiously to the nearest street. The ground was intolerably hard and cold and studded with broken glass. I had no idea where I was. Some housing estate on the outer circle of the city. The Communist architects had cleverly flanked the neighborhood with facing mirrors, which reflected ad infinitum the same littered pavement and block of concrete buildings. I tried to read a street sign and could make no more sense of it than a bowl of alphabet soup from which all the vowels had been eaten. I saw neither dog, taxi, nor human being. Nothing moved on the streets at that hour except stray bits of windblown paper and myself. I walked on, certain by the dreary sameness I walked circles. Eventually, I crossed parallel grooves cut down the length of a street. I followed the grooves to a signpost, and soon after that the first tram of the morning rattled to a stop at my feet. I crawled into the seat at the rear of the car and fixed my gaze out the window to avoid the stares of those boarding at subsequent stops. I did not think about what happened to me. I let my mind go willfully blank.

That the door to my apartment was ajar resolved the problem of how to gain entrance without kicking out the locks. My keys had been thoughtfully dropped on the foyer floor.

The contents of my suitcase, ready for a weekend romance in the quaint historical town of Český Krumlov, lay strewn across the covers of the bed. The suitcase itself was gone and, with it, the Hasselblad camera. The cozy writing corner I had constructed beneath the courtyard window was missing the architectural elements of computer and printer. Across the room, patches of bare shelving encircled by dust proved my portable electronics had been accurately named. I hurried to the kitchen and with scrabbling nails popped the lid of the coffee tin in which I kept my counterfeit bills. The roll remained intact. I glanced at the kitchen clock. Six A.M. Plenty of time to catch my morning train. I dropped onto the bed to rest my eyes and sank into a sleep so oppressive I did not free myself of it until well past noon, missing my train by four hours.

I wasn't naive enough to believe that lodging an official complaint would lead to the arrest of the perpetrators and the return of my goods, but this did not prevent me from taking the nearest taxi to the police station, where at my loud insistence Inspector Zima was summoned from home. I sought to prove by my victimization my innocence of the earlier crimes of which I had been so unfairly if accurately accused.

Contemplating many of my actions then from this cold distance of time and geography, I find that I always acted with a perverse logic others might confuse for irrationality. In my outrage I wanted Zima to acknowledge that I had been robbed in his country, and as a representative of law and order he was personally responsible; I did not then realize he might find the incident ironic. Far from resentful at this interruption of his weekend, Zima was at first solicitous of my misfortune, wanting to know how much I had lost and if I had been assaulted. He listened to my description of the crime behind drifting clouds of cigarette smoke and, when I had finished, asked, "You were drinking?"

"Not enough to pass out."

"How many drinks?"

"I don't remember."

"So many?"

"Just two or so. Double Scotches, on the rocks."

Zima made note of the supposed facts of the case on a small red pad. His eyes looked out at me half dead with understanding. He asked, "Can you remember when you passed out? What time?"

"About two. But I didn't pass out. I think I was drugged."

"Who drugged you?"

"The Gypsies, of course."

"You must tell me which of one hundred thousand Gypsies in Prague drugged you. Then I can arrest him."

"There was a fellow drinking next to me. He was the only one close enough to put something in my drink."

"Please describe this man."

"Dark hair. Dark skin. Bad teeth."

"Nothing else?"

"I didn't pay much attention."

When Zima finished writing my response, he took a lungful of smoke and silently read what he'd written. A brief tightening of his lips betrayed he'd come to some conclusion. He glanced up sharply. "Your friends, why they leave?"

"They had an argument."

"With you?"

"No. With each other."

"Their names?"

"I don't see how that's important."

"Perhaps they know this man with"—Zima glanced down at his notes to deliver an exact quote—"dark hair, dark skin, bad teeth."

"I'm certain they can't tell you anything."

Zima set his pen aside as though waiting for a better answer. Divulging Monika's name seemed a betrayal. No quicker way to end a romance than to sic the cops on your lover, even if she plays the innocent role of a witness. I said, "If they want to give evidence, I'll have them call you."

Zima dug through a desk drawer to his right and handed a form across the desk. I scanned the form and found not a single word of English. He said, "Fill out and return to front desk."

I carefully folded the form into unusable sixteenths. The gesture was not wasted on Zima. With his slack skin and pouched eyes, he looked slow and watchful as a basset hound. He asked, "Is there anything else I can do for you?"

"Yes. Look for a Gypsy wearing a herringbone Armani sport coat and new Italian loafers."

"With this excellent description, we will try our best."

"I have every confidence your investigation will end the moment I leave," I said, and with a curt nod, stood and moved to the door.

"Mr. Miller?" Zima called.

I stopped, turned, grunted with impatience.

"You had with you address of apartment? Written on slip of paper in wallet or in coat pocket?"

"Just in my notebook, but I left my notebook in the apartment that night."

"I ask only because something confuse me."

He stared at me and waited.

"What *confuse* you?" I asked, exasperated not just by the atrocious grammar but by his relentlessly plodding manner.

"When Gypsies stole your keys, how they knew where you live?"

Of course I had written my address down on a slip of paper in my wallet, or perhaps even inked it on the inside label of my sport coat like the mother of a forgetful five-year-old. I simply couldn't remember the details. Other issues concerned me more. I needed money. Twenty thousand Czech crowns and five one-hundred-dollar counterfeit bills had been stolen with my wallet. My credit cards were still safe in a drawer—no reason to carry them in a town that did not accept credit—but no electronic tellers existed from which to draw a cash advance. For the next few weeks it would be unwise to change counterfeit bills in Prague: too great a risk of being recognized.

I called Father at home, seven in the morning Los Angeles time. Of our dreary conversation, I wish to record little. I had hoped to speak with Mother first, as she is by far the easier touch, but Father reported she was out of the house on her morning walk, though quite likely they were arguing again over Father's mistresses and she had gone to spend the weekend with her sister.

No. I mislead out of spite. Father is as faithful as an old dog.

We simultaneously tried to speak, stopped, began again in a second clash of voices. Satellite bounce, the split-second delay between speaking and hearing, an acceptable if obvious metaphor of our strained attempts at communication. Into a sudden gap of silence I blurted, "I've had a little trouble here, was hoping you could help me out."

Father chose not to hear and said, "Several dentists have been calling for you. Claim to be investors in some project of yours?"

"Oh, that," I said, remembering something I'd hoped would be forgotten by all concerned.

"They threatened to report you to the police."

"We all took a gamble and lost. No law against that."

"Your mother and I think you should come home for a while. Your therapist, that nice fellow . . ."

"Dr. Quellenbee?"

"He's been asking about you. He wants to see you again."

"But I have no interest in seeing him. I called to tell you I've been robbed."

A conspicuously long silence preceded Father's question. "Are you okay?" His concern might have gratified me, had it not been delivered in the cautious tone of speaking to someone whose veracity was doubted.

I said, "No. I'm not okay. I could have been killed."

"This underscores my point. You're not safe. You should come home."

I'd given the wrong answer. The trick was to make light of it. I wasn't in any serious trouble. I just needed a little help. I imagined myself a few years hence, laughing over the story with friends. We've dined sumptuously on a meal prepared by my private chef and sit around the fire, drinking brandy. *The most interesting thing happened to me one night in a Gypsy club on the outskirts of Prague, gentlemen. Have any of you ever been intimate with a Gypsy woman?* I said, "Crazy story, what happened. Just one of those things. I went into a Gypsy club. It didn't seem such a bad place. Rather interesting, actually, from an anthropological point of view. I went there with a girl, part Gypsy herself, funny enough. She left early. Long story why. I had a few drinks, woke up the next morning in the alley, stripped to my underwear."

"Had you been drinking that much?"

"You misunderstand. I was drugged."

"You were foolish to go in the first place."

"I was dragged there."

"You already said that."

"What?"

"That you were drugged."

"Not drugged. Dragged."

"If you were dragged to a place like that, the last thing you should have done was get drunk."

"I didn't get drunk. I was drugged. I was dragged there and then drugged."

"Your mother will be very upset to hear you're taking drugs in Gypsy bars."

Impossible. Talking to Father was like that children's game in which one child tells a story to another child who tells yet another, until the story that circles back to the first child bears little resemblance to the original. Whatever I told Father returned to me unrecognizably altered by his opinions of my character and capabilities. I said, "Father, I need some money to tide me over till my next check."

"You know the rules."

"But I was robbed!"

"I'll buy you a return ticket home any time you want."

"With my money you'll buy it. My money, that grandfather gave me."

"He appointed me executor of your trust fund for good reason."

"You just want to humiliate me. You want me to grovel."

"Your mother and I both just want you to be responsible."

"I refuse!"

"Shouting won't solve anything."

"Just send me the fucking money, you fucking bastard!"

The telephone line crackled in the sudden absence of voice. I don't suppose I'd ever shut Father up so completely. That alone was almost worth the risk I'd taken. For over twenty years I had suffered his calm and smothering authority with whining angst and the occasional rebellious act. It hadn't occurred to me to shout obscenities at him.

Father said, "Yes. Fine. I'll advance you one month's stipend. After that, consider all payments suspended until your thirtieth birthday, when the fund reverts to you in its entirety, and you can spend it however you like."

"Father, you have no right to do that."

"One month's advance will be deposited in your account this afternoon. After that, you're on your own. Any time you want to return home, your mother and I will gladly purchase a ticket for you."

The line went dead. I slammed down the phone. He had no intention of ever relinquishing control of Grandfather's money. His lawyers had probably already found a loophole through which to rob me of my inheritance when I turned thirty. Not satisfied with his own considerable fortune, he now wanted mine as well. Had he not given me the perfect excuse to hate him by being my father, I could have admired his trickery. In another week, I would call again, thank him graciously for advancing next month's stipend, and report some fictitious good news to sway him back to confidence in my character.

The beauties of Český Krumlov—a medieval castle and narrow streets vigorously bare of the detritus of industrial society—

hid in Gothic darkness when I arrived by train that night. Monika had not checked into the room I'd reserved at the Hotel Růže, nor booked another under her own name. I tried describing her, but the clerk's English was limited to hotel terms, and no matter how often, slowly, and loudly I repeated myself, he was incapable of understanding sentences more complex than "Room please" and "Change money." He accepted my hundred-dollar bill without suspicion. I penned a brief note to Monika, stuffed it into an envelope, and mimed instructions to tape it within view behind the desk.

Quite possibly she had been delayed. Picking up the phone, I called long distance to the Merkur Hotel and received the desk clerk's report that Monika had checked out that morning. Evidently, her brother had followed, and evasive maneuvers had been required. I stared out the iron-framed window in the far corner of my room, no larger than the window of a jail cell, and watched the silver twist of river and cramped black streets of the old city below. It suddenly occurred to me what had happened. Monika had come to the hotel and, fearing an untimely appearance by her brother, had registered under a false name. Clever woman! The difficulty was that she had so expertly concealed her presence even I had been deceived. That other explanation for her absence I refused to consider, save in bleak and furtive moments, like cracking a door open to a closet full of rats.

The note remained taped behind the desk when I hurried downstairs the following morning. I camped in a stuffed chair in the lobby and waited. I left the chair three times for anxiously cramped micturations and twice for meals in the adjacent dining room, where a carefully positioned chair afforded a view to the lobby. On each occasion the front door swung open or feet padded down the stairs, my heart accelerated and stomach lurched behind. None of the many dark heads that turned my way bore Monika's face. Two days later, I took a return train to Prague.

A postcard awaited me in the morning's mail, bearing a trite view of Charles Bridge on the front and Monika's signature on the back. She wrote:

> *Sven's being a boor. Won't let us go away together. He's terrible when angry! It's best to go home to Copenhagen. Don't be upset with me. I'll write again from Denmark.*
> *Love, Monika.*
> *P.S. I came back to get you at the club, but you were gone. What happened?*

I must have read the card a hundred times before I noticed it had been postmarked in Vienna.

10

P rague suffered a plague of street musicians that year, mostly young American men who sought a sense of self-identity through popular music and wished to get laid by one of the young girls certain to flock like desperate moths to a dull flame. Almost anyone with a guitar singing popular songs on Charles Bridge could draw a crowd, and every night tourists clotted around one in particular who made a small fortune encouraging the crowd to sing along to old Beatles tunes. I crossed the bridge every night going to and from Jo's Bar, and a few nights after the arrival of Monika's postcard, something in a peripherally glimpsed profile ground my heels into the cobblestones. The last musician on the Malá Strana side was Andrew, eyes closed, singing with the desolate passion of the earnest but undertalented. I knew he played guitar, but then nearly every young American in Prague did, to one degree of ineptness or another. I crept closer, considered but rejected the idea of dropping a donation into his hat as too contemptuous a gesture, and instead listened to his voice. He wasn't half bad, on key as far as the music allowed and sweetly angst-ridden, but among the hundred passersby who heard his three minutes of chorus and verse I was the only one to stop. When the final chord strummed out, I clapped my hands. Andrew opened his eyes, surprised at the applause, and, seeing the ironic character of his audience, grinned sheepishly.

"Is this a benefit for your Bosnian refugees?" I inquired, in the manner of a good-natured joke.

Andrew cradled his guitar into its case and slipped shut the locks. He stared as if mystified at the empty hat at his feet, a brown and lumpy old thing he never meant to wear, and for a moment I thought he might do the decently theatrical thing and toss it into the river, but instead he clenched it humbly under his armpit, like a Frenchman might a loaf of bread. As he performed these motions, not unconscious of my presence but not acknowledging it either, I feared he prepared to flee because he thought I mocked him, which of course I did, but only with the best of intentions.

"Come have a drink. We'll talk," I said.

"Can't. I'm meeting someone."

Was he really going to meet someone, or did he find my company so repellent that he invented excuses to flee? Andrew's evasions so terrified me they may have created the only possible circumstance in which I could later tell the truth. I said, "I have something to confess to you. Something important."

"Why don't you give me a call tomorrow?"

"Tomorrow will be too late!"

"It can't be that serious."

I hunched over the bridge's stone ledge and looked significantly at the river below. "How serious is suicide?"

Andrew observed me with suspicion, rightly suspecting I bluffed. I waved him off with the admonition that his meeting was more important. If I wasn't bluffing, he couldn't risk being complicit in the consequences. He led me down a set of stone steps to the Kampa, a small island near the castle side of the river. An outdoor *vinárna* nestled under the arch of the bridge, its few tables overlooking Čertovka, Devil's Stream in English, which flowed between island and shore. We ordered red wine to thicken our blood against the chill night air. Andrew waited for me to explain. I tried my best to look tragic. I said, "What happened to your Bosnians?"

"They're still there. More every day."

"I thought you'd left Prague for the summer."

"If you don't want to talk about what's bothering you, fine, I'll go."

"It's hard to start."

"Start anywhere."

I hadn't planned what to say. Until that moment, it never occurred to me to tell the truth. I said, "I fell in love."

Andrew's laughter cut me open from throat to gut.

"I amuse you?"

"You always seemed too—well, nasty to love anybody. You know, narcissistic, selfish, slightly vicious."

I often think Andrew needed my monstrousness to reaffirm his virtue. I represented a boundary from which he could happily measure his moral distance, knowing no matter what his behavior he could never approach the territory I inhabited. Of course it's possible I'm projecting attitudes Andrew never possessed, that I imagine for myself a metaphysical importance when I might have been a merely unwholesome and sometimes unwelcome presence in his life. I write this account as though understanding the actions and motivations of persons who, as well as I might pretend to know them, have thoughts and emotions inaccessible to all but themselves, and which even they most often cannot or will not understand. My image of Andrew pleases my own desires and compulsions and might be contrary to Andrew's idea of himself. Others who know Andrew might read this account and complain that my descriptions don't fit him at all, that he's someone else entirely. The problem is unavoidable unless I stick to basic facts, such as this and that happened on a certain day, which even then, because the facts were not documented by public record, would be facts privately remembered well after the event and thus susceptible to distortions of convenience and interpretation. I never have spoken to anyone accused of wrong, whether a prosecutable crime or a lapse in judgment, whose memory of events was not influenced by self-justification.

When Andrew asked the identity of the unlucky woman, I described the strange circumstances of my meeting Monika; how her violent response to my vomiting at her feet had inspired feelings I knew existed in others but had never experienced myself. From the tears welling in my eyes to the swelling of my throat, it occurred to me as I told the story that I loved her from the bottom of my heart. That I could feel such an emotion astonished me. Perhaps it wasn't the deepest and most pure love, but the bottom of a brackish pond is still the bottom, no less so than the bottom of an alpine lake. The telling so involved me I never bothered to gauge Andrew's reactions. When I described my near-fatal encounter in the Gypsy club, he laughed knowingly.

I said, "I shouldn't have told you. I've made myself ridiculous."

"Love makes us all ridiculous, you more than others."

"If you saw her, you'd understand my feelings."

"I can't believe you don't see it."

"See what?"

"She conned you."

Whenever that possibility had fluttered into conscious thought I had smashed it; to hear Andrew voice it openly brought a buzzing of blood to my head. "Impossible," I blurted.

"If you hadn't stolen a glimpse at her passport, you wouldn't know her name. If you hadn't followed her, you would have gone to the Hotel Paříž the day after being robbed. The receptionist would've told you there was no recent guest fitting that description in the hotel."

"She had a good reason to lie to me. She was ashamed to be staying in a fourth-class hotel."

"She was making it impossible for you to trace her."

"She was in love with me."

"She wouldn't even sleep with you."

"We were going away together."

"No. You weren't going away together. You were being set up. The night before the supposed consummation you were drugged and robbed and left for dead. Did you tell her you'd be carrying a lot of cash?"

"Of course not."

"You gave her the line about being a famous Hollywood

screenwriter, I bet. She knew you'd have money for the weekend."

Despite Andrew's accusations, I remained willfully dense. I refused to suspect Monika. About her brother I had no illusions. Sven had motive, opportunity, and weapon. I was a rival for Monika's affection. No doubt he wanted to see her an old maid bound to him forever. Sven had to eliminate me once he realized she had fallen terribly in love. Hadn't she written that he had forced her to return to Denmark? The jealous bastard spiked my drink and left me behind to be robbed by the Gypsies. That was the only allowable explanation.

I asked, "What route does the train to Copenhagen take from here?"

"Up through Dresden."

"Not down through Vienna?"

"Exact opposite direction."

She had hastily posted the card between trains in Vienna, not realizing when she wrote that he intended to take her not to Copenhagen—but to where? I pulled a dozen slips of paper from my coat pocket and found like the joker in a pack of cards the receipt from Gerbeaud that had slipped from Monika's purse the day I met her. The receipt had been folded into her passport, next to an open train ticket. "Budapest!" I exclaimed.

"Further south of Vienna," Andrew offered.

I couldn't explain to him how I suddenly knew where to find her; the simple truth would not honor the preternatural awareness, edging by moments closer to absolute certainty, that Monika wanted—no, expected—me to find her. When I need something to be true I invent the circumstances that would make it so and invest the fabrication with the greater reality, so that when presented with the fact of a matter and my memory of it, I'll swear my memory is the more accurate version. The only explanation I can give is a desperate need to conform reality to expectation. Life seems to me a series of injustices, and the only way I can cope is by believing so fervently in what I want to be true that I can no longer distinguish invention from fact. I said, "I just now remembered that, in the event something went wrong, we made plans to meet at a little café we both know in Budapest."

"And you actually think she'll be there?"

"Why wouldn't she be? The only question is when," I answered confidently.

Exasperated, Andrew railed, "Then why are you depressed, why do you threaten to throw yourself in the river, why am I sitting here drinking wine with you instead of meeting my friend?"

"I'm not depressed anymore and you're sitting here because I'm also your friend," I suggested.

"This is a waste of my time." Andrew backed away from the table, the half-liter carafe of wine emptied. "You're buying, I presume."

I asked him to stay and drink another. He refused. Perhaps I chafed about his remark about my wasting his time. I chided, "Off to meet your little clubfoot?"

The line seemed clever the moment before I allowed my voice to sound it, and disastrously rude the moment after. The unchecked compulsion to twist a harmlessly witty remark into something damaging has plagued all my relationships and inspired an untimely end to several. I have attempted to trace this compulsion to its roots but am frustrated at the end by a dense and twisted mass of psychological material that refuses to yield to analysis. Dr. Quellenbee has noted that I'm simultaneously self-aggrandizing and self-destructive, an obvious insight from a quack who does not hold my character in high regard. A psychic I once visited informed me that in one of my past lives I poisoned an entire dinner party of twelve, including my immediate family and closest friends, and that in attempting to poison my current-life relationships I'm acting out what she called *past-life psychic residue*. Like most Southern Californians, I consider myself such a complex character that I require a team of psychiatrists, psychics, astrologers, and tarot and palm readers to sort myself out, yet even with such expert guidance the mystery of my being remains largely impenetrable and my behavior unexplained.

"What did you say?" Andrew demanded, unable to believe I'd said what he thought I'd said. "How did you know about her?"

I pretended not to understand the question.

"You followed me, didn't you? Last week after we met on the bridge.

"Please, Andrew. Everybody in town has seen you with her. I merely heard the rumor and said something impolitic because I was angry."

Andrew looked down at me, mouth still gaped, not believing a word, astonished by how I could so casually follow insult with lie. He said, "She lost her foot to a land mine, you asshole."

I said, "Oops." That explained his sudden desire to teach English to the refugees. "Shall we just forget I said anything?"

Andrew turned and ran out the gates of the *vinárna*. I called his name, said he had misunderstood, pleaded for him to be reasonable. My voice bounced off the stones arched above the *vinárna,* rang clearly across the water of Devil's Stream, but never reached Andrew, who didn't slow or glance back. I shouted at him, shook off a waiter's restraining arm, commanded him to stop, until my throat tightened and strangled me to silence.

11

B y the fourth day in Budapest, I had completed a
check of the more common tourist hotels, rising
early each morning to ask for guests named
Andersen at the front desk of every hotel listed in
my guidebooks. I found two sets, both septuagenarian cou-
plets with tour groups from Copenhagen. Afternoons I de-
voted to staking out Gerbeaud. I never dwelled on the
possibility that Monika was not in Budapest. Several times
each day I spotted her. She was the face on the tram sweep-
ing past, the turned shoulder entering the metro, the sun-
glassed woman in the car stopped in traffic at the light just
ahead, the willowy figure watching me from the railing of a
cruise boat parading the Danube. I once caught her absently
gazing at me from behind the window of a department store

and, shoving through the crowds of shoppers, discovered in her place a fashionably dressed mannequin. That all these apparitions vaporized on second glance did not discourage me. Days passed. The list of pensions and private apartments I visited each morning grew shorter and less reputable. I spent more of my time loitering at Gerbeaud, eating pastries and drinking cappuccino. The constant hope of seeing her visage cross the threshold and the liters of cappuccino and kilos of pastry I consumed each afternoon produced a continuous state of nervous excitement. My hands trembled constantly. I could not speak without stuttering. Any contact with fellow vertebrates brought such stress that I could not breathe. I wore shades in the dimmest corners to curtain a psyche as fragile and vulnerable as cracked glass.

I allowed myself to leave Gerbeaud for an hour each afternoon, reasoning that she couldn't enter, consume her pastries, and leave again in so short a time. Those first afternoons I did little more than nervously circle the block, afraid that a moment of inattention would lose her forever, but as the days passed with nothing more than false sightings, I realized that I needed to make a gesture of faith before she would appear, and scoured the neighborhood jewelry stores, looking for that rare symbiosis of gold and precious stone fit for an engagement ring. What woman could resist the wildly romantic gesture of a marriage proposal from a man who had chased her through half of Europe? Father would be happy to hear I'd settled down at last and, as a gesture of approval, relinquish control of my trust fund. Monika and I would have a small fortune at our disposal. From Budapest we'd fly to Morocco or Greece, rent a villa on an island, lounge on the beach by day, and fill the nights with lovemaking. The prospect sent me into erotic delirium. I found the perfect ring in an antique shop owned by an old man in a wheelchair: twin serpents entwined amid a field of diamonds and garnets. I pointed out the ring and with my finger on the glass display case scrawled a number 25 percent less than the list price. When he attempted to argue I pounded my fist on the glass. We compromised at 15 percent, though the bastard wrapped the ring in tissue rather than supplying the case it deserved. When I returned to Gerbeaud, I examined on vacated tables lipstick-stained glasses and pastry crumbs for evidence of Monika, certain she had come and gone in my absence. I spent the rest of the afternoon vainly waiting for her return, if indeed she had been there at all.

At some point in my vigil I lost contact with normal waking consciousness and became a creature not entirely of this world or any other. Images of Monika consumed me. I played out our past and imagined future thousands of times behind the blank screen of my eyes. When a waitress or lost tourist inquired anything of me so simple as directions or payment I stared as a ghost might at flesh and blood. I had ceased to exist in any dimension beyond self-imposed limbo.

When Monika at last walked into Gerbeaud, hidden behind streaming black hair and sunglasses like a reluctant movie star, my hands trembled cappuccino over the cup edge and in setting down the cup upended the saucer. I lurched back to save my trousers and groped for a napkin. Monika's glance swept the room. She looked for someone. Me, obviously. At any moment she would rush up all tears and laughter. I fumbled for the ring in my pocket. What would I say? I'd rehearsed multiple conversational gambits but could remember none of them. Panic washed my thoughts as clear of detail as unexposed film flooded with sudden light. Monika circled toward me, scanning the seated crowd. The ring wasn't in the first or second pocket I checked, but the third. My fingers responded like wet wood to the command to fetch and unwrap. The clean profile of Monika's face turned to three-quarters. At last I succeeded in ripping the tissue paper back, but when my thumb and forefinger grasped the band the ring squirted free. I stared paralyzed with horror as the ring bounced beneath the table and rolled into the aisle. If she saw me I couldn't ask her to wait a moment while I retrieved the ring. I'd have to abandon it. Without the ring I could say nothing. How quickly the inner certainties of being crumbled to nothing. I dropped to my knees and crawled beneath the table. Hidden by the tablecloth I stretched a long arm into the aisle. By the time I surfaced, she would certainly have found a seat. I could saunter over and present the ring with a roguish smile. *That you and I should meet here by chance proves our destiny,* I might say. Clutching the ring in my fist I peered cautiously over the rim of the table. Monika moved away, toward the corner where each afternoon a pianist skipped through a repertoire of Central European waltzes and preludes. I dusted the knees of my trousers and stepped into the aisle, intent on approaching her the moment she sat.

A robust young man in a purple suit rose to his feet at the far corner table. Monika greeted him with a radiant display of teeth. What sort of man wore purple? Above the burbling crowd I thought I heard a hearty *"Guten Tag!"* German or Austrian. Considering the region's historical alliances, I guessed Austrian. Helmut bent at the waist and took Monika's hand. I thought he might continue the gentlemanly charade by kissing her fingertips, but Monika parried his hand and kissed him on the mouth. The kiss astonished us both. Helmut teetered on his heels. I nearly cried out in anguish. The gesture was recognizable. Monika had greeted me with an identical kiss the night I had taken her to dinner at Parnas.

Distance prevented me from hearing their conversation, but the substance was recognizable enough. Helmut performed verbal acrobatics while Monika listened, a private smile drifting across her face at odd moments seemingly unconnected to his monologue. A raven lock of hair tumbled across her brow, and an impatient toss of her head both disciplined the lock and warned Helmut when her attention waned. Then Monika spoke at length, her fingertips tracing in outline the span of his hand, which silenced him completely. In Monika's company the previous week I had interpreted those same gestures as signs of an exclusive intimacy. It had never occurred to me they were as common to her relationships as a finger pointed to an empty beer glass is to the ritual of public drinking.

No matter how I argued that appearances were deceiving, that I witnessed an innocent tryst between Monika and a man who would turn out to be just a friend, someone who was probably gay, my body betrayed my true suspicions. An alien feeling lashed out in my chest, something very much alive, like a small animal who tasted too late the strychnine in a piece of bait, and thrashed against my ribs in the agony of being so simply and fatally fooled. It occurred to me that I was jealous. Strangely, I had no impulse to kill my rival. Had Monika bared her throat to me, I would have kissed and not cut it. I had always assumed jealousy was a savage, unthinking emotion; in me it provoked violent nausea and the conviction that I had been rendered invisible.

When Monika and Helmut left to stroll the quay along the Danube, I followed. The evening was impossibly romantic; a pregnant moon rose full-bellied over the water, a breeze carried mixed scents of river and lilac bloom, and the air seemed just chill enough to encourage like-minded lovers to clinch against the railing or entwine on benches. Even the rhythmic slap of water against concrete sounded to my ear like copulation. Helmut took advantage of the setting and seized Monika's hand. At times I walked so close behind I could hear snatches of conversation. Near the stringed lights of the Chain Bridge, they paused to admire the view of the palace on the opposite bank. I took refuge behind a screen of bushes on the opposite side of the quay. I was certain he would try to kiss her there. My foot kicked at a stone. I was tempted to throw it. If they kissed I would retch. Helmut leaned close, waiting for the moment she might turn her lips to him, but Monika pretended not to notice, staring instead at the river swirling below, and from a glimpse of her face I saw she spoke of something with feeling. Was she telling him that she was already in love, with a certain young American living in Prague? Or was she reciting from well-worn memory the tragic history she once confided to me with such seeming intimacy?

From the surrounding dark, a voice called a vulgar proposition. I twisted about, startled and uncertain whether I had been addressed or merely overheard. The Budapest equivalent of a Las Vegas blonde stepped from the shadows of the nearest tree. A gap appeared in her teeth when she smiled, like a missing plank in a white fence, and at that distance I couldn't discern whether she had a missing tooth or an inadvertent morsel of food lodged there. Encouraged by my curious gaze, the whore stepped forward to make the offer more specific. In the moonlight, her month-old bleach job framed a face made up like a carnal clown.

"Fuck fifty dollars, you me," she whispered.

My laughter didn't discourage her from reaching to touch my chest, where no doubt she hoped to find my wallet. I looked her over carefully, thinking her appearance at that moment an accident of fate that I must use to advantage. Aware of the intensity of my gaze the whore scooped her breasts together by touching the insides of her elbows, a gesture I supposed was intended to arouse me. I pointed to the couple on the quay and falling into the rhythm of her vulgar patois, advised, "You me no fuck. You him fuck."

We peered down the length of my arm and together spied several moments on Monika and Helmut. The whore tugged provocatively at her miniskirt. "He have girl. You no have girl. I want you fuck."

I pulled a collection of Hungarian currency from my pocket. "You don't understand," I explained. "His girl is my girl."

The whore's eyes sharpened, and the dark gap in her teeth revealed itself to be a silver tooth glimmering in a sex-wise smile. "Cut her," she advised, and lifted her mane of bleached hair to reveal a long red scar slicing up the back of her neck. Glancing back over her shoulder, she caught me in a complicitous glance. "Is best here. No show."

Her suggestion and the sight of her scar, still jagged at the edges, so startled me I joked, "And what should I use, a broken bottle?"

"I sell you knife, fifty dollar."

The whore snapped open her bag and displayed the knife. It was a cheap blade, a stiletto design with a plastic handle. I could have bought its equal for less than half the price, but the poetics of buying such a weapon from a whore proved irresistible. I certainly had no intention of using it, on Monika or anyone else, but imagined myself years hence, comfortably married, the knife something I pull out of a drawer from time to time to entertain my more intimate friends with the tale of how a Hungarian whore once encouraged me to cut my future wife for infidelity. I met her price and doubled it to include Helmut. The money was meaningless to me. While she counted the denominations and stuffed the whole into her purse, I gave her brief but expert direction and whispered, "Action!"

From my distant cover of shadows I could watch but little hear the melodrama unfold. The Hungarian whore opted for a surprise attack. Strolling quietly along the quay, she hesitated briefly upon breasting Helmut and then flung herself upon him with a flurry of kisses, gropes, and fondles. Helmut's mouth fluttered open and shut in protest like the wings of a bird caught by its feet. I jerked my handkerchief from my pocket and stuffed it into my mouth to keep from giving myself away by laughter. At last Helmut pried himself loose from the whore, who changed tactics and berated Monika for what I can only surmise was stealing her man. Monika backed against the railing, properly horrified. Helmut did the gentlemanly thing and stepped between them. This maneuver resulted in a renewed attack from the whore, who directed the bulk of her efforts to the regions south of his belt. I feared she might unzip him on the spot, as did Helmut, who beat a hasty retreat, this time seeking refuge behind Monika.

Movement drew my eye from the scene to a tall and lightly dressed figure hurrying up the quay. I prepared to flee in the event the figure turned out to be a cop; the whore, under threat of arrest or worse, might finger me as the mastermind of this farce. With each stride the figure neared familiarity. Monika jerked at the sound of a voice breaching the distance: Sven. The whore found herself unexpectedly flanked. She protested to Helmut, believing like any good actress in the reality of her role and his past affections. But Helmut was powerless to help even if he chose to do so, which he pointedly did not. Sven spoke a few sharp words which drove the whore back on her heels. She dug in, regrouped, and unleashed a tirade of angry Hungarian. Sven silenced her with a slap. The whore turned and fled. He ordered her to stop and, when she failed to heed, sprang forward and brought her to heel with a twisted arm and fist of hair. A flat leather billfold fell to the pavement. Sven kicked it to Helmut. My whore spat at the ground and hurried off, tugging furiously at her miniskirt.

Helmut retrieved his wallet with an obeisant dip of his head toward Sven that nonetheless conveyed intense resentment. At that distance I could only surmise the conversation that took place among the three of them. Helmut seemed intent on escape, bowing first to Monika, then to Sven, then to Monika again, as though forgetting where he'd started. To my astonishment, she entreated him to stay, leaving Sven's side to place an enticing hand on his chest. The toothy gleam of Sven's smile, and the faint residue of verbal encouragement that carried the distance, convinced me that he, too, didn't want him to go. But Helmut was not to be dissuaded and, in taking several measured steps backward, signaled his firm intention to part company. Brother and sister sandwiched him a few yards down the quay, until, back-slapped and cheek-kissed, he made his way alone. The sound of his brisk footsteps veered away from the river and melded into the background sounds of the city.

Snatches of an angry duet blew in from the river, one voice mocking and the other strident. I was not close enough to make out the substance of the argument; Sven seemed upset about the appearance of the whore or perhaps the German's escape, laying blame that Monika refused to accept. While making one emphatic point, Sven paused and stared directly at me, but like a character in a film or television show his gaze had no substance. I could have stepped out of the shadows with a bucket of popcorn and he wouldn't have seen. A chill of invisibility blew through me; watching without being seen is a defining characteristic of the dramatic arts, but I felt more than the voyeurism of a spectator. From my invisibility it seemed I could direct things and, if not rewrite the script, at least affect the trajectory of the drama. Soon the sound of their voices ceased carrying the distance, and they stood quietly watching the moon over the palace, like any other young couple out for a stroll along the river. When Sven put his arm along her shoulder, Monika reciprocated with an arm around his waist. Such displays of sibling affection, which two weeks before I had thought so endearing, I now found unbearably vexing.

I clung as closely to their single shadow as prudence allowed when they wandered from the quay, terrified that at any moment they might hail a cab and disappear into the vast exoticism of Budapest. But they didn't hail a cab, content to walk the streets coupled like twins joined at the waist, separating only when they reached the Erzsébet, a hotel I had checked for guests named Andersen the previous week. The suspicion that they paid the room rate of $100 a night out of what Sven had stolen from me brought a jabbing pain to my throat. I watched from behind a parked car on the opposite side of the street, and when the curtains of a fourth-floor room flared I approached the desk clerk to inquire about a room for the evening, preferably something on the fourth floor. Signing the credit card slip, I asked with all the casual discretion my anxiety allowed whether or not a couple named Andersen had yet checked in. The clerk tapped a computer keyboard and replied no guests had registered by that name. Taking my room key, I wondered if I'd misread Monika's passport.

Upon reaching the fourth floor, I oriented myself to the street and by counting rooms calculated which belonged to Sven and Monika. When I pressed my ear to the door I heard angry voices. The thickness of the wood stripped words from voices but not the basic emotion. They argued about something. The fierceness of the argument aroused my curiosity. I hurried to my room and in the bathroom peeled the sanitary wrapping from a glass, to better conduct the sound from door to ear. The hour was late, and if by chance someone confronted me I could claim to be a private detective from America, investigating a murder which Sven was suspected of committing. The more I thought about Sven, the stronger I felt he deserved a good beating. It wouldn't have surprised me to discover him a drug addict, thieving to feed a filthy habit. Voices came into focus when I placed the glass to the door, but words remained incomprehensible. I pressed my ear against the base of the glass and shifted its position, hoping to improve the acoustics until realizing Sven and Monika fought in Danish, a language I couldn't understand if shouted directly in my ear.

Later, in my room, I imagined Sven packed his gear into a duffel bag while begging Monika to reconsider her decision to separate. They had quarreled at least twice that day, and they could have decided no longer to travel together. Sven already might have left. If I returned to listen at her door, I might hear a soft and solitary weeping. The door might be ajar, so I could see her, sitting on the bed, face in hands. If I entered the room, she might lift her tearstained face to mine and realize how much she missed me. I don't second-guess my decision to return to listen at the door. I could not stay away. The pull was as strong as a window-framed woman to a voyeur. I glanced both directions down the hall, ears alert to distant clicking lock or hum of elevator. Nothing moved save the low thrum of air through ventilation ducts. I lifted the bathroom glass and carefully positioned it below the numbers on the door.

12

Although it may seem incredible to those who know me, I felt until that moment an innocent, dabbling in various petty evils and certainly guilty of criminal indiscretions, but nonetheless blindly willing to think the best of people even while I thought the worst of myself. One need not be good to be innocent; innocence is a state of blissful ignorance about the nature of others. The cries piercing the glass at my ear made me wise in a way I previously had not imagined. Sven was as loud in his physical exertions as a Bulgarian weight lifter, grunting and groaning under the strain of each thrust. I tried to imagine the stabbed cries accompanying his rough rhythm as belonging to someone other than Monika, but the cadence and timbre of the voice was Danish and undeniably hers.

I didn't return to my room, preferring to run the streets wildly like a poisoned dog. It's possible that I wept. I don't remember. If I did, my grief was ridiculous. Monika considered me less a person than a resource to be stripped. The events of the past week unreeled through memory in sharper focus. The Erzsébet Hotel hadn't registered them under the name of Andersen because Sven's last name wasn't the same as Monika's. They played siblings to better fool their victims. Monika promised passionate sex; Sven hovered nearby to break up any serious attempts at consummation. Between promise and fulfillment something would happen that the victim later couldn't piece together precisely, except the related disappearances of Monika and his money. The stories about her Gypsy grandmother and Count Valdštejn were as fanciful as the tales I told about my successes in Hollywood; a few of the details may have been actual, just as any good fiction contains enough truth to trick the unwary into belief. Her seemingly tragic circumstances and later claims of love had been staged to relieve me of both senses and wallet. The only uncalculated act had been my chance arrival to her table in Obecní Dům. Little wonder she had regarded me then with such cutting irony, like a fox observing a nearsighted rabbit enter its den to nibble a patch of fur mistaken for grass.

That Monika didn't love me disturbed less than having fooled myself into thinking she had. I had willingly suspended disbelief, confusing fiction for reality to such an extent that I had allowed myself the emotions of a lovesick teenager. I sought to reassure myself that such behavior was out of character. I was as incapable of loving as I was of being loved. Monika had merely beat me at a game I had considered myself an expert in playing. As I watched from the edge of Szabadság Bridge the eastern sky lighten to a sodden gray, I realized Monika was more worthy of me than I had previously believed. I admired the consummate skill with which she had played me. I could even imagine that we deserved each other. With a woman my equal in cunning and duplicity I might return to Southern California. We could tell tales and make deals that would spin studio heads, our talents for deception earning us certain success in the chicaning art of Hollywood film.

My emotions were evidence of an obsession—not love—and to feed this obsession I needed to exploit my natural talents in scheming and manipulation. That Monika and Sven were not siblings meant they could be separated. They frequently argued; the arguments I witnessed as both victim and voyeur proved they had not been acting solely to deceive. Monika's sexual provocations angered Sven. The night she pressed herself against me on the dance floor with deliberate sexual intent, he had acted out of jealousy and not simply a role. Though I was not fool enough to believe she cared for me, it was possible to consider that I aroused her. Given the proper circumstances, she might see how well we suited each other; that and physical attraction might form the basis of a relationship.

I had grown so accustomed to despising Sven that it was difficult to consider him from a fresh perspective. I couldn't imagine him plunging into Monika without feeling violently ill, but didn't actively wish him harm. He was a rival who had robbed and left me for dead in a Gypsy club. Had I been prone to the normal primitive emotions I should have wanted him dead. But all I really wanted from Sven was his disappearance. He was not worthy of enmity; I considered him an obstacle to be surmounted or removed. Perhaps we would all be lucky and one last argument would dispatch him permanently from the scene. In my weaker moments I fantasized they argued about me, Monika expressing doubts if not about theft at least about the extreme measures taken.

I returned to the Erzsébet Hotel just past sunrise and ordered a pot of coffee from room service. Every half hour I padded quietly down the hall to listen at their door. When I heard sounds of rising, I descended to the lobby and hid behind a Hungarian newspaper until, just before noon, they emerged from the elevator. No plan had yet emerged to give my surveillance direct purpose. I certainly did not intend to kill or rob them. I had an attitude rather than a definite plan. They had stalked and taken me; now I would stalk them. How to take them I trusted to opportunity and inspiration.

From the hotel they walked the few cramped blocks to the Deák metro station. The noon-hour crowds provided ample cover, and as they had no reason to suspect I followed, it was a simple question of waiting patiently until the push of the crowd concealed my entrance into the metro car next to theirs. Several stops later, when Sven stepped onto the platform, I allowed myself to be swept from the subway car on a tide of disembarking passengers, but caught sight of the raven back of Monika's head, which still leaned against the inside window of the subway car. At the next stop she exited and ascended to a surface which I first mistook for the countryside. The urgency of errand or meeting impelled her steps, and we quickly covered a distance of a few hundred yards before Monika arrived at the edge of a lake, glanced left and right as though expecting someone, and sat in a spot of sunlight on a park bench.

Screened from view by angle and shrubbery, I unfolded a map of Budapest and located our position in a large park within the city boundaries. Sven would be lurking across the lake, having gotten off the metro one stop early to spy on the encounter and make a sudden appearance should events go awry. Taking the chance that I might lose Monika if I guessed incorrectly, I crawled through the bushes to wait by the road that passed near the lake. At five minutes before the hour, a taxi disgorged the familiar figure of the Austrian, dressed for sport in a baby-blue nylon sweat suit. I jogged up to him and, in the friendly way of Americans everywhere, asked if he spoke English.

He regarded my approach without suspicion, likely believing me a lost tourist. His English was heavily accented but serviceable. "Why, you could almost pass for an American," I said, knowing the remark would please him. He confessed that he had spent some weeks in the United States, visiting both Florida and California. What a coincidence, I said; I was a detective with the Los Angeles Police Department. "On vacation?" he asked. "In fact I'm investigating a Danish couple wanted for a string of thefts in California," I said.

Helmut stumbled back as though stunned. The disorienting effect of hormones on his reasoning process aside, I didn't blame him for doubting me. I didn't look like a cop. He stubbornly asked to see my identification. I substituted Esterhazy for Valdštejn, and asked if the Danish woman he was about to meet claimed to be descended from both Gypsies and the Hungarian aristocracy, if she had said there was death in her past and future, and if a tall Danish brute claiming to be her brother appeared inconveniently when sexual promise seemed about to yield to consummation.

Details frightened him into believing me. I knew too much about Sven's scam to be disbelieved once the conversation turned from my incredible claim of identity. Helmut thought I expected him to betray Monika and was relieved to hear that I merely asked him never to see her again. Nobody wanted the woman to go to jail, I said. She'd fallen into bad company with that Danish fellow. The Hungarian police were about to begin deportation procedures. The best solution would be to slap her wrist and send her home. Helmut babbled profuse and awkward thanks. I solemnly accepted them. It wasn't until he turned into a baby-blue streak running to catch a cab that I understood why he had thanked me. Although unintentionally, I had done a good deed. I had saved him from being robbed and perhaps a considerably worse fate. It wouldn't have surprised me to learn Sven was murderer as well as thief. I supposed that even an unintentional good deed counted as a virtue.

Monika exhibited greater persistence than I expected; disbelief that any man would stand her up kept her circling the park bench sixty minutes past the appointed hour. At last she moved purposely away, skirting the edge of the lake toward an odd cluster of buildings which attempted to imitate, simultaneously, a baroque palace and medieval castle, thus achieving an aesthetic of Disneyesque proportions. I strolled casually to a stand of trees not far from the water. Sven stepped from behind a crumbling wall on the opposite shore. From my screen of trees, the angle and sight lines were perfect if the distance imposing. They faced each other in a patch of grass a few yards from the lakeshore, shaking like trees in a wind. Helmut's nonappearance seemed to have become the cause of violent discord. Monika's hands swept the air. Sven swayed on his heels. Angry words flew back and forth between them like a flock of crows. I imagined the argument was absolute and final, knowing nothing of the perverse intimacy couples find in chopping each other to pieces. Still, the violence was unexpectedly sudden when the space between them cracked with the clublike blow of Sven's forearm. I nearly leapt to her defense but cunning held me back. My appearance would so surprise they'd cobble their relationship to meet a common danger. Monika was able enough to defend herself in that public place, though I have little doubt he was capable of murder in more private circumstances. She sprang at him without fear, slapping once through his defenses before he raised his arm and clubbed her to the ground. Had I a gun I would have shot him. To do nothing but watch was torment. No matter how many times he knocked her down she would rise, unwilling to admit the superiority of brute force. My innocence at that time was vexing. Monika sprang at him again, and I so firmly expected broken bones and blood that I did not at first realize she had hurled herself into his arms. Within moments they humped tooth and claw against the nearest wall.

I turned my back and slumped against the tree, not caring to witness how they managed the technical requirements of intercourse. Sometime later, when they strolled arm in arm from the lake, I followed. Though incomprehensible, Sven's power over Monika was unhealthy and dangerous. Twice I had turned events against them, and both tricks resulted in acts of unaccountable passion. I had always taken pride in cleverness, skillfully manipulating people and situations to my advantage; seldom had my machinations achieved such contrary results. Several new scenarios flashed through my imagination. Budapest teemed with twisting alleys. That night, a Gypsy knife or skinhead club could hurtle from the triangle shadow of a doorway.

SCANDINAVIAN FOUND DEAD
Robbery Suspected Motive

Accidents were a common hazard of big-city life. At rush hour the metro crowds thickened to swell the fringe dangerously close to the platform edge. An inadvertent foot or timely jostle as the train rushed through could result in a horrible accident.

TRAGEDY IN THE TUBE
Dane Flattened by Train

When their paths split at the metro station, I followed Sven. I hoped without cause they had enacted the strange phenomenon known as the farewell fuck, and I might see Sven off at the nearest train or bus station. Instead, I waited two hours under a threatening sky as he methodically wined and dined himself in a local restaurant. When the first raindrops splattered on the pavement at my feet, I imagined Sven, grogged with food and drink, stepping in front of a truck speeding on a slick road. But providence would not so serve me, and I lacked the nerve for an act more desperate than standing in a cold rain praying he might choke to death on a chicken bone.

Sven found the cold as little to his liking as I, and after dinner walked briskly across the Szabadság Bridge to the Gellért Hotel and Spa on the opposite bank of the river. I had read about Gellért in my guidebook—described as a famous medicinal bath founded by the Turks in some distant century—and thought it a curiosity appealing to few but Hungarian homosexuals and the occasional Russian taking a vodka cure. Sven passed beneath an imposing stone arch at the mouth of the spa and with an habitué's confidence spoke to a woman in a kiosk. A placard above listed treatments in Hungarian; only those few making use of English loan words were comprehensible to a foreign eye. Sven slipped a few bills across the counter and handed a ticket to a man seated at the entry gate, who speared it on

a metal spike and let him pass into the main hall, an imposing space of mosaic columns gently lit from above by a
stained-glass-trimmed skylight.

I approached the kiosk, vigorously pointed at several
untranslatable items, and hoped I hadn't by chance ordered
a series of colonics. Receiving several tickets, I hurried to
the passage through which Sven had disappeared. A man
in the white uniform of a hospital or lunatic asylum barred
the way. I waved my tickets. He plucked one from my hand
and pointed to a set of stairs ascending to his left. At the
top of the stairs, another white-cloaked attendant issued me
a towel, key, and small square of linen. The third and last
attendant led me to a curtained cubicle, pointed to a locker
where I should secure my personal articles, and snapped
the curtain shut.

As I disrobed, my fingers stumbled across the stiletto the
Hungarian whore had given me the night before. I wrapped
the knife in the towel, picturing Sven found several hours
from then slumped in a corner of the spa. I didn't plan to
murder him. I merely imagined it somehow happening that
the knife should find its way into his chest. The small square
of linen appeared to be a loincloth. After a few unsuccess-
ful experiments, I decided the cloth was to be worn in front
and the strings tied behind. A discreet glance at my neigh-
bor confirmed I wore the loincloth correctly, and following
his mottled pink behind I descended the staircase to a set
of double glass doors opening to wisps of steam. Twin octo-
genarians in loincloths flanked the interior doorway like
sentinels withered by eternal duty, watching a bathhouse
lit by domed skylight. Midway down a tapered arc of Moorish
vaulting, the light diffused in a fetid mist. Slaps of flesh and
water echoed crisply from the tiles, above an indistinct
babble of voices. Through the dull blue pool at my feet,

disembodied torsos waded to drink from the bubbling mouth of a stone chimera carved to the face of a man, the snout of a lion, and the body of a carp. The air beyond the pools thickened to a miasma of steam, minerals, and sweat. The men shuffling past had the wasted buttocks and sagging breasts of old women. I felt a ghost among shades and wondered if Sven had tricked me into the river Styx. The moment I thought of his face I reached into the center of the rolled towel and wrapped my palm around the stiletto. Cloth muffled the click of the extending blade. I edged another few feet forward. A row of flesh sat the bench along the near wall, voices bickering in an alien tongue. If I thrust my hand forward with sufficient force, the towel would compress as the steel pierced his chest, then drape around the blade as it was withdrawn. It would seem I held nothing more menacing than a rolled towel.

A door opened to scalding gusts of steam. The Turkish bath. The shape of the man nearest me vanished into the steam's source and moments later appeared to clamber up a wall. I groped forward. Steam hissed in plumes behind stepped benches where three figures slumped elbows on knees like tired gods, one as exquisitely chiseled as Aphrodite's Adonis. Sven. I turned my back to avoid recognition and sat on the lowest bench. The steam wasn't unpleasant once I became accustomed to it, the heat soothing my anxieties. I needn't do anything violent. The Turkish bath was too crowded to allow action. I listened for the creak of wood or wet slap of foot on tile that signaled arrivals and departures. If we should be left alone for just a moment, I could saunter up to Sven and say *Remember me?* He'd glance up in sullen surprise, groggy with the heat. He'd have little reason to fear. Was I going to call the Budapest police to report a crime I couldn't prove he'd committed in Prague?

I'd say something, like *You wanna fuck something, fuck this,* and give him the stiletto blade first. No. Too vulgar. I wouldn't say anything. I'd laugh at him. And when it was done I'd wipe the stiletto with the towel and drop both at his feet. After a half hour or so someone might notice the blood and discover Sven had fallen into a state of infinite quietude. By then, I'd be dressed and gone. But the pink and yellow parade of new arrivals continued unabated, most lasting only a few minutes before wilting in the heat. I felt as though I'd been pricked a thousand times and through these small holes my very substance leaked out. A beer-bellied man on the bench above slapped his skin, spraying sweat in all directions. Much longer and I'd boil down to nothing. Sweat dripped fast as rain at my feet. My breath burned wet and hot. The beer-bellied man grunted and stumbled off. The heat was intense as a drug. My thoughts shrunk to the size and precariousness of a small ball bobbing on a boiling sea.

The first thing I noticed to disappear was my penis, which I initially suspected had shriveled to nothing from fear and excitement, until I observed that my thighs and knees shimmered oddly. I waved my hands in front of my face. The silver and turquoise ring I wear on my right index finger streaked through the mist. When I held my hands still, the color of flesh paled like milk diluted in water. It seemed I shed corporeality with sweat. The substance of my chest wavered to transparency. I stood and couldn't distinguish my feet from steam. The phenomenon of my invisibility seemed to be transforming from feeling to fact. Far from being alarmed, my dissolution was a moment of great astonishment and satisfaction. I had completely lost myself. I could do anything I wished, and no one would see it.

Sven sat alone on the middle bench. I climbed and crawled along the top bench until I sat directly behind him. His head curled forward in his hands, stretching the skin of his back around a row of vertebrae as fragile as porcelain beads on a string. The smallest slice would scatter him to the floor. I lifted the knife and imagined it plunging into his neck, severing his spinal cord and killing him instantly, silently, with a slight trickling of blood from the wound. I traced the outline of his back ribs, locating the soft indentation between bones through which a knife could reach the back of his heart. The knife in my mind tore through his flesh, but paralysis struck the knife in my hand. My brain's signals to thrust the blade forward were met with an embarrassing silence. I had motive, weapon, and opportunity. But I couldn't act, no more than a ghost can rattle any but imaginary chains.

13

n the hotel bar at Gellért, where he chatted up everything in a skirt while chasing eight beers with eight shots
of vodka, Sven proved himself the swinish sort of man
women adore. First there was a pert blonde, but she
apparently either had taste or a husband too near to permit
an indiscretion, and edged away soon after Sven allowed
his hand casual draping over her upper thigh. Her place at
the bar was claimed by a zaftig brunette who had no such
reservations, greeting him with a sloppy-warm kiss on the
mouth. I was not near enough to hear their conversation
but guessed she was Spanish or Italian, a guest of the hotel,
and they had arranged to see each other that evening, as
two drinks after meeting they slipped out of the bar and
rode the elevator to some undetermined location, the most

logical guess being her room, where they spent the next hour and a half, again the most logical guess, fucking.

Looking disheveled if momentarily sobered, Sven returned alone to the hotel bar. He drank another beer and vodka chaser, glancing periodically at his watch. After a half hour of solitude, another woman approached. Although the dim lighting made it difficult to see clearly, she might have been as old as eighteen. When she extended her hand in shy greeting, Sven pulled her to his chest and kissed her. The girl pushed away but didn't seem displeased, until, about twenty minutes into their conversation, Sven three times took her hand and placed it on the rising promontory between his legs. Sleeping with two women in one day and sniffing a third made Sven too cocksure; the girl giggled at her first touch but panicked at the third and fled.

He spoke to no one else, communicating immediate needs to the bartender by the thump of his empty glass. He drank until he could keep his head no steadier than a buoy in high seas. Just before midnight, he pitched himself from the bar and stood several minutes contemplating the sheets of water pouring from the awning at the hotel entrance. I would have welcomed his hailing a taxi then, content to lose him rather than follow on foot through the rain. He had been fed, bathed, and drained of bodily fluids. His only destination was bed and a sated sleep. But the alcohol lent him false warmth and a misplaced trust in his coordination, and he skittered crookedly into the storm like a man chasing, catching and losing his feet. I fastened the collar of the coat around my neck and reluctantly followed.

Sven crossed the road that led to Szabadság Bridge, stumbled to the edge of the embankment, and howled insults across the Danube. Watching him was an embarrassment. He stomped in puddles, sang snatches of beer-drinking songs, and twice slipped to his knees. Few men were more deserving of death, but I hadn't the nerve or brute desire to murder him. In my imagination I could shoot, stab, hack, and chop him to bits, but my paralysis in the steam room proved me incapable of direct action. I would have preferred to be the sort of man whose actions were circumscribed neither by vestigial conscience nor by failure of nerve. The foul rain and Sven's stumbling drunk conspired to perfect circumstances. All that prevented me from murdering him on the bridge was my idiotic inability to act. I could think of no way of eliminating Sven other than killing him, but as I couldn't bring myself to the moral certainty of murder, he would remain with Monika and I would be denied both revenge and carnal pleasure. I tried to think of a way to arrange his arrest that would leave her free. Any mention of his grift would necessarily involve Monika as his partner. I felt as though I walked in a thick fog, searching for something and certain I passed within feet of it, but unable to see precisely where. Then rough outlines emerged, and I knew I had something.

Up ahead, Sven stumbled into the railing, likely about to vomit over the edge. The bridge provided no cover. To stop and pretend to enjoy the sights of Budapest in so violent a rainstorm would immediately mark me a suspicious character, so with the slightest stutter-step I continued walking across the bridge. I no longer followed Sven; rather, I followed my new idea. That my camera had been stolen posed a serious obstacle. I could borrow a camera from any one of a thousand unwary tourists, but the problems of low lighting and access remained. Perhaps I didn't need a camera to document Sven's infidelity. I could write an anonymous note to Monika, describing what I'd seen and suggesting she follow him the next time he visited

Gellért. If she caught him with another woman his murder would be unnecessary.

Though this idea involved machinations which could rapidly wheel from my control, I no longer felt completely powerless, and this cheered me so greatly that I temporarily lost track of time and place. Sven bellowed at me from the railing. His peremptory challenge caught me unaware. I hoped he was merely drunk and mindlessly belligerent. He couldn't suspect, hadn't made a single gesture or glanced my way all evening. I turned my head aside and quickened my step, hoping to slip past without being identified. I was an idiot not to realize the trap. He came at me from behind with a great springing leap. I waited for him to strike, hearing the scrape of his shoe as he launched himself, the rustle of his coat shifting in the air, the subtle changes in the pattern of rainfall as he passed through space, yet no matter how terrifyingly precise my perceptions I was powerless to dodge or break into a sprint.

As I waited, a terrified thought ricocheted through my cranium: When had he noticed someone followed, did he know who followed or was he merely aware of the fact of being followed, and if he knew precisely who followed would he be as indecisive as I regarding the necessity of murder? A paw on my shoulder whirled me around. The moment our glances struck was exquisitely horrifying. He stared at me with beer-blind aggression, his eyes filmed yellow and face a drunken blotch. Recognition gaped his mouth. He hadn't known. His life was such that I could have been any of a dozen men—victims, husbands, or cops. But Sven was more man of action than thinker, and even though I knew precisely what to expect I was the one to hesitate and not Sven. He clipped my ear with a mistimed left, and threw a fist slow and heavy at my ribs. No matter how clearly I saw it cleave through the rain, I was incapable of moving aside. The blow popped my stomach like a paper bag. I dropped to one knee, and watched his boot hurtle toward my head. My hands remained idiotically pinned in my coat pockets. Sven was too drunk to kick straight. The boot struck me in the shoulder. I struggled upright and shouted, ineffectual and outraged, "What are you doing? What the hell are you doing?"

The question brought Sven to his senses. We regarded the moment in silence, rain-soaked and adrenaline-charged, deciding to what end this incident would take us. We could have decided to step back, curse each other, and go our separate and living ways. But Sven's senses were no less murderous than instinct. His eyes closed off like a guillotine, and he threw me against the railing. He meant to kill me, and I could think of no method of stopping him until my fingers closed around an object shaped like a pen in my coat pocket. From that moment on, I don't recall how many times he hit me or where, the marks upon my body the next morning serving as better documentation than memory. I remember one hand at my throat, another grasping my coat to heave me over the edge of the railing, and the sudden look of surprise on his face as he stepped back and glanced down at my hand fisted at his stomach. A phrase in Danish escaped his lips when he reached down to touch the hole in his jacket. His eyes lifted from the blood on his finger to me, as though not understanding exactly what had happened, and when at last he knew, his stare turned outraged, as though I hadn't so much stabbed as deeply offended him by so ably demonstrating his mortality. A shudder went through him, and when he leaped at me again I stepped aside and whether I pushed or not his momentum carried him over the railing. He turned once, twice, and without a shout or cry slapped into the Danube a hundred feet below.

I can only describe my consciousness during the next ten minutes as merging either in shock or sympathy with Sven's. I don't know if I immediately left the railing or stayed to watch the river take him down. I don't know whether I saw anyone or anyone saw me. I clearly remember standing in the middle of an empty street near the opposite end of the bridge, surfacing as though from some depth, the knife still gripped in my fist. Anyone walking past would have encountered a deranged man puncturing raindrops with the tip of a knife. When I saw what I held, I dropped the knife and ran.

Some blocks later, collapsed against a doorframe to regain my breath, I realized they would search the streets near the bridge if the body was found. I had lacked the presence of mind to wipe Sven's blood from the blade or my fingerprints from the handle. I attempted to retrace my steps but in the dark and rain the streets looked disconcertingly similar. In my haste to escape I noted neither route nor landmark. It seemed as though I searched the streets for hours. As I neared the limits of endurance, I ceased to care, like someone lost in a snowstorm who wishes only the warm solace of sleep. I wandered from street to street, imagining the body had already been found and the police calculated time and drift to place his fall from Szabadság Bridge. Perhaps Sven had not died at all and was recounting to police the story of how I had stalked and attempted to murder him. Within hours or minutes every cop in Budapest would have my description. Whether guided by the unconscious mind or blind luck, I stumbled over the knife where it lay in the gutter, kicking it once before recognizing the search had ended. Seeing the knife, its blade extended and washed free of blood by the rain, I felt unaccountably ill and dropped to my hands and knees. Instead of vomit, a single anguished cry escaped me. I retracted the blade and ran.

Though I had been forced into Sven's murder and had not committed it willingly, I needed to demonstrate to myself that I was capable of tidying up after the crime. The Danube was wide and deep and fast-flowing, the only terrain where a complete search would be impossible. The authorities might correctly guess Sven had been killed and dumped from one of the bridges, and speculate the murderer had chucked the knife over the bridge. They wouldn't have reason or resources to search more than a hundred yards up- and downriver. I ran along the embankment, conscious that dawn spilled tints of red along the eastern horizon, and when I neared the midpoint between Szabadság and Erzsébet bridges I threw the knife with all my strength into the Danube.

The doorman had yet to report to work and no one waited behind the desk at the Erzsébet hotel when I returned. I encountered no one in the elevator, and the fourth floor hall was empty. I entered my room wanting a change of clothes and remembered that my possessions remained in the small pension I'd rented before finding Monika. In the bathroom, I glanced in the mirror and was immediately overwhelmed by nausea. Kneeling over the toilet, it seemed my entire being exploded from my mouth. When nothing remained in my gut save knots of intestine, I stripped and ran the shower. Even beneath steaming water I shivered uncontrollably. My joints felt pricked by red hot pins. Thoughts became as difficult to grasp as bits of broken shell in egg white.

I steadied myself on the sink and saw Sven turn once, twice in the air, before finally I blacked out.

Some hours later, I awoke wound in sheets, eyes pinned shut by a bright blue sky. Several half-conscious minutes slipped past before I recognized that I lived. The events of the previous day strayed into memory like unwelcome guests who, no matter how often I tried to shoo them out, loudly insisted on being served: Monika; Helmut; the attendants at the spa; the pert blonde, zaftig brunette, and young girl from the hotel bar. I turned my back and buried my head beneath the pillow. Sven was the most obstreperous guest of all, clamoring at me like a ghost. I unwound myself from the sheet and sat up. The digital clock on the nightstand clicked 9 A.M. I dialed room service for coffee and a sandwich. It seemed I hadn't slept more than a few hours.

In the bathroom I found my clothes neatly hanging dry over the shower curtain rod. Unsettled by the presence of the mirror above the sink, I turned on the television and paced the room, but couldn't screen my mind from images and snatches of sound from the night before. Though I commanded memory away, not to remember was dangerous. The problem of what to do next couldn't be decided until I remembered exactly what I'd done. I might have forgotten an important detail which if not corrected that morning would hang me. I splashed cold water on my face and, leaning over the sink, willed myself to reconstruct the events leading to and extending past Sven's death. Contrary to expectation, as the night unreeled its comedy and horror, the scenes filled me with more pride than revulsion. Admittedly, I had been unable to act in the Turkish bath, but it was just possible that instinct had held me back. If I had killed him there, I would have been arrested. Sven's death couldn't have been better planned. He attacked me. I killed him. Self-defense, even if I had wanted to kill him all along. I could quibble at not having the courage or determination to act until my life was threatened, but in the end I had acted, and decisively. I lifted my head out of the sink and examined my unshaven face in the mirror, looking for outward signs of an inward change I was certain had transpired. It astonished me to realize that whenever I saw that face in the mirror or in photographs I would be looking into the face of a killer. The notion made me laugh so hard I clutched the sides of the sink for support. Me! A killer! I had completely reinvented myself. I was the freest man on earth.

At the sound of light knocking I slung myself into the bathrobe hanging from a peg on the door and went to answer. Room service, as I expected. A small man with a curiously thin mustache stood anxiously behind a waiter balancing a tray on one palm.

"I am happy to see you are feeling better, Mr. Miller," the little mustached man said, remaining in the hall as the waiter entered the room to set his tray on the nightstand.

I must have allowed my face an expression of bewilderment, as he stepped timidly across the threshold and announced, "We were all quite worried, you see, because yesterday morning the maid found you on the floor and helped you into bed."

"Yesterday?" I asked.

"We were afraid you were very ill, and were going to send for a doctor. You said you didn't need one, that you felt fine, but still, one never knows."

"But yesterday?" I repeated.

"You don't remember?"

Of course I didn't remember. I had slept over twenty-four hours. Sven could have been fished from the Danube. Monika could have gone to identify the body and now be accompanying it back to Copenhagen. I could have lost her. I could have killed for nothing.

The little mustached man said, "Just as I feared. You were really ill. Would you like to see a doctor?"

The waiter brushed past with an empty tray and palm.

"I wonder if you might know a charming Danish girl staying in this hotel, someone I met yesterday"—here I weakly laughed—"day before yesterday, I mean. Do you know whether she's checked out or not?"

"She's still here." He smiled oddly, as though understanding something that had previously puzzled him, and said, "She checked the desk for messages every hour yesterday. Should I tell her you asked?"

I had been an idiot to mention that I'd met her. If she knew I stayed in the same hotel, she might suspect a link between my appearance and Sven's disappearance. I told the manager that I could not possibly be the one from whom she waited to hear. He said he understood and, again cheering my return to health, left me to my coffee and sandwich.

14

A plan spun out of me that morning as perfectly structured as a scenario by Hitchcock, but had I not become a new man two nights before, I doubt I could have summoned the courage and endurance to play the part the plan required. Early that afternoon, when Monika left her hotel room, I followed. By then I knew her habits well enough to realize by the streets chosen that she intended coffee and pastries at Gerbeaud, and sprinted through alley and side street to seat myself comfortably before she arrived. I had almost forgotten the bullet-through-the-throat effect her beauty could have on me when she swept through the door, fetchingly veiled behind Biagiotti sunglasses and a swirl of black hair. She looked for no one that afternoon, striding through the crowd to rendezvous with the pastry counter. Her sweet tooth gave me time to remind myself, as she deliberated between this chocolate and that strawberry cream torte, that though I desired her I was not in love, and this important distinction made her little different from the many women with whom I'd enjoyed my illicit and erotic amusements. I would not allow myself the sudden sweats and lapses in consciousness she previously had aroused in me. I would not go love-simple in her presence. When, tray in hand, she turned to search out a free table, I jumped from my chair and in mock-astonished voice shouted her name.

Monika stood still as if confronted by a mad dog. I waved energetically and grinned. Nothing in my demeanor suggested I suspected her of anything criminal. Indeed, I must have seemed to bystanders the typical young American, an idiotically friendly type who resembles in human form a Labrador puppy on amphetamines. I bounded across the room, clutching the grin in my teeth.

"My God Monika I can't believe meeting you here what an incredible coincidence I was just digging into my torte when I looked up and it was really you after that strange brother of yours and that wild last night in Prague and me thinking I'd never see you again you must sit down at my table and tell me how are you?"

A trembling of her tray was the only evidence Monika gave of not being turned into a pillar of salt. To think I had shocked her into a mineral state gave me immense but false pleasure. I had the feeling of being carefully watched from behind the impenetrable dark of her Biagiottis. As I spoke she took cues from my behavior, preparing a role to suit what she thought I knew and wanted. She would have complained loudly in German if necessary, knowing I didn't understand that language and wouldn't realize what was happening until the café manager's restraining arm allowed her escape. It must have been difficult for her to believe that anyone could be as gullible, as blind, as stupidly innocent as I pretended to be. She could not choose the correct role without knowing what scene we were to play, and the character I portrayed was at odds with what she thought she knew about me. I didn't wonder at her hesitation. When at last she moved and spoke, it was perfect, as I expected it to be. She lowered her sunglasses so that I might see the surprise, the innocence, the wonder in her green eyes as she asked, "Is that really you?"

I wanted to applaud; instead, I offered her a chair at my table. She had little choice but to accept. The clatter of dishes and forks occupied us for a moment, and when her pastries were well arranged I allowed the moment to stretch into uncomfortable silence.

"You got my postcard?" she asked.

"You don't have to explain. I know everything," I said.

Calculations turned behind the faux innocence in her eyes. She gripped her fork like a thing of defense. It occurred to her that I might not be as stupid as I seemed, that I played an end game of which she was but dimly aware. The moment her suspicion veered toward the explicit, I leaned earnestly across the table and said, "It was your brother, right? He wouldn't let you go. He made fine speeches about you being free to live your own life, but in the end he made that life unbearable unless you did exactly what he wanted. Am I right?"

Monika looked away, down at her desserts, away again, and by the time she looked at me again, her eyes had welled with tears. A delicious shiver rippled my backbone. Bergman couldn't have performed better. "A terrible night. Sven was a monster. I never saw him so angry. We fought on the sidewalk outside. It seemed like hours. He wouldn't let me go with you. Threatened to hurt you. Sometimes he can be so violent. He frightens me. So I—" A tear escaped and slid down her cheek. She caught it with her little finger and absently dissolved it on her tongue. "I promised not to go away with you. Then we went back into the club, but—"

"I was gone," I said.

The character of her gaze turned critical again, as she tried to decide whether I anticipated her story through belief or cynicism.

"Would you believe it, one of those Gypsies put something in my drink, a Mickey Finn they call it in English, or knockout drops. I woke up the next morning in an alley. They stole everything. Even took my keys and robbed my apartment."

Monika shook her head as though I said something incredible. "No," she said. "I can't believe it. It's all my fault. I took you there."

"The police were no help at all, of course."

"What did they say?" Asked in tones of casual interest.

"You'll laugh at this one. They actually suggested you might have had something to do with it."

Monika shifted in her chair. I noticed but did not remark that most people naturally position their chairs at right angles to the table at which they sit. Monika had set her chair askew and, with her recent shift in position, sat with her knees only a few degrees off a direct line to the door. I chattered away as though empty-headed.

"I explained that you were incapable of such a thing, that we were in love and going away together. Now Sven maybe, but even he couldn't possibly do something like that, which is what I told the police. Impossible. Out of the question. It didn't help that you disappeared that night, and when I told the police you were staying at Hotel Paříž, they found no record of you ever being there."

"But we were there," Monika insisted.

I knew better, but said, "I'm sure you were."

"What name did they look for?"

A dangerous question to a connoisseur of combs, condoms, passports, and other artifacts of women's purses. "I realized when they asked of course I didn't know your last name, so I told them Monika and then something Danish."

"I registered using my Czech name."

"I knew it would be something like that. And they were looking for a Danish couple, so of course."

"Yes," she said.

My hands fumbled above the table as though spilling water. I remarked, with happily discovered double entendre, "They could look forever and not find you."

Monika grabbed both my hands. I hadn't expected that. I hadn't expected her to touch me. She held me, trembling in her gaze, until she knew I saw in her eyes the sincerity of a wronged soul and asked, "Did you really think I would rob you?"

"Me? No. The police. I tried to tell the police that. But they ask. Suspicious, you know. This and that. Questions. I told them—never." My face flushed hot and red. I heard myself speak sentences breaking up like ice. I could think only with the severest concentration. I said, "But you should have said something. Called. Written. Anything. I was lost."

"I tried to write. A hundred times I tried to write. But what could I say? That I wanted to go away with you, but? But what? I'd start, and then I'd tear it up. My English wasn't good enough. I couldn't admit to you what happened. In English or Danish. That Sven wouldn't allow it. That I'm a complete coward."

The bit about wanting to write I half remembered from a dozen different movies. I knew this scene. Couldn't allow Monika to steal it from me. With her hands touching me, I couldn't think. A gesture was needed. Something dramatic. I flattened the palms against the sides of my head. I started to breathe again. Rhythm and timing were all. Think over-the-shoulder close-ups. Think Frederic March to Greta Garbo.

INTERIOR—GERBEAUD CAFE, BUDAPEST—DAY
A grand fin-de-siècle café. High wooden ceilings. Gilt trim. Central European types huddle over frothing cups of cappuccino and hot chocolate. In the corner, Nix and Monika stare into each other's eyes as though the world is about to end.

> NIX
> You think I didn't know that? You think I didn't feel exactly what you were going through? I know nothing about you, not your age or the name on your passport, but I know you better than anyone in the world. I know you only as someone who loves can know.

CUT TO MONIKA, looking wounded as cut glass. Life is too short, too complicated, too doomed.

> MONIKA
> It didn't work out. We tried, but it didn't.

ON NIX. His eyes burn with passion and destiny.

> NIX
> What happened before doesn't matter. We found each other again. We have a second chance. I'll tell Sven how we feel. That we love each other.

> MONIKA
> He'll hurt you.

NIX

That's a risk I'm willing to take.

MONIKA

What we had together was perfect. A perfect moment
in time. But that moment is gone.

NIX

You can't deny your feelings.

MONIKA

But I must!

NIX

Don't go!

MONIKA

It's over!

Monika rushes for the door but turns at the threshold for a farewell look—

ON NIX, bravely rising from the table.

NIX
(voice choking)

Promise me. We'll always have Prague.

That last line was untouchable. I waited through several
moments of stunned silence, thinking she might come up
with a rejoinder, but nothing can follow a line like that. She
wisely underplayed it, dipping her head in silent assent, then
whirled for the door in a spark of heels. I wanted her to
think me an idiot, to think I loved her, to think she could
get away, yet to feel an inchoate dread that I was not an
idiot, that I did not love her, and that she could never escape. I chased the last of my torte around the dish, wiped
my mouth, and left the café.

Catching up to Monika did not worry me. I knew where she would go, if not at that moment, then soon enough. If she could not be certain of my intentions, she would hurry to her hotel and, leaving a message at the desk for Sven, pack her bags for another hotel or perhaps another country. I anticipated her route from café to hotel and watched the crowds for her brisk strides, timing it to pop out of an alley at the exact moment she crossed it on her return. Even then, Monika clipped by without stopping, forcing me to trot beside her as I exclaimed, "What a coincidence. Don't tell me you're staying somewhere nearby?"

Monika backed toward the street, toes arching, keeping me in front of her like something that could turn on her at any moment. Her voice threatened and was threatened. "Are you following me?"

"What a crazy idea!"

"I said it's over. I can't see you again."

"It's fate, Monika. We belong together."

For a moment, she believed me—not that we belonged together but that I was convinced of it. For a moment, I think Monika pitied me. She would have turned and run had she not believed I might chase after like a faithful dog. Instead, she did what any decent human being does when followed by a likable dog that needs to be discouraged. She said, "We don't belong together. You're an idiot. Blind. Stupid. I don't want you. Do you understand now?"

"Of course I understand." I smiled, amiable, dense, and determined. I took a few friendly steps forward.

Monika shouted, "I don't want you following me!"

People slowed as they passed. One idiot-gallant could step up and ruin the scene. I broke out of character—or, rather, into my true character. I grabbed her by the elbow and said, "Maybe you'd like the police following you instead?"

Monika stood very still, not daring to move or speak. She knew then and finally that I was dangerous. I heard very little conviction in her voice when she said, "Why should I be afraid of the police?"

"You have no idea how well I know you. I have an advantage, because you know almost nothing about me. Nothing true, at any rate. But I won't turn you in, at least not now. I have a business proposition for you."

"What kind of business?"

"The same kind of business you're in now."

"I don't know what you're talking about."

"You're a smart girl. You'll figure it out," I said, and instructed her to meet me that night on the quay leading to the Chain Bridge.

"If Sven learns I'm meeting you, I mean if he finds out you're following me, he'll hurt you."

"You can tell him about me or not. It won't make any difference."

When I let go of her arm she flashed a smile as though she just won something. I knew her. I knew what she was thinking. I dipped my hand into my coat pocket, let show just the corner of a small thin green book, and said, "If you're thinking you won't show up tonight, if you're thinking you might try to leave Budapest, leave the country, check your purse before the train station."

I had taken the precaution at Gerbeaud when she had been distracted by my seeming innocence. Monika dug to the bottom of her purse with the ferociousness of a feral animal looking for a bone. Her passport wasn't there. I had stolen it.

She said, "Bastard!" Then a few other words in Danish, which I didn't need to understand precisely.

I said, "Yes, I am," and walked away.

15

After leaving Monika I felt the triumph of an actor fresh from a successful performance and the insecurity of that same actor in fearing the magic will fail to return for the next. My anxiety was general and overwhelming, though it assumed the guise of particular terrors, which flitted promiscuously from one to the next. The idea of having sex with her terrified. The notion that she carried a second passport and at that very moment rode the elevator to the checkout desk so terrorized me that I hailed a taxi and returned to the hotel. That she had not checked out failed to console me, and I paced about the lobby until, exasperated with my insecurities, I fled to the street, resigned that she would appear with her bags the moment I had gone but not one second before.

Choked by paranoia, I crossed the river and struggled up Gellért Hill until the city was safely distant below, the rumble of traffic and river fading to a single note. Since my first conscious moment I have faced sudden and unexplainable paroxysms of nerves. My throat swells and lungs constrict; the air turns to liquid, and my bronchial tube to a crimped straw. Consciousness diminishes to a white noise not unlike a television channel tuned to no specific signal. I sat very still, drew deep, even breaths, silently counted, and visualized the numbers as I sounded them in my head. When I was small, a child psychologist suggested that my anxieties were little monsters who couldn't breathe if I didn't think about them and thus went to sleep. I still thought of my anxieties in this way, and relaxation as suffocating the little monsters. I didn't need a fully conceptualized plan when I met Monika that night, and she would show as certain as I held her passport. With Sven's disappearance, she had no money and few resources. True to Hollywood form, all I needed was a one-line concept that would sell itself. A dark serenity of spirit settled over me. I was certain I'd found a way of winning Monika and defying my father both.

Monika looked as though she had prepared a role of her own coming up the quay that night, simply but elegantly dressed in flowing bone- and ash-checked coat, eyes cloaked in sunglasses even at that post-crepuscular hour. I watched from behind my familiar screen of bushes and noted the gestures of agitation in her pocket-clenched hands and brisk stride. She hesitated at the railing where we were to meet, turned once to scan the quay, and, torn between impatience for my arrival and the need to conceal her impatience, wheeled toward the Chain Bridge. When deaf to the clip of her heels, I crossed the quay to the railing. I didn't mind allowing her to see me waiting if I knew she waited also. A few hundred feet up the quay, ash and bone checks flashed beneath lamplight. I propped my elbows on the railing and watched the river, marveling at the disciplined hurry of her approach, as though she had not been waiting at all but arrived just now and late. I thought, Sam Spade to Brigid O'Shaughnessy in *The Maltese Falcon*. I thought, Humphrey Bogart.

"Sven is waiting for me," she said, pulling black-gloved hands from coat pockets.

"Where?" I asked, aware I inappropriately grinned.

"Somewhere close enough to hear if I shout."

I did not allow myself to contemplate that her lie might have unintended accuracy. Forty-eight hours of drift would have carried him well past our spot on the quay, possibly out of Budapest, though bodies are notorious for clinging to branches, rocks, and bridge abutments as though willing beyond death to be found. I must pretend it never happened, that Sven indeed waited, vertical and murderous, a few yards distant. I asked, "What does Sven think of our meeting?"

"He wants to take back my passport."

"How does he propose to do that?"

"Beat it out of you."

"I'm happy to hear he hasn't changed."

"You have no idea how violent my brother is."

"I have no idea he's your brother."

She pulled a pack of Gitane Blondes from her coat pocket and cupped her hands to light one.

I said, "Since when did you start smoking?"

"I've always smoked. Just not around marks."

"Nervous about something?"

"Wouldn't you be, someone threatens you?"

♥ 163

"I thought Sven threatened me. Something about a beating, you said."

"Maybe you're too stupid to be scared."

"How long has Sven been your brother?"

"Half brother. I told you the story."

"You remember the afternoon I met you, in the café at Obecní Dům, when I left to attend a meeting?"

"Why would I want to remember something so unimportant?"

"I didn't have a meeting."

A contemptuous spear of smoke glanced off my shoulder. She said, "So. What."

"I followed you instead."

I was acutely aware that she now listened, trying to remember: Where had she gone, what had she done?

"Not to the Hotel Paříž, where of course you never stayed, but to the Merkur, the cheap, no-star, shabby little Merkur."

"What were you hoping to find out?"

"Nothing. It's a game I like to play."

"I've met some pathetic men in my life."

"I bet you have."

"I've had this feeling lately of being watched. It's what you like to do, isn't it? You like to watch?"

And what of it? Artists are voyeurs.

I said, "I like to steal."

Monika flicked her cigarette between my feet. I let it burn. She said, "What do you steal, other than ladies' passports?"

"The same things you steal. The difference is I don't steal for money. I steal for fun."

"Jobs are easy enough to find and the pay is steadier. Don't pretend you know anything about why I do what I do."

"Do you still insist Sven is your brother?"

"Half brother."

She reached into her coat pocket for a knife, a gun. I caught her wrist and held it, asked, "What's it like to fuck your half brother?"

Monika jerked her head aside. She said, "I wouldn't know."

"I followed you. I heard through the door."

"He's not my half brother."

I let go of her wrist. Her palm cupped the pack of Gitanes. I watched her hands shake when she tried to light a cigarette. I took the lighter and lit the cigarette for her. She said, "I could have screamed, you know."

"Why didn't you?"

"Maybe I don't want Sven to hurt you. Maybe I'm curious. How long have you been in Budapest, looking for me?"

A disingenuous question, no less so for the seeming innocence of her asking. I said, "I looked in your purse the day I met you. Saw the train ticket, a receipt from Gerbeaud's, figured you for a regular. Arrived this morning."

"I won't sleep with you, if that's what you want."

I laughed because I did want to sleep with her; I laughed to wound her vanity. Bogart would say, *You'll sleep with me baby and like it if I tell you to.* I said, "Don't flatter yourself."

"What do you want?"

I told her. Not the truth, which she already knew despite my denial, but the concept through which I hoped to obtain her. I said, "Listen carefully to what I'm about to say: *There are no checks in Czechoslovakia.*"

Monika stared at me as though I'd just told her that the rain in Spain falls mainly in the plain. The beauty of the concept was the double entendre, which she failed to grasp until I carefully explained it to her. She was too desperate not to listen. The Helmut thing hadn't worked out. Sven had disappeared two days before. She stayed in a hotel room costing $100 a night. They had quarreled violently the day he disappeared. She knew him well enough to suspect he'd abandoned her for a few days of carnal frolic. She wouldn't mind punishing him with a new arrangement on his return. My fate didn't concern her. Sven would either go along for the money or kill me. She didn't stand to lose much either way. He might beat her, but then they'd make love and everything would be the way it was before. My idea sounded lucrative enough, and I avoided details which might reveal the sketchiness of my plans. Sven was officially alive and murderous, and I carefully included him in the plot, though the starring roles went to Monika and myself. She had a talent for performance but not plotting, and Sven had been a creature of desire and the moment, so even the bare concept I presented to her on the quay was like hearing Spielberg. She agreed to discuss the matter with him but wouldn't promise agreement. I could have been a gentleman and accepted her equivocations, but instinct suggested that Monika admired bastards. I said if she and Sven decided to reject my offer, she would be required to return the money and equipment they had stolen from me. If they decided not to participate in my plan and couldn't return the money, she could retrieve her passport from the Czech police, who might have a few embarrassing questions for her.

"You're forcing me then," she said.

It was a lesson I'd learned game-playing among the tourists in Prague. To have no choice was to act without responsibility, without guilt. Freed from the responsibility of choice, she could act with abandon. This was the look I saw in her eyes, of blaming circumstance for doing something secretly she wanted.

"You can always choose to go to jail," I said.

* * *

Sven officially disappeared the next day. The scene had been horrible, she wept when we met in her room. Sven had become irrationally angry when she suggested they at least temporarily accept my proposal. It had begun with shouting. *If that's how you feel. I knew you liked him in Prague. A cozy threesome. I'll kill the bastard before I ever*—that sort of thing. Then he started to hit her. He had thrown her against the wall and knocked over the mirror. She pointed to it on the floor, propped undamaged against the bureau, as though my seeing it would be the same as witnessing the act that knocked it from the wall. I nodded and cooed, perfectly trained to be a sympathetic listener. Hadn't I heard a dozen women painstakingly recount the exact moment they must have lost their wallet, unaware I had stolen it minutes before? Sven had been terrible. A wild beast. The shouting and crashing grew so loud the hotel manager had been forced to bang on the door to shut them up. Sven had stormed out of the room, his belongings packed into a single bag. When he left, he naturally neglected to pay the hotel bill, and would I be kind enough to take care of it?

The total stretched the limit on my last credit card. Monika's return ticket to Prague claimed the last of my ready cash. That left nothing but a dwindling reserve of counterfeit bills between me and the abject poverty of a phone call to my father, who would make my untimely return a condition of any release of funds. Money concerns humiliated the aristocrat in me, using that word in the American sense of being born from money, even used-car money such as mine. It seemed I was rapidly accomplishing nearly everything I had planned and was dangerously close to having nothing. While Monika slept on the train, I paced the corridor, the din of wheels on track as effective a stimulant as a jolt of caffeine.

Dark shapes of Central European countryside scrolled across the window. One idea jutted into the next until the rudiments of a script emerged. My adventure in Prague and incipient affair with Monika would come to a halt without a quick financial success, and I hoped the little drama I planned would bring just that.

We arrived at the main train station just after 6 A.M., Monika fuzzy with sleep and content to be led to my apartment, where she immediately slipped into my bed and a deep slumber. We hadn't spoken on the train, and when awake she seemed on the verge of tears for reasons unconnected to the moment. We hadn't talked about the deeper meanings of her coming to Prague, other than the financial considerations of a partnership. I knew she mourned Sven, her accompanying me admission that he had abandoned her. I also knew that unless I took care, she would hate me for being her only alternative to his abandonment. I watched her sleep for some time, astonished by the childlike innocence of her face when not animated by the devious turns of consciousness. The sinuous links of thighs and hips, the crescent of belly and carved whorl of navel, the delicate clasp of wrist bones and fingers thinly curved like bracelets: I absorbed her perfections as she slept, like a man who has acquired after hardship a great treasure, which he hesitates to tarnish by touching. Soon, not even the beauty of her on my bed could keep me awake. I slept on the floor.

16

n those first few years after the revolution of 1989, Prague had yet to become money-friendly. With the notable exception of public transportation, nothing and no one worked. There were few shops and fewer goods. Restaurants served food no more sophisticated than pork and dumplings, offered everywhere for less than two dollars a meal. Hotel rooms were criminally overpriced, but beyond that it was impossible to spend money because there was nothing to buy. The only expendable not in short supply was beer. What little money tourists needed they changed at hotels or the State travel agency, where English was spoken, or at banks, where it was not. Money was an alien concept to Czech society. None of the modern technologies for handling it existed east of Germany. When money didn't exist independent of the State and crime was nearly nonexistent, the lack of mechanisms to transfer it safely posed few problems. Credit cards were strictly a foreign phenomenon. The biggest joke of all: There were no checks in Czechoslovakia. It was this weakness in the new capitalism of the East I decided to exploit, happy at the irony of having been given the idea by Inspector Petr Zima the afternoon he threatened to arrest me for robbing tourists.

The man I selected for my first project had the ample, ruddy flesh characteristic of a pork, dumpling, and beer diet. I had noticed him the month before, hovering behind two employees in his newly opened money-changing booth on the edge of Staroměstské náměstí. Every tourist visiting Prague came to the famous medieval clockworks in the tower of the old town hall, and the crowds that gathered at the turn of every hour to gape at the pirouette of clock characters passed his cashiers either coming or going. I speculated he was the son of a Communist Party official who had abused the public trust. Most of the first Czech entrepreneurs were Communists or their relatives, as the rumor went, because the Communists had so long looted the country, they were the only ones with any money.

During my first few days of reconnaissance, I loitered among the tourists, baseball-capped and map in hand, observing his business and habits. Monika slept late each morning, content to wake just long enough to eat and wander the city before returning to bed and sleep. We said little to each other. Silence seemed appropriate to this in-between period, when she worked through the emotional process of leaving Sven and joining me. The Czech, who had the unpronounceable name of Zdeněk, appeared a man of strict habits. Every morning at eight thirty he approached

Staroměstksé náměstí from Melantrichova Street, unlocked the door to the booth, and disappeared into a room hidden from view. At nine forty-five the employees arrived, one young man and one young woman, dressed in matching white and blue. At five minutes before ten, Zdeněk left the change booth carrying a brown satchel and walked up Melantrichova to the bank on Na Příkopě, less than a mile distant. I followed him into the bank on the pretense of needing to change money. He walked to the teller at the far end of the counter. Rainbow bundles of notes flashed across the counter. I glanced into the nearest cage, where another teller sat surrounded by money stacked on the floor by nationality and denomination. Not a single computer in sight. She worked sums on a calculator and scratch pad.

Zdeněk's banking required about half an hour each morning. When finished, he ran various business and personal errands of little interest to me. He returned to his change booth at 2:30 P.M., disappeared again into the back room, and reemerged at three forty-five, bearing his satchel along the now-familiar route to the bank on Na Příkopě. I considered borrowing a motorcycle to snare the bag as he walked, but discounted the idea as not sufficiently clever and, as I had never driven a motorcycle before, too risky. My attention instead focused on the hours between 4 and 8 P.M. The banks closed at four, reducing his competition to hotels and black market money changers. Zdeněk's business doubled to about thirty customers an hour, most changing middling sums to the nonconvertible Czech crown. At eight the stainless steel shutters raked down. He was always careful at that hour to glance warily about when locking up, but he was well in public view and I doubt anyone would have tried to rob him there. From habit he dropped his keys into the outside left pocket of his rose suit coat. He carried nothing in his hands. Most evenings he walked briskly to Marketa's New York Famous Bar, where he stopped to chat up the proprietor and enjoy a quiet drink before departing in a 300 series BMW parked nearby.

When secure in my plans, I brought Monika along to share my observations. Though she had done little the past three days except sleep, she seemed listless, hollowed out. The details of timing and money bored her. Prague bored her. I bored her. Only when I began to discuss her role in the drama did interest spark her glance. What she would wear, the story she would use to mislead him about her identity—the more I explained the details of her performance the more animated she became, as if role and character expanded within her absences to give purpose to her being. The only bit of action at which she balked was the acquisition of his keys.

"I'm not a pickpocket," she said.

"Would you prefer I knock him over the head, like Sven?"

This led to a brief but fierce argument regarding the relative merits of Sven and myself, in which I did not compare favorably. I bit my tongue. It's bad luck to speak ill of the dead. When we returned to my apartment, I donned a sport coat and suggested, "I'm Zdeněk. My keys are in the left pocket of my sport coat. How are you going to get them out?"

Monika slumped on the couch, lit a cigarette, said, "I don't know." She was smoking heavily then, fouling the air of my apartment with a smokestack stream of nicotine and tar. A vile habit, but as one of Prague's few nonsmokers, indeed with all of Europe addicted to smoking, I hadn't the same rights as nonsmokers in California and silently suffered the minutes, hours, and days subtracted from my life with each breath of secondhand smoke. I sat in a chair across the room and focused my entire attention on Monika, watching and waiting, a technique I learned from another director in handling temperamental actresses.

"What are you looking at?" Monika said, annoyed.

"I'm just waiting for you, babe. We can sit here and sulk or we can go to work. Your choice." His words exactly, which I parroted, down to the clipped syllables.

Monika stubbed out her cigarette, said, "You can be a real asshole sometimes."

"I'll make a deal with you."

"What."

"You stop being a bitch, I'll stop being an asshole."

Monika flicked her stub at me with a sexually explicit epithet. For a moment, I wanted to hit her. But I kept my temper, marveling how completely she lost hers. I don't remember everything she called me in the following outburst. The general thrust was regret at having come to Prague with me. I stared dispassionately at the ceiling, ignoring the abuse she hurled, even staging at one point a stifled yawn, which infuriated her to tears. When her rage blew itself out, I asked if she had finished and received a contrite affirmative nod.

"Let me see your hand," I demanded.

She proffered it, compliant as a child. I demonstrated how she must flatten her palm and feel with the very tips of her fingers, as though each fingernail contained an eye guiding her way. Monika was a natural talent. Long and slender, her fingers quickly learned a touch so light even I could have been picked at an unguarded moment; by that evening I had her picking the threads from my coat pocket without disturbing the cloth.

Nothing in Marketa's New York Famous Bar was from New York, nor was it famous to any but the nouveau riche, small businessmen, and fledgling mafiosi frequenting it. Marketa herself was in her mid-twenties, attractive and single, and reigned over her small kingdom with the majesty of a spoiled princess. The bar was too intimate to allow my direct observation; I consigned myself to waiting in a darkened doorway across the street, where I witnessed Monika's arrival at a quarter to nine. She wore a short black cocktail dress and black stockings beneath her flowing bone-and-ash checked coat. Her hair was windblown and her lips an invitational shade of red. When she removed her coat, I imagined every male eye in the bar dilated in response to a sudden release of testosterone.

Zdeněk arrived punctually at nine. A few minutes later, raindrops sparked through bright circles of streetlight. I huddled deeper inside the doorway, deflected the curiosity of a passing drunk, counted trams wheeling toward the main square. I had instructed Monika to play the role of tourist whose boyfriend is later to join her, but who might allow herself the pleasure of a brief affair before his arrival. I much preferred the role of a jealous boyfriend, arriving early if necessary, than to repeat Sven's tiresome role of perverted brother. The plan called for a few minutes of suggestive conversation, the promise of a dinner date, and a quick exit. Though I was confident she could play the role to perfection, her performance was beyond directorial control. She could point me out in the shadows, claim I was an unwanted suitor hounding her, convince Zdeněk to hire a couple of mafiosi to waltz me into the Vltava River. Waiting was unbearable. Standing in any kind of line can inspire intolerable anxiety even on my good days. Fifteen minutes passed the deadline, then a half hour. The idea had been to tantalize but not pick his keys until the following evening. Sixty-five minutes late she stepped out of the bar, not alone as we had agreed, but arm in arm with Zdeněk, who trundled her into his waiting BMW and drove off before I had the wits to hail a taxi.

I walked alone to my apartment, the usual male nightmares tormenting my imagination. He somehow discovered our plan and at that moment Monika was subject to police grilling. He kidnapped her. She had been swept into uncontrollable passion and fucked him in the back of his BMW. She fucked him just to spite me. I had survived the worst of the terrors by the time she swept in, just past one in the morning. She would hate me for weakness if she knew the state I'd been in, so I limited my criticism to a simple observation.

"You didn't follow the plan," I said.

Monika threw her coat onto the bed and filled a glass from the water bottle. I concentrated, tried to remove the petulance from my voice, said, "If you didn't like the plan, you should have mentioned it earlier, saved me a long wait in the rain."

"I liked the plan," Monika said. Water glistened on her upper lip when she pulled the glass from her mouth. I guessed she'd been drinking. She seemed oddly exuberant but not drunk, as though high on some other undefined substance. Adrenaline, perhaps.

"If you liked the plan, why didn't you follow it?"

"Nix, you should relax. You take everything far too seriously."

When Monika said my name, an intimate shudder went through me. She had never called me by name before; so what if a critique of my character followed? "I'm relaxed," I lied. "I just want to know why you didn't follow the plan."

"Zdeněk doesn't always keep his keys in the pocket of his sport coat. Do we have any wine? I need a drink."

I pulled a bottle of white out of the refrigerator and poured two glasses. Monika bolted hers and poured another. I said, "Where does he put them, then?"

"Put your keys in your front pants pocket," she ordered.

"You can't pick the keys from his front pocket. Impossible."

She stared at my trousers. "That's where you keep yours, isn't it? That's where most men keep their keys." She set her drink on the dining-room table and stared at me with disconcerting directness. I glanced away. Had I not become accustomed to her indifference, I would have mistaken her expression as sexual. She traced her fingers over the outline of keys in my trouser pocket. I stood as still as possible, aware that one limb involuntarily moved. No doubt she was aware of my discomfort. Her hand slipped deftly into my pocket and probed the jagged teeth and smooth ring and something adjacent grown equally hard.

"Those are not my keys," I said.

"I suppose not," she answered.

I ground my teeth together, involuntarily pressed my hips forward, said, "You're trying to distract me."

"I know you've been frustrated, baby." She ran the tip of her nail from root to crown and back again. "Is this what you want me to do? Like this?" I reached to touch her. "You can't touch me," she commanded, and clasped my hands behind my back to continue unimpeded her leisurely explorations. "Sven got turned on when I went out with other men. Did it turn you on tonight?"

I opened my mouth to say I thought jealousy a perverse route to eroticism, but the naughty girl in her voice suggested that she spoke in the character of her own sexual desires. I tried to remember the night we had danced at Club Ubiquity, and whether my fulfillment had been her foreplay, but bright lights strobed behind my tightly shut eyelids, and breathing to the rhythm of her hands I focused on a concentration of genital pressure which blotted out my thoughts altogether.

Her laughter jerked my eyes open again.

"What is it?" I blurted.

"Your face." She laughed.

"What about it?"

"You look so ridiculous."

"What?"

"Like you're trying to carry a full bucket of water upstairs, without spilling a drop."

Again, I wanted to hit her. She saw that I wanted to hit her and stepped back, eyes gleefully luminous. She wanted me to want to hit her. I'd never hit a woman before. I could lie, cheat, steal, and sleep around but I had never allowed myself to strike a woman in anger. In Southern California's culture of isms—capitalism, feminism, neo-Puritanism, and New Age spiritualism—hitting a woman is the ultimate taboo. What I'd witnessed with Sven proved she liked things rough. Maybe I wouldn't have to hit her. Maybe all I needed was to grab her forcefully and she'd melt, all coos and kisses. I crossed the room in three great strides, cut off her exit to the front door, and wrapped one arm around her waist.

A gap occurs in this narrative commensurate with the narrator's consciousness. A jump cut, if you will, or a cut to black and slow fade-in. I sat on the floor, staring at cigarette butts scattered along the carpet. I chastised my housekeeping habits and reached to pluck the nearest one. Pain returned me to my senses. I recalled a flash of movement to my left and then nothing. The ashtray that felled me lay upended at my feet. I distinctly remember quipping that I always knew smoking was bad for my health, but a misfiring chain of synapses between brain and tongue reduced the sentence to an inarticulate mumble.

"Missing something?" Monika asked.

She pinched my key ring in two fingers as though dangling a used condom. "Don't ever confuse yourself with Sven," she advised. "I don't know yet if you're smart or just a bullshit artist, but one thing I know, you're not the man Sven is. If you play the game his way, you'll lose."

I said, "I'm very sleepy. I'm going to sleep now," and crawled toward the bed.

Danish and English invective advised me that I wasn't sleeping in the bed, she was sleeping in the bed, and I wasn't allowed to sleep anywhere near her.

I crawled into the bathroom and slept in the tub.

17

I woke the next morning soggy from a chronically dripping faucet. Every joint creaked and each bone cracked. A sneeze convinced me that I was on the verge of contracting pneumonia. Memories of the previous evening shuddered me more violently than the chill. Never had I desired a woman more compulsively, and never had I been so cruelly refused. The more actively I desired Monika, the greater her contempt. She was one of those Zen paradoxes the understanding of which would lead me to supposed enlightenment; I could have her only when I ceased desiring her. But what good would having her be when I no longer desired her? Enlightenment, it seemed to me, was a sham concocted by defeatists.

When I heard Monika's voice I climbed from the tub and eased open the bathroom door, paranoid that she had sneaked someone in during the night, until I realized she spoke to the telephone. Would she be calling someone in Denmark? If so, she spoke English. The possibility that Monika had unseen resources worried me. Perhaps she and Sven had been setting up another sucker in Prague when I propitiously appeared, and they had made the tactical decision to take me and spare the other; she spoke to him now, arranging a fallback in the event I disappointed. I pressed my ear to the crack in the door. She said Sven's name, then paused, and before she hung up, "No new message, thank you."

I banged around the bathroom, flushed the toilet, and ran the taps. Didn't want her to think I'd been listening. Yawning vigorously and my hair suitably tousled, I stepped into the main room. She lay on my bed, face to the wall, shamming sleep. When I tiptoed into the kitchen to prepare a pot of coffee, I heard her rise and latch the bathroom door. If it had been her intent to wound by avoiding me, she succeeded. I lifted the pillow on which she had slept to my face and inhaled as though I held a bowl from which ambrosia recently had been spooned. A fleeting impression attached itself to the scent, like a dream imperfectly remembered; Monika wasn't a goddess but an agent of the goddess, a Fury sent to torture me for my sins against women. The smell of her infused my mouth, lungs, and groin: exquisite torture, the olfactory equivalent of a siren's song.

The whistling kettle called me back into the kitchen. Fine thing if Monika had opened the bathroom door to discover me smelling her pillow like some bicycle-seat-sniffing pervert. I prepared the coffee and carried a cup with me to the table by the window. Better if she finds me hunched over paper and pen, working to recapture *The Prague Conspiracy,* that great American screenplay-in-the-making which had been stolen with my portable computer. Hemingway's lost manuscript hadn't stopped *him.* I scribbled those elements I remembered, such as the title and opening scene description. When the bathroom door opened and Monika emerged, she not only failed to notice my industriousness, she didn't bother to acknowledge my presence on her way out of the apartment. The exponential irritations of sleeping in a wet tub, being ignored, and having to begin all over again with my screenplay loosened my tongue to a rage that shocked me as much as Monika. I railed about her inconsiderateness, her lack of feeling, and accused her of denying the world a future masterpiece when she stole my computer. She had never seen me lose control, and as I vented my feelings I noticed wonder if not admiration in her eyes. When reason fails, the director must outshout even the most vocal prima donna, a lesson I hadn't properly learned until meeting Monika. I had feared my anger would provoke hers, but just the opposite; she only truly listened to frequencies of high passion.

"You weren't my partner then, so how can you blame me?" she reasoned. "Of course I stole everything I could find. Sven made three hundred D-marks from that computer alone. You should be proud I was good enough to take you."

"But my screenplay! Paramount Pictures! Gone!" I protested.

"A six-figure development deal, you said when I met you."

"That's right."

"Then why are you wasting your time robbing poor Czech fools?"

Monika stared at me with faux wide-eyed innocence.

"Research," I said. A great idea. Why couldn't it be true? "The screenplay is about two young Americans who con their way through Central Europe after the fall of the Berlin Wall." The perfect pitch line! Love, intrigue, an international backdrop as big as the end of history! I had to restrain myself from grabbing pen and paper and beginning to write.

"And the CIA, the KGB agent?" Monika asked, her question punctuated by three sharp notes from the downstairs buzzer. I wasn't expecting anyone. Could it be the police, come to harass me again over some minor indiscretion? What if Zima knew I had staked out the money-changing booth and planned to rob it? The buzzer blared again. Bortnyk might be back in town, or one of a dozen women I'd met and escorted through Prague.

"Subplots," I said. Monika probed my face for veracity. Her eyes were sharp and precise as a surgeon's biopsy needle. It was all true enough if I believed it. I edged for the door. I imagined it was Andrew on the street below, leaning on the buzzer for a good ten seconds. If it was Andrew, I could introduce him to Monika and he'd understand why I had acted oddly at our previous meeting. I bolted out the door. Cruise and Roberts as the American couple, of course, myself as Tom Cruise and Monika as Julia Roberts. There would be rumors in *Variety* and *The Hollywood Reporter* that the story was autobiographical, and arm in arm with Monika at the Oscars I'd deflect suspicions with a witty remark—*We're just two average folk out for a night on the town, do we look like a couple of thieves?*—leaving just enough mystery in my voice to give the rumors credence. The scenario so engaged my imagination I neglected to pause at the bottom of the stairwell and spy out who waited behind the glass at the front door. A figure cheerfully waved. I stopped and peered. If a heart could be a ship, mine would be the *Titanic*. He'd already seen me. No chance to slink unseen back up the stairs. I wedged a smile between my teeth and flung open the door, crying with fraternal glee, "Cousin Dickie! What a surprise!"

"Cousin Nix! What's goin' down?"

Dickie held out his hand and our palms groped one another in the ritual greeting of our generation. Timberland boots, faded 501's, L. L. Bean windbreaker, San Jose Sharks cap, and a JanSport frame backpack big enough to furnish a small apartment informed me Dickie was roughing it through Europe the summer after graduating from college.

"You got my letter?" he asked.

"No, this is a complete surprise," I said, and not a pleasant one. I didn't dislike Dickie. Though we had little in common except approximate age, I'd always considered him one of my favorite relatives. His parents were pillars of Newport Beach surf-and-turf culture. Uncle John managed the family dealerships in Orange County. Aunt Buffy dabbled in real estate and home redecorating. With his shaggy blond hair, tanned face, hipster goatee, and taste in appropriate-brand casual wear, Dickie was a mutation, a failed experiment, what happens when nature crosses a preppie with a surfer. We stood awkwardly by the door, Dickie waiting to be invited in and me trying to figure out how best to get rid of him. I'd completely forgotten his letter, only half read and crumpled into a ball. His timing couldn't have been worse—much better if he'd dropped by earlier, when I was in Budapest. I'd have written his parents a nice note saying I'd been out of town on film business and how sorry I'd been to miss him.

"Yes. A big surprise," I repeated, then swung the door open, made a halfhearted grab at his backpack, and said, "But always great to see you. How are Uncle John and Aunt Buffy?"

"Just fine," he said, staggering under the weight of the shouldered pack. "Everybody is, like, real curious what you're up to over here. "

"I'll bet they are."

Rapidly descending footsteps met ours climbing the stairs. Monika swept past as though we were columns on the balustrade. I stopped her at the bottom of the stairs with a shout. By her glance I knew she was irritated at being delayed.

"What about our dinner tonight?" I asked, telegraphing a wink to Dickie.

She flung the answer at me—8 P.M.—and hurried out the door.

"Sorry not to introduce you, old man," I said in conspiratorial tones. "That was Monika. A temperamental actress, as you can tell. We've been spatting all morning."

Your girlfriend? What a beautiful woman, I imagined him saying, and laughed with the sensual daring of a tiger tamer. But he said nothing. I shooed him inside the apartment. "As you can see, the place is quite small, particularly with Monika staying here."

He set his backpack down and collapsed onto the sofa bed. I hurried into the kitchen to pour him a cup of coffee. When I returned, his eyes were closed and he looked on the verge of sleep. "Must be jet lag," he said. "Is it cool if I crash here for a couple days?"

"Sorry. Only one bed."

"That's all right. I can sleep on the floor."

I stared slack-jawed. He meant it. I said, "No, it's not cool."

"It's just that I was, like, hoping to economize, you know?"

I knew. Uncle John and Aunt Buffy had given him a round trip plane ticket and Eurail Pass as his graduation present. My parents had done the same for me when I graduated. He'd want his European summer to be a long one. If he hadn't saved from his monthly trust fund allowance during the school year, his finances would be tight. By the look of his goatee and home barbering, Dickie was going through his Bohemian phase, defined as a one-year hiatus between school and employment in the family business, in which the family turned a collective blind eye to excessive leisure time as a sign he was finding himself. But where would he find himself? In the company uniform on a company lot at the end of the year, shorn of distinctive features and smiling a company smile, selling used cars. He wouldn't stay on the lot for long; after a humbling year of learning the salesman's brash art, he'd be moved to the front office, where he'd be trained to manage his own lot, one of the twenty or so the company owned. Then he'd be able to brag to his children that he'd started from the bottom, washing cars as a teenager (as we'd all done), moving up through the company ranks by sweat and merit. I'd been dodging such a future for years. Dickie was soft and malleable. They'd catch and mold him into a life-size replica of his father. He hadn't a chance.

We passed the hour drinking coffee and chatting about Prague's appeal to the young visitor, which lay primarily in the copious quantity of good and reasonably priced alcohol and the abundance of what Dickie quaintly called "cooze." I entertained him with a few anecdotes from personal experience, circled the clubs on his map which offered the most promising combinations of booze and cooze, and, as the end of the hour neared, suggested a cheap but nice little hotel I knew as preferable to the lice- and backpacker-ridden youth hostels he was initially inclined to approach.

As we walked to the Merkur, Dickie asked the questions the family had dispatched him to ask. Descended from the male line and four years his senior, I outranked him in the family hierarchy, but as my Bohemian phase had stretched three years past the family maximum, Dickie enjoyed the family's trust whereas I did not. He had been sent as a family agent, entrusted to pull me back into line. I asked the obligatory questions about his side of the family and received the usual blather about Aunt Buffy's misadventures with the new house, Cousin Mandy's baby, and Rafe's substance abuse problem.

"Uncle Monty and Aunt Winnie had me over for dinner last week," Dickie remarked. Monty is the diminutive of Montgomery, my father's given name. It's the name he uses in all the TV spots, if you've ever stumbled into the surreal world of late-night television in Los Angeles. Winnie is a mutation of Gwendolyn coined by my cousins, whose young mouths could not form the necessary gutturals to pronounce her name correctly and thus named her Winnie, which they continue to call her despite an assumed improvement of language skills.

"And how did they look? Well, I hope?" I said, sounding appropriately filial.

"They're really pissed. Uncle Monty told me about your trust fund. I understand you wanting to be, like, independent, but don't you think you've gone a bit radical?"

"Best thing I've ever done," I said, in the spirit of a testimonial. His immense backpack prevented me from throwing a fraternal arm over his shoulder. I imagined myself astonishingly successful, giving sound guidance to a confused and directionless younger brother. "Nothing like the fear of poverty to get you moving. I'm tougher, more aggressive, and, the truth is, quite ruthless if the situation calls for it. In fact, Father is punishing me for the very same traits that made Grandfather great. I think Grandfather would be proud of me, and it was his money, see what I mean?"

Dickie didn't, of course. I explained for him the irony of my father, a middling bureaucrat, denying the inheritance of a visionary grandfather to his visionary grandson. It was pure jealousy. Maybe my father saw too much of Grandfather in me, and, still hung up on his own father complex, wanted to punish me for Grandfather's sins against him. Dickie nodded, seemingly sympathetic. There was something spongelike about his eyes. I expected him to soak up what I told him and then pour it into the lap of my father. I hoped the spill was ice cold. What Dickie thought about it later didn't matter; he'd believe me until my father or his father filled him with a different opinion.

The desk clerk at the Merkur likely feared the hotel's faded reputation would be further tarnished by a backpacking guest of Dickie's caliber and, after collecting his passport and money, assigned him an obscure room in the back of the hotel, overlooking the expressway. I tried to escape at the base of the stairs, but Dickie insisted on inviting me up, where from the bottom of his backpack he dug two items he'd brought to me from the States. The first was a small package from my mother containing a pair of nail clippers and a box of Immodium. An accompanying note admonished me to be careful of the water "over there" and asked if I was in any danger because of the trouble in Bosnia, which she seemed to think was a suburb of Prague. The second was a sealed blank envelope. I ripped it open. A letter from my father. I stuffed the letter back into the envelope, unread, and thumbed the official-looking document clipped to it. The seal of the State of California was imprinted at the top, my name and various legal codes inscribed in the middle, and an official signature at the bottom. A warrant for my arrest. I showed it to Dickie and asked, "You knew about this?"

"Everybody knows about it."

"Father broadcast the news far and wide, I'm sure."

"It's not what you think, Nix," he responded. The recrimination in his voice surprised me. "Dr. Cariz dropped Mom as his patient because of this. Nobody in the family can get so much as their teeth cleaned because of this crazy film scheme of yours."

The Cavity of Dr. Caligari had been one of my more successful fund-raising efforts, though the project had eventually collapsed due to creative differences. The concept was simple but brilliant: An oral surgeon secretly hired to implant computer chips in the dental work of CIA agents becomes the target of assassins and goes on the run to discover who wants to kill him and why. I'd read the statistics. Dentists were a depressed lot lacking in self-esteem, killing themselves with greater frequency than any other profession. I pitched the idea to a hundred tooth doctors in L.A. and Orange County—a glamorous thriller about a character much like themselves, in which they might mingle freely with stars such as Harrison Ford and Michelle Pfeiffer. *Just imagine,* I'd say, *you're at the wrap party—that's the party thrown for the actors and cast members when the picture is finished shooting—and you're in a group of people with Harrison*

Ford and more than one beautiful starlet, and someone says, "What do you do?" And you say, "I'm a dentist, just like the character Harrison plays, except of course I don't work for the CIA." The line never failed to get a smile. All I needed was $100,000 to put together a script, attach it to a director and actors of suitable star quality, and what studio wouldn't snap it up for a hefty seven figures? I may have mentioned that Joe Eszterhas was a personal friend of the family—he'd bought a car from us before making it big—and he was so in love with the idea that he'd agreed to write the script for a token sum. The allegations of fraud in the arrest warrant were a complete misunderstanding. Eszterhas hadn't been interested in writing the script after all, and without him I couldn't get Harrison or Michelle, so the studios would have turned the project down had I developed it. The development money was spent on overhead. Sure, some dentists were unhappy that the project didn't meet their expectations, but that's Hollywood.

"It's not that funny," a petulant Dickie cried when I chuckled at the notion that the family was being deprived of local dental care. "Sure, not everybody in the family has been perfect, but nobody's been arrested. This is, like, serious. People are calling the house, demanding their money back."

"And every car our family sells is a good car and all our customers are satisfied customers, is that right? Don't be such a child, Dickie."

"Nobody is threatening to put Dad or Uncle Monty in jail because they sold a lemon."

"I feel the hand of my father in this," I said, holding the document up against the light to examine its authenticity. "How do I know this isn't forged? I wouldn't put it past the old bastard."

"The family thinks you should come back and face this."

"I'm busy right now. I'm not going to drop everything just to answer a bogus set of charges."

"The family thinks you need professional counseling."

"Professional counseling?"

"Sure, you know, like a lawyer, and a—well, you know, maybe a—" No matter how many approaches, Dickie could not leap the boundary of the word he wished to pronounce.

"Are you trying to say *shrink*?"

He meekly nodded, afraid of offending me.

"Fuck the family," I said.

Dickie's lower lip drooped, a sign, I think, that I'd shocked him.

"My father cut off my trust fund because I had the nerve to stand up to him! Did you know I had been robbed and beaten by a gang of Gypsy thieves and when I asked Father for a little advance on my trust fund, so I could go to the fucking hospital because I was still fucking bleeding all over the fucking place, Father said no? *Go ahead and bleed to death for all I care, you're not getting another red cent.* And the family, does it care about me at all? No! It just listens to Father, and when Father says, *Nix needs to be taught a little discipline, he's embarrassing the Family,* does the family come to my defense, does it say, *Nix has a special talent and we should support him in his efforts to follow it?* No! It sends you to tell me I should willingly present myself to be handcuffed and trundled off to prison or the lunatic asylum!"

"I mean, really, we all just want the best for you."

"You don't want the best for me. You want the best for you! You want Nix to straighten up and join the family company. You want Nix in the company straitjacket selling used cars! He won't do it!"

"You're acting, like, seriously paranoid."

"You're acting like a company lackey!"

"Hey, I just graduated. I don't even have a job or anything."

"Three years, Dickie boy. When I'm walking up the aisle come Oscars time, you'll be selling Toyota Corollas on some lot in Lawndale." I flung open the door and was halfway down the hall when he stopped me with a shout.

"I don't agree with the family," he called. "I don't think you're crazy. I just think you're an asshole."

I laughed and continued down the hall. A good joke. Not for a second did I think he seriously meant it. I'd hurt him with the family lackey remark. I'd said it for his own good. Maybe it would shake him from the certain orbit of his current life trajectory.

By coincidence no one manned the front desk when I reached the bottom of the stairs. The Merkur was a small hotel, and when its sole daytime administrative employee felt compelled to attend to biological needs the desk was left unprotected. I tracked the key slots to the number corresponding to Dickie's room and a small blue booklet. I have a weakness for passports. The area behind the desk was easily accessible; I ducked beneath a barrier and snagged Dickie's. I had no intention of stealing it. Just a quick look at the photo and border stamps. A flush of plumbing startled me into pocketing the thing and slipping out the door. I didn't want to get caught in an act that could look illegal, and a quick escape was my best defense against a ridiculous misunderstanding. I fully planned to return the passport to him later that afternoon, or by the next day at the latest. I glanced through the pages and found little of interest. It would serve him right to fly into a panic because of a missing passport. Asshole, indeed. Even meant as a joke the comment was offensive.

When I slipped it into my coat pocket, my fingers brushed Father's letter. I briefly read its two pages on the winding walk to my apartment. The usual drivel. *How could you . . . didn't you think of the consequences . . . why didn't you inform me. . . . all very upsetting . . . wanted to support you . . . didn't raise my son to . . . in your best interests*—I tore the letter into confetti and tossed it into the gutter. How dare he express his venal attempts at control as compassion!

18

By the 8 P.M. curtain time the entire cast had assembled at the Hotel Paříž and waited impatiently for the star. Zdeněk bounced on the balls of his feet near the reception desk. Tourists and hotel guests, cast as extras, cluttered the lobby and café. An octogenarian pianist stumbled through one of the hundred variations of the "Blue Danube Waltz," which by a trick of harmony segued into the melody of "Moon River." I suffered through my usual case of opening night nerves; twice in my apartment I had stifled anxiety attacks, but since arriving at the hotel I felt a light-headed confidence bordering euphoria. In my front trouser pockets warmed four rectangular tins, each filled with wax and held together by rubber bands. Even if Monika managed to pick the keys cleanly from Zdeněk's pocket, he might slap his coat minutes later, alerted by a feeling of absence or an unexpected smooth contour. He would not accuse Monika of theft, but unless the keys were promptly found under chair or table he would rush to that which he feared most losing. The shop would be guarded from that moment until the arrival of a locksmith to change the locks.

My plan dictated that the keys would be missing five minutes, ten minutes at most. Just long enough to press each key between wax blocks and return them to their ring. Later, in the calm of my apartment—I imagined listening to Mozart or Beethoven as I worked—I could carve the flow channels and vent holes required for casting, press the blocks together, and pour in the plaster. The following morning, I would take the plaster casts to a key maker and slip the cutter a few hundred crowns not to ask any questions. With a copy of Zdeněk's keys in hand, I could safely enter his change booth at leisure. The delay of a day or two would so distance Monika from the theft that he could not possibly suspect her role. It was everything a plan should be: meticulously plotted, imaginative, profitable, and completely safe.

Monika's entrance—costumed in stiletto heels, black silk stockings, and a low-cut, thigh-high cocktail dress—agonized the male eye with difficult decisions: Stare first at the wicked stretch of leg, the tantalizing curve of buttocks, the honeyed skin above a delicious rise of breasts, or the delicately sensuous line of bare arm? An elderly Englishman enjoying a quiet drink with his wife choked on the head of his beer. Two German men at the next table fell uncharacteristically silent, save for the popping of vertebrae when she swept past. Zdeněk nearly tripped over tangling feet in rushing to greet her. I'd seen entrances such as hers at the Oscars, from actresses flashing that rare theatrical charisma known as star power. She extended a cool hand to Zdeněk, and when he took it she slowly reeled him in to kiss first one cheek and then the other with the sumptuousness of tasting fruit. His babbling reply carved a smile on her lips. No doubt every man watching concluded he had nothing special except luck. He offered her his arm—a gesture of trite sophistication more than true gentility—and when she took it led her into the restaurant and out of our sight.

I noted the time on my watch: a quarter past nine. Had I wished, I could have kept them under direct observation, but the restaurant was huge and nearly always empty. Even casual surveillance risked a familiarity of face. If he caught her withdrawing the keys from his pocket and she failed to convince him of the innocence of such a gesture, I would need to appear as "the jealous boyfriend" and threaten him with a thrashing. The odds of such a scene were remote, but I had taken great precautions in imagining every possible scenario and making plans to match, so that should action be required I would not *go up,* as the theatrical expression goes, but throw myself directly into the role. The greatest risks are always the unknown and taken for granted. I thrust my hands into my trouser pockets and fondled the tin molds to keep the wax warm and supple. It seemed like forever that Monika had already been inside the restaurant. Certainly she should have appeared, keys in hand, if all was going well. What if Monika sat directly across from Zdeněk, and not in the cozy booth I pictured? I bolted to my feet. What pretext could she possibly find to initiate the intimate contact required to pluck the keys from his pocket? I sat down again, aware that people might be staring. Would she spill a drink onto his lap and sneak them out amid vigorous slaps and pats? Excellent idea! I regretted not having thought of it before. Monika relied too often on seduction. I imagined a discomfited Zdeněk having his privates whacked and prodded with a heavy linen napkin. Perhaps I should take a small peek inside the restaurant and, if the situation warranted, signal Monika. I casually rose to my feet, planning how I might wander in just long enough to catch her eye with a significant look. The brass and oak clock above the reception desk read nine-twenty. I double-checked the time against my watch. I sat down again, observed how slowly the second hand beat against the minute, as though even my own watch conspired against me.

Monika was to hand me the keys outside the door to the women's room, and, after the leisurely accomplishment of her duties there, meet me by the bank of phones down the hall. The entire operation should have taken no more than five minutes. She so ignored me when at last she clipped through the lobby that I could have been a complete stranger. I did not look at her as I approached, holding out my hand as I turned toward an adjacent door to the men's room, but instead of keys I felt a rude pull and an urgently whispered sexual demand.

I stayed in character and stared at her as I would a stranger. Her cheeks were flushed and her eyes dilated as if she had ingested a chemical euphoric. What could she possibly be thinking? Of all the contingencies this was one I had not considered. She repeated the demand in even more explicit terms.

"What, now?" I squeaked.

Monika pushed me through the door into the men's room. Her hands were brutally direct, tugging at the loose end of my belt even as I glanced wildly around for other occupants.

"Where, here?" I squeaked again.

Monika flung open the door to the stall and shoved me inside. A set of keys clanked to the floor beside the toilet. Her fingers tore at the buttons of my trousers. She had already lifted them! Her lips fastened onto my neck as she threaded me through the fly of my boxers. I began to ask how and when she had managed to pick Zdeněk. She whispered "Shut up" and pushed me to my knees. The moment I saw that above her black stockings and below the hem of her pushed-up minidress lay nothing but an immaculately tended ebony and rose garden I forgot about the plan and with the tip of my tongue navigated the folds and oils of her. I'm as easy to arouse physically as any twenty-something man, but passion is not mere biology and her taste went through me like ambrosia. That she had planned this disturbed and excited me. The feint and thrust of her hips dictated pace and motion. When she began to cry out as though each flick of tongue cut her I didn't worry that someone might hear and an offended management throw us out; I sought her mouth with my fingers and let her suck. With her hands pressing the back of my head each thrust bruised my lips, and by the delicate shudders between I was certain she could have ascended to Olympus had she wished but instead I was pulled up by my hair and harshly groped. Finding me serviceable, she bit my neck, pushed me against the wall, and spun around to finger herself while bucking against me from behind. She did not ask me to wear a condom nor give me the slightest opportunity to don one. In that anonymous position and in that environment I could have been anyone to her and probably was. I threw myself against her without tenderness, as she wanted, and she met me with equal if not greater force, determined to finish before my premature delight could disappoint her. Moments after swallowed gasps signaled she had reached her objective, she pulled away and pushed down her dress, leaving me to gush, solo and groping embarrassed for the tissue paper.

Before I finished buttoning my trousers, she cracked open the door and slipped quietly past the urinals. I could scarcely believe in the reality of what had happened. My legs shook so badly I flopped down the lid and sat. My watch read nine-forty. Sex in my experience had always involved aspects of the pornographic; my detached mind watched from above as two bodies, one of which happened to be mine, engaged in activities that stimulated its fantasies. Sex was as real and unreal as film unspooling before a beam of white light. Sex with Monika in a toilet stall was one of my dirtiest encounters and, simultaneously, the least pornographic sex I'd ever had; I felt the experience rather than watched it. After she left, however, my mind returned with a vengeance, questioning whether the incident signaled a change in attitude or if I was merely the beneficiary of an uncontrollable pattern of sexual deviance. I won't pretend to having enjoyed profound insights; rather, these two possibilities shuttled monotonously one after the other, like an endless loop, until my shoes kicking at the keys on the floor brought me to my senses.

I carried the keys to the flat surface on the other side of the sink and laid out the tin boxes. The wax inside was warm and supple—neither cold as I might have feared nor molten after our torrid tryst. I caught sight of myself in the mirror and grinned, thinking, *Quite an adventure, old boy, a little something for the memoirs!* It wasn't until I examined the keys that I noticed the first small flaw in my plan: The key chain held twelve keys, or three times the number of molds I'd prepared. Only two of the keys could be discounted as belonging to the BMW. I had somehow imagined that there would be fewer keys, and the two required to open the doors to the change booth would be readily identifiable either by age or distinguishing mark. Of the ten remaining keys, two were clearly too old to fit a modern lock, which left eight brand-new identical keys. I stripped one at random from the key ring, laid it on a bed of wax, aligned the second half of the mold on top, and pressed the two firmly together. I'd played the lottery often enough to realize that the chances of selecting not just one but two of the correct keys were slim, even with four molds and four chances. I couldn't afford to chance failure. If I failed, Monika would return to my apartment just long enough to retrieve her packed suitcase and try to search out Sven. I snapped the key back onto its ring and pocketed the tin boxes. No reason to panic. The measure of true genius is the ability to improvise.

Monika was not waiting by the phones as arranged when I emerged with the keys. I supposed that our encounter had badly damaged her makeup and she remained in the women's room making repairs. In the odd way that memory works, the sight of the phones recalled Monika's phone call that morning. During her partnership with Sven, no doubt she had foreseen the possibility of a forced escape and made provisions to contact him should they be separated. It occurred to me that I should be a good cousin and check in on Dickie; a call from good old Nix would cheer him had he stayed in for the night, brooding about our conversation. Instead of following this good intention, I identified myself as Sven when the receptionist at the Merkur answered. As suspected, Monika had left a message, saying something particularly unkind about me and asking Sven to leave a number where he could be reached. When the receptionist asked if I had a return message, I told her to inform Monika that I was currently in Moscow with a woman who claimed to be related to the Romanovs, and not to expect me back until winter.

"There's a change in plan," I announced, poking my head into the women's room.

Monika gave me scarcely a glance in the mirror as she limned her eyes with seductive shades.

"I didn't think you liked changes in plan," she answered. Very droll.

"Why didn't you tell me he carried so damn many keys?"

"Why didn't you ask?"

"Because I expect just a little help. You could have said something."

"Don't blame me when you fuck up, okay? Take responsibility. Try to be a man, even if the effort is hopeless."

It was hard for me to imagine that less than ten minutes previous we had engaged in an act commonly considered one of the most intimate expressions possible between human beings. I silently worked my way through half an alphabet of vulgar epithets before advising her that I'd return the keys in approximately forty minutes, and bolted out the door.

During my preparations it had occurred to me that molding and casting the keys might prove needlessly complicated, but I had discounted the most direct plan as involving an unacceptable level of risk. I had no intention of spending my youth in a Central European jail. Zdeněk's money-changing booth was a short walk from the Hotel Paříž. I had the keys. Nothing prevented me from walking into his business and cleaning him out immediately except the fear of getting caught. I hurried down Celetná as fast as possible without breaking into a run. A thick flock of tourists migrated toward Staroměstské náměstí, filled it, and spilled into the narrow streets connecting the square with other city monuments. The gothic hands of the clockworks approached the narrow angle of 10 P.M. I had originally planned to break into the money-changing booth at three in the morning, an hour when the only witnesses would be drunk or bleary-eyed. Tourists flocking at the old town hall fluttered maps and snapped flash pictures to the very doorstep of the change booth. In two minutes, the bell tower would begin to chime, the air would vibrate with the chatter of a dozen languages, and all heads would snap to fittingly reverent angles to observe the sounding of the hour.

What initially seemed a disadvantage was my greatest opportunity. At the first stroke of the bell, every eye turned away from me. Local residents who ventured across the square at that hour were too preoccupied with elbowing through clogs of spectators to notice the baseball-capped fellow in a black windbreaker frantically racing through a set of unfamiliar keys. The lock turned on my fifth try. I squeezed through the door and restrained a triumphant shout as I latched it behind me. Inside the change booth, the darkness was as thick and black as tar. I unzipped the satchel by feel and cast a spotlight around the room: two chairs, a counter with cash drawers, a shuttered window, and, at the back, a door. I tested the cash drawers. Open but empty. The door was locked. The second key I tried opened it. I slipped inside, shut the door behind me, and panned the light across the walls. No windows. No witnesses. The light switch was next to the door. I switched it on.

1 9

The second flaw in my plan became evident when the contents of the room were fully illuminated. It had never occurred to me that Zdeněk would keep his daily takings in a safe. It was a squat little thing, with a black combination dial that looked like a Cyclops eye on an ugly gray face. I gave it a kick and danced around the room one-footed as reward. Brute force was the refuge of those without imagination. The key to the safe lay in my intellect and not my foot. How many caper films had I seen, and once the gang had finished tunneling and sat before the Bank of Mammon, what had they done? I hadn't any explosives but I did have ears and fingers. All combination safes employ tumblers. I lay on the floor and pressed my ear to the dial as I randomly spun the numbers. The only clicks came from the dial itself, and even if the tumblers were perceptibly loud I could only guess what one would sound like clicking into place, if that is what tumblers do. I buttressed a leg against the wall, wrapped my arms around the safe, and pulled with all my might. It didn't move a fraction of an inch. Probably bolted to the floor. Why couldn't Zdeněk have cooperated by purchasing a safe accessible by key? The thing was impregnable. I pulled again, then pushed, and broke into tears like a five-year-old too short to reach the cookie jar.

Zdeněk's desk lay against the far wall. I ferreted through the drawers for anything remotely resembling a series of numbers that might spring the lock. Zdeněk wasn't stupid enough to leave his combination lying about, and I soon abandoned the search. My life crumbled. The first grand caper I'd attempted was a failure. Monika would leave me. I hadn't any money remaining except counterfeit bills. The next morning I'd scrape hands and knees crawling to beg Dickie to forget what I'd said about the family; afterward I'd call Father, whimpering what a bad boy I'd been. Then, the handcuffed humiliation of a plane ride on wired money, back into the custody of my parents like an extradited criminal.

The muted chime of bells caught my attention. I became overwhelmingly conscious of the passage of time. The bell sounded once, twice. I glanced at my watch. Half past the hour. Not only had I accomplished nothing, I was late. It seemed as though ten minutes had passed since I'd left Monika. I laid two tin boxes on the desk and slid my thumbnail between the key-ring coils, methodically working loose the keys to front and inside doors. Even as I laid each in a bed of wax and pressed, I despaired of success. Nothing had worked according to plan and a sudden fit of reason convinced me that something else would go awry between mold and key. I dug out a teaspoon-sized plug of wax from a remaining tin, stuffed it into the hole in the jamb at the base plate, and shut the door. A stroke of genius! Anyone rattling the knob from the outside would conclude it was locked. I lifted on the knob and pushed with my shoulder. The door sprang open. The victory was small but lifted my spirits immeasurably. I repeated the procedure—cracked open the front door and plugged the base plate from the inside—before slipping quietly into the night.

Only when a good hundred yards distant did I begin to run, whipped on by paranoid fantasies of Zdeněk clamping Monika's wrists while demanding the management call the police, which alternated with more realistic fears that his hand wiggled between her willing thighs. My gasping breath drew a startled look from the doorman when I arrived at the Hotel Paříž. The elderly English couple had been replaced by a young American quartet, but the Germans remained, talking boisterously over a small arsenal of alcoholic drinks. I reclaimed my original table, signaled the waiter, and ordered a double Scotch on the rocks. While I waited for my drink, I snuck over to the restaurant, where I ducked the white-frocked maître d' and snagged Monika's eye. Zdeněk's hands were nowhere near the hem of her dress. She laughed at one of his remarks, pretending, while she fondled the flute of a champagne glass, to find him amusing. A brilliant actress!

"Zdeněk invited me to visit a hotel he invested in," Monika taunted when I laid the keys in her palm outside the door to the women's room. "What would you say if I let him sleep with me tonight?"

I shocked myself with the viciousness of my reply. "I'll kill him. I'll break his legs, smash his skull, cut out his tongue and eyes."

Monika backed down the hall, the bright-as-emeralds look in her eyes luring me to an unmarked door that gave with a turn of the knob to a closet of some kind; a wedge of light bisected a shelf of linens until the door shut us in darkness. I felt Monika's hands and mouth everywhere at once.

"And is there very much money?" she whispered.

"More than I can carry," I answered, more or less truthfully.

"I think you should let him fuck me. So he doesn't suspect."

She pulled me to the floor. Various body parts were thrust upon me in the darkness, identifiable by taste and texture, though she moved with such frantic passion I was rarely certain of the relation of these parts to the whole. My most critical buttons gave way, and I was enveloped as though swallowed whole. I haven't much memory of events after that. Never before had I been subject to such passion. I remember grasping something like linen and stuffing it into her mouth to silence her cries, then the sound of a door opening and shutting when she left me wasted on the floor.

A peculiar tranquillity settled over my thoughts as I stared up into the darkness. That evening I had utterly failed at my immediate objective and twice fulfilled my greatest aspiration. I knew what I had to do next. My resources were limited. Even if the molds were perfect, the obvious solution would not have changed. I didn't know where to acquire Semtex, and if I found a few ounces on my doorstep I'd be more likely to blow myself up than Zdeněk's safe. Had I been able to purchase a stethoscope I wouldn't have known what a tumbler falling into place sounded like, and

I didn't know any safecrackers I could hire by the hour. Had I attempted to formulate a plan around any of these possibilities, the plan would have failed. I had expected events that evening to follow my plan, but like the film scripts I attempted to write, my plan was incomplete and unrealistic, no deeper than the one-line concept to which I reduced all ideas.

I straightened my wits with my pants and slipped from the linen closet, pretending to be oblivious to the astonished stare of a waiter who witnessed my exit. He would not soon forget having seen me, but the odds of anyone asking him the type of question that would elicit memory were so remote that I quickly discounted the possibility. I paid my bill and wandered up a garish Václavské náměstí still crowded with foreign teenagers and Czech whores. A drink might serve the dual purpose of quenching my thirst and setting up an alibi for the evening, should events conspire to require one of me. Repré Club, located in the basement of Obecní Dům, always attracted a post-midnight expatriate crowd, and as I found its dilapidated Art Nouveau trimmings more to my liking than the cavernous Ubiquity, I decided to try my luck there, descending a burnished wooden staircase into the smoke-filled din of what local traditionalists liked to refer to as the nightly rape of one of Prague's most significant cultural landmarks.

A few hundred of the 10,000 Americans living in Prague at the time regularly frequented clubs like Lávka and Repré; after a few months of nightly carousings it was easy to spot the regulars among the tourists and the occasional Czech. I smiled and nodded to familiar faces as I pressed through the crush of bodies, making certain they recognized and noted my presence. At the bar, I downed one beer in a long draught and nursed a second. A scribbler of dime detective novels elbowed next to me to talk about his latest potboiler. I politely nudged the conversation to topics of sex, stating unambiguously that I was to meet a beautiful Romanian at Staroměstské náměstí at 2 A.M.; the poor girl hadn't a place to stay for the night so I was letting her sleep in my apartment until the following morning, when she was to catch a train back to her native Bucharest. I cornered a young playwright from Boston with the same story as he stumbled out of the men's room. For the next two hours, I worked my way through the club, disciplining my imagination to repeat the story in unvarying detail to everyone I met, though I couldn't decide whether or not I'd slept with the Romanian girl and thus told conflicting sexual histories of our relationship, from the chaste liaison I'd described to the pulp writer to a more ribald version in which we had abandoned our trousers and inhibitions in a men's room toilet stall at the Hotel Paříž. I doubted the inconsistency would lead to any real difficulties; men are notorious for lying about their sexual exploits and if pressed to explain I could plead either braggadocio or modesty, depending on which answer better served me.

Staroměstské náměstí was deserted by 4 A.M. The few night owls drank their way to sunrise, and the worm hunters remained warm in their beds. A swift yank on the knob and a strategically applied shoulder popped open the door to Zdeněk's change booth. I thought about Monika while I waited in the back room, keeping track of time in the darkness with periodic clicks of the flashlight onto my wristwatch. My new plan was so simple it required little preparation or thought; the principal requirement was to keep my wits when the action began. I couldn't decide whether Monika's behavior signaled a significant and permanent change in our relationship or an aberrance of passion. I had kept my many failures of plan a secret. Was it not possible that my seeming mastery of the situation had moved her to admiration and passion? Of course she couldn't overnight forget the emotional loss of Sven; if she could easily move from one man to the next I could just as easily be displaced. This explained how she could treat me with complete disdain a few minutes after passion had exhausted itself. Her affections would become more constant as her undeniable and instinctual attraction to me gradually wiped Sven from her heart. I imagined us sunning on a beach in the South of France, drinks at sunset on the veranda of our ocean-view penthouse, turning heads as we sweep into a casino at Monte Carlo, dressed cuff to cravat by Armani. . . .

The rattle of a turning lock woke me sometime later. No windows, no light, no way to tell if morning had arrived. I jumped to my feet and fumbled the flashlight, which clanged and clattered to the tiles as loud as a streetcar. I froze, listening. Had he heard? I dropped on hands and knees and felt for the satchel. The room was pitch black. I lost track of left and right, up and down. My hands stumbled over canvas flap and zipper. A blade of blue-white light sliced beneath the door. The scuff of a foot turning, a door thumping shut, a dry cigarette cough: the normal sounds of someone coming to work in the morning. I unzipped the satchel, groped my props, and picked the flashlight from the tiles. Four hours to prepare myself for Zdeněk's arrival and still he had caught me by surprise. I clenched the knife and flashlight between my legs and fumbled with the ends of the scarf. When the key entered the lock my heart thumped as loudly as fists on a door. I couldn't get the loose ends wrapped into a full knot and hadn't time to try again. I gripped the flashlight in my left hand and knife in my right and watched the door swing open, suddenly horrified that it would swing into me. I backed into the corner, holding my knife like a spear carrier in a third-rate opera afraid of tripping up the tenor.

The overhead fluorescents clicked on bright as klieg lights. The room went white. My eyes sparked and burned. Bits and pieces struck my eye—a wall, the door, a rose sport coat. I stumbled forward and kicked shut the door, blinking furiously. I pressed the knifepoint into Zdeněk's back and, my voice thick with what I imagined sounded like a Ukrainian accent, I said, "Don't move or I *keel* you," but the accent took a pratfall in my mouth and I had to bite my tongue to keep from adding, *señor*.

"*Cože?*" Zdeněk said, half turning.

"Don't turn around! Hands, reach for sky!"

Zdeněk obeyed. My scarf slipped off my nose when I spoke, and only by nipping it with my teeth did I keep it on my face. I elbowed the light switch and spotlit the safe with my flashlight.

Zdeněk responded in a language rich in consonants, Czech or one of the other Slavic tongues. I let the scarf slip to my neck. The bastard was trying to trick out my nationality. Brutality doesn't come naturally to me. I reminded myself that I had no conscience. I wrapped my arm around his throat and stuck my knife until I heard him yelp. I told him to kneel. He kneeled. I spotlit the combination dial and told him if he didn't open it I'd kill him. His hands trembled on the dial. I could smell his sweat and the lingering scent of a familiar perfume. I risked removing the knife from his throat to pull the scarf over my face. Most women can be personally identified by a heady mixture of natural and commercial scents. I could smell Monika from across a crowded room. She'd gotten close enough to rub her scent onto Zdeněk. The safe popped open. He sat back on his heels. I kicked the satchel and told him to fill it. When I caught him examining the label I dug the knife tip into the back of his neck. He jerked forward and plunged both hands into the safe. If he pulled a gun I couldn't hesitate to kill him. His hands emerged holding nothing but deutsche marks, dollars, pounds sterling, a fat rainbow of notes arcing from safe to satchel. He emptied the safe in less than thirty seconds. I told him to push the satchel toward the door. He did, and waited for his next instruction, hands on knees.

I hadn't thought how to end the scene. I somehow imagined vanishing, with Zdeněk none the wiser that I'd gone. But I couldn't very well just leave him kneeling like that, able to jump up and shout for help the moment I left his office. Stabbing or knocking him over the head seemed brutal. He looked too vulnerable kneeling before me, head lowered, waiting. I didn't want to kill him. I wanted to be merciful. But still, he reeked of Monika's perfume. What if he'd actually taken her to his hotel? I raised the flashlight over my head and brought the butt end full force onto his skull. He fell onto his side. His eyes looked up at me glazed and vacant. I was sure he and Monika had been up to something. I hit him a second time, harder, in the face.

20

By the looks of his light-socket hair and swollen eyes, Andrew had been sleeping when I had rung and rung again the buzzer to his apartment. His T-shirt, bearing the bleach-faded likeness of Kurt Cobain, bunched haphazardly into jeans buttoned once at the top; at the bottom one dirty white-socked foot scratched another with a gaping hole in the toe. I was happy to see him, not just because I needed to establish an alibi but because I was always happy to see Andrew.

I said, "Did I wake you I'm sorry I just wanted to apologize for what I said the other day I was under a lot of stress and you know I didn't mean it if you hadn't run away I could have explained but I want you to know that it really bothered me and I'm sorry."

He rubbed his eyes as though seeing an unwelcome apparition, and asked, "What time is it?"

"About eight," I lied.

Andrew said, "Look, you don't get it, so I'll spell it out
for you. I'm not your friend, I don't want to talk to you, and
I sure as hell don't want to see you at eight o'clock in the
morning."

"But I've changed!" I protested.

Andrew slammed the door in my face. I left the building
elated. That he had asked me the time was a great stroke
of luck. In this, he was a far better friend than he realized
and I could have hoped. He would soon enough forgive
and forget my unfortunate remark about his cripple. I looped
back to my apartment through side streets and alleys, confident that in the heft of my satchel I carried the resources
to begin leading the life I'd imagined with Monika. I'd suggest a trip to Cannes. At one of those famous little-known
bistros we'd bump into Michael Eisner. He'd mistake me
for someone he'd met and ask about my newest project.
I'd pitch it on the spot and after a half hour of negotiations
we'd shake hands on the deal. Monika was always alluring
in these fantasies; a black haired, green-eyed elegance, the
kind of woman to give a man both confidence and prestige.

A different Monika stared back at me from the couch of
my smoked-out apartment. She sat huddled on the floor,
wrapped in a blanket. Lank and tangled hair spread like an
oil spill down the sides of her face. An ashtray within flicking range overflowed with cigarette butts. Black streaks lined
her cheeks where the mascara had run, and her lipstick had
smeared well beyond the ridged confines of her lips. I mistook her for drunk and, imagining the tawdry scene which
preceded her dishabille, remarked, "Zdeněk gave you a good
fucking, did he?"

The wail that pitched from Monika could have come from a mortally wounded child. She shrieked with pain. My initial reaction was not compassionate; I wanted to bolt out the door or slap her. I dropped the satchel and stared. I felt as if one person repeatedly slugged me in the stomach while a second ran an ice cube up and down my spine. She hid her ruined face in the folds of the blanket. I couldn't fathom how my remark had pierced her; earlier, she had confessed an intent to commit the act I had accused her of and seemed excited by the complications sure to ensue. Her wails quieted to sobs. I crept closer, ready to flee if she should burst out again. Her sobbing neither gained nor lost momentum but fluctuated with the regularity of a looped recording. I allowed my hand tentatively to wander to her shoulder, then, as her sobbing abated, gently wisped away the hair falling over her forehead.

She spoke rapidly, words ellipsed by grief and muffled by the blanket, which she cupped to her face like handfuls of earth. I couldn't make complete sense of her, catching only phrases. Something about fear of abandonment and loss of family. I'd scoffed at the cliché of a melting heart too many times to mention, but mine was reduced to the consistency of chocolate in a boy's pocket on a summer day. She had never before shown me vulnerability. When she said she couldn't stand being abandoned and followed that plea with my name, a seven-headed hydra of virtues stirred in my depths. I said many things of the type that most men regret later having said, such as I'd loved her from the moment I'd first seen her, I'd never leave her, if we were ever separated I'd scorch the earth until I found her. Her hand slipped out of the blanket and grasped mine. Immediately, I got an erection. Shocking, that my finer sentiments could be so directly linked to a sexual impulse. I had always imagined such feelings to be chaste. When I opened my arms she turned her face toward mine and offered her lips. My tongue on a scouting expedition met the solid gate of her teeth. It was the cloistered kiss of a nun, cool and closed-mouth.

"The job went just like clockwork. You should see the fat bundles of money!" I exclaimed with a theatrical enthusiasm, thinking it might rekindle her passion. Twice in twelve hours should have been enough, but Monika's effect on me was priapismic. She curled into my chest. I shifted my body to retrieve the bag but was held in place by the resistance of deadweight. I let her slip into the crook of my arm. Her eyes were closed, and in the soft rhythms of her breath I could hear a faint mewing, like that of a cat chasing mice in her sleep.

Early that afternoon I awakened just enough to carry Monika from floor to bed, where I fell into a dream which would be laughable in its trite iconography had it not been completely terrifying. In the dream, I swam endless circles in a brimstone lake, supervised by Luciferian creatures resembling Inspector Zima and that Hungarian cop, Bortnyk, who prodded me with pitchforks whenever I attempted to land. Most dreams unfold from premise to denouement in seconds, but it seemed I swam forever the same desperate circles.

I woke sweating to the smell of smoke. Monika sat at the table by the window, staring vacantly into space as she sucked on a cigarette. I staggered out of bed, unlatched the window, and stuck my head outside, gasping for breath.

When my lungs filled, I took the ashtray from the table, emptied it in the trash, and opened every window in the apartment. Setting the ashtray back on the table, I said, "Nicorettes."

Monika gave me a blank look.

"Oh, never mind," I muttered, and set about the morning chores of making coffee and straightening the apartment. The satchel lay in the hallway where I had dropped it the night before. If Monika had succumbed to curiosity and glanced inside while I slept, she had been careful not to disturb its position. Cup of coffee in hand, I carried the satchel to the chair opposite hers and emptied it onto the center of the table. She nudged the ashtray to the corner, stubbed out one cigarette, and lit another, her stare fixed at the point where the corner walls met the ceiling.

"Well. Quite a haul," I said.

I imagined that Monika, driven to a mad passion, swept the money onto the floor and we made love at turns violent and tender on a bed of lire, pesetas, dollars, and D-marks. Different movie. She rested her head on the palm of her hand and blew smoke toward the ceiling. I might as well have dumped a satchel of confetti on the table. I sat and separated the notes first by nationality and then by denomination. Even before counting I realized the sum would be significant. The strongest currencies were also the most numerous. Consulting a *Herald Tribune* for current exchange rates and making notes with pencil and paper, I counted just over four thousand dollars, almost half in deutsche marks.

I cleared my throat and said, too loudly, "Half of this is yours. Do you want it now?"

Monika glanced at me as though surprised to find someone else in the room. I pushed a pile of D-marks forward.

She showed no recognition of its value, just stared as though the money represented something making unwanted demands on her concentration.

"Go ahead, take it," I urged.

Monika returned her gaze to the point where walls and ceiling met.

"I don't get it. We went to all this trouble. Here it is, thousands. And you don't seem at all interested."

"It's not the money," she whispered, then ripped a blanket from the bed and took it into the bathroom, where I found her an hour later, sleeping in the tub. I nearly fractured a vertebra carrying her to bed. She slept through the evening, waking just long enough to take my hand from her thigh and turn her back to me when, past midnight, I crawled into bed. It was only much later, after sunrise, that she allowed me to cuddle within a foot of her.

The jangling of a telephone later awakened me to the realization that the lump I had snuggled against was not Monika at all but a pillow. I snapped up the phone to an official voice which requested me by name. My reply was instinctive. "He's not in. Can I take a message?" I jotted down the particulars and hung up. A quick scout of the bathroom proved the tub equally empty. Had I slept so soundly? Naturally, I checked to see if the money and her suitcase remained, not that I seriously believed she would attempt escape after the scenes of two nights before, but nevertheless I was immensely relieved to find both in place.

Over coffee, I wondered what the Vice Consul of the U.S. Embassy could want with me. A stab of paranoia—Zima had checked on my credentials, and the embassy was irate that I had cloaked my criminal activities behind the skirts of the ambassador. More likely, they had heard rumors of an important Hollywood figure in town. The function of any embassy is to brownnose business and entertainment figures as well as the politicians of the host country. Who could blame a backwater diplomat for wanting to rub against a little Hollywood glitter? It surprised me the call hadn't come from Ambassador Shirley Temple Black herself, but then perhaps she did not wish to remind the diplomatic community of her showbiz roots. I dressed carefully before I made the call, donning slacks, sport coat, and tie, all pressed and of appropriate label. The secretary took note of my name and within moments the Vice Consul was on line, introducing himself by name and description of duties, but instead of following with a hearty and personal welcome he asked if I knew a young American man named Richard Greenleaf.

"Well, yes," I answered, after a reflective pause. "He's my cousin."

In highly diplomatic language, which neither assumed innocence nor presumed guilt but outlined the function of the U.S. Embassy in situations such as these, the Vice Consul explained that on the previous day an individual identified as Richard Greenleaf, an American citizen, had been arrested by the police.

I said, "Oh, dear. Oh, my. Oh, my goodness."

The charge was a serious one, the Vice Consul admitted; he was not yet fully informed of the details of the accusation, but the inspector supervising the case had specifically stated that it involved assault. Mr. Greenleaf's parents would be contacted by the embassy, but as I was a relative and lived locally, I could assist my cousin by arranging for the services of a Czech lawyer.

I took down several names of lawyers suggested by the Vice Consul and hung up the phone, wondering how such an innocuous fellow as my cousin could have gotten in-volved in such a thing. Served the sanctimonious bastard right! I imagined the family code words whispered in hushed telephone conversations from car dealership to dealership; Dickie was now the one with *the problem,* the one who could use *a little straightening out,* who needed *profes-sional help.* I relished the impending call from Father, al-lowing that perhaps I should stay in Prague for a while, at least until Dickie was cleared of all charges. Though careful to avoid seeming an opportunist, I'd suggest that Father reinstate my monthly trust fund now that I was continuing in Prague on family business.

Setting aside the U.S. and Czech currencies, I stuffed the remaining bills into a locking Haliburton briefcase, penned a brief note to Monika—a courtesy she had not shown me—and left my apartment. At the base of the stairs, I paused to scrutinize the parts of street visible through the door glass. Though I saw nothing suspicious and quickly blended into a street crowded with tourists, I nonetheless felt as though someone followed at a cautious distance. I tried all the tricks I remembered from movies: stopped at a window display to observe the reflections, unexpectedly whirled to note who veered aside or hid behind a newspaper, and sprinted at the last possible moment to a departing tram. I ran Hlavní Nádraží, the main train station, like a labyrinth, threading through crowds and charging up and down train platforms. Certain that no one could have possibly followed, I stole down a corridor to a shabby room commanded by a frumpy clerk in a floral housedress who, in exchange for a few crowns, took my case and handed me a numbered token. The script had called for a storage locker but none then existed at that station, and after brief deliberation I decided the storage room was less risky than my apartment. A quick read of the schedules in the main hall yielded a train that departed each morning at 7:30 A.M. to cleave the dark heart of Central Europe, terminus Bucharest.

What would be the name of my Romanian sweetheart? I didn't know any Romanians. I puzzled over vowels and consonants while walking back to my apartment. Hanna? Katrina? Natasha? Csiucsiu? As I keyed the front lock to the apartment building, a diminutive figure from my childhood turned somersaults in defiance of the Russian bear. What had been her name? Just when I was on the verge of remembering, a hand nearly clapped me through the plate glass above the lock. I shouted, terrified a half-dozen assailants crowded my back.

"Mr. Miller, no reason to be frighten."

I peeled myself away from the door and stared with disbelief at Inspector Zima's face. What was he doing at the door to my building? Was my apartment being watched? Had he been following me? Had he seen me deposit the case in baggage claim at the train station? Did he know I had robbed Zdeněk? Had he come to take me quietly to a ten-year stint in the uranium mines? He seemed mocking when he joked, "You think I'm jealous husband, I come to beat you for sleeping with wife?"

I laughed weakly, tried to loosen the gag of my fluttering heart. "Not husband," I gasped. "Boyfriend. A Romanian girl. Nadia. That's her name. Ditched him for me. But she left. Train to Bucharest. Still. You never know."

"You are lucky. Is only me."

"Yes, well, nice talking to you," I said, and opened the front door, intent on escape. Zima deftly slipped through the door behind me. I hadn't thought clearly. Was I intending to take him to my apartment and introduce him to Monika and everything he did not already know? I looked at Zima, the door, and at Zima again, as though the two formed an unsolvable equation.

"Mr. Miller, you are nervous. Is true?"

A cagey question. He could have been truly observant, or attempting to unnerve me by suggesting I was already unnerved. I said, "Not nervous. Preoccupied. Us creative types, you know. Head in the clouds."

We regarded each other from behind the curtains of our respective stages, each waiting for the other to begin. I refused to be the first to step out. If he knew something, let him say it. He watched, black-eyed and wary, as though he already knew everything. Still I said nothing, forcing him to the first move, an attempt to pull me out by asking, "Why, you think, am I here?"

"A question everyone asks. The meaning of life. Hell if I know."

"Good joke! No, I am not here for philosophy but to talk of your cousin, Richard Greenleaf."

I replied with a pointed index finger, "You're investigating?" Events moved too fast. I had no time to think. For an unsettling moment, I sensed that my vision was so skewed that I saw little except self-aggrandizing fantasy.

"I could have told my men to pick you up, but is such nice day, and sometimes is better not to be formal. So I think, why not visit Mr. Miller, say, *Let's do lunch?*"

"Do lunch?" I repeated.

"Is not everyday I meet big Hollywood screenwriter."

I wondered if he mocked me. During decades of censorship and repression, ambiguous statements such as his had developed as the national means of communication in Czechoslovakia. The Czechs were as proud of their irony as the Russians were of their tanks. In retrospect, Czech irony had been no match for Russian steel. It wouldn't fare any better against Hollywood glitz.

"Did I ever tell you about the time I met Arnold Schwarzenegger?" I asked.

21

rnold Schwarzenegger, it turned out, was one of Zima's favorite movie stars. As I recounted a tale all the more riveting for its fictionalizations, he led me to a neighborhood *hospoda* redolent of smoke, grease, and spilled beer. Zima was known there by face if not profession, the waitress greeting him with a surly nod and the barman giving a friendly shout. I never would have ventured into such a place alone. We sat at the corner table, away from the windows. I stared at the menu for several uncomprehending minutes, searching for familiar groupings of vowels and consonants, and found only the English loan word *cola*. When the waitress stopped by, I ordered one. She looked as though she waited for me to complete my sentence.

"I forget, you don't speak Czech, do you, Mr. Miller?" he exclaimed, mock-surprised.

"You know damn well I don't."

"Then you must allow me to order," he said, and dismissed the waitress with a brief command.

I watched Zima light a cigarette and smoke, waited for him to address the topic that had brought us together, but the idle task of smoking seemed to satisfy him. I said, "Then there was the time I traded shots of tequila with Clint Eastwood in Baja."

Zima blew the impending anecdote aside with a stream of smoke. "Forgive me. I will be direct. You and I are old friends now. Evidence against your cousin is serious. I know you steal from young girls. Don't protest. No matter. I tell you stop, because it is my job, but I have more important problems, and too much time it will take to catch you. But this other crime, it was not so small."

The waitress slung to the table two beers and accompanying shots of vodka, making four small marks on a slip of paper glued down by a spot of spilled beer.

I said, "But I ordered a cola."

He either ignored me or didn't hear, lifting the shot glass and toasting, "To your health, or, as we say in Czech language, *na zdraví*."

I reluctantly touched the rim first to his glass and then to my lips. Zima downed his in one go and looked at me horrified.

"Please, that is not how to take drink of Slavic peoples," he said, and gestured that I must bolt the thing whole. When I did, he mimed that I should follow with a long draught of beer. "Good!" he exclaimed. "And what you think of Czech beer?"

There is only one answer to this question, which every Czech man will ask a foreigner if given opportunity. I said, "The best in Europe."

Contentment beamed from his face, as though I had complimented a direct descendant. The waitress clattered two more beers and shot glasses to the table, and doubled the slash marks on the tab. It occurred to me that he might be trying to get me incautiously drunk. Just as likely, multiple beers and vodka were Zima's standard lunch fare, as they were for half the male Czech workforce. Nevertheless, I reminded myself to think carefully before volunteering information. Zima lifted his shot glass, bid me to do likewise, and, saying *na zdraví*, emptied it. Maybe I had it wrong. Maybe Zima liked me, or wanted to like me, and staged this lunch to signal a turn in our personal relationship. The idea of having a Czech cop as a friend oddly pleased me. I chuckled into my beer and repeated enthusiastically, "Yep, the best damn beer in Europe."

"And your favorite Czech beer?"

I stole a glance at the label on the glass in my hand. "Městan," I said.

"Excellent choice." Zima beamed. "And your cousin? What kind of young man is he?"

"Cousin Dickie is a happy-go-lucky, well-intentioned, friendly idiot."

"Typical young American, then. Not at all like you." Despite the glimmer of irony in his black eyes, I decided to smile at the compliment. He lit a second cigarette after carefully extinguishing the remains of the first. "This I don't understand. I look at violence of crime and ask, could typical young American boy do such thing? Everyone is capable of violence, this I know. But tourist comes to Prague and commits this crime? No sense it has."

"So you'll let him go?" I asked, trying to sound hopeful. Better if Dickie stayed in jail a few more days, but I wanted to be charitable.

"There is the evidence," he said, as though it damned and nothing could be done about it.

"What evidence?"

"You know what happened, yes?"

Did I? I thought carefully over what the Vice Consul said. Nothing too specific. "Only in general. Something serious. Violence of some sort was involved."

The waitress delivered two plates with another round of beer and vodka. Both plates contained a lump of boiled potato, a shred of green cabbage, and a breaded something which, when cut open and sampled, had the consistency and taste of molten rubber.

"Interesting," I said. "What is it?"

"*Smažený sýr,*" Zima replied, attacking the items on his plate with relish. "In English, fried cheese."

I took a bite and immediately felt my arteries begin to clog.

"Can you tell me what you were doing when it happened?" This, Zima asked around a mouthful of *smažený sýr,* as though he requested the time on my watch. How many times had I seen the same tired narrative device of a suspect admitting something he could not possibly know unless he was the perpetrator of the crime? I would not allow myself to fall for that cliché. But in which crime was he attempting to implicate me? I had to remember that for all my crimes I was an innocent man who knew nothing.

"It would help," I said, clearly and firmly, "if I knew exactly what happened and when it happened."

Zima stared incredulously, a half-chewed lump bulging his cheek. "But I thought you knew," he burbled.

"How could I possibly know?"

Behind our masks, an understanding flickered, however brief and unstated, of the roles we played. He pretended that I was innocent while thinking me guilty, if not of the crime itself then of complicity. I professed ignorance, while knowing far more than was wise to admit. I could read it in his eyes, and as much as I wished to believe my performance was flawless, I sensed he could read my eyes just as fluently. Like actors we could have fooled an audience but not each other. I could admit to knowing nothing more than he told me: an unnamed man had been accosted at 8 A.M. two mornings ago by a thief who had somehow gained entry into his money-changing business and lay in wait for him to arrive. I listened carefully, comparing his version with mine to screen the inconsistencies and variations. The thief had forced the merchant to open the safe at knifepoint and then beat him unconscious. As I listened I tossed down the shot of vodka and attacked the fried cheese. Perhaps the Czechs drink so much because half drunk is the only way they can force down such awful food.

I said, "Dickie would be no more capable of an act like that than he would of flying to the moon on a surfboard."

"And who would be capable?" The implication of the question was clear. He meant me. No. Paranoia misled me. But why had he singled out Dickie if not to get at me? I did not know what to think. He sighed. "Twenty years I have this job, and still, it surprise me what people can do. I want to think your cousin is innocent, if only because we are such old friends, but facts of case are what they are."

"No," I said, growing purposely belligerent. The innocent are always annoyingly self-righteous. "The facts are that for some unknown reason you've decided to harass not just me but my entire family. The only reason I can think of for your behavior is personal vindictiveness. Did that Hungarian cop put you up to this?"

"Please, Mr. Miller! I like you," Zima protested. "But there is nothing I can do. Evidence—"

"What evidence?" I demanded. "I have not heard you utter one shred of proof."

"His passport. Richard Greenleaf's passport." Zima chose that moment to shake another Sparta out of its box, caress the gummed seal with the tip of his tongue, wedge the filter end just off the center mark of his lips, lift his silver Zippo lighter from the table, and bring it to flame; all gestures performed with seeming indolence, as though the outcome of events didn't much matter in the grander scale. After centuries of occupation by Hapsburgs, National Socialists, and Marxists, the Czech has acquired a longer view of time than the average myopic American, and I felt ill-equipped to wait him out.

"What about his passport?" I inquired through clenched teeth.

"First thing we find. Just outside door where crime took place."

The salt in the fried cheese made me thirsty. I bolted half my beer.

"Coincidence," I said.

"Just what we think at first, innocent American lose passport," Zima admitted. But the merchant had identified the thief as an English speaker, probably American, who didn't understand Czech or Russian. About my cousin's height and build, between twenty and thirty years of age, though the merchant had been so badly beaten he couldn't remember much more than that—at present at least.

The improbable location of Dickie's passport just beyond Zdeněk's doorstep confounded me. I blanked, could not remember if I had brought the passport with me, had stuffed it into pocket or satchel, had looked at it while waiting in the change booth, had accidentally or intentionally dropped it as I left. Could I so hate my family that I would commit any self-destructive act just for the pleasure of dragging them down with me? Impossible.

"Please don't look so upset. If your cousin is innocent, sooner or later we know."

Did I imagine Zima's seemingly reassuring remark concealed an intent to prove my cousin innocent but me guilty? "You seriously can't expect a young tourist like my cousin to have an alibi at eight in the morning. He probably didn't get into the hotel until four."

"Why he not have alibi is less interesting, from legal point of view, than fact he not have one."

I tried and could not hold my thoughts still long enough to count the possible ways his passport might have been dropped. The waitress set down two beers and shots of the traditional Czech liquor, Becherovka, reputed to be an excellent digestive, but which always made me faintly nauseous. The marks on the slip of paper began to look like a small stick-figure army. I said, "You confuse a simple accident for something meaningful. Any reasonable person would conclude that sometime during the night, my cousin, probably a little drunk, dropped the passport while making his way between clubs."

"That is not what your cousin say."

"What does my cousin say?"

"At first, nothing. Then he say he give passport to hotel clerk. Never see passport again."

"Well, then," I said.

"But that is not what clerk say." Without a *na zdraví* he tossed down his shot of Becherovka.

My voice raised a frustrated octave, "And what did the clerk say?"

"He return passport to cousin that afternoon."

I hid a pleased smile behind several large swallows of beer. Bad news for Dickie, but extraordinary luck for me. If the clerk insisted he returned the passport, I couldn't have stolen it. I said, "I don't care how bad it looks for my cousin, I can't possibly believe he could do such a thing. You know, he always did have a lousy memory. I still say he dropped it or he had his pocket picked."

"I think instead clerk lies," Zima said.

"Nonsense. No motive," I said, dismissing the idea as unworthy.

"We are nation of ex-Communists and short gray people. We do not tell truth if truth makes us different. When we steal, we steal little things, paper clip here, bottle of wine there, because to steal above crowd is to be caught. We tell little lies. Big lies need imagination, and makes you differ-ent, so is better to tell safe little lies. Like hotel clerk."

"I'm not following any of this," I confessed.

"We are nation of small criminals. Waiter cheat you, taxi driver charge double, but we will not hit you over head or shoot you."

"Well, I guess *we've* drunk enough beer."

"This is why I think you steal cousin's passport from hotel."

I stared, unbelieving. Zima's face lurched in and out of focus. I threw down the shot of Becherovka and heard loud, raucous laughter before I realized it was my own. I said, "I'm sure your reasoning is flawless. I just don't understand any of it."

"Richard Greenleaf is not type to beat man half to death."

"Half to death?" I echoed. Impossible. I'd only hit him a couple of times. He lied, trying to catch me out.

"If passport is stolen from desk, clerk is afraid he lose job. He thinks, Such little lie, what is harm? He later say he make mistake, confuse one guest for other guest. To say he give passport to cousin is just normal lie for short gray man in this country. And if he not give passport to cousin, then someone else steal passport, and that same person, I think, beat merchant. And you, Mr. Miller, were at hotel that afternoon."

I said nothing. To say anything would damn me. I tried to struggle to my feet, but my legs lay helplessly tangled under the table. I gave up, buried my head in my hands, confessed, "This is absurd. I'm hallucinating. A Czech cop did not just accuse me of grand theft and assault with a deadly weapon."

"Please forgive me, we are old friends here, I must ask you question, and you must answer. Where were you two mornings ago, from seven in morning to eight?"

I lifted my head from my hands and tried to fix him with an honest stare, but his face wouldn't hold still long enough for me to catch it with anything more than a frustrated glance, like the eye of a needle which repeatedly evades the thread. I said, "Almost any other morning I would have been asleep in my bed. Two mornings ago, however, I left my apartment about seven to see my Romanian friend off at the main train station."

"Her name?"

"I already said. Nadia."

"Last name?"

"Something unpronounceable."

"Address and phone number?"

"I was sleeping with this woman, not writing her biography."

"You have no alibi, then."

"Is that what I was giving you? I thought you just wanted to know where I'd been."

"I believe is true if you tell me is true, but is my job to judge with proof, and not with opinion, even if I have highest opinion of you. To have alibi, you need witness. Someone who says you were someplace where crime was not committed. *Rozumíš?*"

I understood only too well. "I went out drinking at Club Repré that night," I confessed. "I can give you a half-dozen names of people who saw me at two that morning."

"With Romanian girl?"

"Unfortunately not. I met her later, at Old Town Square."

"Then this Romanian girl, if no one sees her, could be in your imagination. You are famous Hollywood screenwriter. You have big head for imagination."

I made a show of pouncing on memory like a foot to windblown paper, pointed my index finger at Zima, said, "Wait, something else. . . . Of course! I stopped at my friend Andrew's apartment after I left the train station."

"What time?"

"About eight or a few minutes after."

"And this Andrew was home?"

"He was asleep. Woke him up. He was quite angry, I'm afraid." I thumbed through my address book, and cited Andrew's full name and address, as well as the names of those I had seen at Club Repré that night.

He wrote the information in a small black notebook and, when finished, pocketed it with a satisfied smile. "I am happy if information you give is true. It's not good politics now to arrest Americans. Your cousin, he has good lawyer?"

I told him the embassy had given me a list. Zima signaled the barman, who approached the table with a thick wallet in hand and began adding up the pen strokes on our tab. He asked, "Is man named Ladislav Havran on list?"

I ferreted through my pockets, finding on my third attempt the crumpled sheet of paper on which I had written the information. Havran was the third of six names. The barman wrote and circled a number on the tab, something in the range of ten dollars. I reached for my wallet. Zima stayed my hand.

"No, I ask you to lunch, you are my guest."

"Nonsense," I said.

"I insist." Zima pulled from his front trouser pocket a roll of thousand-crown notes as big as his fist. He peeled off a single note and handed it to the barman. I estimated the roll contained thirty or so bills, all the same telltale color. In American money, just over a thousand dollars. The amount stunned me.

"You recommend I hire this man Havran?" I asked.

He pocketed the bills and rose effortlessly from the table. "A case like this has many complications. Many people must be satisfied for cousin to be released. I hope you not take offense when I say you need lawyer too. It's not my job to tell you who to hire. I can only say Havran knows how things work in this country."

I untangled my feet, steadied myself with a palm laid flat on the table, and stood up. The blood rushed from my head as though from a floodgate. The room flared with a bright red light. I opened my eyes to Zima's pouched face, leaning over me. It seemed I had fainted and fallen to the floor.

"I'm perfectly fine," I said.

He helped me to my feet. After a false start, which nearly upset a neighboring table, I managed the mechanics of lifting first one leg, and then the other, until the momentum of my effort carried me to the door. He took my arm and guided me onto the sidewalk. "Really, Mr. Miller," he admonished, "you shouldn't drink so much, not this early in afternoon!"

22

Ladislav Havran sat behind a cubist rosewood desk in an office across from the Hotel Paříž, as ample a physical specimen as I'd seen in a country where corpulence was as cramped as the money supply. On evidence of girth alone, he seemed to have made the transition from protecting ethically disgraced Communists to representing legally compromised capitalists with the efficiency of a parasite able to adapt to multiple host species. He swept open his arms and dipped his head to welcome my entrance, clucking, *"Dobrý den, bonjour, buenos días, guten Tag, vítámé vas, prosím, posejte se."*

"Quite the polyglot, aren't you?" I said.

"Languages are one of my specialties," he crowed, and counted them out with fat, manicured fingers. "I'm fluent in

English, German, French, Czech, Slovak, Russian, Polish, and Serbian."

"Most of us Americans can't even speak English properly," I admitted, pleasantly self-deprecating.

"The Hindus say, 'The wise have no need of language.'"

"Then Americans are the wisest people on earth," I quipped.

He laughed heartily and made note of the remark on his pad. "Very good, sir!" he said. "Very good indeed. This conversation is quite enlightening. Would you give me the pleasure of stating your business?"

Tuning my voice to a frequency between embarrassment and anxiety, I detailed the phone call I'd received that morning from the U.S. Embassy. A half-raised eyebrow, the suggestion of a curled lip, a note jotted quickly on a legal-sized yellow pad—Havran's gestures were concise and comforting, able to convey not only his surprise at the charges but his professional sympathy and mastery of the situation. When I mentioned that earlier in the afternoon I had eaten lunch with Inspector Zima to discuss the case, he laid his pen across the yellow legal pad and folded his hands.

"One of our very finest investigators," he remarked. "How do you know him?"

"I suppose you might say we know each other socially. We met over a silly misunderstanding, but once he learned that I was in Prague to write a screenplay for a major Hollywood movie starring Tom Cruise, well, it wouldn't be inaccurate to say we became better acquainted, even friends."

When I casually mentioned the words *major Hollywood movie* his face glowed as though illuminated by a baby spotlight. "How terribly exciting! Hollywood has so much excitement and glamour—"

"Not to mention sex and money," I interjected.

He laughed appreciatively and observed, "After the bright lights of Hollywood, Prague must seem like a dark little town to you."

"Not at all. Prague is a gothic Disneyland, and the behavior of its inhabitants is as wonderfully exotic to me as the people in Hollywood must seem to you. There was an incident this afternoon with Inspector Zima, for example, which I'm at a loss to explain."

Havran's level of attention heightened, as though listening to a radio program for coded messages. "Perhaps I might assist you in the interpretation?"

"Over a considerable quantity of beer and vodka, Inspector Zima actually suggested that I was personally suspect, due to my close relationship to the accused. That struck me as odd enough, but then he insisted on paying the bill and flashed a very large roll of thousand-crown notes. I mean, what do you think he makes a month, legitimately?"

Havran looked at the ceiling, spread his palms, and shrugged. "A man in Inspector Zima's position, many years of respected service to the State, I would think earns a salary of approximately six or seven thousand crowns a month."

"He carried half his annual salary in his pocket."

"As chief investigator of Prague's most serious economic crimes, it does not seem unreasonable that he carries large amounts of cash, for one reason or another," Havran observed, and his accompanying smile was as bland as the remark was ambiguous.

"Nothing improper was actually said, but I had the distinct impression that he was suggesting that if a little money were to change hands—well, to be perfectly blunt, I thought he was signaling that he could—no, *should*—be bribed."

"One of the unfortunate facts of our poor country," Havran admitted. "Salaries are low, so low even the honest are corrupt. During the unfortunate years of state socialism, the most common saying in Prague was, *The State pretends to pay me and I pretend to work.* In situations like this and a thousand others, it is expected that a little money should pass hands. Perhaps it is easier to understand if you think of it as a primitive form of capitalism."

I felt a momentary love of Prague swelling my heart, because not only could anything be had for money, anything could be had for so little money. I said, "I'm not judging. I come to you because I'm trying to understand how things work here."

"I will tell you exactly. It is a system of lines, forms, and official stamps, controlled by little bureaucrats in little offices. If you wish to convince one of these bureaucrats to stamp your form—and to do anything in this country you need the proper forms and correct stamps—you must offer a gift. If you don't offer this gift, something will be wrong with the way you completed your form. Errors can be found on any form, real or imagined. And if by chance you fill one out so perfectly that even a thousand angels with microscopes cannot find a flaw, well, then, there is no law stipulating when the bureaucrat must give the form his official stamp of approval. He can keep it on the bottom of the stack, or lose it, or simply vanish when you appear. The police inspectors regrettably are no different from the plumbing inspectors in this instance. It is sometimes necessary to give them financial motivation to solve a specific crime when they have so many to investigate, or to clear the unjustly accused when so many—almost everyone arrested, it seems—are unjustly accused."

"You suggest, then, that I offer Inspector Zima a bribe?"

"Despite your youth, Mr. Miller, you seem to be a man of the world, and a man of the world does not need to say such words explicitly. I do not suggest you offer anyone a bribe. Such an act is illegal in this country, and we must always act according to law. But I recommend a retainer be paid for my services, which will be used to take care of certain contingencies. Naturally, upon termination of the case, you will not request the return of this retainer."

"And the size of the retainer?"

Havran puffed out his cheeks and threw his hands in the air, gestures which certified that despite his charade of uncertainty the retainer would be a significant sum. "There are a number of researches I must make before I can answer that question. We do not know for certain the seriousness of the charges." His eyes settled on mine a look both shrewd and curious. "Is this retainer to cover just your cousin or also your honorable person?"

"Inspector Zima has no evidence against me and, frankly, never can. I am absolutely innocent. But my work is far too valuable to risk the whims of police harassment."

"I'm personally relieved to hear you confess your innocence and am firmly convinced we'll prove it to the authorities."

"And once this retainer is paid, we'll have nothing to worry about?"

Havran's smile tightened with the unpleasantness of what needed to be said. "Please don't misunderstand, justice would not be well served if so easily bought. The retainer does not make it certain the case will be decided for you, merely that it will be considered by someone disposed to listen to your advocates. Complete certainty is granted only to those in position of authority to give complete certainty on something of equal value. But rest assured, in most cases, the evidence is not so substantial that complete certainty is required."

"Suppose the proof is substantial."

"A foreigner, high-profile case, it would be most difficult indeed to convince the authorities of the injustice of the accusation and the innocence of the accused." Havran's glance caught mine with frank regret that such a tragic outcome could be possible. A slap of the desk broke the mood and he stood, beaming with vigor and optimism. "But we won't even consider that possibility, no sir! I'm a great admirer of your Power of Positive Thinking!"

I took the cue and rose to clasp his hand in grateful embrace. He walked me to the door, giving my arm an extra squeeze of confidence and good fellowship. "None of these gloomy-doomy European philosophers for me, thank you. American optimism and can-do, that's the ticket! Call me tomorrow, and perhaps I'll bear the good news that this entire affair is the result of an unfortunate misunderstanding."

I left his office convinced that the happier and more optimistic he seemed at the beginning, the more it would cost me in the end.

As I approached my apartment, I heard the phone ringing through the door and, fumbling with the keys, rushed inside to pick up a dead line. I threw down the phone, glanced into the kitchen, and stuck my nose into the bathroom. Monika was not *en manse,* and I didn't see any sign that she had returned and left again in my absence. When the phone rang again some minutes later I let it bleat five or six times, not wishing any more unpleasant surprises for the day, but the hope it might be Monika urged me to pluck it from the cradle. The telltale beep of a long distance line identified the caller before his familiar voice bellowed my name. "Father!" I said, bright tones of happy-to-hear-you in my voice. "What a wonderful surprise! I didn't think you were talking to me anymore."

"What the hell is going on out there, son?" he demanded. Father did not sound pleased.

"Exactly what do you mean?"

The abrupt silence on the other end was punctuated by a static pop. I imagined Father's face, beet red, eyes closed as he mouthed the words to digits one through ten. "Shall we begin at the beginning?" he suggested, politeness quivering his voice like a plucked string. "You are unaware, perhaps, that your cousin Richard currently occupies a Czechoslovakian jail cell?"

"I am not unaware," I said, crowding the sarcasm from my voice. "Nor have I been altogether lax in my family responsibilities to Cousin Dickie. The Ambassador informed me of Dickie's legal problems this morning, and since then I've discussed the case personally with the local chief of police and engaged the services of a lawyer recommended by the Ambassador herself."

"Nix, I'm getting very tired of your lies."

"Father, may I remind you that I did not request this phone call, that you called me?"

"I just got off the phone with Ambassador Black," he announced.

It shouldn't have surprised me that he had secured a personal line to the Ambassador. Father was a significant financial contributor to the California Republican Party. I said, "And she told you I'd spoken with the Vice Consul, who is acting as her agent in this affair."

"That's not the same as speaking with the Ambassador, is it?"

"Absolutely not. It's better. He's a professional diplomat

known for his competence and not for once, as a child, having sung 'The Good Ship Lollipop.'"

"Ambassador Black is a good Republican," Father replied, offended. "I order you not to do anything more until John and Buffy arrive."

"I have Dickie practically sprung and you order me to stop? Father, I think you're the one who needs to see the psychiatrist."

Father said, "Nix—"

"You have no idea how things work out here."

"Nix—"

"You can't expect to wave your American passport and pull Dickie from jail like a bunny from a hat."

"Nix—"

"Uncle John and Aunt Buffy will just screw things up."

"That's enough, Nix."

"You don't live here. You don't give me orders here."

"Please, calm down."

"No. You wise up."

"Nix, answer me, did you have anything to do with this?"

I pulled the phone from my ear and stared at it for several long, hard seconds. Very calm, very much in control, I said, "Are you accusing me?"

"You know you've been having problems."

"I asked, *Are you accusing me?*"

"Richard is not the type to get involved in this sort of thing."

"And I am?"

"You still haven't answered my question."

"Fuck you for using Dickie against me!" I shouted, and slammed the receiver to its cradle.

* * *

Monika returned to find me sitting on a chair in front of the telephone, my face cupped in my hands. The phone rang. The phone had been ringing almost constantly since I'd hung up on Father. Monika flung her purse and coat aside and sat on the couch, watching me watch the phone. It rang fifteen, sixteen times.

"Well, answer it," she said.

I reached behind the base and plucked out the line. The ringing stopped. I lifted the phone from the table, opened first one and then the second window in the double casement, and heaved it into the courtyard two stories below. The plastic gave a satisfying crack when it hit the concrete. I shut both windows and returned to my chair, sitting again with my head in my hands.

"That was a mature thing to do," Monika remarked. I didn't bother to reply. She clanked about the kitchen, devouring anything edible and leaving the dishes piled in the sink for me to do later. The last thing I needed was a bumbling visit from Uncle John and Aunt Buffy. Prague abruptly seemed not distant enough. What was the use of moving halfway around the world if a ten-hour plane ride could yank me back to the dross of a life I had so desperately sought to escape? Monika tromped from kitchen to bathroom, slamming the door behind her. As the dutiful nephew I'd be required to meet them at the airport, carry their bags to the hotel, take them to visit Dickie, listening every step of the way to Aunt Buffy's inane commentary on how shabby everything seemed, not at all like Newport Beach. Uncle John would stare wordlessly out the nearest window, pretending a stoicism all those who knew him better understood as stupidity. And if they had listened to Father, they would secretly suspect I had something to do with landing their innocent son in jail. Hadn't Dickie already hinted they were upset with me over the *Cavity of Dr. Caligari* incident?

"I want to go to sleep now," Monika announced, emerging from the bathroom.

I lifted my head from my hands to stare down her audacity. "I'm in obvious crisis here, and all you have to say to me is you want to go to sleep?"

"It's not my fault the apartment is so small," she said.

Not a word of sympathy or even simple curiosity. I gestured vaguely toward the bed. "I promise to suffer wordlessly, so not to disturb you."

Without making it clear what she wanted—did she expect me to volunteer to sleep again in the bathtub?—but by pouting demeanor making it clear she wanted something, she flicked off the light and under the safety of blanket and bedspread stripped off her skirt and stockings. In my experience, that style of disrobing is hardly an invitation, but the sight of her carefully folding her garments and laying them by the bed aroused me with her indifference. I stripped to my briefs and slid into bed. Before I had approached closer than a foot, she said, "Good night, Nix."

I curled up against her back and allowed my hand a wandering caress. She abruptly shifted positions, elbowed me in the ribs, and complained, "You're suffocating me." I ground my teeth together and stared at the ceiling. The polite thing to do was to let her sleep. My good intentions didn't last more than thirty seconds. I sat up, asked, "Where were you today?"

"Out," she answered.

"And yesterday?"

She rolled to the side of the bed, shook a cigarette from the pack she kept on the floor—never during all the time we lived together did I see her more than five feet distant from a cigarette—and lit it. She said, "Yesterday? Let me remember. Oh, yes. Yesterday I was out too."

"Where do you go when you go out?"

"I go out when I go out."

"Anyplace in particular?"

"Sure. When I go out, I go out*side*."

She stepped out of bed and smoked by the window, moonlight silvering her honeyed thighs. I debated telling her everything: my debacle with Dickie's passport, the visit from Inspector Zima, the disaster of a conversation with Father, the works. As I watched her gaze out the window, outlined in smoke and moonlight, my chest constricted so sharply I gasped, as though I had been plunged steaming into an ice-cold bath. I had fallen in love with her before I had the slightest notion who she was, and now that I realized how truly monstrous she could be, my desire for her controlled me completely. I decided to tell her almost nothing. "Anybody follow you when you go out?" I asked.

"Why would anybody want to follow me?"

"I don't know why. I just asked."

"Do you think somebody is following me?"

"I have no idea."

"Sure you have an idea, or you wouldn't have asked."

"I just think it's smart to be aware, considering."

Monika stabbed out her cigarette and slid the ashtray across the floor. "Are you suggesting we have a police problem?"

"Not at all."

"Sven and I never had any problems with the police."

"Neither do we. I just think it's best to be careful. Because I love you and don't want to see anything happen to split us up."

She walked to the bed and looked down at me. I struggled

against the urge to trace the course of a vein up the skin of her thigh. The electrochemical reactions sparking in her eyes were inscrutable. I gave her my most winsome smile. With a graceful crossover motion of her arms she stripped off her pullover and sat next to me on the bed.

"You're sweet and I'm being horrible," she said.

In the tangled clothing and cramped confines of our previous couplings I had not noticed that on her left breast, directly over the approximate location of her heart, two tattooed snakes consumed each other's tails. The similarity with the entwined snakes ornamenting the ring I had bought for her in Budapest was extraordinary. When I asked her about the tattoo, she cupped her breast and turned it toward the window, so the moonlight might better illuminate the design, but the symbolism of its placement on the canvas of her skin she left unexplained. I took her frank nudity as encouragement and reached for the join between her legs. She deflected my hand and with gentle insistence pushed me onto my back.

"You can't touch me," she said.

"What's wrong?" I asked. Whining was undignified. I thought it humiliating to beg. Neither stopped me from doing both.

"Shhhh," she said, and putting a finger to my lips, let her hand drift to a pink tumescence as tender and hard as an Achilles heel. "You can't touch me because it's wrong to touch me," she said, and when I began to protest she shushed me again. "You can't touch me but I can touch you, baby. Does baby want me to touch him?" She switched to Danish, and though I couldn't understand the specific meaning of her words, the high-pitched singsong in her voice made me feel as though I were a child being addressed by another child. No woman had ever talked to me like a child before, and at first I thought it sexy but contrived, like the breathiness of Marilyn Monroe or any other little girl sexpot, and frankly, her employed style of stimulation was less appealing than its three more comely rivals, but the slightest touch from Monika thrilled me more than circus sex with any other woman. As I began to cry out with pleasure I heard her voice echo mine, and again I suspected it a gesture of contrived eroticism, but her ecstatically clenched face convinced me she felt a genuine if perverse passion, touching herself as she spoke in Danish, lost in the language of her memories and the memories of her desire.

23

The sound of a running tap in the bathroom awakened me to the watery light of early morning. I nipped out of bed, dressed, and slipped back under the covers, feigning sleep until I heard the front door click open and shut. Monika glanced over her shoulder as she crossed the street outside our apartment, forcing me to follow at too prudent a distance, but I felt I could track her blindfolded, guided by an essence as identifiable to me as scent to a bloodhound. I followed not from any specific suspicion but out of curiosity—her every action seemed a mystery, sometimes horrifying and sometimes wondrous but always fascinating—and if that meant spying out an intrigue, I was perfectly willing to benefit by my inquisitiveness. She could have lost me easily at the distance I followed, but after the first few cursory glances she threaded a straightforward route though Staré Město to Václavské náměstí, where she entered a former Art Nouveau jewel transformed to socialist bauble, the Ambassador Hotel.

Screened by the lettering on the front glass, I watched her loitering near the reception desk, absorbed by a sudden and unexplained interest in an adjacent newspaper rack. Several guests dropped keys, checked messages, or checked out. After the arrival of a single woman whose business required no more than a minute, Monika turned from the newspaper rack and strode past the front desk. I selected a copy of the *Herald Tribune* and glanced about the lobby. After a few minutes of observation, I strolled in the direction of her disappearance, which led to a large room with tables and breakfast buffet. She sat alone at a table by the far window, enjoying a considerable repast. I couldn't risk more than a cursory glance and retreated to the lobby, where, loitering near the reception desk, I overheard a Scotsman repeatedly identify himself by name and room number to a clerk confused by his brogue.

I never would have used information gleaned at the front desk, like Monika, to cadge a free breakfast. The risk was disproportionate to the reward. Monika didn't understand the risk-to-reward ratio. Not paying was a principle. I had never seen her pay for anything. Somebody always paid for her, or she figured out a scam to get what she wanted for free. Despite her refusal to pay for anything, she was as liberated from greed as anyone I had ever met. Hadn't her refusal to take a share of Zdeněk's money proven that?

The silver-haired and red-scarfed figure who strode arm in arm with her through the lobby a few minutes later was a dapper if elderly gent whose face, despite dissipated character lines, retained something of its original handsomeness.

They raced through the lobby and out the revolving door before I could fold my newspaper to transport size, and after several failed attempts to get the creases to match I tossed the thing aside and scurried to the window, where I witnessed their approach to a cab at the bottom of the square. When the car pulled away I sprinted to the nearest waiting taxi, snapping open the passenger door to a stringy-haired fellow in tight jeans who touted an advertisement for a local bordello on his dashboard.

"Follow that cab!" I shouted, pointing in the direction of the departing car.

The driver stubbed out his cigarette, reached forward to turn off his radio, and stared at me blankly.

"That cab! Follow it! Follow that car!" I shouted, trying to find a variation that would spark him to action.

He half turned to see what I was pointing at, and by the time it took him to cite a 500-crown fare, the car in which Monika had fled was beyond pursuit.

"Have you considered taking a vacation?" Havran asked in a carefully coded tone of voice. "Personally, I prefer to travel in early summer, before the crowds of August." He watched me over steepled fingers as I fidgeted in the leather armchair before his desk, half fantasizing vulgar episodes involving Monika and a figure old enough to be her father. "It's so much more pleasant to visit a city when one's every step isn't dogged by the touristic masses, don't you think?"

"I wish I had the time," I replied, uninterested in small talk.

"Perhaps you could combine business with pleasure. Research a location in another country. Vienna, Paris, Rome—such beautiful cities this time of year!"

I prepared a brusque reiteration of the fact that I was a busy man, but behind the cheery sparkle in Havran's eyes I noticed a darker glint of warning and shut my mouth to reconsider. "Of course, a writer can work anywhere," I said.

He nodded with vigorous approval. "How I envy you, Mr. Miller! A foreigner, no permanent ties to this country, nothing at all to prevent you from packing your things into a bag and going wherever you please."

"I was planning a trip to Warsaw next month, when the weather warms a bit," I suggested.

"Why wait at all? I've discussed your travel plans with a few key people, who would like to be considered your friends, and all promise that you will enjoy unrestricted travel out of the country. I hasten to add that these friends have urged me to suggest this vacation."

"My situation, then, is grave?"

"I've made a number of inquiries, and what I've heard is not good. Not good at all."

"But I've done nothing!" I protested.

"There is, I believe, a young lady staying in your apartment?"

I didn't confirm or deny, though a reading on any galvanometer would have spiked through the glass. Someone had been watching the apartment. Any connection proved between Monika and me would have a number of disastrous consequences. My cousin's passport found outside the burgled premises of my girlfriend's date that evening—not even I could explain my way out of that circumstance.

"Traveling together can be so much more rewarding than traveling alone," Havran continued, gazing wistfully at the ceiling. "Particularly with such a beautiful woman. How I envy your youth and vigor! She would certainly like to accompany you on your vacation, don't you think?"

I stumbled to my feet, said, "Yesterday, you seemed to think it wasn't so serious."

Havran was at my side before I knew it, nimbly maneuvering his bulk around the desk to clasp my elbow and guide me back into the chair. "Goodness, you're white as a sheet!" he exclaimed. "Would you like a glass of water, or perhaps a whisky?"

I nodded to the whisky and bolted it when he poured a shot from a bottle of Jameson's.

"Your cousin's situation is even more difficult. In this country, it is no easy thing to get out of jail once in. The bureaucracy is imposing—there are simply far too many people to please and regulations to fulfill. Any influence our friends might have is spread too thin to have any real effect."

The shot of whisky and the second to follow steadied me. If Dickie remained in jail, they suspected he acted as my accomplice and would pursue confessional evidence. The longer they tried to pump water from that dry well, the better it would be for me. "Just as well. My father," I said, savoring the bitter taste of that word in my mouth, "has expressed his desire to handle my cousin's case personally. I will pass your name along, of course, though I can't promise he'll be wise enough to heed your counsel."

"Then the retainer will represent your interests, solely?" he inquired, delicately.

"Correct," I answered and, reaching for my wallet, asked the amount.

"Two thousand," he stated.

I slipped two thousand-crown notes from my wallet and laid them on the desk. Havran smiled at the notes like a shortchanged cashier.

"Dollars," he said.

I raised my eyebrows, frowned, cleared my throat, but no matter how discreetly I showed my surprise neither his expression nor the quoted amount changed. I lifted the thousand-crown notes from the desk like corpses and crumpled them into the pocket of my sport coat.

"Just so I understand your price structure, how much would the retainer have been had it included my cousin?"

"I don't believe in hypotheticals, Mr. Miller. Just the facts! And the fact is the retainer will be for you only."

"But you didn't know beforehand that the retainer wouldn't include my cousin, so the fact is, you prepared two bills."

"I can see now you are a clever fellow. If you look at the facts that way, then indeed, the fact is I estimated the cost of a retainer covering both you and your cousin at twice the amount of you alone."

The gross from Zdeněk's safe was just over $4,000. No doubt Inspector Zima was among the group of my concerned friends. The greedy bastards knew the exact amount and were attempting to steal it whole. I felt an intense resentment that all my hard work was going to the benefit of thieves. I said, "For that amount, I trust my vacation will not be a permanent one."

"A temporary measure, we hope," Havran clucked, rising from behind his desk to escort me to the door. "No Euro-pessimism for us, no sir! I sincerely hope you will soon return to walk our historic streets." He tapped twice on my shoulder as he opened the door. "But even if you choose to take a permanent vacation, you must not neglect your Czech friends. This is of utmost importance. They have means to reach you wherever you choose to live, and the last thing any of us wants is a forced return from your vacation."

"I'll bring the retainer tomorrow," I promised.

"You are as wise as you are clever," he pronounced, heartily pumping my hand in farewell. "How I envy you, Mr. Miller. How I envy you!"

The late-afternoon sun slanted across copper-green cupolas and red tile roofs when I stepped onto Paržíšká Street. I did not walk with purposeful direction; instead, I wandered aimless through baroque shadows cast at cubist angles across the cobblestones, ruminating on the profound impact Monika had made on my life as I considered every twenty yards or so the contrast of architechtures in my path—a Romanesque rotunda here against a Renaissance sgraffito facade there—and marveled at the play of light where a gable or spire struck against the sky. Wandering the city served as my chief recreational activity most afternoons and rarely failed to lift my spirits, though that afternoon the thought that I was to leave it oppressed terribly. After some time I arrived at Na Příkopě, a broad pedestrian avenue built on the site of a moat which once defended Prague from foreign invaders, and now served as one of the city's principal attractions to the descendants of those same invaders. I found an empty bench and sat, my face turned sunward, to watch the human panoply: tourists waddling behind umbrella-toting guides; construction workers in blue uniforms as frayed and dusty as their skin; nouveau riche Czechs in ill-fitting German suits and white socks and State bureaucrats in ill-fitting Polish suits and white socks; country Gypsies begging with children clung to flowered dresses; scrawny metal heads from East Germany and robust metal workers from West Germany;

goateed Americans in backpacks and baseball caps and too-loud voices; and everywhere the young Czech girls, high-cheekboned and curious-eyed, tantalizingly lanky and short-skirted and so intensely sexual it hurt to watch them, knowing that in a few short years by the regional curse of reverse alchemy they would turn short and squat and grim as their mothers and grandmothers. I observed with a sense of having missed something vital during my few months in the city, like a man who doesn't realize until the relationship has terminated that he's been in love all along.

Someone calling out my name in public has always startled me like a sudden unmasking, and hearing my name shouted as I approached my apartment building, I scuttled through the door and quickly locked it behind, terrified that it might be Zima or one of his ex-STB henchmen; it wasn't until I turned to glance through the glass that I caught sight of Andrew's frantic wave and grin. I opened the door with a sheepish excuse that I hadn't heard him calling out my name. He laughed—a bright musical sound in his throat, like ringing glass—and jibed, "And you were so angry at me for not hearing your shouts at Jo's Bar."

I summoned the courage to look him directly in the eyes, expecting irony but greeted instead by a cheery twinkle. Surprisingly, he seemed genuinely glad to see me, and suggested a walk through Josefov, the site of the former Jewish ghetto of Prague which bordered my apartment building. I readily agreed. We said nothing for the first few minutes—I was simply too happy to be in his company to risk an off-putting first remark—and it wasn't until we began to circumscribe the walls of the old Jewish cemetery that he observed, "You look troubled. Is there anything wrong?"

After I'd seen nothing but the back of his hand the past few weeks, his sudden concern nearly moved me to tears. I said, "So much is wrong I don't know where to start."

"I think I know. The police paid me a visit this morning."

I feigned surprise. "Inspector Zima? Rumpled and chain-smoking?"

"That's him. He asked if I'd seen you a few mornings ago."

"What did you tell him?"

"The truth, of course. That you woke me up early, about eight."

"I expected nothing less of you, but thanks all the same."

"Did you know a tourist visa is good for only three months?" he asked, seemingly apropos of nothing.

"Sure, but nobody bothers to check."

"Zima did. I've been here three and a half months."

I stopped him with an arm to his elbow and a look of genuine remorse. "He's not going to—no—how awful!"

"I simply can't allow myself to be kicked out of the country now."

"I know a good lawyer," I suggested.

"I knew you'd want to help," he said with a light smile. "Ferida and I are getting along really well. She's the girl who—"

His mouth stiffened and his face flushed dark red.

I tugged him along and said, "Please forget I ever said that horrible thing."

"Part my fault. I shouldn't have pushed you," he admitted, very generously, I thought. "You understand, she's a refugee, she can't just pick up and go anywhere to follow me. And the work I'm doing here is really important. I can't afford to stop."

"You make me feel guilty, Andrew. I'm not doing anything here, not anything of value like you."

"You've engaged this lawyer yourself?" he asked, with an inappropriate intensity.

"Sure. He's not cheap, but he knows the system here."

"Then I don't feel quite so bad."

"I told you it's nothing to worry about."

"You misunderstand. It's not the risk of deportation that worries me. Not anymore. Knowing you have a good lawyer means I don't feel so bad about changing my story."

"Changing your story how?"

"I told him you'd stopped by not at eight but at nine."

"You lied?"

"That's why I came by to talk to you. To warn you. I figured either you or I was going to be deported, so why should it be me? I'm sure the charge isn't anything very serious."

"Grand theft and assault is very serious."

"You didn't do it, did you?"

"Of course not."

"Well then. Nothing to worry about."

"But you're my only alibi!"

"All you have to do is catch a train to the West this evening. You said yourself you weren't doing anything important here." This, Andrew said with a friendly squeeze of my shoulder and a merry gleam to his voice, as though he had not betrayed but merely caught me in a logic trap of my own making. That Andrew had the effrontery to lie about the false time line I'd constructed flabbergasted as much as galled. What was the use of lying about anything if someone else's lie could undo it all? I sputtered a protest that quickly disintegrated to indignant fricatives. Andrew cut me off with a hearty handshake and an encouragement to write when I'd reached safety. "So I can stop worrying about this terrible mess you've gotten yourself into," he said. Then he was off, striding briskly toward Staroměstské náměstí—frequently checking over his shoulder to be certain I didn't follow—and a claimed meeting with his beloved Ferida.

There are moments in everyone's existence, I suppose, that define personal impotence in the face of a universe not just indifferent but seemingly hostile to human will. Moments when events have so conspired against the successful exercise of will that to try at all seems absurd. No matter how I tried to rationalize it, that I was the victim of an indifferent universe or vindictive God or just personally incompetent, I couldn't suppress the horror felt when I entered my apartment and noticed the sudden absence on the floor where Monika's suitcase had been.

Once the first shock passed, brutal as a wall falling, I rushed from corner to corner, upending the couch, flinging open the closet door, charging into the bathroom in hopes of finding that she hadn't left me, but had merely moved the suitcase to another location inside the apartment. When I failed to find it I threw the contents of cabinets to the floor in frustration, searching places a suitcase of that size could not have reasonably been. In the kitchen, I found the note she had left behind, folded beneath an overflowing ashtray:

Nix,
You were right. I am being followed. You know where to find me.

Monika

The cryptic last line maddened me. What did she mean? I had no idea where to find her. We had never discussed how to reconnect should events force our separation. The content of the note seemed designed to assure me of her good intentions when it was evident she had run off with the silver-maned rogue I'd seen accompanying her in the lobby of the Ambassador Hotel. I was reasonably certain she hadn't seen me. Monika was always clever when forced to it. She knew I was wary of her being followed, and so invented that as an excuse to flee. I would not admit to the irony of her having left me because she feared she was being followed by someone who, it turned out, was me.

I paced the apartment, certain at that very moment she stood in the toilet stall of an exclusive hotel or restaurant, skirt hiked and my competitor at her back. No Czech or resident alien would risk taking a cab from Václavské náměstí, the drivers loitering there known for being no better than licensed thieves. He was a tourist, then. I knew almost nothing about Monika's sexual tastes except their unpredictability. He could have been a casual pickup, someone from her past, a mark from whom she planned to con a little traveling money. I knew she hadn't any money. She couldn't survive long without funds. The rogue looked as though he had style if not wealth. But why bother with a con when she had shown such indifference to the proceeds from Zdeněk's safe?

The answer nipped at the edges of consciousness like a small, nervous dog. I kicked it away repeatedly, but each time the idea returned with sharper teeth and shriller in-sistence. I pulled the wallet from my pocket and placed it on the kitchen table. I told myself I wronged her with my suspicions, and, from the very beginning of our relation-ship, she hadn't remained two steps ahead of me. I flipped open my wallet. The claim token to the locked case full of cash I had left at the train station was missing, an absence as large in my wallet as Monika had suddenly become in my life.

24

Lethargy numbed my desire to will any muscle to move, though the involuntary ones continued to pump and flex in the minutiae of an increasingly pointless existence. I don't know how long I sat at the kitchen table, staring at my wallet. Hours, it seemed. A loud knocking once roused my chin from my chest. Sometime later, when it repeated itself with greater insistence, I stood and ambled to the front door, where I peeped a scarlet-faced Uncle John hammering with a beefy fist and shouting things I'd prefer not to repeat. I settled into the chair by the end table in the living room and stared at the dustless square where I had kept the phone, waiting for Monika to call between bouts of consciousness that she couldn't because I had thrown the phone out the window. When I tired of staring at the spot where the telephone had rung, I returned to the kitchen and stared at the fold in my wallet where the claim token had been, like a castled king barricaded behind rook and pawns, shuttling ineffectually between squares.

I could think of nowhere to go without Monika. Despite her coldness and betrayals, I could not imagine life without her. To flee to some strange city would lose her and the money she presumably had removed from baggage claim at the train station. Without those funds, I couldn't pay Havran and prevent my arrest. Clearly, I couldn't leave Prague without some assurance of finding her and the money. She wrote that I knew where to find her. As dawn splashed red the walls of my apartment, I again searched cabinets, drawers, and cracks in walls for some hidden message, and found nothing but lipstick-stained glasses and cigarette butts.

She wouldn't have left evidence in so obvious a place, I reasoned. She feared the police would search my flat; any clues left behind would lead them straight to her. Her cryptic message had been a clever strategy to confuse them but encourage me. She would leave word somewhere obscure yet obvious, a location only I would know to search. But where? The message desk at the Merkur? That was her method of contacting Sven, not me. The Gellért in Budapest? Her memories of our encounter there would not be fond. The men's room at the Hotel Paříž? Certainly memorable, but inappropriate. Where could she be certain I'd look? I retrieved my wallet from the kitchen table and realized with fantastic elation not only the perfect dead-letter drop but the only permissible explanation for the missing claim token.

* * *

The same matron in floral print smock attended baggage claim at Hlavní Nádraží. Rather than wrestle with her limited grasp of English, I snared a fluent passerby who explained, following my instructions, that my claim token had been stolen with my wallet. The argument that followed, in which the matron insisted that I couldn't remove any baggage without a claim token, and I calmly repeated the tag number and a description of the case, ended when she admitted that the bag had been removed sometime earlier, she could not remember when or to whom. I palmed a hundred crowns and slipped it under the service bell. She had been bribed so infrequently the amount shocked her, ashen face blazing as her nubbed nails scrabbled at the bill and swept it into an apron pocket.

"A young woman, very black hair," my translator repeated. "And an older man. Her father? Not Czech. The woman had the claim ticket."

In dashing off her note to me, Monika had misused adverbs; although I didn't know *where* to find her, I did discover *how*. At the Ambassador Hotel, I slipped the desk clerk five hundred crowns and a story about a meeting I'd missed with a gray-haired man whose name I had regrettably forgotten but who had been a guest of that hotel. The size of the tip encouraged a prodigious display of memory from the clerk, aided by a registration card which included the guest's name—Henrík Havas—Hungarian passport number, and street address in Budapest. In my more optimistic moments, I reasoned that Monika had such confidence in my abilities that she had fled knowing I would find her. In my less sanguine moments, I recognized that she had either caught me following her, and fled with a competitor as a punishing ruse, or I had been replaced by a man she would present as "her uncle" when next we met. Either scenario included a new character whose motivations conflicted with mine.

My arrival at the Keleti train station in Budapest was greeted by a sculpture of a man howling, eyes wide and hair electrically aglow, depicted in neon tubes and steel beams bent with the grace of a line drawing. The sculpture was an advertisement for an electronics company, hung just inside the mouth of the arch where all trains arrive and depart, and though it did nothing for the image of that company, it prepared visitors for the horrors awaiting in the city of Magyars. Swarms of neophytic capitalists descended upon the train as it pulled into the station and assaulted the disembarking passengers—mostly American tourists and Germans from Berlin—with offers of rooms to rent and cabs to hire. Such scenes were standard in Central European train stations at the time, renting services to foreigners one of the few methods of securing hard currency in the former Iron Curtain countries. I brushed away those who thrust maps and photographs at me to speak with the swarthy gentlemen who called "Taxi?" in soft voices as I passed. I was keen to find an English-speaking driver who wouldn't rip me off, and after rejecting the first two candidates I selected a short and squat man in his fifties who drove a dark-blue unmarked Russian Lada: perfect, I thought, for surveillance.

From the rear seat, I reveled in the wide avenues and fast traffic of Budapest. With the weekend approaching, I could not be expected to have Havran's retainer until the following week, giving me five to six days to locate Monika and the money, perhaps more if he wasn't quick to alert Zima that I'd tramped without paying the bill. The address listed in Henrík Havas's passport led the driver to a not unimpressive villa in the Buda Hills, just above the Castle Palace. In Los Angeles, a villa of that type in a similar location— say, a tree-lined street in the Hollywood Hills—would have fetched a million. I instructed the driver to park half a block down and across the street and ambled over to closer inspect the premises. Not that I suspected Henrík Havas of being rich; in Budapest a villa like that could have meant anything. Half were owned by the State, and most of the rest by those whose primary currency was good political connections. The villa needed a fresh coat of paint and the services of a competent gardener, but Henrík's name was the only one on the front gate. I returned to the Lada and the task of waiting. Whenever a car drove past, my driver squirmed nervously behind the wheel. The few passersby assiduously avoided eye contact. Occasionally, my glance would cross the driver's in the rearview mirror. He seemed on the verge of speaking, but when I smiled with bland confidence he kept silent. Little doubt he suspected I worked for the CIA.

A thirtyish woman emerged from the villa late that afternoon with two preschool children toddling behind. Old Henrík—he grew older and more infirm the more frequently I remembered him—seemed to have sired a small family to keep him company in his dotage. Monika would certainly be interested in that fact no matter what her scheme. The woman checked the mail, bent over the walk to pull a few straggling weeds, and shut herself inside the house. I debated whether to approach on some pretext—as a lost tourist or claiming Henrík had asked me to drop by when in town—

but before I could decide on a suitable approach a late-model BMW sedan sped up the street and smartly whipped into the drive. I craned my neck out the window to catch a glimpse of passengers in the front or back seats, but the windows were too reflective of sky and flora to pierce. A minute later, he emerged alone onto the front walk, carrying a bouquet of flowers. I cursed. Men bring flowers to wives to assuage a guilty conscience.

Henrík burst out of the villa less than an hour after his arrival, careening down the hill as though making an escape. My driver coaxed a perilous speed from his Lada, which, like most things Russian I'd known, seemed designed to run badly but forever. The BMW turned right on the expressway paralleling the banks of the Danube. Though he could have taken that route to uncountable destinations, I knew then where he headed, passing beneath the castle and along the dolomite cliffs to a familiar Budapest landmark, the Gellért Hotel and Spa.

Natural caution warned me to keep a distance as I followed Henrík into the lobby, until I realized that even if Monika had told him about me, he had no idea what I looked like. He didn't bother stopping at the front desk—another bad sign—but strode directly to the elevators. I waited off his right shoulder, observing with disappointment not only his obvious excitement but a greater than expected youthfulness. Despite his gray hair and lined face, I estimated his age at no more than mid-fifties. He was old enough to be Monika's father, which might act as an unfortunate stimulant to my depraved beloved, yet not so old that age yet presented an obstacle to potency. When the doors chimed open, I followed him inside the elevator, watched him press the button to the fourth floor, and pressed the same button myself. At those close quarters he reeked of cologne and smug self-satisfaction. I had no doubt he expected an evening of sexual entertainment. His sport coat was silver, matching the color of his hair, and below a rugged chin he wore a splash of yellow scarf, like the throat of a vain bird. The scarf was a pretentious touch—perhaps he had reached that age where his neck had begun to wattle—but the clothes were stylish and his coat-hanger frame wore them well. A tuneless whistle of air passed through his pursed lips. I wanted to smash him. Instead, I held open the elevator doors with a deferential smile, allowing him to exit first, and then followed him down the hall. He stopped at the corner room and knocked one-two, one-two-three. I noted the room number and turned down the stairs. I knew who waited behind that door and had little wish to see her just then.

In the lobby, I debated what course of action to take, from affecting a jaded understanding to venting homicidal rage. Breaking down the door to her room would catch her in the simultaneous iniquities of betrayal and theft. I could approach the clerk and ask him to announce I was on my way up, allowing them a few moments to scramble back into their clothes but not enough time to grant Henrík a graceful exit. With nothing except my indecision to divert me, I imagined Sven standing at the bar across the lobby, chatting up a slatternly blonde in red minidress. He turned midsentence, spotted me, and laughed. His flesh had swelled like a gray balloon with the gases of decomposition. I closed my eyes and decided to do nothing, because had I caught Monika *flagrante delicto* it would have destroyed me. Henrík was rich, I reasoned. Obviously, she had designs on his wealth to which his cologned presence that night was key.

She was expert at exciting and then deflecting men's attentions, and no doubt Henrík was turning blue with frustrated passion at that very moment. Paranoia had simply outraced reason once again, and for the sake of my sanity I needed to believe that Monika acted with too great an independence but still within the compass of our partnership.

When, after midnight, Henrík emerged from the elevator, I scanned his face for clues to their recent behavior. His step still had bounce, and by the way he allowed his gaze to trace the curved oak banister of the second-floor balcony he seemed not displeased by the course of events but induced to reverie. My mouth ached from the constant grind of teeth. I wouldn't have characterized him as angry or frustrated. If they hadn't just enjoyed vigorous sex he was convinced it was near enough to savor. Rather than take the elevator I climbed the floors step by step like the stairs to my own hanging. From thorax to appendix I felt crushed and bleeding. Any display of human feeling would only excite Monika with the smell of blood. I had to play the scene for the money. Jealousy was a weakness with Monika. I reminded myself that I wasn't a sweaty-palmed, lovesick adolescent. Not to take a hard line would mark me as a sucker. I'd gutted Sven and beaten Zdeněk half to death. Another shocking example of urban violence could just as easily remove Henrík from the scene. Budapest was a dangerous city, and violent crime the smoke that accompanies the genie of economic reform. The police wouldn't be terribly surprised to find him slumped over the wheel of his BMW one morning, the victim of random violence or capitalist dispute. If he carried any money on him, all the better.

Too great a silence answered my first knocks on the door. I double-checked the room number and knocked again. My anger increased commensurate to the time I was made to wait. I resisted the temptation to pound the door from its hinges. Too obvious an anger would be interpreted as jealousy. In cinematic terms I needed to play the anger as subtext, dispassionate cool a thin crust on the surface of a potentially murderous rage. The door wedged open to a sliver of Monika's eye, and though I feared she would slam it shut at the sight of me she swung it open as though I had been expected. The hard-pitted splash of a running shower reverberated behind her, and she looked fresh from it, wrapped in terrycloth towel and her hair dripping wet.

"Oh, Nix, you found me," she said, in a tone of voice I could not distinguish between disappointment and tenderness.

I opened my mouth to speak, but the words lay as silent in my throat as infants strangled in their bed. Likely she thought I was struck speechless with emotion. The critical piece of evidence was the bed. The room appeared large, even for a hotel as grand as the Gellért. From the doorway I could see the entry hall and part of a large circular room, but no bed. Even if Monika had jumped into the shower to wash away the rank odors of adultery, her bed would reveal the disarray of a romp with Henrík. I ignored the bizarre gleam in Monika's eyes and stepped forward to bring more of the room into view. A bright flash of terry cloth gave inadequate warning that my perspective was about to be flipped. I imagined someone else in the room had lain in wait— a hallucination that Sven had somehow returned to life turned my stomach counterclockwise to the spin of my body to the floor—but a moment after landing to a stunned view of the ceiling I recognized that Monika had thrown me with the same swift urgency with which she unbuckled my belt and tore the shirt from my chest.

"I came for the money, not you," I insisted, but her practiced hands discovered that biology betrayed my words. Her mouth silenced my protests. The scene I had carefully rehearsed vanished from memory. When her robe fell away and she sat astride me like a carnal Diana, my anger alchemized to desire, and later, when we lay at arm's length on the carpet, exhausted, it vaporized to mere petulance.

"You shouldn't have taken the money," I admonished.

"I missed you," she said.

It did not seem possible she really meant it. Perhaps she feared I might harm her and knew passion a certain way to defuse my anger. She might have felt guilty about Henrík and staged an amorous greeting to deflect my suspicions. But she knew I couldn't harm her, no matter how great my anger, and of Henrík not a word had been mentioned. I entertained the wild thought that in the deviant course of her emotions, she might have spoken the straight truth.

"I understand. You thought you were being followed, so you ran," I reasoned. "I might leave a note and take the first train out of town myself, if I thought we were seriously compromised. But I would have left some message where I had gone, which you didn't, and I wouldn't have taken all the money, which you did."

"I knew you'd find me," she said, reaching across the carpet to grasp my hand.

I sat up, stared down at her, refused to be distracted by her unexpected tenderness and the loveliness of her body, by the thin ridge of breastbone like a delicate necklace below her throat, the jewelry of ribs and nipples and labia majora.

"Then why did you steal the money?"

"You don't get it. It's not the money."

"It is the money. Because now you've got it and I don't."

Monika rolled over, hunted for the pocket to her robe and a cigarette. I hoped Henrík was paying for the room, because when I got a proper look, I realized it was a corner suite; she had thrown me to the floor of an octagonal sitting room, six-foot windows overlooking the Danube. A half-closed door led to the sound of running water and what I surmised was the bedroom. She cinched the robe tightly around her waist and watched me inscrutably behind plumes of smoke, debating whether to tell the truth or which truth to tell. When she came to a decision her face lit with a radiant smile. "I didn't steal the money because it meant something to me, I stole it because it meant something to you. I stole the money because I could."

The admission astonished me. Money had no value to her, except as something to steal. I said, "So you made it up. You weren't being followed. You noticed the claim token in my wallet, saw an opportunity, checked out the brief-case, and left me flat broke."

"Not exactly. I took the precaution of borrowing the ticket when I found it in your wallet. I didn't see any reason to trust you. You didn't even tell me you hid the money in baggage claim."

"I tried to give you half and you wouldn't take it!" I exclaimed.

"I didn't need the money then. Only when I noticed I was being followed." Her ambiguous smile could have meant that she knew I had followed her, or that I had offered her the excuse to flee by suggesting she might be followed. "So I did what I felt like doing," she said. "I took the money and left."

"Alone?" I asked.

"Stupid question. Of course alone."

"Do you know how I found you?"

"Sven. You knew I'd come back to look for him." Monika went through a subtle transformation when talking about Sven, the rigidly classical lines of her face softening, and the defensive glint in her eyes collapsing to a rare vulnerability. The cool hardness with which she regarded the world was a mask, seductive but artificial, and in these moments of vulnerability I thought I glimpsed someone far more innocent than she pretended to be. "I've known him forever," she said. "He wouldn't leave me. Not like that. Something happened to him. Here in Budapest."

That only Sven could invoke the vulnerability of genuine feeling enraged me. "And the old guy who visited you this evening, is he helping you to find Sven?" I asked, not without venom.

Monika regarded me without flinching. Her cool was admirable; I could read nothing but a subtle contempt in the smooth mask she presented. She said, "He's a film producer."

I laughed. "A Hungarian film producer? What an oxymoron."

She didn't get it.

"A useless profession," I explained.

"Like a Hollywood scriptwriter, then," she replied.

Insulting but true. I stood and buckled my belt. My crisp blue Oxford shirt was missing half its buttons, and a rip in the sleeve marked it for the rag pile. I wandered to a ceiling-high window, glanced down at the Danube flowing muddy black four floors below, pressed my hand on the door to the bedroom, and pushed it open. The bed linen stretched crisply from head to foot. I smiled, happy that my suspicions were ill-founded, before remembering that beds were not Monika's erotic style.

"He wants me to act in one of his films," she announced, brushing past me to reach into the bathroom and shut off the flow of water from the shower.

A prodigiously arched eyebrow expressed what I thought of that.

"You're the one who gave me the idea I could do it," she said, "with your talk about the movies you wanted to make."

"Excuse me for saying this, but aren't you being just a little bit naive? You don't even speak Hungarian."

"The character is German. It's a German co-production."

I didn't dare insult her with the opinion that Henrík was less interested in her German than other oral skills; if he was like his Hollywood compatriots, his notion of a foreign tongue was not linguistic. I said, "You don't have any experience. You know nothing about cameras, scene work, sight lines."

She dropped the butt of her cigarette into the toilet, flushed it down, and said, "You taught me those things don't matter."

The assertion shocked me. I hadn't been trying to teach her anything. Unexpectedly, I had been cast into the role of an empowering figure. I said, "I never talked about scene work and sight lines with you."

"No, but you talked about development deals, Paramount Pictures, Tom Cruise, Julia Roberts, and what an important Hollywood writer you are."

I didn't get it, stared at her, waited for an explanation. She turned off the lamp by the bed and stripped back the covers. Light from the sitting room wedged through the open doorway. She dropped the robe from her shoulders. The light sliced between her breasts and thighs, splitting her body neatly into light and dark halves. The expression on the lit half of her face was impenetrable, but in her shadowed eye I discerned contrasting glints of admiration and contempt. "I learned from you that I don't need experience or special talent," she said. "I just need to convince other people I have it. It's a con. And if there is something I'm good at, it's convincing others I'm a different person than who I truly am."

25

I f I describe to you the dream I had that first night back in Budapest, it isn't to encourage the Freudian claptrap of analysis but to explain the anxiety in which I awoke that morning to find Monika going through my pockets. Like most dreams, mine was no doubt caused by direct physical stimuli, in this case a tangle of sheets which cut off the circulation to my limbs. In the dream, Monika cradled my head in her hands as I horizontally occupied a shallow grave. The angle of my head prevented me from seeing any higher than the ragged knees of two undertakers who leisurely spooned earth into the hole. My brain's frantic messages to jerk and jump turned to static beyond the border of the third vertebrae. Vocal cords strained and lungs wheezed, and combined they pumped out a barely audible bleat. Monika gazed down at me with the tenderest of smiles and covered my mouth with her hands. The trite stuff of a B horror flick, even by the debased standards of dreams, but when the earth blacked out my eyes I bolted awake, gasping for breath, which no doubt caught Monika by surprise as she stood over the chair on which I'd hung my clothes, flipping through the pages of my passport.

"What are you doing?" I demanded.

She slipped the passport into the breast pocket of my sport coat and dug into my trousers.

"I wanted to order room service," she said.

"You needed to check my pockets for that?"

"Tip money," she explained. "Don't you have any forints?"

"This is Hungary. Tip him in schillings," I said, and, liberating my clothes, escaped into the bathroom. The sharp spray of water brought me to full consciousness. That Monika had my passport in hand was not accidental. Perhaps she thought I kept folding money hidden between the pages. I stepped out of the shower and plucked with dripping hands the passport from my coat pocket. My fingers wet-spotted the pages as I flipped them one by one and paused at three rectangular stamps marking my entry, departure, and reentry into Hungary. Each stamp bore, amid indecipherable symbols and abbreviations, the date of my transit. The lining in my stomach burned and peeled. She was looking for Sven. The dated stamps in my passport proved I had been in Budapest the night he disappeared, and not in transit as I had claimed. She searched for evidence that would implicate me in his disappearance. I shut my eyes and focused memory on the moment I had awakened. She had been thumbing through the pages, I remembered, glancing but not reading. I stepped back into the shower confident that even if she had glimpsed the offending stamps the shock of being caught would make her unsure of what she had seen.

I opened the door to a spread of coffee, orange juice, eggs, and bread rolls on the sitting-room table; Monika had taken the precaution of actually ordering room service. While I had been in the shower she had changed into a canary-yellow miniskirt, net stockings, and sky-blue blouse. After sweetly pouring me a cup of tepid coffee, she did her lips the color of a stoplight, guided by a compact propped against an egg cup. The smell of food reminded me that I hadn't eaten since the train. We traded pleasantries between bites of egg and dabs of lipstick—how did you sleep, what do you plan to do today—and in the same light tone of voice I asked to see the case in which I had kept the proceeds from Zdeněk's safe. She dutifully rose, pulled it from the walk-in closet, and said, "Sorry about the latch."

The surface gouges and twisted frame gave evidence of the primitive tools and violence Monika had used to spring the combination lock. "Haliburton. It was the best," I said. The lid flopped open and a miscegenetic crowd of lire, escudos, drachmas, and pesetas scattered to the floor. A split-second estimate counted less than thirty bills total; not a single mark, pound, or franc. Monika coolly maneuvered a pair of tweezers between her eyebrows and plucked an errant hair. Thirty thousand lire, four thousand drachmas, two thousand escudos, and three thousand pesetas. I dug the previous day's *Herald Tribune* from my bag and calculated the exchange rates.

"Seventy-one dollars," I said.

Monika shrugged and drew a thin black line along the

top ridge of her eyelid. I swept the plates of half-eaten eggs, the pitcher, and cups of orange juice and coffee with her mirrored compact case to the floor. She froze, either from fear or because she couldn't complete her eyelash line without the benefit of guiding mirror.

"Where is the rest of the money?" I asked, very calmly, very much in control.

"You're sitting in most of it. I'm wearing the rest."

I examined the pop fabric and cut of her blouse, the tacky bead bauble dangling from her wrist, and asked, "Was there a sale at Versace?"

She looked at me very seriously and said, "Versace never has sales."

I kicked the plates away from my feet, stood, and jerked open the curtain to the window overlooking the Danube. "I can't believe you're so stupid to have a Hungarian producer on the string and still pay for your own suite." I said. "What is this costing us, if you don't mind my asking?"

"Five hundred marks a day." She retrieved her compact from the rubble of an upended bread basket and returned to painting her eyes. "They made a fuss about payment when I checked in, because I don't carry credit cards, so I paid for the week. The old hag at the front desk just about kissed my feet. They even sent up a complimentary bottle of champagne."

"French?"

"Hungarian."

"I'm *impressed*."

If Monika caught the sarcasm in my voice she chose to ignore it. She dabbed eye shadow onto a feathery brush and lightly swept the tips across a closed eyelid. I sat at the table again, reached out, and clipped shut her compact case.

"Stealing the money was bad enough, but to steal and then spend my half is unforgivable."

A lesser woman would have felt the vestiges of a rationalized guilt, or at the very least exasperation at the rudeness with which I had shut the case, but the stare Monika subjected me to was the guileless product of a superior conscience asking me to rise above the conventions of petty morality. "What fun would it be to steal your money but not spend it?" she asked. "If I still had the money, I'd have to give it back to you. And that would mean I didn't really steal it, wouldn't it?"

While I located the implied ends and unwound the implications of that, Monika took her lipstick, rouge, and eye liner to the bathroom mirror, where she began to concentrate on the volume and line of her eyebrows. The threat of an international arrest warrant might shake her where my righteous indignation had left the pencil tip between her fingers without so much as a tremor. I had never witnessed a woman enhance her beauty with so sharp and practiced an eye, but I had never met a woman as consciously beautiful as Monika. Beauty, like art, seemed equal parts natural talent and willful determination. If I revealed Zima's suspicions and Havran's threats, she might just as easily decide our partnership had become unacceptably dangerous.

She caught my eye in the mirror with a shrewdly seductive look and asked, "Did you like the way I greeted you at the door last night? Didn't it excite you?"

The memory of sex struck me like a shock wave, an incandescent blast of desire that swept all sense before it. I gritted my teeth and stared at the floor tiles, angry that my vulnerability could be so readily exposed.

"And our night in the Hotel Paříž? Do you remember?" she

taunted. "What we did in the men's bathroom and the closet? Did you enjoy that?" She brushed past me in the doorway and picked her purse from the foot of the bed.

I followed her into the sitting room, feeling on the edge of understanding something I might not wish to know. "What are you getting at?"

"It all comes tied together. You can't have one without the other," she said, and blew me two air kisses as she walked out the door.

After months of labyrinthine Prague, I reveled in the modern sensibility of Pest's avenues, broad and straight to accommodate the demands of traffic and open to the sky. I deliberately walked the streets with the busiest midmorning traffic, cars weaving in and out of lanes to jostle for position at the next stoplight. The smell of exhaust in bright sunshine overwhelmed me with an unexpected homesickness for the gridlocked streets of Los Angeles. The streets of Prague were as quiet as a museum exhibit, but Budapest was loud, dirty, vulgar. Street-corner statues depicted the legacy of conflict with the Ottoman Empire, brutal warrior kings wielding shield and ax, fallen Turks at their feet. Even the statues of the Hungarian saints, István and Lazlo, gripped swords in massive fists and scowled down from their pedestals. The inhabitants seemed sprung to life from the statues: alienated, aggressive, borderline violent. The men were short and stocky and favored mustaches the size of a push broom. The women had lustrous black hair and dusty skin, and not one of them looked back at me when I stared in erotic admiration unless it was her profession to do so. The stores sold goods yet undreamt of in Prague, and on every street I noted a restaurant that looked like I wouldn't be risking my life by eating from its menu. Budapest was a modern city, not on the scale of New York or Los Angeles, but I could feel commerce in the rhythms of street traffic and bustling crowds, and, with commerce, money to be skimmed.

I played the tourist through the morning and into the early afternoon, loafing in the gilt and marble splendor of the Café Astoria over a Viennese-style cappuccino and strolling down Vací utca, the shopping promenade where, among flocks of tourists, the black-market money changers and prostitutes plied their trades. Whenever I passed a money-exchange outlet or bank I stepped inside to observe procedures. Our financial situation had not yet become desperate, as I still retained my dwindled stash of counterfeit bills and a portion of the U.S. dollars from Zdeněk's safe, but considering Monika's alacritous spending habits those sums wouldn't last out the week. I had checked with the front desk at the Gellért and discovered she indeed had paid out the week, though I still suspected Henrík had paid and she lied to protect both money and the illusion of virtue. That afternoon, however, I was content to wander without firm direction until the consular section of the U.S. Embassy opened, where I hoped to replace my passport, which had been mysteriously picked from my pocket that very morning.

"I know the exact moment the bastards got it," I told a sympathetic Hungarian woman at the window for U.S. citizens. "Three men were coming out of a door at the same time I was going in, and we got all tangled up. They were gone by the time I knew what happened. Even if I was a little faster on the uptake and managed to catch one of them, my passport would have changed hands about three times by then—you know how they work."

The woman clucked sympathetically and handed me the forms for passport replacement. I needed to provide the consulate with proof of U.S. citizenship—with convenient foresight I had photocopied the inside cover and first page of my passport that morning before it had been stolen—a passport fee of $65, and three photographs, which could be acquired from a photography studio a few blocks from the embassy. It took the photographer three tries and a stern lecture on the proper use of a camera to get it right, but the end result came out rather handsomely, I thought, and by the consulate's closing time I had filled out all the required forms, submitted my passport fee and photographs, and been assured that two days hence I could retrieve my new passport.

I found Monika in high heels and bathing suit when I returned to the suite early that evening, reading script pages to Henrík, who listened to her impassioned German with an air of directorial authority. He actually smoked from a silver cigarette holder, if you can imagine. A half-empty bottle of champagne—not Hungarian but Taittinger—and two full glasses bubbled at his elbow. The dramatization so absorbed Monika that she didn't notice my arrival, and though Henrík was perfectly aware he pretended to focus solely on her performance. The swimming suit confirmed my worst suspicions, but his choice of tactics encouraged me. Only a loser would attempt a trick like that.

I startled Monika with applause at the overwrought conclusion of her speech. Her cheeks blushed with equal tints of embarrassment and pride—a common enough reaction in amateur thespians unused to exposing themselves in public. I addressed myself to Henrík. "Ophelia from Ham-

let, just before she drowns herself, right? I like the swimming suit—it's important to make Shakespeare relevant to
today's audiences."

He embraced her with a congratulatory kiss just off-center
to her lips and spoke rapidly in German. Though I didn't
understand a word, I knew enough about directors to smell
the fumes of fulsome praise. Likely, he had never heard of
Ophelia and thought Shakespeare an exotic African. She
listened with an intensity that portended worship. The intimacy of their dialogue offended me. German had been
selected as the language of choice to screen me out. I wandered over to the window and stared at the twilight, contemplating various forms of objectionable behavior. She
slipped a robe onto her shoulders—a modesty which seemed
directed more at my eyes than his—and continued her
Teutonic prattle. The problem with Europe was its people
spoke too damn many languages.

"Monika say you work at Hollywood," Henrík said, turning at last to offer a limply reluctant hand.

"I've been involved in a few projects," I admitted, aiming
for a tone of modest understatement that would imply a far
greater importance.

"I no like much Hollywood movies," he sniffed.

His jacket, scarf, the cigarette holder and attitude—I suddenly understood that Henrík must have thought himself
French.

"Of course you don't," I said. "Because as long as there
are Hollywood movies around for people to watch, your
shitty little films won't draw an audience."

Henrík glanced at Monika, puzzled. "Excuse, my English
not so good," he said. She spoke to him in German. He
nodded, as though understanding something different than
I had intended, and replied in the same tongue.

"Henrík says he too thinks that Hollywood is destroying the film cultures of Europe and must be stopped," she translated. "He's surprised to hear you admit something like this."

I glared at her, piqued at the mistranslation of my remarks. "I'm surprised to hear Hungary has a film culture. I thought it disappeared with Bela Lugosi and the Gabor sisters."

"Great actors," Henrík agreed.

Monika merely nodded, as though to confirm that had been the gist of my comments. He grabbed my shoulder and grinned. I had become a hit with him, despite my worst intentions. Like most older citizens of the former Iron Curtain countries, his teeth were rotten.

"He says he's always happy to meet another filmmaker," Monika translated, as I attempted to dodge the stench that, at those close quarters, was unavoidable with so fricative a language as German. "Film people understand that great art requires great sacrifice. He hopes you will remember this in the weeks ahead and not let jealousy interfere with my success."

"How could I be jealous of a hack Hungarian schlockmeister with the breath of a dead canine?" I said, smiling and patting him on the back with a friendliness as ferocious as his.

His smile turned to rictus. No doubt he understood at least part of my insult. Monika hurriedly translated some innocuous remark, and the two exchanged question and explanation before she turned to me and said, "He says he also looks forward to seeing your work, if there is anything to see."

We stood together beaming with disguised malice before he lamented the passing of time with a trite gesture of watch and, amid a flurry of script pages and tender kisses to the back of Monika's hand, fled the room.

"You don't actually kiss him on the mouth, do you?" I asked, when the door shut behind him.

She rushed to a cigarette, lit it, and chased the smoke with a sip of champagne. "I'm not fucking him, if that's what you mean," she said.

"That must make him very unhappy."

"Are you jealous?" she asked.

I laughed at the notion.

"Not of Henrík," she explained. "Jealous of me. Because I'm actually doing something, and all you do is talk about it."

"I'm hardly jealous because you got your big break in Hungarian films."

"You know that little notebook you carry around? I looked in it."

I mentally thumbed through the contents for incriminating evidence but could remember having written nothing there except phone numbers, shopping lists, and a few one-line script ideas. I raised my eyebrows, as if to say, *So?*

"It's almost empty. You're not writing anything."

"That isn't how I work," I answered.

"You don't work. You just talk."

"Talking is work. That's how I form my ideas."

"Stop lying. You have no development deal."

Our dialogue had suddenly grown ugly without my knowing precisely how. I had meant to ascertain the truth of her relations with Henrík, and she had turned it into a surprise attack on my character. I had to defend myself, if not for her benefit, for mine. I said, "No, really, it only looks like I'm not working. I wait until the material has jelled in my mind and then I lock myself in a room for two months."

"You're conning yourself with everybody else. There is no Paramount Pictures, no Tom Cruise."

♥ 285

"Sure there is."

"You're a fake."

"I'm not."

"A fraud."

Film was the most important lie of my life, more important than any truth I'd ever known. I had based my being on it. I said, "I do know someone at Paramount."

"You're lying to yourself. That's the sick part. You don't know the difference."

"I could get a script read, and Paramount does pictures with Tom Cruise all the time, so really it's not so unrealistic, my idea of making a film there."

"You're fucked up, Nix."

"No."

"You're a liar, a cheat, a thief, a complete and total fake."

I knelt on the floor, covered my head with my arms, said, "No, I'm not." Monika towered above, watching me like she would an earthworm flooded from its hole, a small pink thing lying prostrate on the pavement. One conscious press of heel and I'd go squish.

"Poor, bad Nix." She sighed.

I nearly burst into tears when, instead of smashing me, she knelt and wrapped an arm around my shoulder. I hid my face in her neck. She smelled of sweat and perfume, a musky odor that swelled my throat. I wanted to explain how, with my ambition and energy, I had achieved nothing but a reputation for dubious word and deed.

"I'm a fraud too," she admitted. "Nobody knows anything true about me."

"But you have talent," I protested.

"How would you know? I read in German."

"I noticed it at the Hotel Paříž. When you walked into

the lobby. It's what movie stars have. People can't take their eyes off you."

"If I have a talent, it's pretending to be somebody I'm not. Just like you. That's what my bad little Nix should do. He should become an actor."

I never should have claimed to be a screenwriter, even one who produces. Lack of substance had hollowed out my claim. That I should even want to write a screenplay was absurd; screenwriting was the most abused and least respected profession in Hollywood. Monika was wrong. I wasn't a total fraud. My problem wasn't a lack of qualifications but a misreading of my talents. "Maybe I should limit myself to producing," I said. "Producers tell other people what to do. I'm good at that."

"Producers have money," Monika pointed out.

"So do I," I said. "My family is filthy rich. My share is in the millions."

She pushed me away, thinking that I joked at best or told a calculating lie at worst, but perceiving in my expression a truthfulness which frankly would have been invisible to anyone else, she asked, "Why didn't you tell me?"

"Before you start scheming how to steal it from me, you should know that I can't touch the money for another four years, and then only if I pay the proper filial obeisance to dear old dad."

"Speak English," she demanded.

"Kiss my father's ass," I explained.

She stroked my hair and coaxed my face to nest again in her neck. "Then kiss his ass, darling, and kiss it good."

I nuzzled her neck and slipped my hands between terry cloth and skin. Her robe parted to a delicate necklace of collarbone and twin pendants set like pearls in the cups of her bathing suit.

"What if, for example, you got a steady job, said you'd found a nice girl, and were ready to settle down?"

Confessing to Monika things I wouldn't even confess to myself twined intimacy with unexpected eroticism. I hadn't anticipated the erotic ramifications of emotional intimacy. The urgency of my desire compelled boldness. I needed to imprint myself upon her, and to prove by her admission of body an equal acceptance of spirit. I lifted her breasts free of cloth and stroked the tips to a ruby-red corona.

"Would that make a difference? I mean, in when you got the money?"

"I could be canonized as a saint, and still I wouldn't be allowed to touch the principal until my thirtieth birthday," I said, and gently pushed her supine. She neither resisted nor encouraged. With the tip of my tongue I traced the line of shoulder to neck, from throat to the crease of skin between breast and ribs.

"I'm sure there's a way. You just haven't thought of it," she advised.

The tips of my fingers slipped the elastic below her belly and thrilled to a rougher texture. Her breast tasted salty sweet. I stretched back the isthmus of her swimming suit, expecting rich oils and perfumes, and cupped instead dry sand. Even the most passionate of women are sometimes slow starters. I edged down her belly, determined that when I dipped my mouth to drink, desert would turn to spring. A sharp click of flint and acrid-smelling smoke lifted my head. Monika stared at the ceiling, arm curled beneath her head while she smoked a cigarette.

"What if your father dies?" she asked.

"My entire family could be wiped out in an earthquake and it wouldn't change the terms of the trust fund. I get the distinct feeling making love right now doesn't interest you."

"You're right. It doesn't."

I sat up, stared down at her with resentment.

"Would you like me to give you a hand job or something?" she asked, I think seriously.

"I want to know how you can just lie there, smoking a cigarette, as though you feel absolutely nothing."

"But it's true!" she protested. "I don't feel anything."

"When I touch you, you feel nothing," I repeated. I couldn't grasp the implication of that and suspected she lied for advantage.

Monika sat up, tied the robe around her waist, and retrieved the champagne from the sitting room. She swigged straight from the bottle, passed it to me, and said, "Normal sex doesn't interest me enough to even pretend I enjoy it. It's like my skin turns to rubber."

I put the bottle to my lips and drank. The champagne tasted sweet, but the bubbles left a bitter aftertaste. "So when I touch you, like just now, you feel what?"

"Bored," she said. She could have said anything else and hurt me less. "You don't excite me. No man excites me, not really, except Sven, and that because of other reasons."

"Why are you lying to me?" I demanded.

"I'm not lying to you." Her expression of wronged innocence meant nothing. She lied with the face of an angel.

"What about that night in the Hotel Paříž? Not once but twice you attacked me."

"It wasn't you. It was the situation."

"And last night. You threw me to the floor, you were in such a hurry."

She grabbed the champagne bottle and fixed me with a look so frankly eroticized I began to tumesce again. "That was great sex," she said. "The night in Hotel Paříž even more so."

"Then how can you tell me you feel nothing?"

"I felt more than you can possibly understand. But it wasn't you, Nix. It was the situation."

"What do you mean, 'the situation'?"

Monika lit another cigarette and set the champagne bottle on a crossed knee. She drew successive lungs of smoke while she observed me; I waited, stoic in body but inwardly squirming with impatience and pain. "Stealing excites me," she admitted, not in the tone of a confession but as a blunt statement of fact. "Some other situations excite me also, but mostly it's stealing. It's the only time I feel sexual. My skin tingles. I think faster. I feel things more deeply. If it's a good situation, I feel like I'm flying a million miles an hour. Most of all, I'm laughing inside. I'm fooling everybody. They want me so badly I can do anything. They can't take their eyes off me, and it turns them blind. That's when the situation is really good. That's when I feel really sexual."

"So I don't matter."

"You're the one who gets me into the situation."

"But your passion is blind. I could be anybody, really, when we're making love."

"It's better when I know the person." She smiled with a beguiling ambiguity and added, "But sometimes it's better when I don't. It all depends on the situation."

"But that isn't human!" I protested. "If that's your entire sex life, it's not just kinky, it's perverse."

"I know it is," she admitted, without the inflections of regret.

"Think of the kind of life it forces you into."

"I know I can't go on stealing forever. I'll end up in jail, no matter how clever I am. Maybe acting will excite me in some of the same ways that stealing does. Because acting to me is the art of fooling people into believing I'm someone I'm not, even if the person I'm pretending to be is closer to the real me than the person sitting here, for example, smoking a cigarette and talking to you. Because she's not real either."

"Then which one of you is real?"

"None," she said. "None and all."

26

My conversation with Monika left me feeling distinctly afterwitted; it seemed I had begun our relationship with a series of assumptions which, when discovered to be false, led me to another set of assumptions equally false. I felt like a cartoon character who walks over the edge of a cliff and stands on nothing more substantial than air and ignorance. Sven, whom I had derided as a brute lacking imagination, had been cleverer than I supposed, having organized his larcenous activities around a relatively safe, simple, and repeatable plan. When aroused, Monika was indiscriminate of partner and place; consequently, he rarely let her out of his sight. His violent reaction to the prospect of a rival consummation was not less genuine for being planned. The perverse nature of her sexual responsiveness made big scores less desirable than frequent ones. I had assumed Sven's intent was to make money, criticized his methods as cheap thuggery, and only that sleepless night realized his central organizing principle had been her sexual needs.

When Monika announced she would be spending the day with Henrík filming a screen test at the state film complex, I despaired that the moment I had discovered the animating principle of her sexuality, I would lose her to a different fetish, which I had helped to create but could not control. If acting inspired an erotic reaction as strong as theft, her first scenes before a camera would culminate in a betrayal certain to terminate our relationship, either by the strangulation of consecutive deceits or with one big bang. With acting as her new fetish, she would have no reason to steal and no need to continue our complicity. And there was always the possibility that Monika had lied about her sexuality. She often lied not just to seek advantage but from habit. She had never given me cause to believe in the veracity of anything she had said, either in passing or in confidence.

A financial crisis complicated these anxieties. Just six notes remained of the ten thousand dollars in counterfeit bills I had brought to Europe. In Prague I could have survived a month on such an amount, but at Monika's rate of expenditure the sum wouldn't last two days. Clearly, we needed a scheme profitable enough to meet immediate expenses and pay Havran his extortion money. Such a plan would take a week to research and execute, and though I had little doubt of our ability to dodge the Gellért for the few days not covered by Monika's advance, I had no intention of remaining celibate so long. I would steal forints from a blind beggar's cup before enduring another twenty-four hours of frustration.

Like Prague, Budapest's banking system relied on bank transfers and briefcases to move large amounts of cash from one point to another. I left the hotel determined to find a way to combine the frequent opportunities for petty theft with the rewards of grand larceny. I stood in a half dozen bank lines, observing customers and tellers. Most transactions involved the paper transfer of funds from one account to another, but just before noon closing time I witnessed a gold-spectacled individual in gray suit, purple shirt, and white socks collect five bundles of 10,000-forint notes. I followed him at a distance of ten yards, surprised at the careless ease with which he carried a briefcase containing more than thirty thousand dollars.

When he turned into a door marked by a gold plaque, I continued on to the consulate to pick up my new passport, contemplating scenarios that would painlessly separate my white-socked friend and others like him from his cash. Witnessing a withdrawal of that amount hadn't been luck; in a cash economy, thousands of businessmen, lawyers, government officials, and crooks used bundles of cash just like checkbooks to fund operations. Carrying large amounts of money from bank to store or office was routine, as it had been in Prague. Routines make people careless. I imagined myself on a Vespa, Monika at my back, snatching the case as I sharply brake and speed away. That I had neither money for a Vespa nor experience driving one mattered less than the cinematic image of Monika and me speeding away with fifty grand between us, scarves blowing in the wind.

Even if jealousy did not allow me the cerebral calms of reason, that Monika had not returned by late afternoon was not logical cause for concern. But as I paced the suite in anticipation of her arrival, I could not help suspecting that the later the hour, the greater the odds of infidelity. Each pair of footsteps in the hall halted my own as I listened, hoping a turn of latch was imminent. In the private screening room of my imagination, Monika's tongue skimmed the masculine line between sternum and navel but instead of encountering my surgically trimmed and shaped member tasted a rough and hooded fellow that brought the fantasy reel to an abrupt end. Eventually, I convinced myself that the watched-pot principle was in effect—she would not return while I so obviously waited—and wrote a note informing her that I visited the spa below. The hotel provided complimentary robe and slippers—marked to my amusement with a request that they not be stolen—and so attired I shuffled down the corridor to a matron in starched whites who locked me into a quaint wire-cage contraption which, with the switch of a massive brass lever, dropped five floors to an entrance reserved for hotel guests. For my five hundred deutsche marks a day, it seemed, I enjoyed unlimited free use of the spa and the prestige of a semi-private entrance.

Considering what had transpired on my previous visit to the Gellért Spa, combined with an environment resembling the interior of the three witches' kettle from *Macbeth,* the mineral baths should have been the last place to regard as suitable for relaxation. Among the octogenarian wraiths soaking in the 100 degree pool I spied a more vital figure who, from behind, so resembled Sven that I tripped over backward in surprise, splashing awkwardly into an opposing pool. I had not intended to make myself conspicuous, and certainly didn't wish to attract the affections of the skinny Turk who gazed at me with lovelorn eyes and none too discreetly paddled to my side whenever I paused to soak. The steam room offered less respite. The sweltering fog so erased the features from every face that every face became Sven's. I knew I suffered from paranoia even as I hallucinated, but the shock of seeing his face superimposed on a dozen milling specters so unnerved me that I crashed through a pair of them, drawing rude protests and a forearm to the back as I careened out the door. Braced against a tiled wall, I clenched my chest to keep my heart from bursting. A Magyar as burly and hirsute as a bear asked if I wanted a massage and gestured toward the adjacent room, where four men lying on steel tables were soaped, pummeled, and hosed like so much meat in an abattoir. I declined and fled to the far wall. In a small room directly opposite, an old man sat on a metal ring perched above a pipe jutting from the tiles below, and by pulling a metal chain shot a jet of water up his ass. The toothless bugger let out such a pleasured gasp I choked with laughter, certain I had been transported into the mise-en-scène of a Pasolini-Mapplethorpe coproduction from hell. I reeled through the mineral baths to the relative sanity of the dressing rooms, where I stuffed a towel between my jaws to stifle a laughing fit which threatened to escalate to hysterical shrieking.

"Shooting late?" I inquired, when Monika stormed into the suite far too late for any excuse to mitigate my suspicions. She hadn't even bothered to dress properly after the act that had delayed her, net stockings torn and seams askew, blouse and skirt creased as though tossed aside in the heat of the moment. I had been waiting with all the lights blazing bright, pacing the suite's diagonals as I reminded myself that ghosts are a projection of the mind, invested with the power to terrorize by belief. Most tellingly, she wore little makeup, and what little she wore looked randomly applied with no great care of accuracy.

"I don't want to talk about it," she said, her tone rivaling the brusqueness with which she brushed past me to shut herself in the bathroom. I was certain it portended the end, and listened disconsolately through the door to the splash of sink water and, more curiously, a single vulgar epithet repeated four times in escalating volume.

"Can I get you anything?" I called, and immediately cursed myself for being so nice. Monika despised niceness in men. When the door snapped open, she held a towel to a face scrubbed clean. Her blouse had been flung to the floor and kicked into a corner.

"You can get away from the door, is what you can get," she said.

I backed away, bitten. She lit a cigarette from her bag and sat on the bed, legs tightly crossed, shoulders slumped around her chest, elbows pressed protectively into her belly. The room filled with smoke. She picked up the phone, pressed a digit, and ordered a bottle of wine from room service.

"Stop staring at me," she said. "I'm tired of people staring at me."

"Problems with the makeup artist?" I asked, injecting into those simple words a venomous irony.

"I don't get what you mean."

"Film companies have professional makeup artists. You came in here looking like a circus clown."

Monika responded by locking herself in the bathroom again. A spatter of water on tiles wafted from beneath the door. Even her need to shower was cause for suspicion— why else would she rush beneath the spray except to wash away the incriminating smells? I did not trust myself to act rationally. She had wedged herself into an elemental crack in my character; the twist of her leaving would split me apart. But I had no evidence that my suspicions were more factual than paranoid. Had she planned to leave, she wouldn't have bothered to confess the strangeness of her sexual desires the night before. In a relationship marked by wariness and mistrust, that moment had been our greatest intimacy.

The room service tray of wine and glasses gave me the excuse to announce its arrival. That brought her out of the bathroom fast enough, wrapped in a robe, her black curls dripping. I clenched my teeth to gate an incautious tongue. She gulped down two glasses of wine and, lighting another cigarette, sipped between puffs through the third. Despite her inexperience as an actress, Monika would be impossible not to watch on screen. She consumed the space around her the way she consumed cigarettes and wine: with a focus sometimes nervous, at other times wearily composed, but always projecting an intensity that suggested her emotions no matter how concealed burned hotter and brighter than everyone else's. She riveted the eye. Her presence shattered my concentration; I could only pretend to ignore her. She dug through her purse for a big-toothed comb and sat on the corner of the bed opposite mine, watching me. I glanced up, trying to appear preoccupied.

"What is it?" I asked.

"Look, I need a situation. Do you think you can do that? Can you get me a situation?"

The timbre in her voice approached desperation. I asked, "Is something wrong?"

"I don't need to talk about it, understand? What I need is a situation."

I tried to flatter myself with the thought that passion for me prompted the request, knowing that I was merely the specific means to satisfy a desire which, at its core, had nothing to do with me. She avoided my eyes and white-knuckled the comb. I began to explain my vision of men carrying briefcases stuffed with money, and how the next morning we might—

"Tonight. Not tomorrow. I need a situation tonight."

Admitting that I did not have a situation for that evening would prove an ill-advised failure. Desperation would drive her to fulfill on her own what I could not provide. I assured her that I had prepared a second plan, which I would reveal when she finished dressing. While she prepared herself in the bathroom, I turned out the pockets of my trousers and coats, searching for the silver and garnet ring purchased when I had first tracked her down in Budapest. I had fantasized marrying her then, and now thought to turn that fantasy into a situation. I found the serpents entwined in tissue paper, buried in the side pocket of the jacket I had worn that day. What I had in mind wasn't so specific as a plan, but a scenario I hoped would be risk free and profitable.

"It looks expensive. Is it mine?" Monika asked when I slipped the ring onto her wedding finger. The silver and garnets sparkled against the setting of her champagne complexion.

I said, "If I told you it wasn't yours you'd only steal it."

She pecked me affectionately on the cheek, taking my remark as a compliment. Though the trace of her lips on my skin did not intend eroticism, I felt my heart accelerate and the tissues in my mouth parch with anticipation.

During the taxi ride we discussed details of character—I supplied her with a troubled past and a rich but jealous husband as part of the role—and right up to the hotel steps I whispered hurried directions to her ear. She wore the fetching cocktail dress from the night we had taken Zdeněk and swept into the Forum with the same eye-catching result. My role in the scenario was not inconsequential, and I mentally rehearsed the demands of the part while I watched through the glass. I've always been more comfortable behind the camera than in front of it—invention frightens me less and pleases me more than performance—but the games I had played with young tourists had been performance of a sort and helped me to prepare. When I estimated sufficient time had passed, I made my inconspicuous entrance. As expected, Monika had not remained long unaccompanied at the bar, though her choice of suitors dismayed me. He towered politely above her, his gangly height topped by a ridiculous cowboy hat. At the reception desk, I identified myself as a guest of the hotel and asked the most touristic questions I could imagine, from directions to the castle which lay in plain sight across the bridge to the safety of the drinking water. Perhaps Monika believed that because he dressed the cliché of the Texas oil man he really was one; more likely the conspicuousness of the target gave her greater thrill.

When certain Monika had the opportunity to spot me, I asked the receptionist a final question—the location of the men's room—and followed her directions to the ubiquitous symbol of a boy pissing into a pot. I hadn't planned on a repeat performance of the night at Hotel Paříž, but if the inspiration moved her I wouldn't object; indeed I found myself painfully prepared the moment I stepped to the sink to inspect collar, teeth, and hair. After several minutes had passed, the door swinging open to series of cramped male faces, paranoia proved a more powerful detumescent than anticipation a stimulant. I had clearly instructed her to knock on the door to the men's room within five minutes of seeing me at the front desk, when she was to whisper the room number of her new friend. A half-dozen explanations for her tardiness raced through my mind: she had not seen me at the front desk, she had misheard and waited in the women's room, she couldn't pry the room number from the Texan, she had unexpectedly improvised or even decided to leave me witlessly behind while she humped him beyond any one of two hundred hotel room doors.

Paranoia escalated to panic when I hurried to view the bar and discovered them conspicuously absent. Straining against the urge to sprint, I approached the receptionist to pry from her the direction they had disappeared. A quick scan of the lobby in passing caught Monika holding the hand of her Texan at the elevator. Their body language—he stiffly anxious and her leaning loose-limbed against his shoulder—spoke clearly of her control. I wondered if she had disobeyed instructions to test or merely gall me. To jump into the elevator with them would destroy the situation. When the bell sounded the arrival of a free car, I charged across the lobby, determined to end it rather than allow Monika free expression of her duplicitous promiscuity, but noticed that she flourished behind her back a slip of paper, which, with quick dip of knee she dropped atop an ashtray stand. When the doors slid shut I hurried to pluck the note from the sand, and anticipating that she had fooled me with a blank cocktail napkin, silently blessed her in reading the number 451.

I gave her no more than five minutes, fearing what she might accomplish even in that brief span of time. Images of a pink-skinned, knobby-kneed longhorn in boxer shorts, T-shirt, cowboy boots, and hat engaging in THE ACT with a passionately compliant Monika inspired titters of disbelief and, moments later, anxious concern. Hadn't she said that it was often better to have sex with strangers than with someone known? Long ago I had given up trying to understand the mysterious process of sexual attraction, and how perfectly sane women were drawn to the worst sort of men, myself included. And Monika was not precisely sane. She might have chosen the Texan not because of his supposed wealth but from perverse sexual attraction. I jammed my finger repeatedly into the call button and impatiently watched the floor lights above each elevator door, my stomach rising and sinking as the cars plunged, stopped, and plunged again. When the elevator arrived I pressed the floor number and waved off a late arrival, fooling him just long enough to allow the doors to close unhindered. I remembered the brevity of sex with Monika, how in the men's room at the Hotel Paříž she had initiated the act and finished it within five minutes. As with any love relationship, I had no choice but to trust her at the same time I knew it was foolish to do so.

Room 451 was conveniently located at the end of the corridor, where the noise of an altercation would not be as readily heard. I paused outside the door to press my ear to the paint. No clanging bedsprings, thumps of wallboard, Texan yeehaws or Danish shrieks, but the absence of voices might also be construed as equally alarming. I would play it restrained, the well-bred husband—the image of Dirk Bogarde sprang to mind—sniffing out an attempt to cuckold him. After deep breathing to focus the mind I raised my hand and delivered six sharp knocks to the door. When that went unanswered I hammered on wood until I heard the latch click below.

Contrary to my fears, the Texan hadn't come to the door in his underwear. Lipstick at the corners of his confused smile proved that some physical contact had been made, and I suspected that at the first sound of my knock he had scrambled back into whatever Monika had taken him out of. I visibly sniffed and remarked, "I don't actually smell sex. Hasn't there been any?"

He stared at me as though surprised I spoke English.

"I believe you were about to have sexual intercourse with a woman who happens to be my wife," I clarified.

The Texan blanched. He said, "You must be making a mistake, this is room four-five-one."

His accent threw me off my rhythm. The closest he'd ever come to a cow was a steak house in Jersey. I shouted "Kristina!" and pushed past him into the room. The Texan blathered indignantly at my back. I glanced around to a conspicuously closed bathroom door. He tried to cut me off when I reached for the knob. I pushed him off balance and flung open the door.

"Come on out, Kristina," I sternly said.

A picture of contriteness stepped out of the bathroom, head hung low, lips pouted, eyes mournfully round. She said, "Nicholas, you found me." In the palm of her hand she clandestinely flashed a hundred-dollar bill.

The Texan picked up the receiver by the side of the bed. His hands visibly trembled and his eyes blanked in terror. The intensity of his fear shocked and excited me. I took two threatening steps forward and pointed my finger at him like a gun.

"In this country, a man is perfectly within his rights to kill an errant wife and her lover, so if you don't want that phone cord wrapped around your neck, I suggest you hang up the phone now."

He set the receiver back onto its cradle and stammered, "I didn't know, you gotta believe me, I was drinking in the bar when she came up to me—"

"You're calling my wife a whore?" I demanded, and brandished a chair over my head, reveling in the moment the fool cringed to the carpet.

"Nicholas, please don't, it was all my fault." Monika snatched the cowboy hat from the foot of the bed and clutched it to her chest. She spoke in the tone of a little girl caught sneaking sweets. "Nothing happened, I swear. I just wanted him to give me his hat."

"You were going to fuck him just to get his cowboy hat?" The notion enraged me. Monika was capable of anything.

"You want the hat, lady, it's yours," the Texan squeaked from the floor.

Without thinking, I kicked him in the head.

"We're both Americans here," he pleaded.

What next? The character I played squirmed and eluded the grasp of my talents. I thought about what he had planned to do with Monika. I should break his neck. One clean blow of the chair back would do it. Monika tugged on my arm. I dropped the chair and raised my hand to strike her. She flinched, eyes shining with excitement. Perfect! I tossed a handful of loose forints onto the bed, said, "That's for the hat," and pushed her out the door.

I bit my tongue to keep from squealing with laughter as we raced arm in arm down the hall to the elevators. Monika cocked the hat on her head and modeled before the polished aluminum doors. The elevator chimed and swished open. The moment we jumped inside she locked her fingers around my neck and straddled my waist. The hat tumbled to the floor. I jerked the hem of her dress to her belly and wondered at what moment she had relieved herself of undergarments— alone in the Texan's bathroom or before? The question both disturbed and excited me. She tossed back her head, exposing a delicate line of neck. Though we were veritable scouts in our readiness to perform, I doubted we could but begin before the sharp drop of four floors opened the elevator to our compromised position. Her sighs when I traced with flicking tongue the line from ear to shoulder quivered through my bones. With practiced fingertips Monika threaded me through my barriers of cloth and flicked a red switch on the control panel. The elevator shuddered to rest between floors.

"Look at me," she commanded.

When I obeyed, I found her eyes not on me, but on our mirrored image at the opposite wall. She wanted to watch me watching her.

"Am I a bad girl?" she asked the image on the wall.

I said, "Yes."

"Then teach me a lesson," she said. "Punish me."

It astonished me that scenarios which would normally trouble even my shriveled conscience excited me beyond reason when performed under her command. Though I did nothing more than what she encouraged, the idea that I punished her brought to physical focus all the slights, hurts, and jealousies of our time together and urged me forward with a brutal vigor. A series of sharp, short cries signaled that in the genus loci of guilt and desire she found momentary release from both. We untangled ourselves, straightened our clothing, and as the elevator descended and the doors opened to the ground floor she so distanced herself that we might have been strangers.

In the back of the taxi leaving the hotel, Monika looked at the floor, her purse, the scenery flitting out the window, everywhere but at me. She said, "It was a porno film."

I thought she had made a comparison to the torrid scene we had just enacted in the hotel elevator, but the remoteness of her voice and the lack of any comparative adjective prodded me to ask, "What?"

"Henrík," she answered. Her voice was small and weary. She stared out the window again. "That was the film he was making. Did you know Budapest is now the capital of the European pornography business?"

♥ 305

"No," I said, cautiously.

She asked the driver if she could smoke. He shrugged. The wind when she inched down the window drew out the smoke and whipped her hair into an angry black swarm. "He had me in a bathing suit, like before, reading lines from a script. Then he asked if I minded doing a love scene first, and introduced me to my costar. My costar was completely naked. He was pulling his thing with one hand and wanted to shake my hand with the other." She drew deep breaths of smoke with resignation rather than her usual nervous energy. "Henrík locked me in a closet when I wouldn't go along with it. That was why I was so late. He told me he could make it a rape scene if I didn't cooperate. I threw a bottle at his head. Finally, he gave up and let me go."

I bit the insides of my cheeks to keep from laughing in relief. Five days of jealousy, terror, and depression over nothing more than a deceitful pornographer! Images of Monika and me adventuring through the cities of Central and Eastern Europe fast-forwarded through my imagination. Kiev, St. Petersburg, Moscow, Warsaw, Talinn, Kraków—any city where the happy confluence of primitive banking and corrupted order gave an enterprising young couple the advantage. The elevator would be only one memorable scene in a compilation of erotic escapades in public locations. We would make love above the heads and under the noses of the unsuspecting, on rooftops, balconies, and stairways, in trains, trams, and funiculars, amid toilet stalls or statuary, any nearest place when our courage and wits combined to complete a situation. And fresh from a string of victories through Europe, we'd attack Cannes the following spring to pitch our life story to the chief of Paramount Pictures, who would be so charmed he'd hire me to produce and Monika to star!

"It's nothing to smile about," Monika acidly commented.

"Of course it isn't," I protested. She must not see me smiling. She must not think I'm happy. "It must have been absolutely awful for you. And I won't say I didn't have my suspicions about Henrík from the very start. I smiled because I was thinking how pleasurable it would be to kill him."

"You're such a bullshitter at times I can't help but laugh," she said, with surprising fondness.

"I'm serious. I'll kill him if you want," I insisted.

She dismissed me with a flick of her hand.

"I've killed before," I asserted.

"Sure," she said.

"Some guy came at me with a knife."

"And where did this happen?" she asked, in tones of a humoring disbelief.

"Right here in Budapest."

She looked at me sharply, sniffing something I should have been careful to leave buried. "When was this?"

"Before I met you." Vanity had played me for a fool. I could have said anywhere but Budapest. "When I first came to Europe. This February. I hadn't intended to kill him. But he attacked me, and I reacted."

"Who was he?"

"Some skinhead. You know the type. Maybe I didn't really kill him. I mean I didn't take his pulse or anything."

"I'm sure you got him." She sighed, losing interest. "You're a real killer." She lit another cigarette and stared out the window. "I feel like shit," she confessed. "I want another situation."

"It's late," I objected.

"It's never too late when I want one."

"Don't you think we're a little tired?"

Monika bolted forward and shouted at the driver, "Stop the cab! Right here."

The driver swerved sharply to the curb in a squeal of brakes. I peeled myself off the back of the front seat. Monika clawed at the door handle. I should have known better than to patronize her.

"Where are you going?" I asked.

"It's very simple. I get what I want. When I don't get what I want, I go elsewhere."

She opened the door and put one foot out. I pulled her back. To the driver, I said, "Hotel Inter-Continental."

27

Most addictions are safe and controllable at the start and only become dangerous when the desire for gratification escalates to absurd proportions. Monika terrified me because she was uncontrollable. I would reach a depth of perception from which I hoped to influence the course of her behavior, only to discover ignorance had acted as a drag, and my new understanding allowed me to be pulled along more readily in her wake. Her thrill of speed could be sated only with greater speed. I couldn't brake her and I couldn't trust her instincts of self-preservation to check the velocity. Nor, because of my own addiction, could I peel myself away. The prospect of mutual immolation at the terminus of such a lifestyle was an event not to dread but to celebrate as a final consummation, a vindication of my feelings since meeting her of the rightness of our union.

With greater recklessness we began our second situation of the night, seeking in audacious risk the jolt to satisfy our addictions. The Inter-Continental was a modern concrete and glass hotel situated just off the Danube, charging top rates and attracting an exclusively Western clientele. The bar, located in a cozy corner of the lobby, had been charmingly named the Gipsy Bar, though any Gypsies plying their trades within a hundred yards would have been hustled into the Danube.

As midnight approaches in almost any bar, restiveness hits that percentage of the clientele which, no matter what the avowed reason for spending such a disproportionate amount of time in low surroundings, either consciously or subconsciously is looking to spend a few hours in the embrace of a stranger. The solitary arrival of a beautiful woman in a provocative black cocktail dress radically shifts the focus of the room, as single men pretend glances in her direction are truly idle, and male friends with slipping concentration try to maintain a grasp on the threads of conversation.

Showing a long stretch of leg as she sidesaddled a chair at the bar, Monika played to the room like an actress plays to a camera, allowing herself to be watched seemingly unaware she was the focus of attention. The tapping of a pack of cigarettes against her thigh signaled she knew too well the symbolism of lighting a cigarette to risk it until she had made her decision. A few of the more alert men scrambled to palm incendiary devices should she glance around for a light. When she slipped a cigarette from the pack she turned in an unexpected direction, toward the only male pair of eyes to remain aloof, which belonged to a trimly dressed man whose reserve marked him as a Japanese business-man even at my distance of observation. He seemed sur-prised at her attention and visibly started when she spoke. I feared she had been too forward, but a smile broke his stern countenance, and he readily lit her cigarette, even taking one that she—with lowered eyes and demure smile—offered to him. Silently, I approved her choice of targets; Japanese men are relatively wealthy, polite, fearful of for-eigners yet notorious suckers for Western women. An en-raged gaijin bursting into his room would terrify him into easy submission.

Monika worked the Japanese with admirable economy; by a suggestive glance here and a curl of lip there, she com-municated between the lines of their dialogue a seductive-ness coolly arousing. Once her choice had been made clear, the focus of the bar dissipated. Some still watched with determined fascination, ready to move forward with their own ploys should the Japanese prove inadequate or un-willing. Others marked her as a professional and, though undeniably beautiful, less interesting. The Japanese warmed from initial reserve to gregariousness with surprising speed, laughing frequently and talking with great animation. The artfulness of her approach made it impossible to judge from whom first came the suggestion to leave the bar for more intimate surroundings. They simultaneously began the ritual bill paying and collection of personal effects, and moved toward the elevators across the lobby as though they headed to bed for the hundredth and not the first time.

As before, she casually dipped at the ashtray stand, and even turned a dazzling smile over her shoulder meant for me. When the elevator doors safely enclosed them, I hur-ried to retrieve the scrap of paper she had dropped in the sand and watched their progress by floor in the lights above.

The note, when I unwrapped it, was alarmingly incomplete, containing just the numbers 2 and 2, preceded and followed by question marks. The number 22 never stands alone in a multilevel hotel, so 22 what? Or what 22? I calculated sixteen possibilities in an eight-floor hotel. The lights marked the elevator's progress, pausing at the second floor and continuing uninterrupted to the eighth. I couldn't escape the dread that she had planned this careful obfuscation because we had already made love this evening and she needed someone new to satisfy her ever more jaded erotic tastes. That the elevator had stopped on the second floor was the worst possible luck, with nine rooms bearing the numbers 2 and 2. Only with fortunate guesswork and frenzied effort could I prevent a deceitful consummation. As I raced up the stairs I could hear her protest with self-righteous innocence that it was my fault she had fucked him; my failure to appear as scheduled had left her no choice but to continue to play the scene to its implied conclusion.

The first door I knocked on at the second floor summoned neither answer nor sound from within. I moved quickly to the next, which yielded to an offended matron in pink nightgown, who scolded me in the Queen's tongue for waking her and slammed the door at my back. I ran to the opposite end of the string of numbers, and hammered at the far door. A man with a belly the size and color of a slab of beef answered with a sleepy *Ja?* I wished him *Gute Nacht* and pounded the door across the hallway. It opened to a Mediterranean who, when I told him I was looking for my wife and a Japanese man, stared at me as though I was either drunk, stupid, or insane. I moved one room toward the center. The language of the gentleman who flung open that door was incredibly rude, no matter what its Romantic origins. Doors opened up and down the hallway, and persons in various states of national undress peered and stumbled into the light. Soon I was being cursed in half the languages of Europe.

I judged the distance and obstacles to the bank of elevators down the hall as too daunting and sprinted up the nearer stairs. The arrival of hotel management, considering the clamour I'd caused, was a realistic fear. My legs and lungs began to cramp by the fourth flight of stairs, slowing my progress to a staggering climb. When I knocked at the correct door, I would not play my role with restraint. My wronged husband would not be a civilized man of good breeding but a raging primitive. By the eighth floor, I must have looked as maniacal as I felt. My heart threatened to pound from its cage of ribs, and sweat half blinded me. I tracked the room numbers to 822, paused to focus my concentration, and knocked so gently on the door I might have been caressing it.

That the Japanese was still crisply dressed moderated my anger. He stood openly in the doorway, blinking in confusion as I ranted about the perfidy of wives who cuckold their husbands. That word, which so appropriately if approximately rhymes with vulgar slang for coitus, seemed to alarm him. He stepped back and attempted to slam the door in my face. I wedged my foot at the base and threw my shoulder into it. The Japanese was a slight man, no more than 140 pounds, and I knocked him well back into the room. Monika stood at the side of the bed, glowing with excitement, the cocktail dress peeled down to her waist. The sight of her unsheathed breasts enraged me, not just with jealousy; she had revealed her most identifiable mark, the snake tattoo adorning her left breast. I called her a dirty whore and meant it, which excited her all the more.

The Japanese nattered at me in his incomprehensible

tongue from the moment I breached the threshold. When I felt his hand on my sleeve I ripped my arm away, turned and threw an overhead right which not only missed its target, but was used by the Japanese to his advantage in flipping me to the floor. I rolled in time to evade a karate chop aimed at my head. Monika laughed and poured herself back into her dress. Her laughter infuriated me. I jumped to my feet and charged, but the Japanese inconveniently moved aside, thrust out a hip and, employing some martial-arts mumbo jumbo, turned me onto my head. I spun free and scrambled back to vertical. The Japanese stood lightly balanced on the balls of his feet, waiting for me to reveal the depth of my stupidity by charging again.

"Go get him, killer," Monika laughed, zipping herself up the back.

I picked up an ashtray and threw it at him, and after that did damage to his hand in deflecting it, I threw a lamp, which struck him on the back. He fell stunned against the wall. I lifted the desk chair above my head; the backrest swinging down clipped his shoulder and made him howl. He ran to the bathroom and slammed the door, crying, "Thief! Help! Thief!"

How could I possibly act out a scene with someone not just on a different page, but with an entirely different script? "Not thief!" I shouted, pounding on the door. "Husband! Jealous husband!"

The urge for sexual gratification did not occur to us in the elevator descending to the lobby or in the taxi we hailed on the street outside. The incident left us dry and bitter. Her attempted act of infidelity and derision at my being thrown were unforgivable. She crouched in the far corner of the taxi, sullenly smoking. I huddled in the opposite corner, seething. The stupidity of showing her breasts to the Japanese was maddening. Had I arrived just five minutes later, the question of their consummation would have been unanswerable. She would assure me she hadn't and I would be almost certain she had. Not once did she look my way. Her anger enraged me. She had no right to attack me with so hostile a silence.

"Sorry I came before you could, dear," I remarked. "Do you want me to give you a hand job?"

Her two-word reply assured me she didn't.

"Showing him your tattoo was idiotic," I charged.

"That was his interest. Tattoos. It's some Japanese thing."

"Why didn't you just give him your name and address?"

"The whole stupid scene wouldn't have happened with Sven. He'd throw that little man through the wall."

"Sven is dead," I said.

Monika did not hesitate. She did not think or plan. She sprang at me claw and fang. Her hands seemed everywhere at once. She slapped, slugged, kicked, and bit. My ears rang with murderous shrieks. The taxi careened from curb to curb. I fastened one hand to her side and struggled to catch the second. Her teeth found the soft spot below my jugular vein. Headlights raked the cab and horns bellowed. The rip of metal on metal signaled a violent shift in direction, and I soared through the cab as though launched in zero gravity, Monika at my throat. The pebbly texture of the vinyl which covered the back of the driver's seat came to my attention as I ascended above it, then the black vortex of hair on the back of the driver's head sucked me in to indeterminate moments of stunned calm. I don't think I lost consciousness as much as the will to move. The steady bleat of a horn roused me, if slowly, like an alarm sounding in an adjacent room. I peeled myself off the back of the driver's seat and pushed Monika upright. Her mouth was smeared in blood, and I feared she had been badly injured, until she smiled, dazed but oddly happy, and I realized the blood was my own.

A mustached man in a windbreaker jabbered at me when I stumbled onto the street. At that late hour, traffic was thin. Only one other car had stopped, the one we had struck. Traffic slowed, detoured around the wreckage, and sped on. I assumed the man was the driver of the other car, which had fared much better than the Romanian Dacia in which we had ridden. The taxi driver remained slumped over the wheel. Monika staggered out the opposite door and began to laugh as though she had just disembarked from an amusement park ride. I opened the driver's door and shook his shoulder. He didn't move or groan. I hadn't bothered to look at him when I had jumped into the cab and shouted our destination. I pulled him back from the wheel. The horn ceased bleating. The only visible damage to his face was a small cut above his left eyebrow. Blood dripping from my neck stained his shirt. I removed my hands. His head lolled to the side like a ball of cotton candy on a broken cardboard tube. The other motorist nudged around my shoulder to look. The impact of the collision and the force of our bodies striking him from behind had snapped his neck. The dead face looked so wronged I tried to apologize. Monika grabbed my arm and pulled. I turned and ran and did not stop until the fire in my lungs burned the features of that face from memory.

The wound, as I examined it in the bathroom mirror of our suite, was oval in shape and dark purple in color, like the mark of a leech. Over the shoulder of my mirror image, I watched Monika sit on the closed lid of the toilet and carefully feel with thumb and forefinger her bruised lips. We hadn't said a word as we had run through the streets of the old quarter and across Szabadság Bridge. I had waited in the lobby with a Hungarian newspaper hiding my bloody shirt while Monika, mouth washed from a rusty spigot, had claimed the room key. Even in the safety of the hotel room, we couldn't bear to look at each other directly. Her fingers probed her twin arch of teeth for loose fittings. The accident had left her miraculously unhurt, and I think she so minutely examined herself not from vanity but hoping to find in some small cut or scrape a pain to lessen her guilt.

"If you're missing any teeth, I think you'll find them in here," I joked, grinning wryly and pointing at my neck.

She jerked her fingers from her mouth and stared at the tiles. I pressed a warm cloth against my neck to clean the tooth marks, then a cold cloth to ease the swelling. I pitied her. Holding the cloth to my neck, I searched the bedroom and found an opened pack of cigarettes on the floor by the lamp. Monika craned her neck around the door to watch me. That was the most touching part. She followed me around by foot or glance, afraid of being left alone for more than a moment. I crouched at her feet, speared the center of her lips with a cigarette, and lit it.

"It was an accident," I said.

She swept the hair from her eyes and nodded. The wound on my neck made me wince when I stretched to kiss her brow. I returned to the bedroom and called room service for a bottle of wine. When it arrived, I washed down four aspirins with the first glass. Monika sat on the floor and smoked. Smoking was a return to life. The more she consumed, the healthier she seemed. I pressed a glass of wine into her hand. She took a distracted sip, then gulped it down whole, her gaze fixed on the opposite wall.

"I killed him," she said, matter-of-factly.

"He killed himself," I answered.

Monika smoked, drank, thought a moment, and carefully replied, "No. I killed him."

"He killed himself by driving a shitty car."

"He killed himself by picking us up," she countered.

"It was an accident."

"I killed him. I should have killed you instead."

I let that one go for a minute, then returned, walked around it, sniffed at it, and, unable to resist, picked it up. "Why should you have killed me?"

"The poor fool was just trying to make a dollar. Two people get into his cab one night, have an argument that has nothing to do with him, and then he dies."

"But why me?"

"Because you're foolish enough to love me."

I stared at the ceiling and thought profound thoughts about chance and destiny. Closing my eyes, I summoned, detail by detail, the first critical moments of our meeting. Clear as a strip of film projected in a dark theater, I watched Monika shout obscenities as I lay prostrate at her feet. That our relationship had begun with such a wretched scene, and by determination I had willed our love into being, exulted me. "Amazing to think how the simple act of our meeting each other—remember that night at Club Lávka?— could result in a chain of events that would end the life of this perfectly anonymous being. How else can you explain it, except by fate?"

"What night at Club Lávka?" she asked.

"You won't remember this because I never told you," I began, certain the moment had arrived when we would begin to mythologize the initial circumstances of our meeting and mating, like all lovers who feel their love was destined from the start. "We didn't meet that afternoon over coffee, but two nights before, at Club Lávka. It was just after midnight. You were seated at a table by the river. I had gotten into some silly argument with a friend, and to say I was a little drunk is an understatement. I was ripped. Then somebody elbowed me in the stomach, and I hurried to the railing, because I had to, you know, because I felt sick, but I didn't get there in time and threw up at your feet."

I was laughing by the time I completed the last sentence, expecting to hear her exclaim *That was you?* I imagined ourselves older and wiser, years hence, still laughing over the incident.

"But I wasn't at Lávka that night," Monika complained.

"Of course you were," I insisted. "At a table by the river. You were incredibly angry, but I fell in love with you at first sight."

Monika retrieved her purse from the sitting room and searched it for something she failed to find. She looked up, annoyed. "I wasn't even in Prague two nights before we met."

"One night before then," I tried.

"Sven and I arrived from Budapest that morning. We checked into our hotel and went straight to the café." She tossed her purse aside. "I wanted to show you the train tickets, but I guess I put them someplace else or lost them."

"It's been a long night. You're just confused," I suggested.

"I'm not confused!" she shouted. "I hate Lávka. I never go there."

I stared at her, astounded. "How could you possibly forget a man throwing up at your feet?"

"Exactly," she replied.

28

When dealing with an intellect as naturally devious as Monika's, reasonable suspicion was difficult to separate from paranoia, and the effort of keeping the two apart nearly unhinged me. As the escalating volume of her snores marked the passing hours, I increasingly disbelieved the veracity of her supposed amnesia. My remark about Sven's demise goaded her into an attempt to hurt and disorient me. She remembered well enough that first night at Lávka but would not admit it. After gulping three-quarters of the bottle of wine, she slept through the night peacefully enough. Little wonder I felt like a wreck when the door began to rattle at the hinges, and I bolted up to find myself alone in bed.

Henrík! I thought. That silver-haired sultan of smut! By the insistent strength of his fist on the door I was certain he had returned to abduct Monika into a life of hard-core hell. I sprang from the bed and struggled into my trousers, imagining the running motion of his feet as I lifted him by the seat of his pants and dropped him out the window. The banging shook the entire suite. I hurried to the walk-in closet that separated sitting and bed rooms, still fumbling with zipper, button, and clasp. Through a crack between hinge and doorjamb, I watched a sliver of Monika unlock and swing open the front door. No sense in rushing out half undressed. I plucked a polo shirt off the shelf and found the sleeves with my arms. When he thought himself alone with Monika, I'd leap from the closet, grab him by the scruff of the neck, and hurl him into the nearest blunt object. I slipped the polo shirt overhead but neglected to unbutton the top, and when my forehead got stuck in the opening I experienced a comical moment that cut to horror as I pushed my head through the womb of cloth to the figure of István Bortnyk standing just inside the entry hall.

His voice at that distance was barely audible. I ransacked memory for any mention to Zima or Havran about recent or impending trips to Budapest. Bortnyk had once vowed to hunt me to the grave, and though I considered his threat ridiculous at the time, I cursed myself for the hubris of committing crimes in his territory. I should have pulled Monika out of the country on the day I arrived. He palmed something that looked as though it might be a small picture. I imagined he sought my identification. He had traced Monika through her name on the hotel registration. She looked at the object in his palm and nodded. Had she just betrayed me? I could tell nothing from her reaction. I glanced wildly about the closet for a shelf large enough to conceal me and considered crawling under the bed. Bortnyk would just drag me out by the collar like a dog. Better to fight. The closet was unbearably small. I fought the urge to bolt out the door, shove him aside, and run. The air stifled. I took successive deep breaths that turned to gasps. If I ran, I could knock him cold and escape before he warmed to consciousness. My breathing sounded ragged and sharp, like grinding metal. Impossible that he didn't hear it; Monika's nod had informed him of my presence and my rasping lungs pinpointed my exact location in the suite. I searched the closet for something to bludgeon him into submission, but found nothing more deadly than a heavy sweater.

I retreated to the bedroom, jerked the lamp cord from the wall, and gripped the base by the light socket. Monika nearly took a panicked blow to the crown of her head when she walked through the closet to retrieve her purse. I took her by the arm and mouthed a one-word question. Monika looked through me, not just without recognition but as though I had ceased to exist. I might have already struck her on the head by the dazed look on her face. She turned to unhook my fingers—those inanimate things snagging her blouse—and walked away.

Though the clatter of footsteps marked their progress out the door, I waited several minutes in silence, suspecting a trap. Lamp cocked above my shoulder, I crept cautiously into the sitting room, feeling like a character in a bad suspense film about to be fooled by scrambling cat or windblown shutters. Such cinematic canards lull the character into a false sense of security while on the periphery the killer lurks, but a thorough search assured me I was alone in the suite. I chain-latched the door and raced from room to room, jerking out suitcases and clothes.

Remaining in Budapest would invite my own beheading, or whatever the style of execution in that barbaric country. I would pack my belongings, draft a note to Monika instructing her to meet me in Warsaw, and flee to the train station. That Bortnyk had not searched the suite proved he did not yet know we were partners. But where would we meet in Warsaw? I'd never been to any Central or Eastern European cities other than Prague and Budapest. And if I thought of a foolproof meeting place, could I be certain she would join me? My breath raced so quickly I could not catch it. I darted to my wallet on the nightstand for a snapshot of my finances, and discovered I hadn't enough money to take a taxi to the train station. Monika had pilfered me while I slept. My heart beat so violently I feared I would vomit the thing. After several blank moments, I found myself on hands and knees, lungs barking for air.

A towel soaked in cold water and molded over my face restored a less hysterical pace of breath and a return of my senses. Monika was a good enough actress to convince Bortnyk of the falseness of any accusation and keep my identity secret, if she wished. To abandon her would not be just foolhardy, as she would in turn abandon me, but would be an act of cowardice branding me unworthy even to my own conscience. I breathed slowly in and slowly out. If she failed to return by late afternoon, I would notify the Danish ambassador and seek the counsel of a local lawyer, careful to screen my identity from both. Bortnyk could not possibly know anything. She would certainly return. He could not have tracked Monika so quickly without a name and passport number, which implied he wanted her for something other than last night's debacle. But his mere arrival on the scene commanded my departure.

I struggled to my feet, breathing deeply, breathing evenly, and retrieved from the walk-in closet the rolled-up pair of socks I used to keep my capital hidden from Monika. Six counterfeit bills remained of my original horde, a few Austrian schillings, and about seventy dollars in forints. Train travel within the former Warsaw Pact countries was still cheap. I judged three bills sufficient for two one-way tickets to Kiev or Warsaw and left the rest of the money in place. In front of the mirror, I costumed myself in bright orange shorts and white Nike cross-trainers, an Atlanta Braves baseball cap and a University of Georgia T-shirt, replete with helmeted, football-toting bulldog. With a pair of faux-aviator sunglasses as the final touch, I looked like the type of backpacking dimwit who would consider changing money on the black market a good deal.

The Gypsy on Vací utca who asked in the tritest of stage whispers if I wanted to change money was true to type, a wolfish man in blue jeans and jacket who leaned against the corner of a Hungarian crafts gallery with no obvious occupation other than watching the crowds of pedestrians. I scrutinized his face carefully before deciding I hadn't changed money with him on my previous trips to Budapest. I acted slightly nervous, like a high school kid on a drug buy, and agreed to the rate he proposed. Like most money changers he had a friend nearby; the weaselly accomplice who materialized the moment we fixed a price looked uncomfortably familiar. I long suspected money changers were organized by a local mafia. Possibly his accomplice had apprenticed with a changer I'd used before. Their hands were too friendly as they walked me to a side street—undoubtedly the jostles and arm clasps were reconnaissance forays to the suspected positions of my valuables. I was accustomed to such tricks, and had left my wallet and passport at home. When they pulled me up just inside a doorway, I turned away from the accomplice, fearful that he might recognize me just as I thought I might have recognized him. I concentrated on the money changer's hands, and so intensely watched for the anticipated switch of good bills for bad that I initially failed to notice his pause extend beyond the normal. I glanced to find him watching me with what might have been suspicion, had I been able to read between the inscrutable lines of his face. My best look of startled innocence prompted, if not belief, at least motion. He reached to pluck one of the three hundreds from my thumb and forefinger. I stubbornly held onto the bill, allowing him to test the color and texture, which, as the counterfeit had been made from a bleached dollar bill, had a look and feel identical to a genuine note.

"Only one hundred," he said.

"But I have three!" I protested.

He shrugged as though that didn't concern him and counted out his bills. An Olympic judge would have been hard pressed to rule which of us disappeared with the greater speed and agility once the hundred-dollar bill and roll of forints exchanged hands. I glanced over my shoulder as I approached the Vací utca promenade, and saw neither heel nor coattail. One of the skills of the trade, I speculated, was the ability to disappear into the surroundings. In the safety of the crowd I flipped through the roll of bills, and in several worthless Bulgarian notes discovered the cause of their hasty departure. The shortchange was about 20 percent, a common enough trick and difficult to spot under the best of circumstances. About half the money changers managed to cheat me in this way.

♥ 325

Although it irritated me to be cheated, the fact that they had accepted the counterfeit bill assured me that I hadn't been recognized.

At the far end of Vací utca, I was solicited by a gentleman who, by his polite manner and the businesslike cut of his slacks and sport coat, so distinctively violated the money-changer codes that I was certain I had never seen him before. He was older than the other changers as well, into his forties, and I suspected he might be a plant until, after a few conversational exchanges, I realized I might have discovered the only honest money changer in Central Europe. As he led me to a quiet corner of the public square that fronted Gerbeaud Café, he tried none of the usual dodges of his younger, less reputable colleagues. Although someone could have been watching from a distance, no accomplice was in visual evidence. He unfolded a roll of bills the size of a cabbage, and while asking how I enjoyed my visit and at what hotel I stayed, counted out the two hundred dollars in forints, first to himself, then to me, with meticulous accuracy. The man so completely charmed me I almost regretted cheating him. Before we parted ways, he warned me against taxi drivers and other money changers, whom he considered no better than thieves, and wished me a happy stay in Budapest.

The citizens of the former Warsaw Pact nations are cramped, cold, and unfriendly sorts, not like Americans, who greet strangers on the street like old friends and casual acquaintances like beloved relatives; the acts of unsolicited kindness I'd experienced since arriving in Central Europe were too infrequent to bother remembering. The old changer's kindness so disarmed me that I did not pay strict attention to my surroundings and failed to suspect that I was being followed until well advanced into the quiet web of streets between Vací utca and the hotel. I did not panic, though paranoia counseled me to scream and run. For the next block, I vowed not to allow my hyperactive imagination to make a fool of me. At the corner I kneeled suddenly to tie my shoelace and descried in a parked car's side mirror the image of the weaselly-faced accomplice, who followed thirty yards behind. I didn't bother with the niceties of reasoning out my predicament, but bolted up and out of the crouch like a sprinter at the starter's pistol. A hurried glance over my shoulder assured me I had caught him by surprise.

I was laughing with the exhilaration of escape when a jeans-jacketed figure materialized at the far end of the street and another rounded the adjacent corner. I pulled up, looked about frantically for a side street, alley, or open doorway. The accomplice was a far less imposing physical specimen, and I turned to attack in his direction, but the sight of the two additional thugs who joined him braked me. I backed into the center of the street. At five to one the odds I could prevail were slim to none. I screamed at the top of my lungs and charged the two at the far end, looking once over my shoulder at the motorcycle racing up from behind and not spotting the waved helmet that brought me down until too late to duck.

I have no interest here in milking to full dramatic effect the beating I took. The only reason the savages didn't kill me was the time of day and witnesses attracted either by my screams or to the spectacle of my slaughter. I managed to struggle to my feet a few moments before they converged upon me. I didn't fight back as much as flail out in all directions simultaneously. The image in my mind now is that of a cartoon character trying to vertically climb from the center of a whirling melee of fists, feet, and teeth. When the number and ferocity of blows overwhelmed my defenses, I sank to the pavement and curled into a ball. The kicks and punches stopped hurting after a while, and the attack slowed to a spiteful kick here and there. I felt hands rip at my clothing. It seemed a miracle that I could take such abuse and still live. Fingers pressed at my face. I struggled at first, because I imagined, horrified, that they looked for gold fillings to dig from my teeth, but when I peeled open my eyes I saw the face of the good money changer staring down at me. He smiled. I smiled. He stood and lifted his foot. I read the imprint of his heel as it descended to black out my eyes.

Sometime later, I found myself staring into a gruel of blood, motor oil, and saliva. I looked up, expecting to be run over the next instant, but some good Samaritan had dragged me out of the street to bleed against the curb. No doubt I had impeded the progress of his vehicle, and he had shown the kindness of dragging my body out of the way rather than running it over. I didn't manage to hold myself upright on the first try, or even the second, but by persistent effort I pushed myself to a sitting position, and with the help of a car bumper and hood ornament I stood on wobbly legs. The walk from there to the hotel was accomplished with a determination equaled only by desperation. I leaned against buildings, cars—any object that helped me claw another few feet toward the safety of the suite. I had no sensation of a specific pain. I thought of Arnold Schwarzenegger, severed in half but still crawling in *Terminator II*. The image struck me as inappropriately funny. Me, Arnold Schwarzenegger! I laughed up blood and bits of tooth. The curious stopped to watch as I made my way, but no one approached or offered to help. Two steps into the suite I passed out on the floor.

29

What I experienced couldn't be considered sleep, as it brought me little rest and no dreams, nor was I completely unconscious; I remained dimly aware, though unable to muster the complexities of the simplest thought. My body felt immensely heavy, as though the blood flowing through my veins had stilled. I did not feel pain or comfort, but something in between that was equally neither. I suspected myself of being dead and wondered if I was in heaven or hell. I feared it might be purgatory, and I was damned to stare out petrified eyes for eternity, mouth mute as the ambulance attendant zips the body bag over my head, deaf to the coroner's sternum saw raging through my rib cage, and blind to the mortician's farewell wink as he presses the ashes-to-ashes button on the conveyor belt to the incinerator.

When I first felt the slow drip of water onto my forehead and glimpsed beneath slit eyes the blurry figure of Bortnyk crouching over me, I did not jerk or cry out in alarm. As a dead man, I was beyond the reach of the living. He balanced a water glass in hand and tipped it out one drop at a time. I felt like a statue might feel; decades of steady dripping might wear a groove in my brow but a few drops couldn't make flesh of stone. Only as he began to slap me gently about the face did I feel pain and thus disappointedly discover that I had not died. My eyes involuntarily blinked back water. He tossed the balance of the glass into my face. I rolled over and tried to sit up. Bruised, crushed, and severed nerve endings in every quadrant of my body let out a howl.

Bortnyk said, "When I heard you were in Budapest I was happy that at last I'd have a chance to smash your face, but it looks like somebody has beaten me to the punch."

I groaned and could rise no higher than elbows and knees. He could finish me off and not only would I be powerless to prevent him, I might welcome it. My left eye had swollen to a slit. The light striking it splayed out in all directions, like light through a jammed lens. He seemed to be grinning, either with regret at a lost opportunity or at the cleverness of his pun. My ribs ached. I was certain the bastards had cracked at least one and probably more. Any fraction greater than a quarter breath cut flesh on bone. I crawled to the wall and leaned against it. Bortnyk squatted in front of me like one animal cornering another, in no rush to end the hunt with a swift killing.

"Who did this to you?" he asked.

"Money changers," I said, the words dull in my swollen mouth.

"You tried to change a few American dollars on the street?"

"With the Gypsies on Vací utca," I confessed.

"You mean the Arabs," he corrected.

I peered at him through my one good eye, trying to judge by his expression whether he joked with me. I said, "You know, the Gypsies. The guys wearing the blue jeans and jeans jackets. If you look like a tourist, you can't miss them."

"They're Arabs. Mostly Syrians. Came to town during the time of the great socialist brotherhood. But to you, I guess anyone with dark skin and black hair looks like a Gypsy."

Attempting to disorient the suspect is a common police tactic. Confuse a suspect regarding simple facts, and he can't possibly keep something as complicated as a story straight. I had to remain above simple mind games. I nodded, pretending to agree that I had been mistaken, when it was plain everyone knew they were Gypsies— whoever heard of Arabs in Budapest? I said, "Sure, with the *Arabs,* then."

"Changing money on the black market is illegal," Bortnyk chided. "I could arrest you for that."

I laughed at him. "I'm robbed, beaten within an inch of my life, and you threaten to throw *me* in jail. The U.S. Embassy would love to hear that one."

His expression darkened when I laughed at him. I suspect he thought he could harass me at will. Defiance strengthened me. A cornered animal fights all the fiercer. He dipped his hand into his coat pocket and thrust a small black-and-white portrait of Sven into my face.

"Know this man?" he asked.

I hadn't counted on the possibility that Monika might report Sven missing to the local police. The portrait had been oddly taken, with his eyes shut, and although the photo was perfectly focused, his features looked blurred. I speculated that Bortnyk's visit was less menacing than it seemed. He investigated Sven's disappearance, at Monika's request. He knew nothing about the felonies of the previous evening.

"Sure," I said. "That's Monika's ex-boyfriend."

"When was the last time you saw him?"

I made a great show of counting days and weeks. "Back in Prague, about a month ago, I guess. At a Gypsy nightclub. I'm sorry, I mean *Arab* nightclub."

"We fished him out of the Danube three weeks ago."

Bortnyk pocketed the photo, which, I just then realized, had been taken of Sven's corpse. Amazing how similar a photograph of a well-prepared corpse looks to that of someone sleeping off a hangover. The discovery of Sven's body shocked me, though I tried not to show it. I always assumed the thing would float out to the Red Sea, or wherever the Danube flows.

"We found his wallet, so we knew who he was. But we had trouble getting someone to claim the body. The woman renting this suite was his only relative."

"Relative?" I faintly asked.

"You didn't know they were brother and sister?"

"We never discussed him," I lied. Another attempt to confuse me! I refused to believe it. Monika was a clever liar. Conceivably, she could have convinced even the Danish government they were related if it suited her interests. "How did he die? Did he drown?"

Bortnyk flipped open a notebook and jotted a few lines. I couldn't summon the strength or will to move. He asked, "Who knows you were in Prague three weeks ago?"

I listed the usual names, American, English, and Irish expatriates so frequently drunk they had difficulty remembering with certainty the events of the day before; a month previous was well beyond their range of recall. They could testify on my behalf with coached memories and clean consciences. Wincing at the possibility of a second betrayal, the final name I gave was Andrew's. That Bortnyk didn't bother to note any of the names I'd listed made me wary.

"Passport," he demanded.

I fought to hide a triumphant smile. No doubt he hoped amid the border stamps to find proof that I had the opportunity to murder Sven. I cautioned myself that I did not officially know that Sven had been murdered. The precaution I'd taken in securing a fresh passport had saved not just my relationship with Monika, but possibly my life. I wondered if she had seen the offending stamp and tipped off Bortnyk. Paranoia. She hadn't betrayed me. And if she had, they could prove nothing without a passport. I tried to stand, but searing pain brought me down again with a squeal. I stretched out my left leg. My ankle looked as if it had swallowed a gopher.

"Must be painful," Bortnyk observed, backing away.

I expected a helping hand and received a malicious grin. With the support of the wall I pushed myself to my right foot and hobbled into the bedroom. Determination to wipe the smile from his face proved as fierce as the not inconsiderable pain shooting through my body. My passport was on the nightstand. Flipping first to the pages reserved for border stamps but finding them blank, Bortnyk frowned and, noting the recent date and local issue inside the front cover, inquired, "You lost your passport?"

"I lost it at the train station to a Gypsy—I mean *Arab*—pickpocket." I bit the inside of my cheeks to keep smugness from spreading to a smile.

He tapped the passport against a clenched fist. "Then you can't prove you weren't in Budapest," he said.

"I have witnesses in Prague," I repeated.

"This is much better than I'd planned," he said, and jammed my passport into the breast pocket of his windbreaker. "The lack of an entry stamp in your passport would have been difficult to get around. Our judges might reject a case that depended on you smuggling yourself across the border. Now I can suggest you destroyed your old passport because it contained an incriminating stamp."

"But I didn't!" I protested, though of course that was exactly what I had done.

"This is very good luck for me, and very bad luck for you. In fact, my good luck is shocking. I come here this morning to identify a dead body, question the relative—all quite boring, routine work—and suddenly out springs your name! My very best friend, here in Budapest, my city, where I can entertain him any way I wish!"

His ironic tone was too much to tolerate. The man had the emotional maturity of a psychotic three-year-old. Painfully, I lowered myself into a chair.

"At first, I thought I would beat you up, maybe throw you out the window," he admitted, pacing the suite with vindictive energy. "But—another stroke of luck—somebody had already beaten you up for me. So I'm thinking now, what can I do that's new and exciting? I have on one hand a corpse, a murder victim by all outward evidence, and on the other hand, I have you. The two of you, I'm thinking, might just go together."

"Murder?" I asked, careful to sound surprised and properly horrified.

"Stabbed to death and dumped into the river. You wouldn't like to make it easier for all of us with a quick confession, would you?"

"But I didn't do it!"

"Of course you didn't," he soothed. "You're a seducer and purse snatcher. Anyone who knows you would agree that you haven't got the guts to kill anyone, and certainly not with a knife. That isn't the point. The point is what I can prove."

"But I have witnesses who will swear I was in Prague!"

"And I have witnesses who will swear you were in Budapest. I'm sure I can talk to the border officials and convince one of them that he remembers stamping your passport on any date I wish to name. Without your original passport, how can you prove he lies?"

Though my witnesses were as fictitious as my innocence, I felt a moral outrage that he would stoop to similar invention, and sputtered, "But you can't just make things up!"

"The lucky thing is, with a case like this, I can get the coroner to swear that death occurred any time I want. A body in the water, the rate of decomposition depends on a number of factors, such as temperature, drift, and so on. Even with your witnesses, who frankly our judges won't be so likely to believe, I can create a time line to hang you."

For the first time in my life, it occurred to me I might be in serious trouble. The film financing schemes, the games of amorous larceny I'd played with young women, and the mugging of Zdeněk had all produced uncomfortable moments, but nothing beyond the powers of extrication. If Bortnyk bothered to check, he could find ample evidence that I'd been in Budapest at the time of Sven's murder. Credit card records and a hotel registration form to start. Then the hotel maid would remember finding me passed out on the floor, and the manager would testify to my odd behavior. With real evidence at hand, Bortnyk could turn his perjuring talents to the manufacture of eyewitnesses and murder weapon. I had no friends in Budapest, and even if my family rose to my defense the most it could accomplish would be a phone call from a U.S. Senator. It galled me to be framed for a murder I in fact committed.

"Please," I begged, "can't you see I've suffered enough?"

"No," he flatly answered.

"Not even you could hate me so much."

"But I do," he insisted.

"Look, I'm really sorry, but I didn't know she was, you know, your fiancée. Don't you think you're being just a little bit unreasonable?"

"Jail will come first, and your beating from the Arabs will seem like foreplay compared to what the guards will give you. I might even be able to arrange a psychotic sodomite as your cell mate. Then the trial, the death sentence, the months of waiting, filled with beatings and other small pleasures. And I'll be with you every day, every step of the way. Because, Mr. Miller, revenge never should be *reasonable*."

I quaked and gnashed my teeth. Lucifer could not have terrified me more. "My family is rich," I confided. "Filthy rich. Name a sum and they'll pay it."

The offer gave his malice pause. I imagined the call I would make to Father, begging his forgiveness. I'd offer to wash cars at the family dealership for a year. I'd promise to don suit and tie and attend sales training seminars. I would allow them to plant inspirational can-do messages in my parched soul. Father would be moved by my humility and quote some obscure biblical passage about the return of the prodigal son. At the end, we'd be shedding tears of filial and paternal joy.

"Just say the word and I'll arrange to have a car shipped to you tomorrow," I offered. "Any color you want. Or cash. I'll have the funds wired direct to your account from my bank in L.A."

Bortnyk smiled with what I imagined was avaricious glee. "On the other hand," he said, "I'm not inhuman. I want revenge but I'm not a monster. To begin, it's plain you need a doctor. Are you in much pain?"

Every breath lacerated. "Excruciating pain," I said.

"Stand up. Let me take a look at you," he commanded.

I took his offered hand and inwardly rejoiced at the power of money to transform and unite all to a common interest. He probed the cut above my swollen eye, the abrasions on my cheek, my split lip and bruised jaw. "I'm not a doctor but I've seen enough beatings to know what to look for," he bragged. I winced and grunted when he pressed on my rib cage. He turned me around and probed the muscles and inner organs at the lower back. "There's no swelling or sign of damage here," he observed. "Didn't they work you over in this area at all?"

My kidneys were thankfully free of pain. "I'm lucky," I joked. "Seems like they missed at least one part of my body."

"Fucking amateurs," he said. "If you really want to hurt someone, that's the best place to do it."

The first blow cut my spinal cord in half and blasted a rocket of red light through my skull. When my knees buckled he pulled me up by the hair and held me face first against the wall. I squirmed and thrashed but he was bigger, stronger, and expert at that type of beating. He pinned me with a forearm to my neck and drove his fist into one kidney and then the other with a force that shook the wall. With each blow I shuddered as though he reached into my guts and ripped me apart from the inside out. The final blow burst my brain like a blown-out bulb.

"Don't try to leave the hotel," I heard a distant voice say. "Someone will be posted in the lobby, someone else on the street outside." Then, as a measured afterthought, the voice said, "Have a nice day."

The smell of smoke revived me like salts. I rolled onto my back. Monika sat against the far wall, arms curled around knees, smoking a cigarette.

"Thank God you're back," I groaned.

She knocked the ash from the tip, took a drag, and said nothing.

"I feel like I'm dying." I confessed.

She glanced down at her feet—she wore a T-shirt and jeans but no shoes—and wedged the cigarette into a corner of her lips to pick at something between her toes. Never before had I seen her dressed so casually. Ribs and kidneys fiercely resisted my attempts to stand. I pushed to hands and knees and crawled into the bathroom. She had not seemed to recognize that I had been in the room. Like most actresses, she was not of a naturally stable temperament, and the death of the taxi driver the previous night had partially unhinged her. The news of Sven's death might have delivered such a severe blow to her psyche that the lid had come all the way off.

The sight of my face in the mirror staggered and disoriented me; the beating had reorganized my features into an

unfamiliar terrain of lumps, bumps, and gashes. The ob-
longish sphere that rested above my torn and bloody shirt
bore as much resemblance to the original as Frankenstein's
did his. I clawed open Monika's bathroom kit—a bangled
new Versace model—and amid the jumble of cosmetics
plucked a bottle of acetaminophen, which I joyfully discovered was laced with codeine. The manufacturer recommended two. I took six.

A cool shower stripped my skin of sweat. The water
pleasantly stung my open wounds and dulled the pain of
the closed ones. When I stooped to examine the subcu-
taneous purples and blacks that mottled me from ankle
to neck, pain thundered from my lower back and nearly
brought me to my knees. Bortnyk had been right: Kidneys were the best place to hurt someone. In the sink, I
opened the tap until the water ran cold and clear. I soaked
two towels and hobbled into the bedroom, where, reclined
against stacked pillows, I draped one towel around my
swollen ankle and applied the second as a cold compress
over my left eye and jaw.

When Monika entered the room, accompanied by ashtray and cigarettes, I said, "I heard about Sven. I'm sorry."
I didn't rue killing him, but regretted her discovery of his
death. She sat on the floor across from the bed, lit another
cigarette, hugged her knees to her chest, and smoked.

"That Hungarian cop told me. He found me lying on the
floor, just after the Gypsies beat me half to death. It's lucky
I'm still alive."

Although my vision was skewed to one good eye and I
couldn't be certain of what I saw, she seemed to watch me
with an inhuman coldness. I felt like a wounded animal,
stalked by jackal or wolf, which patiently waits just beyond
striking range. I discounted my unease as paranoia. "I know
how much he meant to you," I said. I needed to be sensi-

tive and caring. A time of crisis just might draw us closer together. I remembered the voice of Dr. Quellenbee, soothing me while I stewed on his couch in silent fury, and tried to reach the same compassionate pitch. "There's so much about the two of you I don't understand. I know you were brother and sister. You don't have to say anything, but if you want to talk, I'll listen. Sometimes, it's not healthy to hold these things in."

She said nothing. She smoked and watched me. Her green eyes had always seemed exotic and not quite human. Now they looked bestial. Her silence offended me. I had been thrashed by a vicious gang of Gypsies, beaten by a psychotic Hungarian cop; I lay bloodied and broken, crippled in one leg and unable to draw full breath. Not one word of sympathy, not a compassionate glance or merciful expression of concern. She looked at me as though I might be a lump of meat waiting to be cut up, chewed down, and shat out the other end.

"Only a couple of bones broken, thank you, some damaged organs and internal bleeding, but other than that, I'm perfectly fine," I burst out, finally unwilling to fence my resentment.

She stubbed out one cigarette, thumbed the flint on her lighter, and lit another. Had I the strength, I would have smashed a chair over her head.

"I'm hurt," I pleaded. "I think I'm hurt really bad. I need you to help me. I need you to at least talk to me. Please, just say something."

She inhaled smoke, exhaled smoke, tapped the tip of her cigarette against the glass rim of the ashtray, said nothing. When I first noticed my body trembling I thought I had succumbed to the first stage of shock, and only after I shouted, "You're a monster. A bloody, brother-fucking monster!" did I recognize it as rage.

It was like I jabbed a stick at her. She recoiled and stared at me, bluntly murderous. She said, "You killed him, didn't you?"

Though I anticipated her suspicions I had not foreseen a direct accusation, and stared at her amazed she would say such a thing. We had lived together the past few weeks, if not in complete bliss at least with an intimacy that should have tempered her accusation with a modicum of doubt. A dozen protestations and denials vied for simultaneous expression and twisted my tongue into a useless, sputtering appendage.

"I should have guessed it earlier." Her voice was flat, unemotional. "He disappears, and you show up a day or two later. You seemed so confident that I'd go along. You couldn't be that confident unless you knew he was out of the way. But who would have thought a runt like you could kill a man like Sven?"

I told myself she didn't mean the accusation, she had no evidence, she tested me, and all I needed was to hit upon the magic formula of denial and cajolery to convince her of my innocence. But when I opened my mouth I could not articulate a scenario of plausible deniability. The best I could manage was to sputter in my defense, "Ridiculous."

She wrapped her lips around the filtered tip, sucked, and blew a rage of smoke across the room. She said, "You didn't have the guts to face him. You stabbed him in the back and pushed him into the Danube."

"In the back? Who told you he was stabbed in the back?"

"I saw his body," she said.

"But in the back?"

She stared at me with bestial coldness. I imagined her teeth ripping a bloody coil of entrails from my abdomen. I closed my eyes and tried to remember that night on

Szabadság Bridge. Had I invented his whirl and challenge, the beating I'd taken, and then the desperate plunge of knife that sent him over the edge? Had I instead stalked him from behind and stuck the knife into his back? Unable to bear such a cowardly act, my conscience might have fabricated a more heroic scenario. I had lost not only the ability to distinguish between truth and fiction, but the ability to differentiate between fictions. The wound to his back might just as easily have been caused by a propeller or other sharp object encountered as he bobbed along the Danube. But then she couldn't have seen a wound to his back. Bortnyk would have stripped the sheet from the face of the corpse, and no more.

"Don't believe anything Bortnyk tells you," I warned. If I couldn't lie convincingly about Sven's murder, I could protest Bortnyk's mutilations of the truth. "A few months before I met you, I had an affair with his fiancée. He threatened to kill me over it. He doesn't believe I'm guilty. He told me so this afternoon. But he said he'd frame me for the murder, because he wants me dead. If he can kill me in a legal way, all the better."

"You left a message at the Merkur, pretending to be Sven. You figured out that was how we contacted each other. I really thought it was him. I thought he left me. That was the only reason I ever let you touch me."

"You want me to admit that? Okay. I called the hotel. I was jealous. Wanted to convince you that he'd taken off with somebody else. But I had no idea where Sven was." True enough. I thought he still floated in the Danube!

She stabbed out her cigarette, lit another, watched me. I couldn't tell if she believed me or not. She waited for something, but for what? The idea that Bortnyk would soon return bolted me up in terror. Perhaps she'd watch with a similar cruel patience while he murdered me in my bed. "We have to leave," I said. "Pack your things." Abruptly, I yawned. The first wave of an irresistible fatigue hit me. I fell back against the bed. Monika moved cigarette to lips but nothing else. If I fell asleep, she might pack her bags and steal away. These could be our last moments together. If she seriously thought I'd murdered Sven, she would be gone when I awoke. My emotions toggled between terror and indifference. Monika's assertion that she hadn't been at Lávka on the night we had met had shaken all my assumptions about the significance of the past month. If indeed it had been some other woman at whose feet I'd cast gastric roses, then Monika was not the fulfillment of a romantic destiny but a mistake. I had fallen in love at first sight with one woman and transferred my emotions onto a chance being; I'd involved myself in a completely arbitrary relationship that was in the process of destroying me. But Monika had lied to confuse me. She had been at Lávka that night. I had not made the error of mistaking chance for fate.

"It was the Gypsies," I blurted. "Sven had stolen some of my counterfeit bills, remember?"

Monika's glare varied neither by glance nor gesture.

"Look at my face!" I cried. "This is what they did to me. Sven probably made the same mistake. They chased him to the bridge, caught and killed him."

"There were five hundred deutsche marks in his wallet when he was found," she said. Her inflectionless voice made the implication no less clear; Gypsies would have robbed him before dumping his body into the river.

I tried to sit up and face her, hoping that if she saw my sincerity and adoration she would believe, but my limbs had turned to sand. The muscles in my neck seemed composed of millions of disconnected cells. My head collapsed onto the pillow. I could no longer see Monika and hadn't the strength to turn to look. "According to who?" I asked, sounding distant to myself, as though voice spoke and ears heard in separate rooms. "You can't believe anything Bortnyk says. He planted the money. Sure, the Gypsies did it. Killed Sven, tried to kill me. You have to pack. Get us out of here." Pain receded to a red-hot mist somewhere beyond my body, and consciousness drifted fast behind. My ankle, face, and kidneys throbbed an edematous lullaby. What did any of this matter, compared to the delicious beauties of sleep? I must get the swelling down. "Soak these in cold water, will you?" I called, but sentience slipped out with the request.

A drugged sleep is not sleep but a clumsy burial of consciousness, wherein the corpus of thought is earthed but the odd sensation juts out like a stray appendage. The drug weighted and wrapped me like a winding sheet. I sank into the covers and springs, carpet, wood, and concrete, through the soft blanket of soil and rocky mantle to the warmth of the earth's core. Perhaps I would meet Bortnyk wearing the double horns of a cuckolded devil! I remember laughing once. Something tugged at my arms. I dimly imagined Monika's attitude had softened and she prepared me for bed. A coolness draped my face from brow to chin. She had decided to tend my wounds with a cold compress. For a brief moment, I felt warm and loved. I drew a deep breath, prepared to sigh in contentment. The smell was familiar but not immediately identifiable, something I associated with Monika but nothing so common as perfume or cigarettes. She voiced my name and several unintelligible words that ended with *Sven*. The scent locked into the region of the brain that matches olfactory stimuli to memory. Lighter fluid? The coolness ignited to sear my face with heat and light. I screamed and jerked my hands, reached instinctively to pluck the burning thing away, but something firmly secured me at the wrists. I hallucinated that Bortnyk sat at my head, clamping my arms while my face burned. I screamed Monika's name, writhed, and nearly shook my neck from its socket. The burning cloth dropped to my chest. I bucked and rolled. It slipped from my chest to the floor, where it flamed to ignite the carpet. My arms held fast, secured to the bed frame by Canali silk ties. Secure in the privacy of the suite, I could burn to death, screaming, with no one but her to hear. I kicked the covers to the floor, swiveled my legs over the bed, and stamped at the flame.

She stood just beyond the bedroom door, listening and watching. I couldn't see, but I knew she was there. The room reeked of lighter fluid, charred fibers, singed hair, and burnt flesh. I moaned and cried, called her name, and begged for mercy. She did not bother me with the courtesy of a reply. I did not see her leave. The door clicked once upon opening, and again at closing.

This is how I remember her when plagued by the banal aches of lost love, as I imagine she looked the moment she left, not as the compelling mask of eye shadow, rouge, and lipstick I so ardently loved, but stripped of makeup and dressed in something as plain as jeans and T-shirt: a stranger, someone so unremarkable that I could share an elevator with her for the twentieth time and not recall her face a moment later.

30

The desire to escape the past and reinvent oneself in an imagined, better future are intrinsically American virtues. That morning I hoped to prove myself all-American. A towel draped my head as I hobbled toward the spa elevator, and in my hand I carried a gym bag, which might have contained a swimsuit and a few essential toiletries. The corridor was empty of both guests and plainclothes cops at that early hour. I rang the call bell and waited. The starched-white attendant greeted me with a cheery *Guten Tag* when the elevator arrived, and for once I was only too happy to be mistaken for German. I replied in kind. Though not quite a Hungarian Lourdes, the Gellért Spa has a faithful following among Central Europe's chronically crippled; visits by the stooped and lame are not extraordinary, though the sight of my face might alarm her. She locked me into the wire-cage and pulled her brass lever, beginning our descent. I pulled the towel over my face like a cowl.

"Arthritis," I confided, clutching my hip when once she looked my way.

"Ach! Arthritus," she commiserated.

I tipped a hundred forints to ensure her continued sympathy, and followed helpful directions to the spa's central hall. Instead of continuing to the mineral baths, I turned more immediately down a tunnel parallel to the indoor swimming pool, white legs awkwardly bobbing in blue-tinted portholes along the way. A locker room waited at the end, quiet at that hour except for a few restless old men and one scampering grandchild. I claimed a corner locker and donned jeans, T-shirt, and casual sport coat, as though I had just completed a swim and dressed for the day. From my gym bag I extracted a California Angels baseball cap and a pair of Ray-Bans. Although any contact with my skin induced grunts of pain, a glance in a mirror conceded the accessories helped to conceal my swollen and skewbald face. At a distance in dim light, I looked almost normal.

If Bortnyk had posted a man at the spa's exit, I would need a better disguise than cap and sunglasses, but I entered the central hall confident I had outwitted him. Adrenaline proved as effective an analgesic as codeine, allowing me a stiff-legged stride. When I breached the entry arch, I paused to enjoy random sunlight spilling from a broken sky. Figures no more threatening than the old and infirm approached. The avenue flanking the Danube buzzed with Škodas and Ladas and the occasional Mercedes. The pockets of my sport coat held my old passport, three counterfeit hundreds I dared not attempt to change, and just over $70 in forints. When a streetcar clanged to a stop across the street, I hobbled off the curb and pulled myself onboard. No one shouted or shot at me. I curled up on a seat as though wishing to doze. A quick peek beneath my cap confirmed that no one looked at me as though I was out of place. People are probably beaten senseless in Budapest all the time, I reasoned, exulting in my luck.

A family of Gypsies begged in the subterranean plaza at the mouth of the train station, where I ascended from the metro. As usual, the father was off somewhere, leaving the mother to beg in her colorful rags, infant at tit and two children at her skirt. I had learned months before that a simple passing glance encouraged them to chase you open palmed, the children in particular. I limped past, deaf to entreaty, and pulled myself up the stairs one game step at a time to the bird-cage arch of the main station. Above the departing trains flickered the sculpture I had noticed on my arrival three days earlier, depicting in neon tubes and steel beams a man with electric hair, his mouth in open howl. Below, a signboard listed arrivals and departures in German, Russian, and Hungarian, demonstrating by language the unfortunate fact of Hungary's geography. The first international train left for Vienna immediately. The next headed to Bucharest in less than an hour.

I approached the ticket counter with cap pulled over eyes and head down. On a slip of paper I had written destination, time of departure, and guidebook-instructed Hungarian for a one-way ticket. Let them take me for a mute; I did not wish to identify myself as American by voice and language. Second-class fare was just under 10,000 forints. The sculpture of the howling man watched over my shoulder as I counted out the change. I collected the ticket and skirted the sides of the station, determined to keep clear of the platforms until the last possible moment. I wished to do nothing that might attract attention to myself. A chill up my back warned me that someone watched. Bortnyk had posted my description throughout the city with instructions to shoot to kill. Paranoia. He thought I still slept, a hotel prisoner without passport. Only the howling man watched, his head afire with a neon glow. I reasoned it wise to avoid so obvious a place as the train platform, in the event that someone observed from habit or specific instruction, and scuttled back down the steps to the subterranean plaza at the mouth of the metro. It was safer and cooler there; no one would notice my deformities with so many to choose from in the bustling crowd. For several minutes, I wandered aimlessly, until the feral pains gnawing at my every step drove me against a wall.

If the old ascetics were correct in believing that suffering purifies the spirit, I felt whipped and chaffed enough for sainthood. Though my conscious mind mocked such superstitions, I secretly suspected that I was being punished for the crimes of my character. Only through suffering would my character be purged of offending elements. I was a loathsome, vile, selfish human un-being, congenitally crippled in spirit and with newly matching deformations of the flesh. Until my skin healed, no one would accept me as a dashing filmmaker from Southern California, traveling through Central Europe to research the newest Tom Cruise vehicle. They would see me more precisely as I was, and not as I pretended to be. They would look at me and think, *monster!*

I vowed that in Bucharest, or in whatever city I chose to claw a new foothold of identity, I would devote myself to a new concept of being. First, I would get a job, however poorly paid, that might benefit others and thus ennoble the spirit. I could volunteer for the Peace Corps or apply to Greenpeace. English teachers were needed everywhere. I would even be willing to go hungry in the service of a good cause. A job peddling syntax and vocabulary would teach me humility, and in side comments to the main lecture I might instruct my ex-Communist charges in the glories of Western culture. They would revere me as a role model, and I would strive to be worthy of their respect. Of my artistic ambitions and accomplishments, I would remain mute. Those passing my garret late at night might see a light still burning in the window and wonder what so feverishly occupies that nice young teacher who devotes his spare time to working with orphans. Some years later, they might gasp in surprise when, at the local cinema, they saw my name splash across the title credits of the newest Hollywood blockbuster; until then, I wouldn't breathe a word. Relations with my father would remain cool for some time, but after a year or two, even he would notice that I'd changed. He might not approve when I informed him that I planned upon turning thirty to donate Grandfather's inheritance to charity, but he would respect me for it. After some time, I might even allow him to talk me out of it.

At my train's imminent departure, I decided to make some initial gesture of faith, demonstrating the seriousness of my conversion to a more reputable character. I had 500 forints remaining from my second-class ticket. In my bag I carried enough water, fruit, and bread for the journey. I needed little else. Forints were a nonconvertible currency. I would never return to Hungary. To keep the money would be the same as throwing it away. The Gypsy family still begged in the center of the square. Other families begged by the steps and at the entrance to the metro. Their takings were meager. Twice or thrice during the half hour someone had paused to drop a small coin into one of their hands and hurry on. Barely enough for a loaf of bread, poor beggars. They were a misunderstood race of people. I had been as guilty as most in romanticizing and reviling them. I arrived in Central Europe believing them a nomadic tribe of fiddlers, when I thought of them at all. Though I saw them on the streets every day, dressed as businessmen, workers, beggars, whores, and thieves, though I had cheated them and they had beaten me, and though I had fallen in love with a woman who claimed a Romany heritage, I knew nothing about them, and my ignorance had cursed me.

It was time to make my peace and go. An offering would rid me of maledictions. I folded the bills into neat halves and approached the woman in the center of the square. She turned from one callous passerby to the next, murmuring pleas for mercy and charity. At my turn she thrust her baby forward, as though I might have some personal responsibility for the unfortunate creature's existence. I stopped and admired the child. Somehow, she managed both to cradle the infant and press her hands together at the palms, as though praying to me. I counted out three bills and set them on the infant's swaddling clothes. Her two children obediently flocked to me with open palms. I couldn't tell how old they were—children's ages always confound me. Though the sight of begging children fills me with horror, I graced each of their palms with a hundred-forint note.

I was not surprised when they failed to thank me, but instead pocketed the money and proffered their palms anew, as though I was a cash machine which had unexpectedly begun to spit money. When I limped toward the stairs, the woman continued to thrust her baby in my face while the two children backpedaled ahead.

"No more," I said, good-naturedly.

Two more children materialized to tug at my coat from behind, and another Gypsy woman, older and fatter than the first, beseeched me with clasped palms. I brushed the children's hands aside and sternly shook my head at the fat one.

"No," I commanded.

She grabbed a child and flung her at me. The thing had no shoes and a face as dirty as her feet.

"I have no more money," I explained.

She clutched at my sleeve and loudly proclaimed, I supposed, that she was worthy of my charity. I pulled away only to be assaulted by a swarm of squalid brats and Gypsy women who shoved their palms and babies under my nose. I held my hands up helplessly. The women chattered and the children whined with excitement, like pack animals on the hunt. Hands pressed and grabbed my clothing. The infants thrust to my face blinded me to the hands below. I gasped and wheezed for air. They felt for my wallet. I was a fool to expect a little charity would earn either forgiveness or respect. They looked at me like meat on the hoof. I couldn't breathe in such a ravenous crowd. The Gypsies were part of a conspiracy, organized by Bortnyk and Zima to hound me to my death. My train was departing that very moment. I didn't think about consequences. I panicked. I swung my bag like a club and knocked the nearest children sprawling on their backsides. The women screeched. Two fell to their knees and huddled over infants. The fat one stepped up to shout at me. I slapped her out of my way and clubbed her sister with my elbow when she reached out to claw me.

The children were slow to understand the nature of the hunt had changed and continued to grab at trousers and coattails. I kicked them away and ran. The boys gave chase, shouting insults. I looked back over my shoulder when I reached the stairs. The plaza was as still as an auditorium, the bystanders and passersby locked between steps like an audience in its seat. From the entrance to the metro, three young men, dark and lean as wolves, sprinted. Despite the spurts of adrenaline charging my body I could not manage the stairs quickly enough with my swollen ankle. One of the beggar boys caught hold of my bag midway to the top. I dragged him along, banging his skull into the steps, but the stubborn creature refused to let go. I dropped him and the bag and scrabbled to the top on hands and knees.

In the web of tracks I searched and found the strand that railed the train to Bucharest. My legs churned with nightmarish reluctance, as though I ran, drugged, in deep sand. Behind me I heard the lupine yips of the three lean young Gypsies. Even as I ran, I argued that I was being pursued not due to a chance encounter but because my suffering and persecution were part of an elaborate mechanism of fate, the workings of which were too complex to understand. A blue uniformed train official a dozen paces ahead held a whistle to his mustached lips. His eyes bulged at me when he blew. The public address system blared a message distorted by volume and indecipherable language. *Warning, comrades! An imperialist dog runs loose in the station! Women, protect your children! Men, to arms!*

If I had a camera and filmed these last moments, I would begin the sequence framing at foot level a desperate character who hobbled along a train platform swarming in baggage carts and embarking passengers; then with a quick move of camera I'd catch and race abreast his swift pursuers, lens focused upon the thrust and churn of loping muscles here, the carnivorous slant of an eye there, and craning high into the station's arch view his impending devourment from the perspective of the howling man sculpture, neon hair sizzling as the camera passes through its open howl. A last scheme came to me as I neared the rear passenger compartment and a hopeful escape. If they caught me, I would shout *Cut!* and, looking up at the skylights, call, *Was that good for camera? Good for sound?* To my pursuers I'd announce, *That's a wrap. Thank you for your cooperation. We'll shoot the dismemberment scene tomorrow.* Like actors on a set their chase would abruptly break, and I could escape to travel east, as those with suspicious pasts once traveled south, to a place where no one knew me and I could pretend again to be anyone I wished.

I shrieked with laughter and lunged for the compartment door.